PETER JAMES

'Edge-of-the-seat reading . . . formidable – a British Alex Cross.'
THE SUN

'An ingenious and original plot. Compulsive reading.'
RACHEL ABBOTT

'A deliciously twisted and fiendish set of murders and a great pairing of detectives.'
STAV SHEREZ

'Avon's big star . . . part edge-of-the-seat, part hide-behind-the-sofa!'
THE BOOKSELLER

'An explosive thriller that will leave you completely hooked.'
WE LOVE THIS BOOK

Paul Finch is a former cop and journalist, now turned full-time writer. He cut his literary teeth penning episodes of the British TV crime drama, *The Bill*, and has written extensively in the field of children's animation. However, he is probably best known for his work in thrillers, crime and horror. His first three novels in the DS Heckenburg series all attained official 'bestseller' status.

Paul lives in Lancashire, UK, with his wife Cathy and his children, Eleanor and Harry. His website can be found at www.paulfinchauthor.com, his blog at www.paulfinch-writer.blogspot.co.uk, and he can be followed on Twitter as @paulfinchauthor.

By the same author:

Strangers
PAUL FINCH

avon

AVON

A division of HarperCollins*Publishers*
1 London Bridge Street,
London SE1 9GF

www.harpercollins.co.uk

A Paperback Original 2016
5

A catalogue record for this book is
available from the British Library

ISBN 978-0-00-755131-6

Set in Sabon by Palimpsest Book Production Limited,
Falkirk, Stirlingshire

Printed and bound in Great Britain by
Clays Ltd, St Ives plc

MIX
Paper from
responsible sources
FSC
www.fsc.org   FSC™ C007454

For my Dad, Brian, who never lived to see any of my published novels, but who if he had would have been 80 this year. You were always the spark, Dad. You lit the flame that burns in these books.

Prologue

Four years ago . . .

Michael Haygarth didn't look much like a man who'd raped and murdered two women, but then Lucy had already learned that there was no set physiology for the deranged. He sat on the bench opposite her in the rear of the unmarked police van. Throughout the journey here he'd remained perfectly still, his head hanging low as though the muscles in his neck and shoulders couldn't support it.

It was an awkward posture. Haygarth was tall, about six-four, but lanky too, and, folded into this confined space, his sharp-tipped knees came almost to his chest. He was somewhere in his forties, she surmised, though she couldn't be sure exactly, and balding, what little hair he had left around the back and sides shaved to grey bristles. His skin was brownish, tanned – as if he'd spent time abroad or maybe was of mixed-race, though apparently neither of those applied. With his weak chin, snub nose and buck teeth, he had a rodent-like aspect, and yet there was something oddly innocent about him. From his glazed eyes and vacant expression you'd have wondered if he wasn't all there. There was

1

certainly no hint of violence in his demeanour. Rather than a murder suspect, he looked the sort of hopeless, unemployed oddball who'd sit on park benches all day.

And yet he'd confessed. Under no duress whatsoever.

With a *crunch* of brakes, the van ground to a halt, presumably on the unmade track leading into Borsdane Wood, though it was impossible to be sure because the only windows in the rear of the van were small, mesh-filled panels set in its back doors, and only gloom penetrated past these, unaided by their dim, smeary glass. There was muffled movement as the other detectives crammed into the back of the vehicle stirred. Metal bumped and clanked as they sorted through the pile of spades and picks lying along the riveted steel floor.

The van's back doors were yanked open from the outside. Frigid air flowed in, smoky breath weaving around the tall, lean form of DI Doyle and the shorter, stumpier figure of DS Crellin. They'd already donned their white Tyvek coveralls and disposable gloves, and now stood with torches in hand.

'Michael, it's your time,' Doyle said, flipping open her pocketbook. 'I've got all your instructions written down. But I want to confirm them with you. We're at the end of this track now, where the bollards are . . . so we go on foot from here, approximately forty paces north, yes?'

'Yes, ma'am,' Haygarth replied in his wavering, flutelike voice, still not looking up.

'We go that way until we come to an old rotted log lying crosswise on our path, correct?'

'That's right, ma'am.'

'From there, we walk thirty paces west . . . until the ground slopes upward?'

'Yes.'

'We don't ascend the slope, but navigate along the base of it for another fifty paces . . . until we come to a clump of silver birch.'

2

'They're not all silver birch, ma'am.' He still didn't look up, but his words were slow, thoughtful. 'But there's a few silver birch in there. You won't be able to miss it.'

'Let's hope not, Michael . . . for all our sakes. There's a clearing in the middle of this clump, somewhat unnatural because you cleared it out yourself some time ago. And that's where the two graves are?'

'Correct, ma'am.'

'How deep did you say you buried them again?'

'A foot or so. You'll find both bodies in a few minutes.'

The officers pondered this in silence. Haygarth was in custody for the rape and attempted murder of the seventy-five year old woman who lived next door to him. The admission that he'd raped and strangled two prostitutes three years earlier and had buried their bodies out in Borsdane Wood was unlooked for and had come completely out of the blue during the course of his very first interview. At the time, no one had known what to make of it, but a rapid-fire check on the system had revealed that in roughly the same time-zone two Crowley-based sex workers, a Gillian Allen and Donna King, had been listed as missing persons. No trace of them had been found since.

'One final thought on this, Michael,' Doyle said, voice clipped and stern. 'If we get lost, we'll come back for you so you can show us the location in person. But I warn you now . . . I won't be impressed if that's the case. These directions had better be good.'

'They're right, ma'am. You'll find it.'

Doyle backed away, Crellin alongside her as the rest of the team lumbered to the doors. Lucy, who was handcuffed to the prisoner, had to change position first, switching across the interior to sit next to him. One by one, the rest of the team, now armed with shovels and spades, jumped down outside, where Crellin handed them each a set of overalls.

'No shoe covers till we get to the actual scene,' Doyle

said. 'We'll be tramping through God knows what kind of crap before we reach it.'

In the milky twilight of this dull February evening, the wood was a leafless tangle, the unmade road snaking back away from them beneath a roof of wet, black branches. Lucy glanced at her watch. Just before five. Another forty minutes and it would be pitch-dark. Unless they'd already uncovered physical evidence by then – in which case the entire arc-lit circus would be summoned – there'd be nothing else they could do until morning, which perhaps explained why everyone was in a hurry, Crellin's voice issuing gruff instructions as the sound of their boot falls receded.

Only Lucy and DI Mandy Doyle now remained.

She was an odd-looking woman, Doyle: tall, lean of build, pinched of face and often dressed messily in skirts, blouses and jackets that never seemed to match. She walked with a slight stoop and had longish, straggly brown hair streaked with grey, all of which combined to make her look older than she probably was, which couldn't have been much more than thirty-five. In particular, Lucy found her attitude puzzling. A woman who'd fought her way up through the ranks, one might have thought she'd welcome the arrival of a young female officer on her first CID attachment, but from the outset Doyle had seemed to find Lucy's presence frustrating.

'She just wants to get ahead,' Crellin had confided in Lucy earlier that week. 'She doesn't feel she's got the time to break in trainees.'

'I'm not exactly a trainee, sarge,' Lucy had protested. 'I've been six years in uniform.'

'Sure, sure . . . you don't have to convince me. But Mandy's a bit funny like that. She's got this idea that the team's only as strong as its weakest link. If you're going to work with us, she'll expect you to pull your weight.'

'I'll pull my weight, don't worry.'

'I know that, I've seen your record.' He'd winked. 'And I'm sure Mandy knows it too.'

Lucy was less sure about *that*. Especially at present.

'Hang onto this fella like your life depends on it, Detective Constable Clayburn,' Doyle said, her limpid gaze flicking from Lucy to the prisoner and back again. There was rarely a hint of friendship in her voice, but on this occasion her tone was especially ominous. 'Though I suppose we mustn't exaggerate . . . it isn't your life as much as your job. Because for the next hour at least this suspect is *your* responsibility. Do I make myself clear?'

'Perfectly, ma'am,' Lucy replied, straightening up dutifully, but irritated to be addressed this way in front of Haygarth, who gave no indication that he was listening but could hardly have failed to overhear.

Doyle droned on in the same menacing monotone, as if she hadn't received any such reassurance. 'Be warned . . . if anything happens while we're over there digging, anything at all – your fault, his fault, the fault of some squirrel because he distracted you by shitting on the roof – it doesn't matter. Anything happens while we're away that is prejudicial to this enquiry, *you* will carry the can. And if, by any very unfortunate circumstance, you manage to lose him, well –' Doyle cracked a half-smile, though typically it was devoid of humour '– in that case, the best thing you can do is sneak off home and send us your resignation by snail-mail.'

'I understand, ma'am,' Lucy said.

'Don't engage him in conversation. If he tries to talk to you, just tell him to shut up. If he tries anything fancy, and he gets out of hand . . . remember, you've got your radio and we're only a hundred yards away. You've also got Alan in the driving cab . . . you only need to shout and he'll come running.'

Alan Denning was one of the bigger, beefier detectives in Crowley CID. He was thinning on top, but had a thick red moustache and beard, and the meanest eyes Lucy had ever seen. If it kicked off, he looked as if he'd be more than useful. But in truth the last thing they needed was for something bad to happen. Haygarth hadn't been charged with anything yet, but assuming it all went as planned, he'd be facing lots and lots of prison time, and though he might be acquiescent now – perhaps struggling to come to terms with what he'd done to the harmless OAP next door – in due course he'd realise the big trouble he was in. So at all costs they needed to avoid handing him something his legal reps could use as leverage, such as an injury. It didn't matter whether it was inflicted on him in self-defence or in an effort to prevent him escaping, any time police officers assaulted suspects these days it exponentially increased said suspect's chance of walking free.

'But I don't think you're going to try anything silly, are you, Michael?' Doyle said.

Haygarth didn't reply. His head still hung; his posture was so still it was almost creepy.

Lucy, on the other hand, was churning inside. It wasn't just the embarrassing warning she'd been issued. Even without that, it had now dawned on her how serious this shift was turning out to be. The strange, distant man linked to her right wrist might actually be a multiple killer. It was unnerving, but it was exciting too. After several years in uniform spent ticketing cars, chasing problem teenagers and nicking shoplifters, *this* was what she'd really joined for, *this* was why she'd applied again and again for a CID post.

'Michael, can you hear me?' Doyle persisted.

'Uh?' Haygarth glanced up. As before, he only seemed half aware what was going on. 'Erm . . . yes, ma'am.'

'Yes what?'

'Yes, I'll be good.'

In actual fact, Lucy didn't think the guy would pose much of a threat even if he wasn't. He was tall, but rail-thin, whereas she, who was about twenty years younger, was in the best shape of her life. Okay, she didn't represent the Greater Manchester Police women's hockey and squash teams any more, but she regularly ran, swam and visited the gym.

'Excellent,' Doyle said. 'That's all I needed to know, Michael. You play fair with us, and we'll play fair with you.' She turned back to Lucy. 'Remember what I said, DC Clayburn.'

'Certainly will, ma'am,' Lucy replied.

The DI made no further comment, just slowly and purposefully closed the doors to the van. For what seemed like a minute, her trudging footfalls diminished into the woods. After that, there was only stillness, though other sounds gradually became audible: a faint metallic clicking as the engine cooled; the hiss of dead air on the police radio; the dull but distinctive murmur of music and voices from the cab at the front, most likely Radio One. Beyond all that, the silence in the encircling trees was oppressive. Borsdane Wood wasn't as idyllic as it might sound, covering several hundred acres of abandoned industrial land on the town's northern outskirts, not far from the old power station and sewage plant, and ultimately terminating at the M61 motorway. In summer it was trackless and overgrown, and in winter bleak and isolated. Bottles, beer cans and other rubbish routinely strewed its clearings; more than once, drugs paraphernalia had been found. No one ever came here for picnics.

Lucy rubbed her gloved hands together. The temperature inside the van was noticeably dwindling, mainly because the engine had been switched off so the heating had deactivated. She glanced sidelong at Haygarth. Someone had given him a coat to wear over the white custody tracksuit, but if he was feeling any chill, he wasn't showing it. His head still hung, while his hands, which looked overlarge and knobbly at the ends of his long, thin wrists, were clasped together as though in penitential prayer.

This had certainly been his attitude since DI Doyle had arrested him earlier that day. It wasn't unknown for violent criminals to occasionally feel guilty, or even to turn themselves in through remorse. Others coughed because their life outside prison had become unendurable, because they needed a more stable and disciplined regime. But neither of those possibilities struck Lucy as a given where Michael Haygarth was concerned. Perhaps they might if his only offence had been to attack the lady next door, but the conscience thing didn't seem quite so likely when you considered that up until now he'd been happily sitting on the deaths of two other women.

Unexpectedly, he looked up and around. 'Ma'am . . . I, erm . . .' His eyes widened, in fact bugged, while his wet mouth had screwed itself out of shape as if he suddenly felt distressed about something.

'Best not to talk, Michael.' Lucy refused to make eye contact with him. 'It's for your own good.'

'But . . . I need to relieve myself.'

'You'll have to wait, I'm afraid.'

'Seriously . . . don't think I can. Didn't Miss Doyle say they might be an hour or more?'

'It's honestly best if we don't talk.'

'But this is ridiculous.' His voice thickened with feeling as he stared down at the floor again. It was his first show of emotion in several hours, since he'd been arrested in fact, and yet still there was that air of the pathetic about him, of the beaten.

'Michael . . . it's just not possible at the moment,' Lucy said, angry with herself for having started conversing with him.

'All I want is a toilet break, and . . . now you're not letting me have one.'

'You never mentioned you needed a break back at the nick.'

'I didn't need one then.'

'We've only been out here ten bloody minutes.'

'Sorry, but I can't help it. It's all that tea you kept pouring down my throat in the interview room.'

'Just try and wait, Michael . . . you're not a kid.'

But he now sat stiffly upright, his face etched with discomfort. 'What if I released it down my leg and messed your van up, eh? All because I couldn't hold it? I bet you'd have a right go at me, wouldn't you?'

Lucy thought long and hard.

It wouldn't be the first time a prisoner had urinated on her, and quite often that had happened inside the back of a police vehicle. It wasn't always their fault; some of them were losers in so many aspects of life. And it wasn't as if clothing couldn't go in the wash or that she herself couldn't just step under a warm shower. But it always took so long to get the smell out of the car or van. This was a pool vehicle, of course, and different officers would drive it every day, so it wouldn't solely be her problem . . . except that she was the one who'd get blamed for it, and on top of that, she'd be stuck in here tonight with the stink for God knew how long.

'They probably won't be more than an hour,' she said, though it was as much an attempt to convince herself as Haygarth, and in that regard it didn't work.

Most likely they'd be much more than an hour. They might even be several hours.

He muttered something else, his voice turning hoarse. She noticed that his bony knees, formerly wide apart, were squeezed together. He'd begun twitching, fidgeting.

Could it really do any harm?

'Alright,' she said reluctantly. 'We go outside and you pee against the nearest tree, but you'll have to do it one-handed because you're staying cuffed.'

9

'That's fine.' He sounded relieved and waited patiently while Lucy reached down, found the release lever on the door and flipped it upright.

If Alan Denning in the cab heard the *clunk* of the rear locks disengaging, he didn't respond. Most likely, he couldn't hear it with what sounded like Rhianna blaring away. Lucy thought to call him anyway, for the purpose of extra security, but decided that Denning, being the epitome of the big, unfeeling, hairy-arsed male copper, would most likely respond with: 'Don't be so soft, Clayburn! Make him fucking wait! He can tie a fucking knot in it!' Or something similarly enlightened.

She kept her mouth shut as she climbed out onto the road, Haygarth following, grit and twigs crunching under their feet. Proper darkness now enveloped the woods, the source of the constant dripping and pattering completely invisible. Lucy's torch had been purloined by one of the others, but there was sufficient light spilling from the back of the van to show the nearest tree-trunk, a glinting black/green pillar standing on the verge about five yards away, with a huge hollow some eight feet up it, where a knot had fallen out. Haygarth made a beeline towards it, but Lucy stopped him, first peering down the length of the van to see if anyone else on the team was hanging around at the front, maybe having a smoke. From what she could see, there was no one. The glow of the headlights speared forward, delineating the concrete bollards that signified the end of the track. Those too sparkled with moisture. Beyond them lay a dense mesh of sepia-brown undergrowth. Nothing moved.

'Okay,' she said, proceeding to the tree. 'This'll do. Make it quick.'

Haygarth grunted with gratitude as he assumed the position. Lucy stood alongside him, but turned her shoulder so that, even by accident, she couldn't glance down and catch sight of anything. It fleetingly occurred to her that, given,

Haygarth's alleged form, this voluntary blindsiding of herself might not be the wisest policy, but it was done now, and he had the air of a broken man in any case – plus Alan Denning was only a shout away.

She heard Haygarth sigh as liquid splashed gently down the bole of the tree.

'That's much better,' he mumbled. 'God, I've been waiting for this.'

'DC Clayburn, what the hell's going on?'

Lucy turned, surprised. Behind the blob of torchlight approaching from beyond the bollards there was an indistinct figure, but she knew who it was. The clumsy, slightly stooped gait was the main giveaway, but the harsh, humourless voice was added proof.

'Ma'am, the prisoner . . .' Lucy's words tailed off as everything suddenly seemed to go wrong at once.

First, she sensed movement alongside her. When she glanced around, Haygarth, who was six foot four – and with one arm extended upward could reach to nearly nine feet – was rooting inside the tree-trunk cavity.

'What're you . . .?' she said, fleetingly baffled.

Next, DI Doyle ran forward. At the same time, with a metallic thud, a driving-cab door swung open in response. Then there was a plasticky *crackle*, and Haygarth laughed, or rather giggled – it was a hyena-like sound rather than human.

Lucy tried to grab his arm, but he barged into her with his left shoulder, knocking her off balance. And now the object he'd been groping for inside the tree came into view. It was only small, but it had been swathed in a supermarket wrapper to protect it, so its make and model were concealed. And it was anyone's guess what calibre it was.

As Lucy fell to the ground, he swung the object around. Its first booming report took out Doyle's torch. She was only about ten yards away, but her light vanished with a *PLOK*.

By the way she grunted and gasped and doubled over, the bullet had punched clean through it, tearing into her midriff.

Lucy, prone on her back, was too numb to react. Hideous, unimaginable seconds seemed to pass before her training kicked in and she tried to roll away – only for her right arm to pull taut where it was handcuffed to Haygarth's left. As she struggled to escape, he turned a slow circle, still laughing, a black skeletal figure in the reduced light, a man of sticks, a living scarecrow. And yet so much stronger than he looked. With embarrassing ease, he yanked her backwards, throwing her hard onto her spine, and pointed his bag down at her, smoke still venting from the hole blown at the end.

She kicked out, slamming the flat of her foot against his right knee. There was a crack of sinew, and Haygarth's leg buckled. He gave a piercing squeal as he collapsed on top of her, at the same time trying to hit her with his weapon. She blocked the blow with her left arm, and fleetingly their faces were an inch apart, his no longer the melancholic image she'd seen earlier, but a portrait of dementia, foam surging through his clenched buck-teeth, cheeks bunched, brow furrowed.

He headbutted her. Right on the bridge of her nose.

The pain that smashed through the middle of Lucy's head was so intense that she almost blacked out, and as such didn't see the weapon as he swept it down at her again, twice in fact, both times catching her clean on the left temple. A double explosion roared in her skull. As awareness faded and hot, sticky fluid pooled over her left eye, she saw him kneel upright, sweating, drool stringing from his mouth as he bit at the plastic wrapping, exposing the gleaming steel pistol underneath, and then pointed it down at her face – only to go rigid as a massive blow clattered the back of his own head.

Consciousness ebbing away, the last thing Lucy saw was Haygarth's thin, limp form as it was hauled roughly off her by the brute force that was Alan Denning.

Chapter 1

Now . . .

He said that his name was Ronnie Ford and that he was from Warrington. By the looks of his heavy build, weathered face and chalk-grey hair, he was somewhere in his late forties. Apparently, he ran his own business – an auto-repair shop, which explained his ragged sweater and oil-stained canvas trousers – but he added that he was now on his way home for tea. Weirdly, the longer the woman rode alongside him, the more she came to suspect that he'd picked her up for honest, even gentlemanly reasons.

For the first fifteen minutes of their shared journey, he'd kept his eyes firmly on the road, chatting amiably, covering every subject under the sun, from the unseasonably mild autumn weather, to the poor state of the Malaga hotel where he and his wife had spent two weeks last August, to the latest and, in his opinion, even-more-hopeless-than-usual contestants on the new series of *X Factor*. It was all very affable and light-hearted.

So . . . a bit of a father figure, Ronnie Ford.

Or at least, an avuncular uncle type.

13

But ultimately he was a man too. And seemingly as red-blooded as so many others.

When he parked the car in the quiet lay-by and she climbed out, he climbed out as well. When she ran giggling to the stile, he followed her, expressing open if feigned admiration as she climbed it with lithe efficiency, despite her tight, knee-length skirt and four-inch heels. It helped, of course, that she did it sexily, wiggling up the rickety ladder and stepping prettily over its topmost rung before descending into the field on the other side.

At this point, he shouted. 'Hold up, love! Whoa . . . wait a minute!'

He'd lost sight of her, thanks mainly to the autumn twilight. It was early October and not yet seven in the evening, so it wasn't what you'd actually call dusk. It wasn't even what you'd call cold. They'd had an Indian summer, which even now was only dissipating slowly, but light *was* leaching from the cloudy sky and dim traces of mist rising in the under-growth.

In the field, hacked stubble was all that remained of a recently harvested crop. It was roughly the size of a football pitch, but as the woman already knew, there was a clear pathway running straight as a ribbon to a belt of reddish-leafed trees on its far side. She hared off along this, still giggling. She had no idea why men found that 'cheeky giggle' thing fetching; she supposed it harked back to those daft naughty schoolgirl fantasies that generation after generation of saucy movies and top-shelf lads' mags had impressed on British male society.

From behind, she heard the clump of Ronnie Ford's feet on the wooden rungs, and his loud grunts for breath. A non-too-fit avuncular uncle then, but evidently a man who now felt he was on a mission.

They usually were in the end. It was always so pathetically easy.

She'd only needed to remove her black knitted beret and shake out her blonde locks, ease down the zip on her anorak just sufficiently to reveal the skimpy blouse underneath, and then cross and uncross her legs a few times while he'd attempted to drive.

The surreptitious sidelong glances had started soon after. And then, about quarter of an hour into the journey, when the suggestive conversation had commenced, she'd known he was hers.

'It's okay to check me out,' she said in what was almost an apologetic tone. 'I know I'm a bit of alright. Men are always saying crude stuff like that to me. I've got used to it now. So if it makes it easier for you, I don't mind you looking.'

'The problem is,' he replied, heat visibly flaming the back of his neck, 'I've got to concentrate on the road. Where did you say you were heading for again?'

'Liverpool.'

'I can drop you off at Warrington bus station. You'll have no problem getting a connection to Liverpool from there. It's not too far.'

'That's very kind of you.'

'Not at all.'

Despite having permission, Ronnie still only glanced furtively at her. Possibly he was even more of a gentleman than she'd first thought. Or maybe it was just his age and upbringing. She'd all but invited him to ogle her, but his initial reaction seemed to be to try and resist, to try to avoid getting drawn into those huge doe-eyes, which had gazed on him so beseechingly when he'd first pulled up alongside her, as if to say: 'Are you here to help? Is it possible you are genuinely here to help? Or are you only after one thing too?'

That always added to the allure, the 'little girl lost' approach.

15

She resumed that teasing conversation, again crossing and uncrossing her legs so that the hem of her skirt started to rise.

'Warrington's still quite a ride from here,' she said. 'And I've nothing to pay you with.'

'Doesn't matter,' he replied. 'I'm going that direction anyway.'

'Yes, but you should get something for your trouble. I'm Loretta, by the way.'

'Erm . . . nice to meet you, Loretta.'

Somewhat belatedly, he fiddled with the radio, trying to find a different station, something smoother than the hard-edged rock jarring out at them. After twenty seconds jamming and prodding, he located a slow, bluesy saxophone and turned it down a notch so that it could clearly be heard but at the same time they could talk.

'What about it?' she asked again, watching him. 'How do I make it worth your while?'

'Don't be daft, Loretta . . .'

But she wasn't being daft. And he knew it.

The revealing attire, the improper pose, the Marilyn Monroe combo of sweet, innocent kid and pulse-pounding vamp.

'Look . . . I don't mean to imply anything, but . . .' He cleared his throat awkwardly. 'I don't have much cash on me.'

'You're paying your way by giving me a ride,' she tittered. 'I'm just wondering if I can return the favour.'

'Don't taunt me like that, love,' he said, driving less than steadily. 'You'll make a sad old man even sadder.'

'No, I'm serious,' she responded. 'I want to make it up to you any way I can. You'll find I'm very broadminded.'

'Yeah?' *Though it wasn't really a question.*

'Look . . . just ahead there's a turn,' she said. 'That's a

backroad. It leads to Abram eventually, but about half a mile along it there's a lay-by for lorries and such. There's a chippie van there during the day, but it'll be closed at this hour. We could park up.'

He glanced at her wonderingly. Whatever he'd been about to say died on his tongue, his eyes diverting down to where the zip on her silver anorak had completely descended, exposing a deep, creamy cleavage, and then even further down, to where a pair of black stocking-tops were revealed, along with shiny clips and taut, white straps.

He looked again at her beautiful face, this time askance. And then he grinned. Broadly if somewhat disbelievingly. 'Is this for real?'

'Maybe. You'll have to find out.'

And if nothing else, he was keen to do that. Which was why she was now three quarters of the way across an empty field, with the darkling trees in front and Ronnie Ford about fifty yards behind.

'Loretta?' he called, huffing and puffing as he attempted to follow. 'Come on, eh?'

He wasn't just unfit, he was clearly unhealthy. Just climbing over the stile appeared to have sapped him of energy. Perhaps it would be necessary to give him further encouragement. The wood stood in front of her, the path leading into it through a natural archway amid the nearest trees. As soon as she entered, and was fleetingly out of view, the woman hiked her skirt up and slipped her lacy white knickers down, stepping nimbly out of them and hanging the garment on a nearby twig.

Giggling again, she hurried on into the darkness. Any reservations he might still have harboured ought to evaporate completely now.

'Loretta?' He tried to make a joke of it as he breathlessly entered the wood. 'As you've seen, I'm approaching the autumn of my years. I might be like a fine vintage wine, but I can't chase around the countryside anymore.'

She watched him from about forty yards in front, from behind the clump of rhododendrons she'd been looking for on the left side of the path.

Approximately five yards into the trees, he stopped and pivoted round. Suddenly wary.

She wondered what he was thinking.

A blue murk was spreading amid the gnarled stanchions of the trunks. Here and there, ground-level bushes hung heavy with dew. There was a reek of woodland decay, of fungus and leaf-mulch. All was deathly still.

It looked as if he was about to start retreating. But then he stopped short.

Ten yards to his right, he'd spotted the pair of knickers suspended from their twig.

Hurriedly, he lumbered over there, fingers twitching, apparently eager to fondle that soft, pliable material.

Yeah . . . so much for the avuncular uncle.

He yanked the garment down and spread it out in two hands, to check its authenticity no doubt. Then he folded it into a small, neat square and inserted it into his left hip pocket, before ambling back to the path and proceeding along it towards her, penetrating deeper into the ever-gloomier trees but now with a big lewd grin on his mug.

She'd have laughed aloud if it wouldn't have given her away.

The poor stupid sod really thought he was going to get some.

Chapter 2

The Hatchwood Green estate was a sinkhole even by the standards of Crowley, which was one of Greater Manchester's most deprived boroughs. It had been constructed in the 1950s, along with the rest of the district's many council estates, though this was one of the largest, having been built on extensive brownfield land – a site formerly occupied by the long defunct Manchester Railway Company – and in so many ways it embodied the decline of the council housing dream in post-war Britain.

Brand-new, spacious living accommodation for Crowley's working class had soon turned sour for its residents as they'd found themselves isolated from the town centre and other amenities, and often from jobs. More to the point, this new community was broken from the outset, as its members had already sacrificed the old social networks they'd formerly built up in order to move. Follow that with decades of neglect, the gradual deterioration of cheaply built properties due to their having exceeded their expected lifetimes, and the increased and often twin ravages of drugs and crime, and you were left with a truly depressing environment. Years later, even with right-to-buy in force,

Hatchwood Green still had the aura of desolation and menace.

To PC Lucy Clayburn's jaundiced eye – and she couldn't help but see it this way as a copper – there was something inherently soul-destroying about these immense, sprawling housing estates: all the domiciles built from the same red brick, their doors existing in repeating patterns of pale blue, pale red or pale yellow; the patches of grass between them boasting no other distinguishing features – no trees, no bushes, no flowerbeds – though they occasionally hosted the relics of kiddies' playgrounds. And of course, when they had dropped into disrepair, as this one had, with dilapidated housing and broken fences, their inhospitable aura reached a new low.

So it was with the usual air of stoic boredom that, one Wednesday night, she and PC Malcolm Peabody, the twenty-year-old probationer she'd been puppy-walking for the past couple of months, drove their liveried BMW saloon onto the Hatchwood, to attend 24 Clapgate Road in response to a reported domestic.

This house was in no better or worse state than those around it: a small front garden, which was mainly a trash heap (though it hadn't used to be, Lucy recalled), a rotted gate hanging from its hinges and thick tufts of weed growing through the lopsided paving along the front path. They could hear the hubbub inside as soon as they pulled up. When they actually entered – the house's front door having opened immediately to Lucy's firm, no-nonsense knock – the interior looked as if a bomb had hit it, though it was difficult to tell whether this was a new mess or just the usual one. Dingy wallpaper and mouldering carpets implied the latter, but it was hard to make out whether the bits of strewn underwear, or the beer tins, dog-ends and other foul bric-a-brac, were recent additions. The atmosphere, of course, was rancid: a mingled fetor of sweat, cigarettes, booze and ketchup – which was sad as well as sickening, Lucy thought, because again, that hadn't always been the case at this address.

The occupants were Rob and Dora Hallam, he a displaced and unemployed Welshman, she a local lass who'd recently been sacked from her supermarket job for being light-fingered. They were both in their late thirties, though they looked older: ratty-haired, sallow-faced, gap-toothed. Rob Hallam was short, stumpy and overweight, Dora thin to the point of emaciation, her facial features sunken as though the very bone structure was decaying. At present he was wearing Y-fronts, a vest and a pair of dirty socks. She was in flip-flops, pyjama bottoms and a Manchester United shirt.

Both were streaming blood, Rob from a split eyebrow and gouged left cheek, Dora from a burst nose, which as she sniffled into a handkerchief, continued to discharge itself in a constant succession of sticky crimson bubbles.

The main set-to looked to have occurred in the lounge. That was where most of the wrecked furniture and broken glass was congregated. The door connecting the lounge to the kitchen, which now lay wrenched from its hinges against an armchair, was also a giveaway. But whatever violence had erupted before, it was over now, primarily because the combatants were too exhausted to continue. They stood apart, one at either side of the room, panting, glaring. In between them, quite surreally, the television played away to itself, screening the crazy antics of *Cow and Chicken*.

'So what am I going to do with the pair of you?' Lucy asked, having stood in stony silence during the predictable exchange of accusations and counter-accusations, and refusing to give a moment's thought to Rob Hallam's meandering explanation that the squabble had started over his wife's 'fucking stupid' assertion that the Red Guy, Cow and Chicken's nemesis, was supposed to be imaginary and not the real-life Devil.

'You've got to arrest him,' Dora whimpered, seemingly surprised that this hadn't happened already.

'Arrest him?' Lucy said. 'Dora . . . every time we try to arrest him, you either go ballistic as soon as we lay hands on him, or come rushing down to the station and insist he hasn't done anything wrong.'

'You can see that this time he *has*.' Dora yanked her hair with bloodstained fingers. 'Look at the state of me.'

'And look at the state of Rob.'

'But I had to defend myself . . .'

'What did you use?' Lucy asked. 'A meat-grinder?'

Dora's mouth dropped open, guppy-like with incomprehension.

'The point I'm making, Dora,' Lucy said, 'is that you're both as bad as each other. Every time you have a drink, you have a fight, usually over nothing . . . and you wake the whole neighbourhood up. And it's not just every Friday and Saturday. Now it seems it's weekdays too.' She glanced at Rob. 'And what've *you* got to say for yourself? And don't give me some bollocks excuse about kids' cartoons!'

Rob regarded her hollow-eyed. 'She's right. I need locking up. Even if she withdraws her complaint, you can do that, can't you? You said that last time.'

'That's right, Rob . . . but this isn't a straightforward assault, is it? You're going to need at least as many stitches as she is. Your brief'll have a field day. Unless I lock you *both* up, of course.' Lucy knuckled her chin. 'I could charge you *both* with wounding, breach of the peace, causing damage to council property . . . that might get a result.'

'Both of us?' Rob looked startled.

'Both of us?' Dora echoed, as if this had never been part of the plan.

'It's the age of equal opportunities, love,' Lucy replied. 'Spousal abuse works both ways these days.'

22

Dora's mouth slackened into another bewildered gape.

'Course,' Lucy added, 'ultimately, it'd be a waste of *all* our time, wouldn't it? Not to mention expensive . . . when what you really need is to go and get some counselling.' She stepped across the wreckage-strewn room, and took a framed photo from the cluttered mantelpiece. It depicted a little blond boy, smiling happily despite his missing front teeth. 'When Bobbie died, it changed everything for you two, didn't it?'

Rob slumped onto the couch. He shook a can, sipped out a last dreg and discarded it onto the floor. 'I can't remember a time before that,' he said.

'You need to try,' Lucy replied.

In response, he reached into a carrier bag next to the couch, took out a fresh can and ripped it open.

'What do you mean counselling?' Dora asked.

'Grief counselling,' Lucy said. 'Look, I *know* Bobbie's death changed your lives, Dora, because I never had to come here in the middle of the night before then. But it's five years ago, love. And it's still tearing you apart. So you need some professional help. There's something else. You need to stop hitting the pop.' She snatched the can from Rob's grasp and placed it on the mantel. 'You can get some help for that too . . . but you've got to *want* it first.'

Rob gazed blearily up at her. 'So . . . I'm not getting locked up?'

He seemed puzzled rather than relieved, though perhaps now that he'd calmed down a little, it was dawning on him that the advantages of being allowed to sleep in his own bed outweighed the disadvantages of being cooped up in a vomit-stained police cell.

'That depends.' Lucy indicated the broken door. 'What about this?'

'Suppose I can fix it.'

23

'Definitely?'

'Yeah.'

'When?'

'Soon as I get round to it.'

'Not good enough, Rob. I'm back on duty tomorrow afternoon. I'll make this my first port of call. Will it be fixed by then?'

'Yeah.'

'Sure? Stare me in the eye and say it.'

'Yeah,' he said again, though he looked too haggard to be totally convincing.

'Okay . . .' Lucy pondered. 'Before I leave here, I want a solemn promise from you two jokers that, for the rest of tonight . . . no, let's not cheapen it . . . for the rest of this *year*, I won't get a call-back to this address.'

'Promise,' Dora said quietly.

Rob nodded again.

'You have to get some help, you understand?'

'Yeah,' he said.

Lucy knew they wouldn't. It might be all quiet now, but in a few days' time tempers would flare again over something completely ridiculous. The Hallams were too stuck in this rut, too damaged by events, too drunk on misery and hopelessness to effect any kind of change in their own fortunes. For anyone to keep proceeding down a dark, dank tunnel there had to be at least a flicker of light at the end. But in truth, Lucy didn't really care a great deal. She couldn't afford to. At times she was so tired out by these mini disasters in the lives of others that all she wanted to do was shut them down any way she could, even if it was only temporarily.

'Alright . . .' She put her radio to her lips. '1485 to Three, receiving?'

'*Go ahead, Lucy,*' Comms crackled back.

'Yeah, I'm finished at Clapgate Lane. No offences revealed. All parties advised, over.'

'Roger, thanks for that.'

'That was so cool,' Peabody said, as they climbed back into the panda.

'Cool?'

'The way you defused that situation.'

'It defused itself.' She put the car in gear. 'They were too knackered to keep fighting.'

'Yeah, but we could've locked them both up. Plenty of reason. Instead, you calmed it down, had a few words, put them right, spared them a difficult time . . .'

'And saved us a raft of paperwork.' Lucy drove them away from the kerb. 'That was my main motivation.'

Peabody chuckled. 'Can't fool me. You just didn't want to bring any more crap down on them . . . you're getting soft-hearted in your old age.'

He was a rangy, raw-boned lad, red-haired and freckled, and to an outsider his tone might have seemed a tad impertinent given that Lucy was a ten-year veteran of the job and he'd only been in it a few months, but a few months on the beat in a town like Crowley counted for a lot. Even a few days spent side-by-side on the frontline could bond coppers together like no other job outside the military.

'Well. . .' Lucy swung them towards the south end of the estate. 'It's not like they haven't had a lot to deal with.'

'What happened to the kiddie, anyway?'

'Run over.'

'Christ!'

'On the way home from school. Horseplay with his mates . . . ends up stepping off the pavement in front of a bus.'

'Sounds messy . . .'

'It was.'

'You were there?'

'First responder. But there was nothing anyone could do. After that, I had to deliver the death message.' She sighed. 'Not among my favourite memories.'

Before Peabody could say more, the air was shattered by a burst of static from the radio.

'November Three to all units, urgent message . . . female reported under attack in the telephone kiosk at the top end of Darthill Road. Anyone to attend, over!'

'1485 and 9993 en route from Hatchwood Green!' Peabody shouted as Lucy spun the car in a U-turn and blazed back across the housing estate, activating the blues and twos as she did.

They were three miles from Darthill Road, which ran from top to bottom of a steep hill; on its south side it was lined by houses but on its north it gave way to arid spoil-land. As such, there was only one real approach to it, but other patrols had been closer and by the time Lucy and Peabody arrived at the phone-box, Sergeant Robertson in the Area Car had got there ahead of them. A Traffic unit was also in attendance, alongside an ambulance, which rather fortuitously, had already been in the area. From the radio messages bouncing back and forth, it sounded as if the assailant had fled on foot.

Lucy and Peabody jumped out and dashed forward.

The girl, who was clearly young but too bloodied around the face to be recognisable, sat crying on the kerb, two female paramedics kneeling as they tended her cuts and bruises. Robertson was on his phone to CID, but a quick conflab with the Traffic guys, who were already deploying incident tape, revealed that the attacker had dragged his would-be victim a few yards onto the rough ground, before she'd fought him to a standstill. He'd then had to punch her repeatedly to subdue her, after which, thinking he'd knocked her out, he'd started going through her handbag – only for her to suddenly jump up again and leg it. Having already lost her mobile to the bastard, she'd scrambled into the phone-box and called 999. The assailant was kicking the hell out of its door when she managed to get through. That was when he finally did a runner.

Lucy raced back to the car and leapt in, Peabody hurriedly following.

'Get onto Comms,' she told him, flinging the vehicle around in a rapid three-point turn. 'Tell them we need India 99.' That call sign wasn't officially used any more in GMP, but some police terminology never changed. 'We want the eye in the sky.'

'So where are *we* going?' Peabody asked.

'The other side of the Aggies.'

'You think he'll have got over there already?'

'He'll have heard our sirens, Malcolm . . . if that doesn't put wings on his heels, nothing will.'

'This time of night he'll break his bloody neck.'

'Most of these scrotes grew up round here. They'll have played there as kids. Don't underestimate their local knowledge. Now get me that bloody chopper!'

The Aggies was one of numerous spoil-heaps in Crowley. A former hotbed of coalmining and cotton-weaving, the township was sandwiched between Bolton and Salford, November Division on the GMP register. It had definitely seen better days, the glory years of muck and brass having long departed. Most of its factories were closed, either boarded up or redeveloped into carpet warehouses, while its collieries were totally gone, pitheads and washeries dismantled, even some of the slagheaps and derelict brows flattened and built over, though for the most part these remained as barren, grey scars, sometimes covering hundreds of unusable acres.

The Aggies was typical. A hummocky moonscape dotted

with the ruins of abandoned industry, no road led over it. Lying between inner Crowley and Bullwood (an outer district that was almost as depressed as Hatchwood Green), it was rectangular in outline, which meant that someone trying to get clean across it on foot, so long as he knew his way, had a reasonable chance of reaching the other side ahead of someone in a car, as the latter would have to drive the long way around. And it wasn't as if Lucy could activate the blues and twos. At its lower, western end, the Aggies terminated in a swampy region caused by a polluted overflow of the River Irwell, and a mass of black and twisted girders marking out the remnants of the old Bleachworks, which had burned to cinders twenty years ago. Aside from that, it was wide open down there – there were no other houses, and the stretch of road looping through that section, Pimbo Lane, was unlit, so anyone crossing the Aggies from south to north, especially on the higher section in the middle, would clearly spot the police car's beacon as it raced around to intercept him.

But if nothing else, the day and the hour were in the officers' favour. All the way down Darthill Road, they met not a single vehicle coming the opposite way, and as they swerved onto Pimbo, only a night-bus cruised past, and its driver had the sense to pull into the kerb to allow them swifter passage.

Meanwhile, messages crackled on the force radio. They broke constantly and the static was loud, but it was just about possible to glean from them that the AP, who had only just turned eighteen, had suffered facial injuries and wounds to her neck and chest, but that otherwise she was safe and well. Apparently, she'd described her assailant as somewhere in his late twenties, blond-haired and wearing a green track-suit with white piping. Peabody scribbled this down as Lucy steered them at reckless speed along the swing-back lane.

They arrived in Bullwood five minutes later, Lucy slowing to a crawl and knocking the headlights off as the BMW prowled from one darkened side street to the next. She'd zeroed in on several rows of terraced houses, each one of which terminated at the edge of the Aggies. Superficially, you couldn't gain access to the wasteland from any of these residential streets – in some cases there were garages there, in others wire-mesh fencing had been erected. But the local urchins enjoyed their desolate playground too much to tolerate that. Thanks to the various holes they'd made over the years, passage through was easily possible if you knew where it was.

The only question now was did their suspect know all that?

Assuming he had come this way at all.

The first three streets were bare of life, nothing but cars lining the fronts of the identical red brick terraces. Most house lights were now off, given that it was almost midnight. But in the fourth street, Windermere Avenue, they glimpsed movement, a dark figure sauntering out of sight into the mouth of a cobbled alley. Lucy turned her radio down to the minimum and indicated that Peabody should do the same, before cruising on past the top of the road and pulling sharply up before the next street, Thirlmere Place.

'Leave your helmet off,' she whispered, opening her door.

Peabody nodded and slipped out onto the road, just as a walking man appeared from Thirlmere, turned sharp right and receded away along the pavement. It was difficult to distinguish details in the dull streetlamps, but he wore a light-coloured T-shirt, which fitted snugly around a muscular, wedge-shaped torso. More important than any of this, he also wore tracksuit bottoms, and had a tracksuit top tied around his waist by its sleeves.

If this was the guy, one might have expected him, on

hearing the chug of the engine, to try to hide, but instead he was going for "normality", Lucy realised; rather than skulking in some backstreet and probably drawing more attention to himself, looking to brazen it out by hiding in plain sight – like he was just an everyday Joe on his way home.

They walked after him, padding lightly but gaining ground quickly, hands tight on their duty belts; Lucy clutched her CS canister, Peabody the hilt of his extendable Autolock Baton. When five yards behind, they saw sweat gleaming on their target's thick bull-neck, dampening his fair, straw-like hair. They could also see his tracksuit properly – it was green with white piping.

'Excuse me, sir,' Lucy said. 'Can I talk to you?'

He walked on, not turning, not even flinching at the sound of her voice.

They closed the gap, at any second expecting him to bolt.

'Excuse me, sir . . . we're police officers and we need to speak to you.'

What Lucy didn't expect was for him to whirl around and throw a massive punch at her, but she was now so used to these situations that her reactions sat on a hair-trigger. She ducked the blow and wrapped her arms around his waist.

'*MALCOLM!*' she shouted.

Peabody might have been a newbie, but he threw himself forward and crooked his own arms around the assailant's bullet-shaped head, crushing his Neanderthal features in a brutal bear-hug, and at the same time dropping down with his full weight, dragging the guy to the pavement. The three of them landed heavily, the suspect on top of Peabody, Lucy front-down on top of the suspect. The two men got the worst of it, the suspect primarily as Lucy dug her left elbow into his solar plexus and drew her CS spray with her right hand, ejecting its contents into his gagging, choking face. He squawked and convulsed. With a satisfying *click*, Peabody snapped one bracelet onto his brawny left wrist.

'You're locked up, you bastard!' Lucy gasped down at him as he writhed, using her right forearm to compress his throat. 'You're bloody locked up!' She put her radio mic to her lips. '1485 to Three . . . re. the attack at the phone-box on Darthill Road. One detained at the junction of Pimbo Lane and Thirlmere Place. Require immediate supervision and prisoner transport, over.'

'Pig-slut!' the prisoner choked. 'You'll fucking die for this . . .'

'What did you say?' Lucy asked, levering herself backwards now that Peabody, who was clearly stronger and handier than he looked, had got both the prisoner's hands cuffed behind his back. She grabbed the guy's throat in a gloved claw. 'Eh?'

'Nothing,' he gagged. 'For Christ's sake . . . I said nothing!'

'Nah . . .' She shook her head. 'Sounded to me like your response to caution was "okay, I did it . . . you've got me banged to rights". Did you hear that confession too, PC Peabody?'

'Absolutely, PC Clayburn,' Peabody replied. He wasn't just handier than he looked, Malcolm Peabody, he was in the right job too. 'Abso-bloody-lutely!'

Chapter 3

Lucy groaned with relief as she stripped her gear off in the female locker room: the straight-leg combat trousers, the duty belt with its various appointments, the stab vest, the radio harness, the high-viz jacket. After twenty hours on duty it all seemed a dead weight. She stepped gratefully into the shower and braced herself against the cubicle wall as the hot spray lashed over her.

Making an important arrest just before the end of shift always guaranteed you hours of overtime, which was sometimes a good thing if you needed the extra cash, but was rarely desirable when it kept you busy all night. Lucy checked the time as she towelled down, and then climbed into her underwear and picked up her motorbike leathers. It was almost eight. Beyond the confines of the locker room, the rest of the station was humming with life, but given that the morning team were now out and about, she had this quiet little space to herself. At least, she thought she did.

'PC Clayburn?' a voice said.

Lucy glanced around, surprised to see that while she'd been in the shower cubicle, an Indian woman, somewhere in her early fifties, had entered the locker room and was now perched on a bench near the door, fiddling with an iPad.

'Who's asking?' Lucy said.

'Oh good . . . hostility from the word-off.' The Indian lady stood up, stiffly and rather painfully, and dug into her coat pocket. 'Just what I'm in the mood for.'

Lucy eyed her warily. Whoever she was, she was plump featured, with a short, squat stature, her thick, greying hair tied in a single, rope-like ponytail. She wore a heavy waxed jacket over jeans and a scruffy grey sweatshirt. The look didn't especially suit her. Most likely it wouldn't suit anyone of that barrel-shaped built. But for this reason alone Lucy now suspected she was in the presence of someone who'd reached a stage in their career where appearance counted for little compared to reputation.

The newcomer flipped open a leather wallet to reveal her warrant card.

'"Priya" to my friends, "Detective Superintendent Nehwal" to you. I appreciate you've been on all night, PC Clayburn, but I'd like a quick word if poss . . . without the attitude.'

'Certainly, ma'am. If . . .' Lucy was briefly tongue-tied. She didn't know DSU Priya Nehwal personally, but she certainly knew *about* her. Everyone knew about her. 'If . . . if I can just finish getting dressed . . .?'

Nehwal glanced at her watch, as if this itself was an imposition. 'I'll wait outside.'

Priya Nehwal was a thirty-year veteran and ace thief-taker, a status for which she'd been decorated many times. She was now one of the most senior investigators in Greater Manchester's Serious Crimes Division, having solved many more high-level offences – like murder, rape, robbery and arson – than anyone else currently serving. She was something of a poster-child for the women entering the job, especially Asian women.

Lucy hurried to finish getting dressed, and left the building through its side personnel-door, rucksack on her back, crimson motorcycle helmet tucked under one arm. The aptly named Robber's Row wasn't just a police station but the N Division's administrative HQ, and as such a massive multi-floored redbrick monstrosity of a building, which occupied an enormous plot of land running alongside Tarwood Lane, the main thoroughfare into Crowley from Salford. It shared a forecourt with the local fire station, though when Lucy walked out there, nobody was waiting for her. She checked in the personnel car park at the rear of the nick, and even around the garages and in the vehicle pound, but again it was no dice. She finally found Nehwal some ten minutes later, in the small park on the other side of Tarwood Lane, where she'd unwrapped a plastic bag and was breaking up a squishy cheese-barm, fragments of which she scattered for the ducks clustered at the pond's edge.

She didn't bother looking round when Lucy approached.

'Ma'am?' Lucy finally said, feeling strangely self-conscious.

At a slim five foot eight, physically fit, with long black hair and handsome, feline looks as yet unlined by her years of police service, Lucy was aware that she cut quite a dash, especially when kitted out in the leathers she wore to ride her gleaming red Ducati Monster M900. But the presence of a living legend like Priya Nehwal, however much a raga-muffin she was in appearance, made Lucy feel gawky and awkward. It didn't help, of course, that Nehwal had blazed a trail for female detectives though many decades of impressive work, and that Lucy had completely ruined her own CID chances in the very first week.

'Heard you had a good lock-up last night?' Nehwal said.

Lucy shrugged. 'Common sense bobbying, ma'am.'

'And now you're the woman of the moment.'

'I wouldn't go that far, ma'am.'

Nehwal brushed crumbs from her hands and scrunched the plastic wrapper into her coat pocket. 'Neither would I . . . but when you're back on Division you've got to talk the talk.'

She pulled on a pair of fingerless woollen gloves. It was October 15th, and though it had been a mild month so far, this particular morning was fresh to the point of chilliness.

'Is this something important, ma'am?' Lucy asked. 'Only I've just finished a double-length shift . . .'

'Ready for bed, are you?'

'Well . . . the armchair. No point going to bed when I'm not actually on nights, but a couple of hours can't hurt.'

'Yes, well . . . sorry to rain on your parade, PC Clayburn, but sleep may not come so easily after this. Even so, it'll be your call.' Nehwal produced a morning paper, unrolled it and offered it to her. 'What do you think?'

Lucy gazed at the front page, which in a massive banner-headline, read:

JILL THE RIPPER!

Underneath it, colour photographs depicted two side-by-side images. One was of a rural lay-by with a silver-black Lexus LS 430 parked in the middle, CSIs in Tyvek unspooling incident tape around it. The second one, clearly shot from a helicopter, displayed woodland from a high angle, with a red circle indicating an only partly visible forensics tent erected beneath the cover of the trees, and more diminutive Tyvek-clad figures.

An equally eye-catching sub-header read:

Police bosses admit Lay-by Murders could be work of _female_ serial killer

Beneath that, a tower of grainy, black-and-white headshots portrayed mass murderesses from former decades: Myra Hindley on top, with Beverley Allitt and Joanna Dennehy underneath. The opening paragraph to the sensationalist lead read:

In a stunning turnabout, senior detectives investigating the brutal sex-murders of four men are considering what might at one time have been unthinkable – that the perpetrator could be a woman!

The recent Lay-by Murders have been occurring across the north-west of England at a rate of one a month, with the latest victim, Ronald Ford (48), a garage owner from Warrington, found dead last week off a secluded road near Abram in Greater Manchester. All had been brutally beaten and repeatedly stabbed . . .

Lucy glanced up. 'So you're not looking for a gay suspect anymore?'

Nehwal shrugged as she fiddled with her iPad. 'I never thought we were, if I'm honest. None of the victims were known or even suspected to be homosexuals. I know some men lead double lives, but four of them one after another without a hint of it in their background? Seemed progressively less likely the more we were able to put names to their emasculated corpses.'

'So you're now looking for a woman? Seriously?'

'Shocking thought, eh? That there are girls out there as badly behaved as the boys.'

'But this is correct, ma'am? You're hunting a female sex murderer?'

'We're hunting a lunatic, PC Clayburn. The fact it's a woman is no more a problem for me that if it was a man. Evil knows no gender.'

'I get that, but it'd be a rarity . . . surely?'

'First time for everything.' Nehwal turned the iPad around. A grainy video was playing. 'Couple of days ago, we recovered this CCTV footage from the slip road connecting a filling station outside Atherton to the A579.'

At first, the moving picture wasn't easily distinguishable. The camera was clearly located some distance from the slip-lane, but the image had been enhanced sufficiently to display a vehicle cruising down it, and slowing and stopping just before it reached the main drag. Here, a female figure – female because it had longish, fair hair under a beret-like hat, an hourglass shape and, by the looks of it, was wearing a tight skirt or dress, and high heels – approached from the verge, spoke to the driver through an open passenger window, and then climbed in. After that, the car sped away.

'Lexus 430,' Lucy observed.

'Correct,' Nehwal said. 'Belonged to Ronald Ford, the last victim – the next time anyone saw him, apart from the murderer, he was lying dead with his skull bashed in and his dick and balls severed.'

Lucy pondered that. It certainly matched the MO. So far, the APs had all been found in isolated locations but close to busy roads. In each case they had been beaten with a blunt instrument like a hammer, which was thought to have rendered them semi-conscious. They had then had their genitals cut away. Most had died from the subsequent blood loss, though one had also suffered a severely fractured skull, and might already have been dead when he was mutilated.

Though these horrible eviscerations were widely known about inside the police, the taskforce had deliberately been vague with the press, publicising that in all cases death was caused in the same way: first, blows to the head to weaken the subject, and then knife-wounds to the lower abdomen to finish him off. That latter detail wasn't untrue of course,

37

but they'd withheld it that the sexual organs had been removed in order to weed out any serial confessors, of whom there had already been several since the news had broken that a new killer was on the loose.

There were lots of questions here, though.

'Gave the nice old lady who was out for an early morning walk with her poodle a turn that she's never likely to recover from,' Nehwal added conversationally.

Lucy said nothing as she watched the video play through a second time and a third.

'You look doubtful,' Nehwal said.

'It's nothing, ma'am . . . just, wasn't the second victim a big heavy bloke?'

'That's right. Larry Pupper, a lorry driver. Weighed in at about twenty-five stone. We found him just off the East Lancs, near Worsley.'

'And yet I seem to remember reading that he'd been dragged something like a hundred yards before being dumped in some thickets.'

'You've been following the case, PC Clayburn?'

'You can't get away from it. It's all over social media.'

'Well, wait till this story hits Facebook. Jill the Ripper, eh? You can't beat a novelty, even where serial killers are concerned. Anyway, yes . . . that lorry driver thing was easier to understand when we thought we were looking for a bloke, but there are as many oddities in this case as there are theories.'

'Could the killer be a cross-dresser maybe?'

'Got a good figure if he is.' Nehwal closed the iPad. 'It isn't a bloke, though. There's been no semen found at any of the murder scenes. Okay, that isn't uncommon with sex crimes these days given the public's knowledge about DNA evidence. But killers are rarely as careful as they like to think they are. More telling is the footprint we identified.'

'I didn't realise we had,' Lucy said.

'We're sitting on it,' Nehwal replied. 'For the time being at least. There was a whole mess of footprints in the area surrounding all the murder scenes. Most were boot or trainer prints. Hardly unusual given that they were on or near to public footpaths. But then we found the imprint of a high-heeled shoe close to Ronnie Ford's body. That would be uncommon in a woodland area, which made it suspicious. However, it was only identified as a size seven, which meant that it most likely had been left by a woman rather than a man.'

'If it's a woman she'd have to be unusually strong.'

'Uh-huh.'

'Or she's got company . . .?'

'We've considered that, but serial killers working team-handed are even rarer than go-it-alone women.' Nehwal tapped her iPad. 'And as we have to go where the evidence leads us, at present we're only looking for one.'

'So that little miss on the video is your prime suspect?'

'I wouldn't call her little. Even allowing for her heels, we estimate she stands about six feet. Plus she's stacked, as you saw for yourself.'

'Prozzie?'

'Most likely.' Nehwal sniffed. 'Could be a hitcher, but a tight skirt and high heels . . . you ever known a hippy chick hit the road dressed like that?'

'If nothing else, it should be easy enough tracing her.'

'On the contrary . . .' Nehwal cracked a cynical half-smile. 'It's proving anything but. Surprisingly so. And there are other complicating factors. Hammond, Pupper and now Ford were all killed in Greater Manchester, but Graham Cummins, the third victim was found in a ditch near Southport, which is in Merseyside, having apparently picked his murderer up – we *think* – just outside Preston, which is in Lancs. So before you ask, their lordships are about to announce

Operation Clearway, a specialist taskforce comprising officers from all three forces.'

Lucy nodded. 'And, just out of interest . . . why are you telling *me*?'

'It's simple.' Nehwal slid her iPad back into one of her apparently capacious pockets. 'We need women, and lots of them. Younger women, preferably . . . but they'll need at least a bit of experience.' She eyed Lucy carefully. 'You tick both those boxes.'

'You're aware, ma'am, that my last CID attachment was a bit of a disaster?'

'Yeah, but that's not an issue. You won't have an investigative role.'

'Okay, so let me see . . .' Lucy's brief thrill of interest rapidly deflated. She arched an eyebrow. 'When you say you want young women, you mean you want secretaries to run the MIR?'

'Erm . . . no.' Nehwal cracked another smile, again minus humour. 'The job you'll be doing won't be anything like as clean and safe as that.'

'Decoys then? You want undercover decoy units?'

'Well . . . you won't be decoys as such. The killer's not targeting women. But unfortunately, if you take this job it still means you're going to be out there in your tarty gear, rubbing shoulders with the girls who work the roads.'

'Covert enquiries?'

'Basically. Hang around with them, talk to them, make friends. Collate as much intel as you can.'

'Sounds like a pretty desperate ploy.'

'No . . .' Nehwal re-rolled the newspaper. '*This* was a desperate ploy. Releasing that it's a woman to the press. But the new footage means the time's come to openly warn the travelling salesman crowd. So we're not just in the papers, we'll be on all the news bulletins too. Whether it works'll be anyone's guess. Some of these fellas couldn't keep it in their pants if a one-eyed hunchback flashed her knockers at them. But basically you're right . . . we've got to nip this thing in the bud right now.'

'What's the actual process going to be?'

'Just what I say.' Nehwal headed towards the park gate. 'Start pretending you're a hooker. You'll each have a body-guard, of course. We're bringing a few Tactical Support Group lads in. A couple will be parked up covertly wherever you're walking your pitch. Others'll be driving round undercover. They'll pick you up from time to time. Make it look like you're working. But I'm not going to pretend it isn't going to be a bag of crap. You'll have nasty-piece-of-work johns to deal with, not to mention hostile pimps and aggressive suspicion from the real working girls. And a lot of the time you'll have to deal on your own. We can't have the TSG monkeys showing their hand for every little thing. It's going to need to get very tasty indeed before we blow our cover. But you've done this sort of thing before, haven't you?'

'Ish,' Lucy replied.

They reached the edge of the pavement. Rush-hour vehicles trundled back and forth in front of the towering Victorian façade of Robber's Row.

'Just don't take too long making your mind up,' Nehwal said. 'We go live on Monday, and before then I've got to see twenty other girls.'

'Any chance there's a way back into CID for me, ma'am?' Lucy wondered. 'I mean if this thing comes off.'

Nehwal mused. 'We never say "never".'

'They more or less said "never" when I fouled up last time.'

'Jill the Ripper has changed every priority, PC Clayburn.' Nehwal strode forward as a break opened in the traffic. 'All bets are off from now on. Anything can happen.'

Chapter 4

Lucy was home by nine, though, strictly speaking, it was her mother's home. Several years ago, Lucy had bought herself a bungalow on Cuthbertson Court, in another part of town. It was little more than a crash pad really, and at the time she'd acquired it mainly as an investment with a possible view to renting it out at some point. It had been in a poor state of repair back then, and to an extent it still was, Lucy increasingly seeing it as a long-term project, something she could slowly but surely refurbish when she finally got around to it. Whatever she opted to do with it when it was finally finished, in the meantime she was still in her old bedroom in her mother's small terraced house in Saltbridge, another former mill district close to the border with Bolton.

She yawned as she wheeled her Ducati through the back gate, and opened what had once been the coal bunker but now had been adapted into a shed with a felt and plastic-lined waterproof roof. She pushed the vehicle into the interior, which, though unlit and stinking of oil, was all very orderly. The tools with which she maintained the majestic beast were arrayed neatly on the walls. There were cleaning materials on the shelves, and several spare canisters of Ultimate Unleaded stored in a locker in the corner.

As Lucy closed and padlocked the shed door behind her, her mother stepped out from the kitchen. Whereas Lucy was dark-haired and coltish in build, Cora Clayburn was fair haired and buxom. She'd been quite a beauty in her day, or so Lucy would imagine – she *had* to imagine, because they had no other living relatives and she knew no friends from her mother's early life who could confirm this. Though age was catching up a little – Cora was now fifty-three and a lot of that lovely fair hair was running to silver – she was still trim and shapely, an appearance she preserved through careful eating and regular exercise. Lucy had always thought that her mum looked amazing in the pink Lycra top and tight, black tracksuit bottoms she wore each day for her five-mile evening constitutional. Less attractive, though, was the shapeless blue smock with the plastic name tag she was currently clad in for her role as assistant manager at the Saltbridge MiniMart.

'Now?' Cora said, looking relieved. Shortly after midnight, Lucy had left her a message that she'd be late, but it wouldn't have stopped her worrying. 'Long shift, that?'

'Yeah, but a good one.' Lucy pulled her gauntlets off and tucked them into her helmet. 'Bloody maniac grabbed this eighteen-year-old lass on her way home from baby-sitting.'

'My God . . . where?'

'Top of Darthill Road.'

Cora didn't look surprised. 'The Aggies?'

'The edge of it.'

'I wish they'd take action about that place. Build on it, or something.'

'No chance, Mum . . . they'll want to find a nice green space for that.' Cora sidled past her and went indoors, where the mingled aromas of cooked bacon and fresh coffee set her empty stomach rumbling. 'Anyway, the bastard – pardon my French – gave her a real smacking. Smashed her teeth, broke her nose and cheekbone.' She unzipped her leather jacket and peeled it off the thin, sweat-damp T-shirt underneath. 'I got him over in Bullwood. He still had her phone and purse in his pockets. Talk about banged to rights.'

'Thank God for that,' Cora said. 'Who is he?'

'A total lowlife called Wayne Crompton.' Lucy folded her leather over the back of a kitchen chair, and stretched. 'He's got form as long as your arm, but this time he'll be off the streets for a while. Charged him a couple of hours ago . . . robbery, GBH and attempted kidnapping.'

'Like you said, a good night's work.' But Cora's tone remained neutral, as it always did when Lucy got enthusiastic about cop stuff. 'But I thought you were back on duty this afternoon?'

'*Was*,' Lucy confirmed. 'Not any more. They offered me the money or the time in lieu, dropping extra-strong hints that they wanted me to take the time. So I'm going to – today.'

Cora nodded approvingly as she shrugged her mac on.

'Mum, there's something else I need to talk to you about,' Lucy said.

'Tell me quick, because I'm running a bit late.'

'It's okay . . . it's not important.'

Cora stopped by the door. 'Go on . . . I can tell you want to.'

So Lucy did, all about Operation Clearway, not specifying the exact role she'd be playing of course, but outlining the basics of the case and the new lines of enquiry the taskforce would shortly be embarking on.

Cora frowned. 'So what are you saying . . . you're a detective again?'

'Not quite. It may be a way back for me though.'

'I'm surprised you want a way back in after the way they treated you last time.'

'Mum, come on . . . I'm lucky I'm still in the job.'

'Some of us wouldn't mind if you weren't.'

'I know that, but look –' Lucy embraced her '– this is me. It's my life, okay?'

'Yes, yes, I know.' Cora returned the embrace but a little stiffly. 'And we've had this conversation before . . . so stop going on about it, you silly old trout.'

Lucy pecked her on the cheek. 'I've never called you "a silly old trout".'

'You've thought it, I'm sure.'

'The thing is, I'm mainly going to be working nights for the next few weeks.'

Cora considered this with visible apprehension.

Lucy knew why, and that it would be unrelated to her mother's own safety.

With its edificial industrial ruins and rows of red-brick terraced houses, Saltbridge was not the most salubrious part of Crowley. Like so many working class neighbourhoods in the post-manufacturing era, it was extensively unemployed, drugs and alcoholism were rife and it suffered higher than normal crime rates. But Cora had lived here all of Lucy's life at least, a dauntless single mum who'd never once been oppressed or intimidated by the environment in which she'd been forced to raise her child. These days, having held a management position for several years, she could probably afford to move out to the suburbs if she wanted to, but she had friends locally and was comfortable here.

'How long will this assignment last?' Cora asked.

'As long as it takes. Could be a few months. But don't worry. I'm not going to be in harm's way.'

'I bet you thought that last time too. And then look what

happened. You were relieved you didn't lose your job. All that mattered to me was that I didn't lose my child.'

Lucy smiled tiredly. It was tempting to retort with the provable fact that uniformed patrol, her current role, was one of the most dangerous jobs a police officer could undertake, and that detectives didn't encounter violent criminals half as often as bobbies on the beat did. But that would hardly help. Perhaps if Lucy had earned herself some stripes by now, or maybe an inspector's pips, things would be different. She'd be able to con her mum into thinking that each shift was spent in the hermetically sealed environment of a supervisor's office, rubber-stamping reports all day. But though Lucy had already passed both her sergeant's and inspector's exams, she hadn't received the call just yet. Positive discrimination was a big thing in the service these days. The top brass were keen to advance the careers of their female underlings, but perhaps not when said underling was the child of a single parent from the wrong side of town – a child who didn't even know her father, and especially not after that foul-up in Borsdane Wood.

'So you'll be here this evening when I get home?' Cora said, opening the back door.

'Certainly will. I'll have tea ready and waiting.'

'Lovely. That'll make us square. Your breakfast's in the oven.'

'Oh cool . . . I'm starving.' Lucy pulled on a padded glove and drew out the hotplate, and was delighted to see bacon, eggs, sausage, beans, grilled tomato and toast. 'Mum! You shouldn't have gone to this much trouble.'

'I know I shouldn't, but I have to make it worth your while coming home, don't I? Otherwise one day you might not.'

'Don't be silly.' Lucy kissed her on the forehead. 'Go on . . . you'll be late.'

46

Chapter 5

An executive decision was taken to locate Operation Clearway's Major Incident Room, or MIR as it was known in the trade, at Robber's Row. The taskforce took residence on its top two floors, where suites of offices were available which already were well equipped and close to all necessary facilities. The MIR itself was on the lower of these, the station's fourth floor, where the N Division's Sports & Social Club had once been: over a hundred square yards of floor-space with a raised stage at one end and a bar at the other, though both of these were now defunct. Robber's Row was one of the last nicks in GMP with a section-house attached, in other words sleeping quarters for junior officers. Few of these comfortable but basic one-bed domiciles were used any more; in fact most of them would need to be aired out at the very least, but the proximity to the MIR of such a purpose-built bunkhouse was perfect, given that, as prom-ised, nearly half of the two hundred officers attached full time to Clearway had been brought in from outside the GMP area.

The whole thing would be a home from home for Lucy,

who'd worked out of Robber's Row for the last four years, ever since she'd transferred away from Cotehill Crescent, the sub-divisional nick where she'd been posted until the incident at Borsdane Wood. But the atmosphere would be different in the MIR. A little less formal perhaps, with everyone in civvies and relatively few newbies involved, but with less margin for error than would normally be tolerated. The thought of having Priya Nehwal in command was a little unnerving – she was the best, so she expected the same from her staff. But in truth, she was only one member of the top brass on Operation Clearway, Deputy SIO in fact. According to the bumph circulated by email those first couple of nights, the rest of the senior supervision would comprise Detective Chief Superintendent Jim Cavill, also from GMP's Serious Crimes Division, who was SIO, and Detective Chief Inspector June Swanson from Merseyside, who was Office Manager. Both of these characters were unknown quantities to Lucy, so it was anyone's guess what their overall management style would be, but given the general experience of the taskforce, it was to be hoped that it would be pretty relaxed.

It all started reasonably well that first morning.

As part of the Intel Unit, as they'd now be referred to, Lucy found her induction briefing on the top floor in what had once been the classroom where the N Division Training Officer had put probationers through their paces. From here on, this would be their base. It was airy and spacious, with rows of neatly arranged tables and chairs, and a large desk and widescreen VDU at the front. It also had a locker room attached and a small anteroom, which the DI running the Intel Unit could make use of as a private office. If nothing else, it was a relief to be in there, given that downstairs it was already a tale of chaos, taskforce detectives doing their level best to work amid the bedlam of delivery guys tramping in and out wheeling desks, filing cabinets and computer equipment, and techies hammering and banging as they installed new electrical fittings. Not that the Intel Unit didn't feel a little crowded itself. That first day, approximately thirty young female officers were assembled there, mostly seated, while a row of fifteen blokes stood at the back.

'Morning, everyone,' DI Geoff Slater said from the front. 'Chuffed to bits to see so many of you here . . . but if I don't sound overly excited, apologies in advance. We've got a shedload of work ahead of us.'

Slater was another GMP Serious Crimes Division man, but to Lucy's eye he looked more like a TV cop. He was somewhere in his late-thirties, tall and lean, but with an air of virility. He had a thatch of unruly black hair and rugged, lived-in looks. His shirt, tie, jacket and trousers were all vaguely rumpled. He didn't seem especially happy: he wore a serious, rather sullen expression – and yet it all hung together nicely.

'You all know why you're here and what a ball-acher of a job you're going to be doing when you're out there,' Slater said. 'Hopefully you all gave deep consideration to this assignment before you stuck your hands up – I hope so at least, otherwise you might find you're in the wrong place. I'm certainly not going to do you the disservice of trying to sugar-coat this, because that'd be a total waste of time. Likewise, I don't want to spend time we can't spare making formal introductions, aside from to introduce myself, which I already have done, and your two immediate line-managers, detective sergeants Sally Bryant from Merseyside and Maureen Clark from Lancashire.'

Two of the seated women stuck their hands up to indicate who they were.

'You'll obviously need to get to know each other,' Slater

said, 'but you can do that on your first tea-break. You're all wearing name-tags anyway, so that should help and there're a couple of charts on the wall that you might find useful.'

Lucy glanced up. Among a mass of other paperwork, mainly maps and photographs with marker-pen notations all over them, there were two colour charts, one for women and one for men, each bearing ordered and neatly blown-up headshots, with essential details like name, rank, collar-number and police force of origin listed underneath. She skimmed through. Several of the women were already serving detectives, though the majority were PCs like herself. The male officers, she'd already learned, had largely been drafted from the Tactical Support Group, which meant they'd most likely be ex-military, which their burly physiques and hard, truculent faces also seemed to imply. Their role was basically to keep an eye on the women, but also to drive up in unmarked cars every so often, posing as customers, so as to maintain the illusion that the girls were working prosti-tutes.

'What I will say is this,' Slater said. 'We're a small but vital part of a very big operation. I've been a detective for sixteen years and I've never known a case where as many resources were being chucked around. I could put my cynical hat on and say that if we were investigating the usual type of serial murder . . . i.e. drug-addled hookers getting sliced 'n' diced rather than the white, middle-class men who use their services, there wouldn't be half as much media attention and nowhere near as much pressure on us to get a result. But I'm not going to. I don't know if that's the case, and frankly I don't care.'

His gaze roved across them. His delivery was a low, taut monotone.

'Mine's a school of thought where *all* lives are valuable,' he said. 'Where each one that gets snuffed out leaves a hole in people's lives that will probably never be filled. None of these fellas asked to get murdered, much less tortured. And that's the other thing. That's the really nasty bit . . . someone's out there using a butcher's knife to carve off these blokes' crown jewels. Now I'm sure everyone here knows some misogynistic pillock who in one of your lighter moments you'd happily say deserves such a fate. But you've still got to ask yourself the question . . . do you really want someone wandering the streets who's capable of this kind of sadism? I mean, disregarding the mistreatment she may have suffered at the hands of men, because that's irrelevant to our role here . . . do you really want this woman walking about free? Because who gets it next? Not just the bloke who propositions her or offers her money . . . maybe the bloke who makes a politer approach, offering her a drink or asking her out on a date. Maybe the bloke who opens a door for her, or simply gives her a smile when he's out walking his dog. And this is the real rub, ladies. Because when *you* get out there, this could be the very same person you're swapping banter with when you're fixing your make-up in the bus station toilets. It could be the girl standing on the next streetcorner, the one who comes over every five minutes to scrounge a ciggie off you.'

He scrutinised them carefully.

'When policewomen usually do decoy work, they're standing among the prospective victims. This time you may be standing with the killer. And for that reason if none other, you're going to have to stay sharp. You'll be working four days on, three days off, four till four. You'll not be on the same pitch all the time, though I'm not going to allocate any one of you more than two or three pitches, the whole purpose of this being that you get to know the other girls who work there . . . that you talk to them, find out who *they* think might be doing it. But for your own safety, at no time can you take your eye off the ball. I mean not once. Because if you let something slip about who you are, and Jill the Ripper picks up on it, and you're stuck with her all night on a lonely road . . . I wonder who's *not* going to be heading home again when the shift finally ends.'

Lucy had already considered this discomforting possibility, though by the looks on the faces of some of the others, primarily the younger girls, they hadn't. There was no safe way to perform this kind of work. At the best of times, the women they'd be interacting with were likely to be damaged. They wouldn't all be bad people; there'd be tired mums trying to make ends meet, students with college bills to pay, actresses and models who couldn't get real work. But it was an unforgiving profession. There'd be thieves among them too, addicts, mental patients, disease carriers. And now one of them could be a murderer.

'And if that hasn't scared you shitless,' Slater said, 'sorry . . . but next up we're going to run through the details of the enquiry. And this isn't going to be pleasant either.'

He called various images onto the VDU as he outlined the progress thus far. As expected, the crime scene photos were graphic in the extreme, and yet, from a purely analytical perspective, there were startling similarities between them. The most recent victim, Ronald Ford, lay on his back in the roadside woods near Abram, with a pool of blood and brains beneath his broken skull, and his trousers and underpants pushed down to his shins, exposing a gore-glutted cavity where his genitals used to be. Two of the other victims, William Hammond and Graham Cummins, who were found in lay-bys near Chadderton and Southport respectively, lay in exactly the same posture, suffering from exactly the same fatal injuries. Only the second victim, Larry Pupper – the heavily built HGV driver, who'd been dragged a considerable distance – lay on his side in a muddy, litter-cluttered ditch on the outskirts of Salford. His trousers were tangled around his feet, as though he'd been trying to take them off altogether, which suggested the killer had waited until he was most off his guard in order to attack, and his face was battered savagely and extensively, implying that even then he'd put up a fight. Perhaps even after the beating, he'd struggled, which might explain why he'd needed to be dragged still further from the East Lancashire road. Whatever, it looked as if he'd died before he'd reached his final destination – in the photo he lay draped on his side, his arms twisted out of shape as though partly dislodged from their sockets. The gaping wound where his genitals had been hacked off was less bloody than the others.

Medical examiners now felt certain the actual implement used to achieve this ghastly effect was a knife with a thick, serrated blade – the sort a butcher might use to saw through bone and gristle. There were plenty other lines of enquiry too, though few had borne fruit as yet. Slater hastened through them anyway, skimping on detail where he could – primarily because this was mainly of use to the girls as background info. They had no investigative brief, and so the DI was much more interested in those factors that had potential relevance for the role they would be playing.

In which case he now summoned the mugshots of three living men onto the VDU.

'A bit of intel on the kind of people you are likely to hear about,' he said. 'I doubt you'll encounter any of these characters personally – I sincerely *hope* you don't – but you definitely need to know something about them. As you're probably aware, we have a wide range of crime syndicates trading in the north-west. But tough as they like to talk, on the whole they are all dominated by these maniacs. Anyone know who they are?'

Lucy eyed the three faces with interest. All looked to be in early middle age, but at second glance there was no doubting their chosen professions.

'The Crew,' one of the other girls spoke up.

'That's correct,' Slater said. 'This is the infamous Crew. For any of you who've spent your police service on another planet, the early noughties saw the formation of a particularly dangerous cartel here in the north-west of England . . . they're known simply as the Crew, and they control most of the high-level crime in Manchester, Liverpool and various of the two cities' satellite towns. As I say, it wasn't always thus. Back in the day, the numerous gangsters we had up here were too busy fighting each other to actually make any money. At least, that was the case until one of our leading Manchester hoodlums –' he indicated the middle face '– a certain Bill Pentecost, decided enough was enough.'

Lucy looked in fascination at the image of Bill Pentecost, the north-west's legendary boss of bosses. At first glance there was nothing immediately brutal about him, but on closer inspection something wasn't quite right. He was weasel-faced, with a shock of greying 'wire-wool' hair. His features were lean and sharp-edged, and he wore steel-framed, rectangular-lensed glasses over a pair of narrow, ice-blue eyes.

'Pentecost started his career as a council estate money-lender,' Slater said. 'His trademark was extreme terror; he would punish those who failed to pay up by crucifying them on doors. But he built his larger empire on drugs and extortion, finally coming to occupy a position as one of Manchester's top godfathers. As such, his vision gradually broadened. He decided that he'd rather make deals than engage in crazy violence, and so arranged a meeting of all the heads of the region's main gangs, at which he proposed the set-up of a kind of overarching north-west crime faction, in which they'd all participate and which in due course would become known as "the Crew". Members would have an equal partnership and an equal say in all major decisions affecting the governance and protection of crime in this region, the endgame being to establish permanent peace and prosperity.

'And guess what . . . with a few minor exceptions, it worked. Harmony wasn't just restored to the north-west crime network, all these years later the Crew is still the leading underworld power in this region. It's got a controlling interest in just about every racket you can think of, and Bill Pentecost, now in his mid-fifties, is firmly cemented in place as top dog.'

He paused to take a breath, and for the first time smiled – a rather tired smile, Lucy thought, the smile of a guy so used to thinking how unfair it was that these killers were all millionaires while the average copper spent so much of his time worried about his pension that if he didn't laugh about it he'd cry.

'As I say, you're unlikely to meet him,' Slater said. 'He never gets his own hands dirty anymore. He's got umpteen layers of fall-guys between him and the streets, but it's important you know who he is, because quite a few of these girls are likely to be on his pay-roll, albeit indirectly. Which brings us to the second name you need to know, and this is someone it's just conceivable you *might* meet up with.'

He indicated the left-hand image. This one portrayed a younger man, perhaps only his mid-forties, but again lean and feral of feature, an impression enhanced by a vaguely insane smile. His head was completely shaved, and his eyes sunk into pits. Lucy had the notion that if some Photoshop genius added a goatee beard and a pair of antlers, it would be a perfect spit for the Devil.

'As I say, the Crew have many rackets,' Slater said, 'and one of the most lucrative is the sex trade. So this is their pimp-in-chief, the ludicrously named Nick Merryweather, more accurately known as "Necktie Nicky" thanks to his preferred method of despatching those he doesn't like. For the record, Serious Crimes Division has two unsolved murders on its books wherein the APs, both of them underworld players, were found with their throats cut and their tongues pulled out through the wound. They're suspected to be Crew hits, and Necktie Nicky, though a Crew lieutenant rather than a soldier, was almost certainly the assassin. So this is someone to be especially wary of, though most likely, if you do your job properly, you'll be a flyspeck beneath his notice. That's assuming he bothers coming out to check on business. He has lots of madams and under-pimps to do that for him.'

He moved along to the third and final mugshot.

'Now . . . prostitution being what it is in the age of Internet-fuelled home industry, not even a terror like Necktie Nicky can exert ownership over the entire field. He doesn't actually run any brothels – he protects them, in other words he takes a big share of all their profits. That's the way the Crew work, which makes it hard if not impossible to hit them with any real criminal charges. But as I said, there's so much sex-for-sale out there now that even Nick Merryweather can't cover the entire spectrum. So to help him, he relies on this charmer, fellow Crew lieutenant Frank McCracken.'

McCracken's face was in some ways the scariest on show, because it was the most normal. There was a hardness about it, for sure, but he was also a handsome man, square-jawed, dark-eyed, his lightly greying hair worn in a sharp crew-cut. His eyes were chips of glass – there was no doubt that this character would kick you to death if you said a word out of place. But he too was in his fifties, and if you weren't on the look-out for villainy, it was possible you could pass him in the street without giving him another glance.

'Anyone know what McCracken's official role in the Crew is?' Slater asked.

Another girl put her hand up. 'The Shakedown.'

'Correct again,' Slater replied. 'And you even use the underworld terminology, so ten out of ten. Frank McCracken's role in the Crew, ladies and gentlemen, is what they call "the Shakedown". If ever a lucrative theft is committed in the north-west area, like a robbery, a high-end burglary or fraud, or if pimps, dealers and bookies are active who aren't "officially approved", it's McCracken's job to ensure the Crew gets its cut. And trust me, he's very good at it. Some of his methods, at least those reported to us as hearsay, are beyond imagining. On the upside, McCracken is another who only comes out to play if the opposition gets serious. It's unlikely that small-time operators like you will actually encounter him.'

He paused to look them over. Everyone was maintaining a suitably serious aspect, but quite a few of the girls, again mainly the young ones, had noticeably paled.

'I'd imagine none of you are feeling any the less nervous after what I've just told you,' Slater said. 'Sorry about that, but how would it help if I lied? This just underlines the importance of the front you put out when you hit those streets. As I said, the Crew don't control all the sex-for-sale in the north-west. It's too diverse, involves too many people and is too technology-driven. From your POV it's a good thing that you won't be the only freelancers out there. But it's important that each one of you gets a good cover story and gets it right – who you are, where you live, why you're on the game, etc. In the first instance, you won't be going out there cold. Vice have loaned us one or two working girls who also happen to be snitches – but only the most trustworthy, so that means there's no more than a handful of them. They won't be able to hold all your hands all the time – and at some point you are going to be asked questions.

It'll happen less out there on the fringes of town, where everything's a bit wild and woolly, than it would on the backstreets around Piccadilly and Whalley Range, but it's going to happen and you're going to have to be ready for it. Now you'll all have protectors, you know that . . . but some crap you'll just have to deal with. Any questions so far?'

'Most punters would be surprised to learn there's any kind of prostitution out on the road networks,' one of the girls said. 'People drive around all day and never see anything.'

'That's true,' Slater replied. 'We're going to train you up on that as well. Because you start openly touting at some service stations and you'll be locked up by Traffic before you can say "Cynthia Payne". It's the quieter spots the girls tend to work from: lay-bys, lorry parks, picnic areas – especially at night, when they're deep in shadow. Again . . . sorry not to sweeten this for you, but it's in those shadows where you'll need to be. And it isn't going to be nice.'

They broke for coffee at around eleven, and were on their way down to the canteen when Slater sidled up alongside Lucy.

'PC Clayburn, is it?' he asked.

Lucy waited to let the others pass. 'That's right, sir.'

He stopped next to her. 'You were the one involved in the Mandy Doyle incident?'

Lucy's heart sank, but there was never any option these days other than to admit her error and hope to brazen it out. 'Right again, sir.'

He regarded her with an odd kind of indifference, which she found more unnerving than she would if he'd been openly angry. 'So . . . what?' he said. 'You just admit it like that? No excuses? No convoluted self-justification?'

'None whatever, sir. I dropped a total bollock, and that's why I'm here now . . . I'm trying to make up for it.'

He readjusted the pile of paperwork under his arm. 'I worked with Mandy Doyle on the Drugs Squad. We were partners for three years.'

Lucy's cheeks reddened. 'I'm just glad she's alive, sir.'

'So am I.' He yanked at his tie to loosen it even more. 'She's an idiot, by the way. Always was.'

Lucy thought she'd misheard. 'Sir?'

'Mandy,' he explained. 'Spent her entire career trying to prove she's as tough as the lads. Made up for her lack of imagination with a bolshiness that extended right across the board. Difficult enough when you were a similar rank. But if you were lower, you could expect to put up with a whirl-wind of shit. But why am I telling *you* that, eh?'

Lucy was temporarily lost for words. 'I . . . didn't know her that well.'

He shrugged. 'Lucky you. Or unlucky. She obviously had to blame someone once she went and got herself shot.'

'Strictly speaking, sir, it was me who went and . . .'

'Uh-uh.' He shook his head. 'I read all about it, PC Clayburn. You had a guy in custody on suspicion of raping and brutalising an old lady, yeah? But by his own admission, and as later excavation of the deposition site revealed, he'd also murdered two young women. That should have put him in a different category. That meant he was physically pretty adept, and yet your gaffer went and left you – five days into CID – on your own, handcuffed to him.'

'There was a police driver . . .'

'The driver's irrelevant. He was in a separate compartment of the vehicle.'

With Radio One playing, Lucy reminded herself.

'He couldn't necessarily have known what was going on in the back,' Slater added. 'Even if Haygarth hadn't produced a gun, he might still have overpowered you.'

'I was still a police officer, sir.'

'Your loyalty to DI Doyle is touching, if a tad misplaced. She spent the next year saying you'd almost got her killed, when the reality was exactly the opposite – it was her who almost got *you* killed.'

Lucy preferred not to ponder that, even though her mum had – excessively. You didn't dice with death every day as a copper, but it happened more often than in most civilian occupations. It didn't pay to dwell on the near misses, to wonder what *might* have happened rather than what *did* happen. That was a sure fire way to cost you your nerve for future such situations. But sometimes it was an effort to suppress those distracting thoughts.

'You never should have been left in that vehicle on your own,' Slater concluded.

'I still looked the other way when I shouldn't have.'

'Oh hell . . .' For the first time, Slater's blank expression slackened; he almost smiled. 'I wouldn't have fancied watching a scrote like that take a piss either. The fact is there should have been two of you, minimum. And that was Mandy Doyle's fault. She had tactical command, so she ought to have taken care of it.'

'I'm glad you see it that way, sir. Not everyone does.'

'Shit, Lucy. . .' He walked again; she followed. 'You know what this job's like. Fill a form in wrong and it can follow you for the rest of your career if it suits someone's purpose. But DI Doyle's gone now on a medical, so theoretically that's a clean slate for you.'

'I want to get back into CID.'

'I know. Priya told me.'

'Can you and DSU Nehwal make it happen?'

'Is that your burning ambition?' he asked. It sounded like a genuine question.

'It's what I joined up for in the first place.'

This time he *did* smile. 'So what were you watching as a kid? *Cagney and Lacey*? *Prime Suspect*? No offence intended . . . with me it was *Miami Vice*.'

'Yeah, well . . . I guess we all got a bit of a shock when the reality hit us.'

'Telling me. Anyway, the truth is, Lucy, we *need* detectives. Urgently . . . and I mean everywhere. Special units too, not just Division. Too many people are joining up these days who are only interested in fast-track promotion, and CID's the wrong place for that.' He halted at the entrance to the canteen. 'So if you're serious, and you do a job for us . . . we might be able to assist. It's early days though. I mean we've got to catch a killer first.'

'And you really think the Intel Unit's going to have a role in that, sir?' she asked. 'Isn't it more likely forensics'll nab her? Or some good old-fashioned detective work?'

He shrugged as he walked inside. It was already noisy and crowded, mainly with plain clothes and civvie admin staff from the MIR, though uniforms and traffic wardens occupied some of the tables. They threaded their way through to the service counter with difficulty.

'We're dealing with someone who's deadly serious about what she's doing,' Slater said over his shoulder. 'You can tell that by the scorecard she's racking up. It's always going to be shoe-leather that brings someone like that to heel. Whether that's Plod going door-to-door, detectives bouncing around the MIR having great ideas, or you lasses walking those grubby roads in your kinky boots . . . it doesn't really matter.'

'We just nab her any way we can.'

'Correct.'

But Lucy was under no illusion. Slater was clearly disposed to be her friend – possibly because, at thirty, she was older and more experienced than most of the other Intel Unit girls and maybe, therefore, was someone he felt he could look to. The Mandy Doyle incident aside, her record was pretty good – so that could only help. Alternately, he might just fancy her. But even that was tolerable if, when all this was over, it meant he and Priya Nehwal could exert some influence in her favour. And by the sounds of it, there was one sure way to make that happen – feel the collar of Jill the Ripper.

No pressure then.

Chapter 6

'You sure no one's going to see us?' Barney wondered
tautly.

Kev rolled his eyes in that exasperated way he'd so perfected
during the many years of their relationship. 'You tell me,
Barn. Who's actually going to see us? Look . . .' He pointed
through the van window at a patch of diminutive lights
twinkling some distance away. 'That's Bickershaw.' Now he
pointed in the other direction, indicating a similar scattering
of lights, so distant in this case that they were only noticeable
because all other landscape features were hidden by the
autumn darkness. 'And that's Leigh. So where are we, Barn?'

Barney didn't know for sure, even though he'd driven
them both here in his uncle's shuddery old van. The truth
was he didn't even think this area of wasteland had a name.
As far as he could recall from his daylight travels, it was a
patch of emptiness lying just east of the B5237.

He shrugged, helpless to answer.

'A shit-tip where nobody lives,' Kev said irritably. 'Where
you'd be lucky to find rats, because rats are generally not that
fucking stupid. Nobody wants this place. So not only is no
one likely to see us . . . why should it matter if anyone does?'

Even to Barney – who was a bigger, heavier lad than Kev, but tended by instinct to defer to his lifelong mate on all matters where complex thought was required – the answer to this one was more than obvious.

'Because it's public land and fly-tipping's illegal.'

Kev snorted. 'But it was alright to dig coal mines out here, wasn't it? And dump mountains of slag?'

'I'm just saying,' Barney cautioned. 'Let's be careful.'

'We'll be careful. But for fuck's sake, don't let these bastards guilt-trip you.'

'These bastards' was Kev's signature phrase, and his catch-all term for anyone he perceived to have higher control than himself, be they employers, bailiffs, police officers, the local authority, central Government itself, or anyone at all who qualified in his mind as part of the establishment.

'Hypocrites, the lot of 'em,' he ranted on. 'If they wanted a rubbish tip out here they'd soon okay it . . .'

'I said alright!' Barney didn't normally interrupt his mate in mid-flow, but of the two of them, he, ultimately, had most reason to be nervous.

They'd spent the whole of that dreary Sunday clearing out Kev and Lorna's new flat, which the couple were about to move into at mates' rates because its owner was Lorna's brother-in-law. He'd offered to lower the asking price even more if they disposed of the pile of rubbish that the previous tenants, a bunch of art students at the local Technical College, had left behind. There were boxes of broken brushes, paint pots, turps bottles, easels, torn canvases, along with the ruined carpet from the main lounge, the festering contents of several bins, two mattresses, and even the bedding as well.

It had been a lot more work than the two lads had expected, taking them several hours to bring it all downstairs and load it into the back of Barney's uncle's van, which ensured that all the municipal recycling centres were closed by the time it came to dump the stuff. Having opted – at Kev's insistence – for this other, simpler solution, it now looked as if they'd be at least another hour out here, on a one-time colliery wasteland which it had been quite a challenge just to access. They'd prowled its edges for half an hour or so, both driver and passenger tensing every time another vehicle drove past, before locating a track of sorts. This was little more than a ribbon of rutted, rubbly ground, but at least it was driveable and it led away from the B5237 in a straight line, running a couple of hundred yards before terminating in front of what looked like a burned-out Portakabin.

They halted here, and even though it was a desolate spot, the undefined outlines of rocks and stunted vegetation standing left and right, the pale flood of their headlights picked out a muddy footpath on the other side of the ruin. Barney was glad they were at least away from the road. He switched his headlights off and climbed out, glancing around and listening, before walking to the rear and opening the van doors.

Kev went with him, saying nothing as he dug into the mountain of refuse inside, hefting out a box filled with bric-a-brac, and strutting away through the gutted shell of the Portakabin. Almost by unspoken agreement, they'd decided to chuck the stuff somewhere on the far side of it, using the broken structure as a final shield between themselves and the road. But as Kev vanished along the meandering path beyond it, Barney thought he heard something.

He spun around.

A clacking, or clicking.

Most likely it had been branches rattling in a gust of wind.

There wasn't much starlight penetrating the cloud-cover, but his eyes were finally adjusting to what little there was. Scrub-like thorn breaks were clumped to either side of the track, interspersed here and there by the odd stunted tree; the sort of charmless, twisted vegetation you saw so often on former coal-tips like this but rarely anywhere else. His vision didn't spear very far into it – a few yards, but that was sufficient to show nothing moving.

Barney shuddered as he zipped his fleece. This desolation was the last place he wanted to be in right now. It was ten o'clock at night, and the nearest habitation – either Bickershaw or Leigh – were both miles away.

'You're one to talk about guilt-trips,' Barney mumbled as he humped a roll of heavy, stinky lino onto his shoulder and stumbled through the Portakabin, following the same route as Kev. 'Reminding me I owed you a few quid from when I was short, and calling this an opportunity to pay you back. It was only a few quid, lad.'

Naked bushes clawed at him as he pressed along the path beyond the ruin. Some sixty yards later, it opened out onto a flatter, harder surface – what had once been the concrete floor to another industrial unit.

'This'll do, here,' Kev said from just ahead, as he dumped his load in a kind of unofficial centre-spot. Barney followed suit. They stood there, breathless, glancing round.

The B5237 was about three hundred yards behind them. The streetlights over the top of it were just barely visible, but their own vehicle was concealed by the trees and undergrowth.

'Tell you what,' Kev said in a "go on, I'll humour you" kind of tone. 'If it's really bothering you, why don't we build it all up into a bommy? I mean, it's Bonfire Night in a couple of weeks. If some copper comes wandering around here, he'll probably just think its kids. Won't cock a snook at it.'

'If you say so,' Barney said, not feeling convinced.

'There'll be bommies everywhere this time next week. We'll completely fox the bastards.'

Barney nodded again, before noticing that Kev was watching him – and only belatedly realising that this meant it was going to be his job to construct said bommy. While Kev lurched back along the path towards the van, he got to work, piling the rubbish together, and then looking for spare bits of timber with which he could form that distinctive pyramid shape.

A few minutes later, job done, Barney was also on his way back to the van. They passed each other in the process, Kev's arms wrapped around a bulging bin-liner. They passed each other again a short time later, Barney this time hefting a couple of armfuls. And so it went on, the two of them working in relays until Barney was headed back to the van for what seemed like the fifth and surely final time – only to stop dead when he came in sight of it.

Because another vehicle was now parked at its rear.

Blocking it in.

The only conclusion – the only conclusion *possible* – was coppers.

For half a second, Barney's world collapsed. He felt his bowels shrivel inside him. It wasn't a serious offence, fly-tipping . . . except that he was currently on probation for pinching lead off a church roof. And he had no idea how much another conviction, even a minor one, might damage his chances of staying out of jail.

But now, slowly, he began to notice things that reassured him a little.

In the dimness, he couldn't distinguish much about the car parked behind his van – he could only see the offside of it, and he certainly couldn't identify its make or colour. But there were no Battenberg flashes down its flanks. Nor was there any kind of beacon or visi-flasher on top of it. That didn't necessarily mean it wasn't a police car, but its engine had been switched off and there were no headlights showing. Surely, if they were coppers, they'd still be sitting inside, waiting for the miscreants to come back?

Barney trod forward warily. Even drawing closer, it wasn't possible in this gloom to determine whether or not someone was inside it. But then a voice addressed him.

'Excuse me . . . can you help?'

He swung right, to find a woman sliding into view around the front nearside of the van.

Barney was shaken to see anyone at all, but this lady was the last person he'd have expected. Even in the dimness, she was a stunner: quite tall, an impression enhanced by her high-heeled boots and long, shapely legs, which were clad in spray-on black leggings. Her hands were tucked into the pockets of a shiny, silvery anorak, which was partly unzipped, exposing the best amount of cleavage he'd seen since last accessing the *Butts & Boobs* section of *SexHub*. She had a pretty face as well, and a nice smile. What looked like an awful lot of blonde hair was tucked beneath a smart black beret.

'Erm . . . miss?' he stammered.

'I said can you help me?'

Barney remained tongue-tied; he was smitten. But it now struck him that whoever this lady was, she was still a potential witness to his crime. Even if she failed to recognise him again, she might recognise the registration mark on the van. Trust him to let bleeding Kev talk him into using his uncle's vehicle.

'I've broken down, you see,' the woman said, apparently oblivious to all this. 'I don't know what it was but I just kept losing power and stalling. I'd only just managed to get off the road when I saw your vehicle. I could really use someone to look at the engine.'

'Look at the engine . . .? I'm, whoa . . . I'm not a mechanic.'

'Please help,' she said, her smile faltering, her voice softening with distress. 'I don't want to get stuck all the way out here.'

'Can't you just call a garage?' he said, and immediately

cursed himself. That would be all they needed, a vehicle-recovery team showing up.

But now the woman spoke again, taking a couple of steps towards him, unzipping the front of her anorak. To his disbelief, he saw that she wasn't wearing anything underneath.

'There must be something I can do,' she said, 'to make you change your mind.'

'Miss, I . . .' Barney turned hoarse, his mouth dry of spittle. 'You can't be . . .'

She beckoned him with a long, crimson-tipped finger, before slowly backtracking.

Barney wondered if he was actually unconscious and dreaming. Even though a voice inside kept telling him that this didn't happen in real life, he followed her anyway – back around the front nearside corner of the van and down along the flank of it towards the deep shadows where her own vehicle was parked.

As Kev made his way back to the van, he quietly fumed.

A small man, of thin, wiry stature, the last item he'd taken – the larger of the two mattresses – had almost overwhelmed him with its size and weight. He'd dropped it several times en-route; it had subsequently smeared mud all over the front of his white shell-suit top.

It was no one's fault obviously, but Barney was still going to cop it verbally.

A bloke his size ought to have gone straight to the heavier items, rather than leaving them for his mate. And where the fuck was he anyway? They ought to have passed each other again by now. Kev was secretly hoping that, whatever remained in the van – and it couldn't have been much – Barney would take care of it all himself.

But then he came in sight of the vehicle. And stopped short.

Who the bloody hell had been so inconsiderate as to park up behind them?

Surely to God Barney hadn't been right and, by a one in a million chance, some lazy-arsed copper had happened to drive past and spot what they were up to?

'These bastards!' Kev said under his breath, spittle seething through his clenched teeth.

But then he realised that the other vehicle wasn't a police car. At least, not a marked one.

He padded forward, wondering why both vehicles appeared to be unmanned. If nothing else, Barney still ought to be hanging around. Unless he too had thought the new arrivals were coppers, and had headed for the hills.

That would be so fucking typical.

The big daft prat never watched the news, of course. Dear Lord, they weren't even sending burglars down these days. Did Barn seriously expect they'd find prison space for fly-tippers? Of course, even if such stupidity explained why Barney was absent, it offered no clue about the car behind. By the looks of it, it was a relatively new Ford Mondeo. A posh bit of kit to be driving on a rubbish-strewn wasteland like this.

Then, without warning, the van's headlights came on, catching Kev in their full beam. He backed away a step, raising his hand to block the dazzle.

'Whoa!' he shouted. 'Barney, that you?'

The van's engine chugged and coughed, and grumbled to life.

With a CLUNK, it was thrown into gear – and then rocketed forward.

'*Jesus!*' Kev screamed.

It crunched headlong into him, its front bumper-bar slamming his thighs with sledge-hammer force, snapping them both like sticks of celery, its windscreen smashing into his face with explosive force.

70

Kev was carried forward for several yards, spread-eagled, before the driver hit the brakes. The van screeched to a halt in front of the Portakabin, and he slumped to the ground. At the same time, a heavy, cumbersome form catapulted down from on top of the van's roof, and landed with a thud on the gritty floor next to him.

Kev was only vaguely aware what had happened. His body felt like a heap of disjointed wood. There was no feeling in it, and when he tried to turn his head sideways, his neck burned with a bone-deep fire. Even so, he managed to focus on the prone figure at his side. This too was in a broken, bedraggled state, but its face, which had been worked over with some heavy implement until it was gory pulp, was just about recognisable. As Barney.

This made no sense to Kev.

Barn had been on the roof of the van?

Who put him there?

A pair of feet trudged up behind him. Kev wanted to glance around, but his neck was hurting too badly. With a slow exhalation of breath, someone sank to their knees.

'Two trophies for the price of one,' a hoarse voice snickered.

To Kev's incredulity, his flies were pulled down and someone started unbuttoning his skinny jeans.

'Did you really think you were going to get some?' the voice whispered. 'You little shit! You little rodent! Did you and that brainless hunk of meat seriously believe you were going to tap this perfect arse?'

Kev still didn't understand. Chill air embraced him as his underpants were ripped away.

These bastards, he thought as he ebbed into unconsciousness.

Chapter 7

The Intel Unit convened that first Monday, in their office on the top floor at Robber's Row – to find that some wag from somewhere else in the nick had already attached a paper sign to the door, which read:

Ripper Chicks

As a general rule, there was dark humour, and then there was black humour, and then there was police humour. It was a psychological defence mechanism, of course. The best way to fend off the stress of spending every day steeped to your armpits in human misery was by laughing at it. But even by those standards, this was seen by several of the girls as a little close to the knuckle. Some, on the other hand, thought it rather catchy.

'Kind of rolls off the tongue,' PC Julie Ebbsworth from Oldham said. 'We are the *Rrrriiipper* Chicks!'

'Well, the blokes have always had cool nicknames, haven't they,' DC Val Ashworth from Preston replied. 'They've had the Shots, the Protectors, the Sweeney. Why can't we be the Ripper Chicks?'

Perhaps if they'd been investigating the ripping apart of female victims, consensus that they weren't offended by it would not have been achieved so quickly. It might also have been the case that, given what they were all about to undergo – and no doubt this had been preying on several of their minds for the whole of the weekend – this mischievous rebranding of their unit by an outside party did not seem such a big deal.

When agreement was reached, DS Sally Bryant agreed to leave the sign there. In fact, she said she'd take it home with her after shift and have it laminated so that it could be a permanent fixture on their office door.

After this, they got down to business, using the locker room attached to the briefing room to change from the casual attire they'd worn to travel to work, to the street-gear they hoped would help them blend in when they hit the streets.

Lucy had chosen a clingy blue camisole with lacy ribbons down the front rather than buttons, blue satin hot pants, fishnets and blue suede thigh-boots with platform soles. Over the top, she wore a black plastic mac. Her hair hung loose, while her make-up was loud and garish. All the girls affected similar transformations, looking each other over approvingly before deciding they were ready. There were some titters and sniggers, but an air of nervousness prevailed as the realisation finally dawned that they were going out there more or less alone. They'd have their phones and their 'guardian angels', as the plain-clothes TSG guys were now being referred to, but none of them would be carrying radios or wires. If they got into a cat-fight, they'd been advised, they'd have to see it through on their own (unless it turned very nasty), because it was always possible that communications devices could be exposed through yanked or torn clothing.

Lucy was only thirty, but she was actually one of the oldest present and certainly the most experienced. Deferring to this, more than a couple of the other girls came over seeking words of comfort or encouragement, neither of which she was able to offer in abundance. Detective Sergeants Bryant and Clark were in a similar boat; technically, they were the girls' line-managers, but in reality they'd be role-playing themselves and thus unable to act as normal supervision.

Shortly after three, DI Slater appeared, having run through several pointers with the male members of the team in the next room along. He now went through everything again with the girls, and then gave them a quick pep talk.

'This isn't going to be easy,' he said. 'You don't need me to tell you that. Ordinarily, we'd put you through a month's training for a job like this, but there simply isn't time. It may interest you to know – and this is totally embargoed, so don't go blabbing – we've got another couple of APs. Both were found this morning on wasteland near Bickershaw.'

There was a dumbfounded silence in the room. If there'd been any doubts in any minds about the necessity of this action-plan, they'd been expunged now.

'They may be ours, they may not be,' Slater said, 'but . . . well, they probably are. All the signs are there. If so, that makes it six victims and counting. Ladies, this assailant is absolutely relentless and the public is getting wind of it. When this next two hit the headlines, there'll be a total circus, which'll mean extra pressure on the investigation team, more stress, more mistakes. We need to pull together and get it sorted. So go out there and do your job, but watch your backs as well, and I mean watch them closely. The more men die at the hands of Jill the Ripper – sorry, I hate using that name but I don't see what difference objecting to it will make now – the more vulnerable you people are going to be.'

Lucy would find out for herself what Slater meant by this approximately one hour after arriving at her designated pitch, which was a small picnic area – in reality little more than a thinly treed grass verge – just off the stretch of the A580 dual carriageway, better known locally as the East Lancashire Road or 'East Lancs', that ran south-west from Boothstown towards Lowton.

Her guardian angel that evening was PC Andy Clegg, a TSG officer in his early twenties. He was a bullish lad, well built around the chest and arms, but whose regulation-cut dark hair, ruddy, chubby features and permanently grave expression only served to underline his youth. Lucy wasn't sure whether to be encouraged by this or unnerved. When they chatted before setting off, Lucy seeking nothing more than an informal introduction, he responded to her questions in taut monosyllables, which suggested that he was either very focused on the job, which was good, or that he was tongue-tied and abashed in the presence of a female officer who happened to be showing leg and cleavage, which wasn't so good. There was a time to be embarrassed, and this wasn't it.

Clegg would be sitting in an unmarked car on wasteland on the other side of the East Lancs – a battered old relic of a Ford Focus, equipped with a pair of night-vision binoculars. Without doubt he'd have the physical ability to help her, and the willingness to get stuck in – young male coppers were nothing if not reckless in their efforts to prove themselves. She just hoped he had the judgement to go with it.

And this was to be tested as soon as they arrived at her pitch.

Lucy was dropped off at the picnic site by an unmarked van with fake company logos on the sides. The hoped-for impression was that she'd just successfully serviced a bunch of navvies. The TSG lads inside the van assisted by beating on its sides and whooping aloud as the vehicle roared away. Following this, she stood out in the open, which wasn't difficult given the proximity of the streetlights and the semi-leafless state of the autumnal trees, brandished a fistful of twenty-pound notes, and commenced a slow, deliberate count.

It had the desired effect.

Two girls were waiting nearby, only half discernible in the dank shadows. One of them was black, one of them white; both wore leather jackets, short skirts and heels. They sauntered towards her side-by-side.

'Who the fuck are *you*?' the white girl wondered, her accent strong Scouse.

'Who's asking?' Lucy replied, tucking the money up the sleeve of her mac.

The black girl leaned forward menacingly, an impression enhanced by an old scar that diagonally bisected her mouth and was still clearly visible despite a preponderance of emulsion-like lip gloss. 'What the fuck's it got to do with you, you gobby bitch!' she snarled. 'This is our pitch and you're fucking trespassing!'

Lucy shrugged, but her spine was already tingling. 'Don't see a signpost, love.'

The black girl snapped her hand out, and a gleaming blade sprang into view. 'I'll slice your fucking tits off, you cow!'

'Or alternatively, you can pay up,' the Scouse girl said.

Lucy gazed from one to the other, affecting dimness. 'What?'

'We share everything here. And we know you're not short of cash given that road crew you've just balled . . . so cough up.'

Even from across the dual carriageway, Lucy heard a *thud* from the back of the Ford Focus, as if Clegg was already getting set to intervene. That'd be great. She could just picture him clumping across the blacktop in his army surplus trousers, hoodie top and baseball cap. He'd save her of course, but it'd be quite a coincidence – that the moment the new girl was threatened, a tall, dark stranger stepped in.

But by a miracle, perhaps suggesting that he was smarter than she'd thought, he held off.

'So I have to pay you two for the privilege of standing here?' Lucy said. 'On this stretch of public highway which anyone else can use free of charge?'

'See,' the Scouse girl said to her mate. 'Told you she was clever.'

'You've got to be joking,' Lucy said, suspecting they were bluffing but now knowing she had to call that bluff.

'This look funny to you?' The black girl offered the blade again.

Though its glinting steel tip was now right under Lucy's nose, less than an inch from severing her septum, she was determined to remain composed. That was all you could ever do in this job, pretend. It didn't mean that, deep inside, her heart wasn't going like the clappers.

'Go on then,' Lucy said. 'Cut me up. I wonder what would make Mr Merryweather angrier? That . . . or the fact I had to share his hard-earned to buy you two off?'

The two prostitutes didn't exactly flinch, but the blankness of their expressions said more than words ever could.

'You don't work for Nick Merryweather,' the Scouse girl finally replied.

'Not directly,' Lucy agreed, 'but we know whose pocket you'll ultimately be picking, don't we!'

She was onto a winner; she could tell. No one would believe that she had some kind of hotline to the Crew's whoremaster-in-chief, but the mere fact she knew who he was would indicate that she was no novice, that she wasn't just playing at this.

'So go on, cut me!' she urged them. 'Or maybe you can put the sodding blade away . . . and just to show there's no hard feelings, because yeah, I am trespassing a little bit, I can give you something to be going on with.' She filched

77

two twenties from under her sleeve, and offered one to each of them. Oddly enough, probably because this kind of thing had never happened before, they were hesitant to take them.

'I've never seen you round here,' the black girl said, still snarling, but the blade now lower. 'Who the fuck are you?'

'I'm Keira,' Lucy said.

'Keira?' The black girl hooted. 'Jesus wept, couldn't you think of anything more fucking original?'

'Who are *you*?' Lucy asked her.

'I'm not telling you my fucking name.' The girl pocketed her switchblade, but snatched the twenty and backed away. 'Just piss off, you silly fucking mare.'

The Scouse lass gave Lucy a long, searching look – as if somehow suspecting this thing still wasn't right – then helped herself to her own twenty, taking it almost gingerly between thumb and forefinger, before turning on her heel and hurrying to catch up with her mate, the pair of them dwindling off along the leaf-cluttered verge.

Lucy watched them as she slowly calmed herself down, wondering if any kind of bridge had been built there or perhaps if it was quite the opposite.

'You won't make friends that way, love,' a voice said from somewhere to the right, seeming to answer the question for her. 'They'll just mark you as a soft touch and try and scam you again.'

Lucy turned to the trees and had to squint through the darkness under their half-naked boughs. The dull yellow glow of the streetlights didn't penetrate too far. However, her eyes were now attuning, and she realised that a third party was close at hand. Another girl, younger than the others by the looks of her, with longish red hair and a very short dress, was seated on top of a picnic table, high-heeled shoes resting on the bench in front of her, as she swigged from a bottle of vodka.

'And you're not part of Necktie Nicky's stable neither,' she said, screwing the cap back on and giving a satisfied belch. 'You wouldn't dare give that much of his dosh away if you were.'

Lucy ambled towards her. 'I admit I've never met Mr Merryweather personally . . .'

'No one has who's so far down the food-chain that they have to walk these streets, love. Anyway, you can spare me the bullshit . . .' The red-headed girl climbed down. 'I know what you really are.'

Lucy held her tongue, unsure how to respond.

The girl slid the bottle into her shoulder bag, and struggled with the zip of her scruffy fleece jacket before finally drawing it up. She was shapely but short, not much more than five feet tall. There was no threat here, but the last thing Lucy needed was to be outed on her first night. She wondered what it was that might have given the game away.

'You're an independent, aren't you?' the girl said.

Up close, even in the gloom, Lucy could see that she had a pretty face, though she smelled strongly of alcohol. If Lucy hadn't been very used to it thanks to all the drunken prisoners she'd wheeled in over the years, it would have been nauseating.

'And you're *new* to the game,' the girl added. 'You know how I can tell? Because you haven't got the thousand-yard stare. I'm Tammy, by the way. And that's my real name too. I was christened Tamara. Can you fucking believe that?'

It was an odd way to introduce herself; delivered in a casual, only half-interested tone, as if the information barely mattered.

'Keira,' Lucy said.

'Yeah, I heard. So what's the story, Keira? Lost your job? House repossessed? Kids hungry?'

'Something like that.'

'And you thought this'd be a piece of piss?'

'Not exactly a piece of piss.'

'Easy money then?'

Lucy shrugged, took the wad of notes from under her sleeve and screwed it up into a ball. 'You telling me I just got lucky when I met that gang of workmen?'

Tammy eyed the money as it disappeared into Lucy's bag. 'Sometimes we get lucky, I suppose.' She took a step back, this time eyeing Lucy herself. 'You don't look the worse for wear considering you've just been star-attraction in a back-seat gangbang.'

Lucy realised her mistake. She should have smeared her lippy and mussed her hair a little. But it was too late now. She could only brazen it out.

'How many were there?' Tammy asked.

'Three.'

'Jesus! Talk about getting off to a flyer. Anyway . . . your minge must be killing you, which means *this one's* for me.'

Lucy hadn't realised it, but another vehicle had drawn up at the verge just behind them: a grey SUV with tinted windows. The front nearside window rolled downward.

There were two guys inside it, one behind the wheel and one in the front passenger seat. This immediately struck Lucy as a potential problem, though if Tammy needed the custom, who was she to object? As the girl teetered across the grassy verge in her ridiculously high heels, the passenger grinned, white teeth splitting his thick black beard. He was somewhere in his early thirties, brawny and wearing a lumberjack-style plaid shirt.

'You gents looking for a good time?' Tammy tittered, leaning down at the window.

Plaid Shirt's expression rapidly changed – from lewd grin to twisted scowl.

'*YOU MURDERING SLAGS!*' he screamed, before throwing something into her face.

Lucy caught a fleeting glimpse of a dark, lumpen object wrapped in what looked like white tissue. The next thing, Tammy's hoarse voice rang out, an exclamation of horror and disgust, as she tottered backwards. The SUV sped away, howls of mocking laughter echoing from its interior. When Tammy turned to face Lucy, the excrement was smeared down her left cheek and around the side of her mouth. Solid fragments of it spattered her décolletage; a strip of filthy toilet paper had tucked itself into her cleavage.

Quite clearly, the two most recent murders had finally hit the headlines.

'Dirty bastards!' Tammy stammered, eyes glimmering with tears of shock.

Lucy hurried over to her. 'Here, let me help.'

She had some face wipes in her shoulder bag, but Tammy tried to pull away, too embarrassed in front of the new girl to allow herself to be assisted.

'No,' Lucy said, refusing to release her arm. 'Let me help.'

'Not here, for fuck's sake!' Tammy snapped, voice turning nasal as the tears flowed. 'God, the stink!'

'I can clean it off,' Lucy insisted.

'Yeah, but not out *here*!' Tammy yanked her arm loose and strutted quickly away, working her way deeper into the copse of trees, heels clacking as she joined a paved pathway, which snaked from the road into denser shadows. Lucy followed, shoving the wipes back into her bag. Fleetingly, Tammy was invisible in the darkness ahead – it was only possible to follow her by her footfalls and sniffles. By the sounds of it, she'd quickly got on top of the tears. Probably couldn't afford not to in this line of work. Lucy accelerated and fell into step alongside her. The path weaved away from the picnic area towards what looked like an open, well-lit space, though they passed several more girls before they got there, most of them standing talking quietly, indistinguishable in the darkness, only the tiny red pinpoints of cigarettes and the occasional whiff of cannabis revealing their presence.

Tammy sniffled again and tried to wipe under her eyes, inadvertently smearing her fingertips with excrement. 'Bastards!' she hissed. 'Can't fucking believe this!'

'Nor me,' Lucy agreed.

'Yeah, but you're new. I ought to have learned my lesson by now.'

The path ended at the edge of what was actually a lorry park. This was a rectangular dirt lot, rugged and rutted at this time of year, and about thirty acres in size. It was still close to the East Lancs, extending along it in a southerly direction, but was encircled on three sides by trees and undergrowth. At the far side stood a single-storey red-brick building, a combo of service garage and lorry drivers' cafe.

'There are some toilets round the back,' Tammy muttered as they walked over there, passing numerous trucks and wagons, some old and some new, some with curtained interiors.

When they reached the building, they circled round it, away from its glazed, brightly glowing frontage, passing a row of bins and a pile of spare but rusting auto-parts. At the very rear, two doors stood covered with flaking paint. One was marked 'Gents', the other 'Ladies'.

Two more girls were standing here, chatting as they smoked. One of them, a bottle-blonde in a fur coat and a preponderance of mascara, spotted them as they approached. Initially she looked shocked, but then she grinned,

'And what happened to you, Tammy, love?'

'What's it look like?' Tammy replied sulkily. 'Some bastard threw a turd at me.'

The bottle-blonde coughed cigarette smoke as she guffawed. 'Oh my God . . . sorry, love, but rather you than me!'

The other woman, who was older, grey-haired in fact, and

considerably heavier – and thus looked awful in her matching red mini-dress and stilettos – seemed completely unmoved. She simply took in the night air, expelling streams of smoke through her flaring nostrils.

'They were a lot of help,' Lucy said when they'd entered the toilets, to which Tammy only grunted.

The Ladies was a small, boxy room with white-tiled walls and a damp concrete floor. There were four cubicles, three of them marked "Out of Order", and two large mirrors over two side-by-side washbasins. The mirrors were grubby and smeared. Across the top of each one, some past comedian had used a black marker-pen to offer his opinions on the unfortunate women who'd routinely imprint their faces in the glass below in order to fix their make-up. The one on the left read *Blowjob Queen of Manchester!*, and to ensure there was no misunderstanding, an arrow pointed downward. The one on the right was signposted: *Takes it up the arse! Yukkity yuk!*

Lucy handed the face wipes over so that Tammy could clean herself, though it was already apparent that the girl was going to need to go home and take a shower. Throw enough shit and some of it will stick, as the old saying went – sometimes, as in Tammy's case, in your hair as well.

However, if Lucy had anticipated a range of expletives from the young hooker – and here in the stark white light of the drab toilet, she could see just how young she was, clearly not much more than twenty – she was to be disappointed.

Tammy merely sighed to herself as she rubbed and scrubbed at her face, occasionally wrinkling her nostrils, accepting the odd bit of help from Lucy.

'Digby'll go spare if I go home without earning tonight,' she muttered. Again, this was spoken matter-of-factly, without feeling, as if all this awfulness was simply routine.

'We can probably get most of it off here,' Lucy said, in attempted consolation.

'Gimme a break, love. No john's going to want to give me one now, is he? The first whiff he gets, he'll chuck his tea up.' Tammy continued scrubbing on her own. 'Can't believe we're actually getting blamed for these *murders* now.'

'Yeah, how about that,' Lucy said.

'You picked a good time to start out, I'll tell you.'

'That's what *I* was thinking.'

'Don't worry . . .' Tammy actually managed to crack a smile.

In the process of cleaning away the filth, she'd also removed most of her slap, but she was none the worse for that. She had rosebud lips, a snub nose, a dusting of freckles and a pair of fetching green eyes – there was something of the saucy minx about her. Lucy couldn't help wondering how so pretty a youngster had finished up in this profession.

'I've got just the thing for us,' Tammy said. 'Look in my bag.'

Lucy did as instructed, and alongside Tammy's purse found the vodka bottle. It was still half full.

'Help yourself,' Tammy said.

'Nah . . .' Lucy shrugged 'I'm teetotal.'

'What the fuck!' Tammy broke off cleansing herself to gaze at her new pal in disbelief. 'Aren't you full of fucking surprises? You're the hottest thing I've seen up here in yonks, you chuck your money round like there's no tomorrow and now you don't imbibe!'

'I used to, but it never did me any good.'

'Never does me any good either, but that doesn't mean I don't like it. Hand it over.'

Lucy obliged, and Tammy took several large swigs, a quarter of the bottle vanishing in one fell swoop. She screwed the cap back on and belched again.

'Ahhh . . . nothing better when you've had a chocolate log chucked in your face. Anyway –' she grabbed the handbag and shoved the bottle back inside it '– gotta make a move. Nice meeting you. What did you say your name was?'

'Keira,' Lucy replied. 'But my real name's . . .'

Tammy held a hand up. 'Best if I don't know your real name.'

'You told me yours.'

'Yeah, but I'm a fuck-up . . . as you've seen. Bad stuff always happens to me, but it's usually for a reason. Anyway, thanks again for your help.' Tammy turned back from the doorway. 'Listen . . . if you need someone to show you the ropes, the blonde bimbo outside, Sandy, can be alright. She's a bit of piss-taker, but her bark's worse than her bite. Just watch the other one, Tomasina. If she finds out you've got that much dosh in your purse, she'll have the lot. And she'll kick your face to mush in the process.'

Lucy nodded and smiled in thanks. And then Tammy was gone, the toilet door slamming, the sound of it echoing through the damp cell that appeared to be their one and only indoor refuge on these cold, wet autumn nights. She turned back to the mirror, the sheet of grimy glass with *Blowjob Queen of Manchester!* scrawled over the top. A foul stench emitted from the sink. When she glanced down, she saw that someone had vomited into it. And now, just to complete the picture, it was also crammed with Tammy's screwed-up, shit-stained tissues.

Lucy regarded her sallow features in the tarnished glass.

This was going to be a vastly more challenging stake-out than even she'd anticipated.

Chapter 8

As a policewoman, Lucy counted herself an old stager. She'd dealt hands-on with all the horrors of urban living, from child abuse to fatal road accidents, from violent brawls on Saturday nights to forgotten OAPs so long abandoned there were only bones remaining when someone finally found them. Nothing shocked her, nothing upset her – she simply refused to let it. But possibly thanks to her being in a semi-disorientated state due to the new work patterns, not to mention the strange nature of the new work, she couldn't help but brood on what she'd seen that night. The memory alone was hardly conducive to sleep: that dank, soulless location; those wet woods and rain-washed roads; that grubby little lorry drivers' caf with the rubbish heaped behind it and the nasty little toilet in its guts. And then the shadowy forms on the edges of her vision: the girls themselves, the pimps, the addicts, the muggers.

Lucy's alarm was set for two o'clock that afternoon, but she gave up on bed around seven-thirty a.m. When she tottered downstairs in a sweater and pyjama bottoms, her mum was still in the house, dressed for work but clearing away the breakfast things in her usual efficient way. The explanation Lucy offered was that she'd try to snatch some zeds later but that for now she wanted to catch up on what was happening, which was at least partly true. She curled on the couch and tuned the television to one of the all-day news channels, from whose coverage of the two latest murders she immediately detected a change in tone.

The news teams were now all over it, to the exemption of any other item. It was still early, but various anchormen had already departed the studios. One was broadcasting live from outside Robber's Row, which was almost hidden from view behind a wall of press and TV vans, while another was intoning into a microphone on the edge of one of the north-west's many interchangeably bleak and featureless waste-lands. In this latter case, dog-teams, both the officers and their pooches clad in hi-viz jackets, could be seen progressing slowly across the grey clinker-desert.

'Two of them this time, apparently,' Cora said, placing a cup of tea and a plate of buttered toast in front of Lucy as she sat riveted to the screen.

'Yeah, I know . . . I heard last night.'

'They don't think these two were actually up to anything.'

Lucy glanced at her. 'Sorry . . . what do you mean?'

'According to the news, they were just a pair of lads trying to sling some rubbish.'

'Yeah?' This was first Lucy had heard about the new murders in any actual detail, and it surprised her. She turned back, refocusing on the breaking story.

It seemed that two young men from Hindley Green, Wigan, Kevin Crumper, aged twenty-five, and Arnold 'Barney' Hall, aged twenty-seven, were thought to have been fly-tipping on the evening of October 18th, on a stretch of former colliery wasteland at Bickershaw, when they'd encountered their killer.

Twenty-five and twenty-seven.

Two robust young blokes.

Again, Lucy wondered if there might be more than one assailant. If there was – say if there was more than one prostitute involved – it meant that she and the rest of the Ripper Chicks would have to step even more lightly. One twisted killer was dangerous enough, but a conspiracy of them? Under those circs, you had to be extra wary who you got friendly with and who you asked questions of. But still . . . there had only been that *single* figure on the Atherton CCTV video.

What kind of girl would a single killer have to be to overpower two red-blooded young guys on her own? In her mind's eye, Lucy pictured a kind of Amazon, an unfeasible example of the female form, someone part way between an Olympic athlete and a supermodel. Unless, of course, she'd used guile rather than brute force. Both men had not necessarily been killed at the same time, for example. They could have been separated from each other first.

But even then it couldn't have been easy.

On reflection, Lucy wasn't sure which theory was more *unlikely*, the Amazon Queen or the tag-team from Hell. Whatever, in this particular case it was certain the two victims had fallen foul of the same person, or persons, known as Jill the Ripper. According to the TV, the causes of death had now been determined by medical examiners. Both men had been brutally beaten with a blunt instrument, probably a hammer, and then mutilated with a knife, subsequently dying from blood loss.

She pondered this as she sipped her tea and nibbled her toast.

It was noticeable and understandable that the taskforce was still withholding the detail of the severed genitals, but adding that there were unspecified mutilations was more information than had been given out previously. The probability was that they were seeking to ram it home to the public just how sickening these crimes were and thus make it more likely that someone, if they knew anything, would talk.

The choice of victims was a bit of a right-turn, though. Two lads dumping waste.

Lucy knew from her own experience, which admittedly wasn't extensive in this field – though she had worked on the periphery of murder investigations before – that repeat sex-killers didn't always stick religiously to their MO. Inevitably, some targets had to be targets of convenience. This 'double-event', as reporters were now referring to it, was also responsible for a new tone of sobriety in terms of the coverage. Beforehand, while the press hadn't exactly demonstrated an air of frivolousness with regard to these crimes, there'd been the usual morbid fascination but minus any attached horror and dismay – as if kerb-crawlers were asking for trouble anyway and maybe, just *maybe*, were getting what they deserved. Now the attitude was markedly different

For her own part, Lucy always tried to avoid making any such rushed judgement.

From what she'd seen, men who used prostitutes didn't always have sinister motives. Often, they were lonely or had problematic sex lives at home, or they simply didn't wish to offend their wives or girlfriends by asking for fetishistic things. Certainly there were oddballs and weirdos out there – they existed too, but it didn't sound as if Crumper and Hall were especially wholesome characters either. They'd been in the act of committing an offence when they were attacked, but of course had no record for being sexual predators, so the press at least was prepared to cut them some slack.

'What's the latest?' Cora asked, sitting in the armchair, also sipping tea.

'I think it's all about to move up a gear,' Lucy replied.

'You anywhere near catching her?'

'Not as far as I'm aware, though this could change every-thing. New crime scene, new evidence. We'll have to wait and see what the forensic teams make of it.'

'At least she's only killing men,' Cora said.

Lucy glanced round at her. 'Personally, I'd rather she wasn't killing anyone.'

'So do I, but, well . . .' Cora shrugged and sipped again. 'I know lots of women who've had a rough time over the years thanks to the fellas in their lives.'

If Lucy had been surprised by the previous comment from her normally mild-mannered mum, she was even more surprised by this. Cora's friends, whom she sometimes went out for a couple of drinks with at the Labour Club, all seemed pretty normal: mostly married and with grown-up kids, the majority of them hard-workers and gentle souls.

'But all this dirty business, you know . . .' Cora shook her head, a pink dot on either cheek. 'Girls going out at weekends, making a show of themselves. You've seen them in the town centre. Practically nothing on. And they're not even prostitutes. Blokes sniffing round them like dogs at the butcher's dustbin . . .'

'Mum, for God's sake!' Lucy exclaimed.

'Well, what do you expect to happen, Lucy? You're not telling me that won't lead to trouble. But maybe now that it's trouble for the men things will change.'

'It's not *all* men, Mum.'

'No, of course it's not all men. But look at the problems only a handful have created.'

Not for the first time, Lucy found herself wondering about the father she'd never met.

Dan the Bus Driver.

That was the only name she'd ever had for him; she'd never even been told what his surname was. She knew next to nothing about him as a person, except that he'd apparently been a happy-go-lucky rogue. It was true that the only stories she'd ever heard involving him had been amusing, not least the one concerning Dan and Cora's very first get-together.

At the time, Cora was nineteen and still living with her own parents in Moston. She'd been resisting this guy Dan for quite some time, but allegedly he was so smitten with her that he'd turned up one Saturday afternoon outside her parent's little terraced house while still in his bus, to beg her for a date. He was supposed to be driving his route at the time, so a whole bunch of bemused passengers had found themselves peering out through the vehicle's windows and in through the windows of the Clayburn family's front room.

Quite a surprise for Cora's father, who at the time was watching the racing from Kempton.

Old Mr Clayburn had taken an instant dislike to Dan the Bus Driver, as he apparently didn't trust anyone with 'that much of the gab'. And he hadn't been especially sorry when Dan had later fled the scene, even though he left Cora pregnant.

Both Lucy's grandparents had died before she was old enough to get to know them, so she'd never been able to verify these stories. But why should her mother have lied about it? Unless the truth about the laugh-a-minute bus driver was actually not so amusing.

Lucy glanced at the clock on the mantel – it was now ten past eight. Plenty of time to try and get some shuteye before she had to head to Robber's Row. She still had to pen her end-of-shift report from last night and email it in, but that wouldn't take long. There wouldn't be a great deal to include. Normally, it would be anything she'd deemed pertinent to the enquiry, and aside from the incident with the switchblade, there'd been precious little of that.

The other Ripper Chicks, who were dotted all over Greater Manchester from here to Stalybridge, would be doing exactly the same thing now, though in truth she doubted many would even have got out of bed yet. Most would have been exhausted by their first 'hooker shift', even if they hadn't had to spend it wiping the shit off a pretty girl's face.

Chapter 9

The next few days weren't anything like as eventful as the first. As there seemed to be more girls hanging around the lorry park and the lorry park café, Lucy made that her pitch rather than the picnic area. The café owners didn't mind the girls coming in for a coffee or a cheese roll, but they didn't want them touting for business inside or round the front of the building. So long as the girls were out of sight and out of mind, that was fine; as such, they mostly congregated at the rear of the caf or out across the lorry park, under the cover of the trees.

Even so, the twelve-hour shifts could be tedious. To maintain appearances, Lucy would drive away with a 'customer' at least three times per shift, usually for about an hour on each occasion. Most often it was with lads from the Tactical Support Group, who were almost invariably young and hunky, which to a degree raised her standing with the other girls.

But of course, there were times when she had regular johns to deal with too, and though it was easy enough sending them off with a flea in their ear when they were obvious losers driving ramshackle, rust-bucket cars, that wasn't the case indefinitely, as she discovered on the fifth night of the undercover operation.

'What's up, babe . . . rich man's money too good for you?' a guy in a silver Jaguar XE said through his powered-down tinted window. 'I've got plenty of it . . . look.'

He cruised the edge of the lorry park, one ring-bedecked hand on the steering wheel as he dug a side-stitched pigskin wallet from inside his pinstriped jacket. It was fat with notes.

'I don't have to get into any car I don't want to, sir,' Lucy told him for the second time. 'And I don't want to get into yours. So goodnight.'

As Lucy increased her pace along the kerb, he accelerated sufficiently to stay parallel. Older than her by about fifteen years, with longish grey hair, designer stubble and a gold crucifix glinting in the fuzzy chest-hair exposed through the open collar of his shirt, he wasn't Lucy's type at all, but he wasn't exactly odious. And he was clearly loaded. The main problem of course was that he wasn't one of hers.

'You cheeky mare!' he laughed harshly. 'You've got some nerve, walking around out here like the princess of the night, looking like the best shag on the A580 . . . and you won't even give me the time of day? *Me*, of all people!'

'Goodnight, sir.'

'I'll tell you what, I like a challenge. So I'll pay you double your going rate. Triple even.'

'Goodnight, I said.'

'Babes, I want that sweet, satin-clad arse of yours.'

'Hey pal, fuck off!' She spun to face the car again. 'I'm not interested . . . you got it?'

'You snotty bitch!' he called as she changed direction, leaving him stranded. 'I hope some weirdo fucking strangles you.'

A group of the other girls had gathered nearby and now

regarded her curiously as she strode away from him. They'd taken in the flashy motor and were wondering what the problem was.

'Don't make me tell you what he asked me to do,' she told them in a disgusted voice.

They didn't look much less bemused even after that, so it was a relief half a minute later, when a Ford Focus slid up beside her and Andy Clegg wound its window down.

She leaned quickly into it. 'Hello, sir . . . looking for a bit of fun?'

'Everything alright?' he asked quietly, clearly having observed the incident.

'It's fine. Here . . . drive us about for a while.'

At first, Lucy's air of apparent superiority played a little bit into her hands, when, the following night, Sandy, the bottle-blonde, was finally moved to speak to her conversationally.

'Try not to knock back *all* the social rejects, eh?' Sandy said. 'They end up coming to me.'

Lucy shook her head. 'Call me picky, but I've got to like what I see before I can get into a car with them.'

'Good job you get so many lookers then.'

'Suppose I'm lucky on that score.'

'Nah, you're a doll.' Sandy shrugged. 'Don't know what your story is, but you're too good for this place.'

Tomasina, a constant, chain-smoking presence at Sandy's shoulder, still said nothing, her face like a gaudily made-up breezeblock, though within another day, even *she* started to open up, snorting with laughter the next night when they were all sheltering under the café awning during a rainstorm, and Sandy said that her hair was ruined, only for Lucy to comment that she didn't know why they both-ered tarting themselves up as a recent news report had offered stats allegedly proving that the majority of internet porn browsers went in search of "granny" and "old bag" sites.

'I'm a granny *and* an old bag,' Tomasina said in a husky, smoke-damaged voice. 'And I don't get any more action than the rest of you. I saw that report too. If it was true, I'd be a bloody millionaire by now.' And from that point on she and Lucy spoke regularly, as if they'd been friends for years, though there was never any substance to it. The reality was that few of these women had anything in common other than a sisterly need for companionship on the edge of the dark, dangerous world that was Punterville.

As a further indication of the strangeness of this existence, hostilities one day might be completely forgotten the next. A week and a half after the incident at the picnic area, when the black girl – whose name was Bianca – had pulled the knife, Lucy met her in the café toilets, where they were both looking to fix their make-up.

'Evening, Keira,' Bianca said as if they'd never been enemies. 'Different day, same shit, eh?'

'Yeah,' Lucy responded, trying not to look fazed that she was now shoulder-to-shoulder with a woman who for a brief time had been a potential suspect in the case.

Lucy had filed a separate report concerning Bianca after her very first shift, because the woman carried a blade and had used it threateningly – but in due course it had been marked "No further action". There were two main problems with Bianca as a suspect. Firstly, the knife she'd pulled was nowhere near big enough to be the murder weapon. Secondly, and more conclusively, Jill the Ripper was thought to be white whereas Bianca was black.

Not that Lucy was entirely comfortable in her presence, even if they did now stand side-by-side applying fresh lipstick.

Bianca glanced at the marker-written slogan over the top of Lucy's mirror. '"Blowjob Queen of Manchester" . . .? That the secret of your success? Getting all these young, clean-looking lads, I mean?'

Lucy shrugged. 'Wasn't head-girl at school for nothing.'

Bianca chuckled. 'I'll bet you bloody weren't. But it's no surprise you can afford to turn all those ugly buggers down, when you get so many hunks as well.'

'Gotta keep my standards up,' Lucy said jokily, but at the same time making a mental note that if so many of the other girls had now clocked that she seemed to attract more than her fair share of punters who were young and square-jawed, it wouldn't be long before they decided this was odd.

She rang Slater at the first opportunity to request a couple of older, scruffier specimens. Accordingly, her first customer the following evening was Des Barton, a DC from the Serious Crimes Division, who was somewhere in his late forties. Des was of West Indian descent, short, tubby and balding, the only hair left on his head growing in thin, grey tufts behind his ears. Lucy would come to learn that both he and his beaten-up old Volkswagen Beetle existed in a permanently untidy state, the car dented and scratched, while Des's shirt and tie always looked to be in need of an iron and his shabby beige overcoat was a cliché all of its own.

He was clearly aware of this, and apologised that first time he picked her up.

'Sorry about my dishevelled state,' he said in a broad but cheery Moss Side accent, which he had to shout at her in order to be heard over the grumbling engine. 'Yvonne didn't have time to sort me out this morning.'

'Yvonne?' Lucy asked as they chugged down the East Lancs.

'The wife.'

'Your wife needs to sort you out?'

'Yeah, but she can't. Got six nippers, you see. The eldest's only thirteen. Bloody bedlam in our house. Especially this weekend. She's doing a Halloween party for the little 'uns.'

'It never enters your head to sort yourself out?' Lucy wondered,

'Well, that's what Yvonne says,' Des replied. 'But we're all busy, aren't we?'

'Perhaps it's you who should be sorting Yvonne out?'

'Ooh, you're wicked!' He gave a squawking laugh. 'Nah, I didn't mean it like that. Only kidding, chuck.' He laughed again, rather infectiously. 'Anyway . . . got any leads for us?'

This made him the first of Lucy's 'clients' to enquire about her progress, but of course Des was a detective, not a TSG man.

'Not much, I'm afraid,' she replied. But then she thought about it a little. 'The most talkative is this girl, Tammy. I looked her up on the system. Didn't expect to find her, only having a first name to work with . . . but there she was, bold as brass. Tammy Nethercot.'

'Lots of form?' Des asked.

'Yeah. All petty stuff. Sad case really. But she's the most likely to give me something.'

'Nothing solid yet, though?'

'Nothing yet.'

Lucy hadn't expected to see much more of Tammy, having moved her own pitch to the lorry park, but it wasn't long before Tammy was popping up there too. Perhaps her 'tough girl' act of the first night was all for show and the experience of having excrement thrown in her face had made her feel a little vulnerable out there on the edge of the dual carriageway. In the lorry park, which was still close to the road but where there were plenty more people around and lots of parked and idling vehicles, it was likely the punters would keep a lower profile. She also seemed to enjoy Lucy's company, seeking it out whenever she could.

As they drove on in Des's car, Lucy thought long and hard about her new 'friend'.

Tammy was twenty-two and still had her looks, just about. Her hair was thick and copper-red and hung past her shoulders. She also had those bright green eyes, which, when they weren't glazed with alcohol, possessed a remarkable lustre. She might only have been five feet tall, but she had a slim waist, curved hips and a sizeable burst, which always looked good in the mini-dresses, shiny tights and high-heeled shoes she favoured. Even in late October, with the leaves spinning down from a slate-grey sky, the wind ever colder and filled with spattering rain, she affected the same get-up, her only modification as the weather deteriorated a warmer fur jacket with a zip and a big collar which came down to just under her ribcage. The overall ensemble looked great from a distance, especially when Tammy remembered to wiggle her way across the lorry park rather than drunkenly trudge.

But with Tammy the drinking was a problem that would clearly never go away. She wasn't soused every time Lucy met her, but she always smelled of it, which was never a good sign. The kid often got loaded before she even turned out. Lucy smelled it on her breath whenever they hooked up. And if she didn't do it before she appeared, she would definitely do it afterwards. There was never an occasion when Lucy didn't glance into Tammy's shoulder bag and spot a bottle of vodka, from which the girl would take regular swigs. But even without the booze, Tammy was reckless. She wasn't the sharpest tool in the box anyway, but combine this with her lifestyle choice, and it was a disaster waiting to happen.

Three nights before, for example, Tammy had confided in Lucy that she was finishing early as she'd had a good day. To illustrate, she'd revealed a rubber-banded brick of tens and twenties even though she'd only serviced three clients.

When Lucy had asked how she'd managed this miraculous feat, Tammy had replied that the last one had wanted to go bareback with her and so had offered double the asking-price. Tammy had then boasted that she'd held out for treble before consenting. When Lucy had called her 'a little fool' and told her she must never take such a risk again, Tammy had responded by telling her to 'naff off', before laughing drunkenly, kissing her on the cheek and saying that the john 'was an old coot who looked dead respectable – shirt, tie, suit, driving a Jag . . . he's not going to have anything bad, is he?'

'It depends how many girls he goes bareback with, doesn't it?' Lucy had replied. 'If that's his thing and he's got the money, it could be quite a number.'

Tammy'd told her to 'naff off' again and stumbled away.

The following night, Tammy had tried to withhold some money from Digby, her pimp. She'd decided she needed another bottle before she went home, so she'd concealed three twenties in the most personal place she could think of. Digby, who was about six-four and always dressed like a cowboy, even down to the heeled boots, drainpipe jeans, big-buckled belt and fancy-patterned shirt, hadn't been fooled – and had found the missing readies by lifting her dress and cramming his hand down the front of her knickers. Right out there on the café car park. He'd then frogmarched her to a quiet corner where his own vehicle was parked, a black Land Rover with tinted windows, put her in the back, removed that big-buckled belt of his and dealt it to her bare backside at least twenty times.

Tammy had merely shrugged afterwards, sitting down at a café table opposite Lucy, but only delicately. 'That's Digby's thing,' she'd said, sniffling back what remained of her tears. 'Fuck it, I don't mind. There are plenty punters want the same thing . . .'

99

'You still with us?' Des Barton asked, interrupting Lucy's thoughts.

'What . . . oh yeah, sorry. Miles away.'

'You were saying about this Tammy Nethercot . . .?'

'Yeah.' Lucy related the latest event in the young prostitute's life, the one involving Digby. 'Like I say . . . sad case.'

'Aren't they always?'

'Don't know what her home-life's like. She never mentions a boyfriend.'

'That prat, Digby, will have been her boyfriend once,' Des said. 'Least, that's what he'll have told her. That's usually how they get them into it. I think I know who you mean when you mention him. Big goon . . . real name's Carl Bretherton. Dresses like Gary Cooper.'

'Gary who?'

'Don't wind me up, I'm not that much older than you.'

Lucy smiled.

'He may dress like Gary Cooper,' Des said again, 'but when he opens his gob all that nasal Salford shite comes out. Used to be a bouncer. Think he spent time clamping cars too.'

'Suppose there's a kind of thread there,' Lucy observed. 'First he bullies drunks, then he bullies motorists, now he bullies hookers.'

'Way it is, isn't it?'

She shook her head. 'I really wanted to do something, Des. I mean, I know we have to be careful . . . but the way he was marching her across that car park to belt her on the arse . . . I so wanted to do something.'

'Be thankful you didn't . . . or all our arses'd be on the line now.'

'Thing is . . . Tammy's been around a bit. I know she's only a kid, but I get the feeling she's been on the game quite a while. She's gradually slipping me more and more titbits.

Who works for who, which pimps are the worst, which punters to avoid.'

'But she's never once mentioned Jill the Ripper?'

'Only to say "that lass is doing a job for us".'

Des threw her a look as he drove. 'She didn't . . .?'

'No, she didn't mean anything. All the ones I've spoken to . . . they're indifferent to it really. It's like it's just more of the same violence they see and hear about all the time. They get brutalised themselves often enough.'

'It's bigger news than *that* surely? It's all over the papers and telly.'

'Well, Tammy doesn't read the papers. I don't know whether she watches TV. She drinks that much she probably can't focus on the screen.'

'Perhaps it's time you cultivated a new contact?'

Lucy considered this viewpoint. There was more than a modicum of sense in it. In all probability she'd already got what she realistically could from Tammy. Why should the girl open up any more than she already had? They were friends of convenience, nothing more. It might be that in due course they'd come to mean more to each other, but how long would that take? Weeks? Months? Even the most pessimistic analysts attached to Operation Clearway expected they'd have a suspect in custody before then.

Lucy glanced from the car window. The normal process whenever she got picked up by whoever it happened to be was to head as far away from the Boothstown lorry park as they could so that she wouldn't get spotted by any of the other girls or punters, and to keep driving, staying on the move for at least an hour so that by the time she'd returned it appeared that she'd given her client a full service. They'd already pulled off the dual carriageway and had switched roads several times while they'd been chatting. It was pure coincidence that a lay-by now appeared on their left, with a static fish-and-chip caravan at the eastern end and large sections of the rest of it, particularly around a stile in the middle of its rear hedgerow, barricaded off by stands of fluttering incident-tape.

'Hey,' Lucy said. 'Isn't this . . .?'

'Yep,' Des replied as they cruised past. 'Where that Ronnie Ford got murdered.'

She was surprised to see no police personnel on the site, not even a uniform to stand guard. 'CSIs finished with it now?'

'Probably,' he said. 'They were here two weeks.'

'Stop, will you?'

'Why?'

'Humour me, Des . . . stop the car.'

Shrugging, he steered his Beetle into the lay-by, pulling it to a halt at the western end. Lucy buttoned her plastic mac over her saucy gear, before climbing out. It was now just after five-thirty in the evening, and dusk had fallen properly. But she could still see the desolate autumnal fields to the north, only dotted here and there with farm outbuildings. Whatever lay south was screened by the hedgerow, but she already knew that extensive woodland lay somewhere over there. She pivoted around, scanning each direction to its horizon.

'Not much out here, is there?' she said.

'Well . . . there's a chippie van.' Des sounded pleased. He slammed the driver's door, and dug into his coat pocket to see what change he had. 'Seems a shame not to sample his wares while we're here.'

'You not had any tea?'

'None whatsoever.'

'There you go.' She closed the passenger door. 'What could be more convenient?'

Des locked up and they walked along the lay-by.

102

'You eating too?' he asked.

'No, but I'll have a chat with him.' She brushed her hair with her fingers to try and straighten it. She was aware of her overly heavy make-up, but there was nothing they could do about that. 'I don't look too tarty, do I?'

'You look gorgeous.'

'That doesn't answer my question.'

'He's a chippie man. He won't care as long as your money's good.'

They skirted past the taped-off section in front of the stile. Beyond it, thanks to the twilight, only a vague glimpse was possible of the farm field across which Ronnie Ford had traipsed to his death.

'Just out of interest,' Des said, 'if you're thinking of asking if he saw anything, I wouldn't bother. He's been interviewed half a dozen times already.'

'I wonder if anyone asked him the right questions though.'

'Eh?'

'The other day I was looking at some of the bumph I got sent when we started this thing,' Lucy said. 'These murders are all very organised, aren't they? For the most part, well-planned?'

'We think so, yeah.'

'And Jill the Ripper *brought* Ronnie Ford here, rather than it being the other way round?'

'That's the theory.'

'So how did she know about it?'

'This lay-by?'

'And that wood? How did she know there'd be a quiet, hidden spot a hundred yards past the stile?'

'Maybe she lives round here.'

Lucy expanded her arms. 'No one lives round here, Des.'

'So . . . what're you saying?'

'She must've scoped the place out beforehand. Look . . .

he picks her up at Atherton, which is quite a few miles away. They drive all the way here together, and suddenly she gets him to park up. This happened after seven in the evening. Which is long after this chippie van closes, yeah?'

The fish-and-chip caravan – which was logoed *Mark's Eats: fish, chips, burgers, pies* – was still fifty yards ahead, but they were approaching it fast.

'Again, that's the theory,' Des replied. 'The vendor had certainly gone home before it happened.'

'Which is further evidence that Jill knew about this place in advance.'

'Not necessarily. It could be that she got lucky in the timing. The murders of Crumper and Hall were very opportunistic.'

'I don't think this one was,' Lucy said. 'At the very least, she must've known what time the chippie van would close.'

'Or she just saw that it was closed when they happened to drive past.'

'Okay . . . well she must've known that the footpath on the other side of the stile would lead into a wood, not to a housing estate or a farmyard or something, where there were likely to be witnesses around.'

'Okay, but I'm still not sure what point you're actually trying to make . . .'

'That she'd already been here on a recce!' Lucy said, exasperated. 'The next question is who's to say the chippie van was closed when she did *that*?'

Des seemed bemused. 'Lucy, me and you are *not* part of the investigation team. You're aware of that?'

'We're still coppers.'

'Hang on a minute . . .'

They'd now almost reached the caravan. A large male figure in a white apron, his sleeves rolled back on meaty forearms, stood behind its serving-hatch.

'Just leave it to me,' Lucy said. 'I'm only asking him a couple of questions.'

The guy behind the hatch leaned on his elbows to watch as they trekked the last twenty yards. He was somewhere in early middle age, his mop of black hair greying at the edges and combed over in a 1970s-style side-parting. Up close, there was something of the bulldog about him, his unshaved face etched with a truculent frown. He wore blue, semi-translucent gloves, while his white apron was strangely pristine.

'Evening,' Lucy said.

'Evening.' The guy's tone was almost weary.

'You Mark?' she enquired.

The question seemed to weary him even more. 'It's a company name, love.' He straightened up. 'But while we're asking, who are *you*? . . . as if I didn't know already.'

Des flipped open a leather wallet to show his warrant card.

The chippie man nodded. 'Don't tell me . . . I've got to close up again?'

'Sorry . . . what?' Lucy said.

'I've lost weeks of business thanks to you lot,' he grumbled. 'They wouldn't let me anywhere near the place till they'd finished checking every square inch of ground. And now, even though they've gone . . . half the bloody lay-by's still taped off. So not only isn't there much room for customers, how many of them are seriously likely to show up here if they still think the coppers are hanging around?'

'You *are* sitting next to a murder scene,' Des pointed out, distracted by a chalkboard menu hanging at the side of the hatch.

'And how is that my fault?' the chippie man wondered.

'I'm not saying it's your fault,' Des replied. 'I'm just trying to explain.'

'I've had it explained. About fifteen thousand times, so don't waste your breath . . .'

'Whoa!' Lucy interjected. 'I think we've got off on the wrong foot here.'

'What do you want exactly?' the chippie man asked. 'And if it doesn't come with chips, I won't be impressed.'

'Well . . . I'll have two battered sausages, large chips and gravy,' Des said.

'Oh . . .' The chippie man looked surprised. 'Why didn't you say that in the first place?' He moved to comply, shovelling a mountain of chips onto a Styrofoam tray.

'We want some information too,' Lucy said.

'You don't think I've been asked a raft of questions already?' He didn't glance up as he used tongs to add the sausages, and ladled on the gravy. 'I'll say it again . . . and for the last time. I close at six o'clock in the evening. I wasn't even here when this bad thing happened.'

'I want to know if you saw anything any other days?' she said. 'For example, was there anyone . . .?'

He shook his head as he pushed the tray of food across the counter. 'I've seen no one except people who were buying chips.'

Lucy looked sceptical. 'You're seriously saying the *only* people who ever stop here are coming to buy food?'

'Not *just* that.' The chippie man mopped up with a paper towel. 'People park to make phone calls, to check road maps. Lorry drivers stop here for a kip.'

'How many of this general crowd are women?' Des asked, taking a plastic fork from a receptacle on the counter.

'Plenty,' the chippie man replied.

'What about on the days leading up to the murder?' Lucy asked.

'Like I say, plenty.'

'Okay,' she said. 'What about women who parked here

and then climbed over that stile back there? I'm sure there can't have been too many of those?'

The chippie man shrugged. 'More than you might think. Quite a few ladies come here to jog. I *assume* it's to jog – they've usually got running gear on. They park up, first thing in the morning or around lunchtime, climb over the stile and away they go. There's probably a track through the woods. But as I say, I've told your lot this already.'

Lucy pondered. Undoubtedly, this was a fly in the ointment of her theory. But if this place was a regular haunt for female joggers, that might also have provided cover for their suspect.

'Do they go jogging alone or in groups?' she asked.

'Sometimes in twos and threes, sometimes alone.'

'Any of these lady joggers particularly catch your eye?' Des asked, chomping his way through a batter-encrusted sausage. 'Outstanding assets, that sort of thing. Sexy.'

The chippie man regarded him with distaste. 'I don't have time to give every lass who comes here the eyeball. I have a business to run.'

Inwardly, Lucy had cringed at Des's question, though it was probably in line with the other questions that detectives in the team – male detectives mainly – were likely to have asked. With no e-fit of the suspect's facial features, and no certainty that her blonde hair was real, all attempts to identify her had inevitably focused on her buxom shape and 'lady of the night' apparel, and while no one expected the murderess to wander the streets during daytime dressed the way she did when out on the midnight prowl, given that a lot of modern running gear was rather snazzy, all figure-hugging Lycra and so forth, it was perhaps understandable that Des might think this way. Though that was a bloke all over. If the suspect *had* been here during daytime, even if she was a genuine statuesque stunner, Lucy knew that she'd have been able to dress herself down very subtly if she'd wanted to, to literally turn herself into such a plain Jane that no one would notice her.

There was one other detail though, which perhaps none of her fellow detectives had thought of yet.

'This one would only have been gone ten minutes or so,' Lucy said.

Both men looked quizzically round at her.

'I'm quite serious,' she added.

A keen jogger herself, Lucy was well aware that any fitness session lasting less than half an hour was unlikely to be much use; most fitness types trained for a minimum of forty minutes at a time. But it wouldn't take anything like that long to make a quick reconnoitre of these woods.

The chippie man still looked puzzled.

'Okay, how long do these lady joggers usually go for?' Lucy asked. 'I mean you must notice from time to time. They park up here, they climb over the stile and they're away . . . and then, at some point, they're back and their cars are gone again. How long does that normally take?'

'I've just told you, love . . . I barely notice these women. And now you're asking if I put a stopwatch on them when they're running? Seriously?'

'Fair enough.' Lucy tried not to sigh. Perhaps it had been a dumb question after all. She indicated to Des that they were done. 'Thanks for your help.'

'Wait a minute, whoa . . . you've just made me think.'

Lucy turned back to the hatch.

The chippie man's eyes glazed as he recollected something. 'Now you mention it, there was *one* girl who struck me . . . and this would have been in the right timeframe too.'

'Yeah?'

'The reason I remember her is she had quite a decent motor,' he said. 'Little sporty thing. Not sure what make or model, but it looked expensive. I remember thinking I wouldn't have liked to leave that here. I mean, there were people around . . . but you know, you hear about these high-end car thefts. Anyway, she had the jogging gear on. I assumed she'd be gone a good hour or so, like they usually are. But then she was back within ten minutes and drove off. Made me wonder if she'd got cold feet about leaving the car.'

'What did she look like?' Lucy asked.

'Blonde.'

'Blonde?'

'Yeah. Longish hair, because it was tied in a bun. Wearing a trackie top and shorts. The usual thing.'

'Height?' Des asked.

'Hard to say.'

'Tallish?'

'Maybe.'

'Any distinguishing features, tattoos or what-have-you?'

The chippie man snorted. 'Gimme a break, mate. I wasn't standing right next to her.'

'Anything else you remember about the motor she was driving?' Lucy asked.

He gave it some thought. 'Only that it was sporty. And red . . . bright red.'

'This was definitely a few days before the murder?'

'About that, yeah. One lunchtime, between twelve-noon and two.'

'You seem sure about that at least.'

'That's when I get busiest, and there was a queue of fellas standing here at the time.'

Lucy tried to process the intel. It was intriguing for sure, but it was still far too vague.

'It would obviously be useful to us,' she said, 'if you could try and pin down the date on which this happened. Bearing in mind that Ronald Ford died on October 6th.'

109

The chippie man blew out a long breath. 'I can't be any more specific except that it was about a week before then. I reckon you're looking at the last day of September-ish. But you've got to take a couple of days either side to be absolutely sure.'

'Would you recognise this woman again if we showed you a photo?' Des asked.

'Probably not.'

'What about the car?' Lucy said.

He mused. 'Don't think so.'

'Okay.' She stepped away. 'You'll be here if we need to come back and get a statement?'

'I'm here every day, Monday to Saturday.'

'Thanks. That's quite useful.'

'And those were belting.' Des nodded to his empty Styrofoam tray, before tossing it into a plastic bin next to the caravan. 'Cheers.'

'They were also three-pound-fifty,' the chippie man replied.

'Oh yeah . . .' Des gave a sheepish grin. 'Sorry.'

'So what do you think?' Lucy wondered as they walked back.

Des unlocked the Beetle, and they climbed inside.

'I think it's interesting,' he said. 'But it's the longest of all long shots. You realise that?'

'But it *is* interesting?'

'Just remember, Lucy . . . this isn't in our remit. And when you go and write it up for the brass, they'll inform you of that in no uncertain terms.'

'You've got a dab of gravy on your tie.'

'Shit.' He scrubbed at the offending mark with a clutch of tissues, which only served to smear it lengthways. 'Glad you saw that before Yvonne did.'

'Doesn't like you making a mess, does she not?' Yet again, Lucy eyed the vehicle's cluttered interior.

'Doesn't like me eating crap food.' He switched the engine on, and drove them to the lay-by exit, where he halted to allow for a gap in the traffic.

'Where does this road lead from here?' Lucy asked.

'Right takes us back the way we came, ultimately towards Tyldesley. Left takes us towards Abram.'

She pondered. 'I wonder which way she headed?'

'Well there are only two options,' he pointed out rather unnecessarily.

'Let's try left.'

'Shouldn't we be getting back?'

'Humour me again, Des. One last time.'

'Lucy, you're not a detective.'

'*You* are.'

'Yeah, but I'm attached to you lot.' He looked frustrated. 'Here I was, anticipating some nice, easy work.'

'This *is* nice and easy.'

Despite his moaning, they headed left and within five minutes had come to a roundabout with a large pub called the Rake and Harrow on the far side of it. As they waited at the broken white line, Lucy spotted traffic cameras in various locations around the circuit.

'This'll be easy work for you too,' she said. 'Pulling the footage from those cameras for between twelve-noon and two o'clock in the afternoon on all the days between and including September 27th and October 3rd.'

'Looking out for red sports cars, you mean?'

'Yeah.' She glanced round at him. 'Of which there won't be a great many, will there? Even by the law of averages.'

Des contemplated this as he navigated the roundabout and headed back the way they'd come. 'You know . . . that's not a bad shout, even if it is a million-to-one. That was a good question, about how long she was gone for. Clearly no one else had asked him that.'

'Seemed like an obvious question to me.'

'How long were you in CID?'

'A week,' she said.

'Well, they either taught you a lot very quickly, or you've got a natural aptitude for it.'

'So you think this is a lead?'

'Could be. We'll have to push it upstairs though.'

'Fine, whatever it takes. So long as you let them know it came from me.'

He laughed. 'I'm not going to tell them *I* went off the grid to do it.'

Chapter 10

It was nearly seven o'clock when they got back to the café car park. Des pulled up to the left of the building, alongside the bins. The only other vehicle round there was a scruffy high-sided van, a mucky brown in colour. It was idling rather than parked, its engine pumping plumes of exhaust in the frigid autumn air. By the glinting pinpoint of red behind its steering wheel – a cigarette no doubt – the driver was still inside.

There was something vaguely suspicious about that. The two cops knew it by instinct, but then all sorts of non-too-wholesome things went on around here, and at present they were otherwise engaged. Lucy drew down the passenger seat sun visor, wiped the blurry sheen off its mirror and attended to her make-up. Not that it had been messed up while she was out driving, but it was important to make it look as if it had.

'Getting a coffee,' Des said, opening his door. 'Want one?'

'Yeah, but I'd better not.' She carefully rouged her lips. 'I don't know too many prozzies who get treated to a brew when business is concluded.'

'Okay, I'll not be a mo.' He slipped out and left her to it.

As Lucy tarted herself up, she kept half an eye on the idling van. It could be here to pick up a girl, to buy or sell drugs – even to rob the café. But none of that really mattered. There was only one target on their agenda at present.

And then she heard the sound of someone crying out in pain and confusion.

At first she thought it might be coming from the van, but then she realised that it was actually somewhere to the rear of her. She adjusted the sun-visor, initially seeing nothing but the brick wall of the café and the egg yolk-yellow glow of the sodium street lights along the East Lancs. She adjusted it again, and this time spotted a pair of figures approaching Des's Beetle from behind, though coming at it diagonally as if from across the lorry park. Fleetingly, the figures were only visible in silhouette, but by her diminutive size and buxom shape one of them was recognisable as Tammy. The other one was lean, tall and quite clearly male. Moreover, he had a grip on Tammy's left arm and was dragging her forcefully alongside him.

Is this the awful Digby again?, Lucy wondered, a sinking feeling inside her.

As always, her complete lack of options out here served to deepen her despondency.

It went completely against the grain for a police officer to turn a blind eye to such casual brutality. And yet here she was, unable to protect one silly, drunken girl who yet again had managed to antagonise the vicious boor she'd voluntarily enslaved herself to.

Despite all, Lucy hit a button on her left and powered down the passenger window as the twosome struggled their way past – and now she realised that it wasn't Digby.

This guy, who was someone she hadn't seen before, was quite young, and in physical terms was a beanpole, with a mop of fair hair and, when she glanced up as he passed, a juvenile snarl on his thin, acne-scarred face.

'It's dead simple, love,' he shouted over Tammy's tearful

114

protests. 'You're under arrest for prostitution. You can have it easy or you can have it hard, but either way you're coming with me.'

Under arrest?, Lucy thought. *For 'prostitution'?*

There was no such criminal offence.

They veered towards the van. The guy was wearing track-suit bottoms, a sweatshirt and a shimmering yellow pair of Nike Air Max trainers. He was twenty at the most. Few cops were out and about in plain clothes at that age. As she watched, scalp tingling, the back doors to the van swung open. Another figure climbed out and came round the vehicle to meet them.

Lucy was approximately thirty yards away. In the late October gloom, it was difficult to distinguish him, but he was of relatively small stature with thin shoulders and a hunched posture. He halted in front of the van, glancing warily left to right.

'What's that?' Lucy murmured to herself. 'Making sure no one's here to see what you're up to?'

Evidently, the two men hadn't spotted that she was inside the darkened Beetle. Once Des had gone into the caf, they'd thought the coast was clear.

'And how old are *you*?' she wondered. By his slim build, she put this one in his late teens, maybe even less than that.

This was all very wrong, but, of course, as usual, Tammy was too drunk to have worked that out for herself, or, if she had, too drunk to resist them adequately.

The second character now took hold of Tammy's right arm, and despite her increased wailing, he and his mate hauled her around to the rear of the van together. There was a double slamming of doors. The van's headlights speared to life, and it lurched forward, engine growling.

'Shit!' Lucy glanced back towards the front of the café. 'Des . . . come on!'

But there was no sign of him. Most likely he'd be queuing to get served. And there wasn't even sufficient time now to jump out and go looking for him. Besides, to openly seek his help inside the café would be to risk her cover.

The van rumbled past the Beetle. Lucy turned and peered after it. Its back doors were firmly closed and there were no windows in them. Equally absent was a seam of light running down the middle, shining through the narrow gap between those doors to indicate that conditions inside were at least tolerable for the prisoner.

She pulled her mobile from her shoulder bag, despite knowing there wouldn't be time to use it. A frantic readjustment of the rear-view mirror showed the van swinging left onto the East Lancs. At this time of night, with rush hour over, it would be gone in seconds.

'Shit!' she said again, heart racing.

She glanced right. Des's key still hung in the Beetle's ignition.

'Sorry, DC Barton,' she said. 'I've no bloody choice.'

She levered herself up and over the gearstick and into the driving seat, and turned the key. The engine juddered to life. Snapping her seatbelt into place, she got her foot down, spinning the car around in a fast three-point turn, and gunning it towards the exit and out onto the dual carriageway beyond. Thankfully, there was minimal traffic, and the high-sided van came back into view some ninety yards ahead, keeping a steady pace. Lucy accelerated in pursuit, but discreetly – the last thing she wanted was to create the impression that she was chasing it.

As she did, she took her mobile out again and thumbed in Des's number.

'Yello!' he said jovially. She could hear women laughing in the background. It sounded as if he was exchanging banter with the girls behind the café counter.

'Des, it's Lucy,' she said. 'I've borrowed your car.'

'Yeah, that's . . . *what*?'

'Sorry, no time to explain. You've just got to trust me. I'll be back as soon as poss.'

'But . . . where are you going?' There wasn't much joviality in his voice now. 'Lucy, hang on . . . this is no bloody good! *What do you mean you've borrowed my sodding car?*'

'Look, just stand by, okay?' To Lucy's surprise, the van swung sharply off to the left. She hit the pedal hard to try and catch up. 'I think a bunch of scrotes have just abducted Tammy.'

'Lucy, what the hell are you talking about?'

'I'm not sure, I'll tell you when I know more.' She cut the call, thoughts racing.

The left-hand turn now approached. It connected with what looked like a single-track lane. She swung into it, and brought the Beetle to an abrupt halt, grit and leaves spraying from her tyres. She shouldn't be doing this. Even if what she suspected was true, she was endangering her covert status and therefore the status of the entire operation.

But there were some things you just couldn't sit by and ignore.

As quickly as she could, she called Des again.

'What the hell is going on?' he yelled.

'Des . . . listen. I don't want to get personally involved in this unless I absolutely have to. So I need some divisional support. Can you get on the blower . . . do it discreetly obviously, and try to get some uniforms to investigate the first left turn-off north of the café? Be economical with the facts, eh? Don't tell them I'm a copper . . . say an abduction's been reported by an unnamed member of the public who's currently in pursuit, or something like that. Look, I've gotta go if I'm gonna keep tabs on them. I'll stay in touch.'

She rammed her foot down again, grinding more grit as

she tore down the lane, which immediately began curving and twisting. In truth, this was a nightmare scenario. Even assuming the local lads responded immediately, it would take minutes for them to get all the way out here . . . and how far away would the target vehicle be by then? She'd only dallied a second or two and she'd already lost sight of its tail lights. Ahead, trees were now ranked thickly down either side of the lane, their leafless branches interlocked overhead – it was more a tunnel than a road. But there was still no sign of the van. Lucy accelerated again, pushing up from forty to fifty to sixty.

Signposts and farm-gates flickered by in her peripheral vision.

With no clue about the geographic layout at this end of the East Lancashire Road, she had no idea where she was, except that she was about six miles from her home-patch in Crowley, and at least twelve from Manchester city centre.

Another turn-off veered into view ahead, this time on the right.

Lucy smashed her brake pedal flat, screeching to a halt over thirty yards.

This new turn led onto a dirt track rather than a metalled lane, and meandered off into total blackness, probably leading to a field or a barn or something; a regular road to nowhere. Even so, she backed up and spun the wheel again, to try and see better in the flood of her headlights. Her gaze fell on recently churned tyre-marks in the track's muddy surface. It was still a gamble that they'd come this way, but if these guys were some bunch of scumbag rapists, as Lucy suspected, they wouldn't be heading anywhere easily accessible to the general public.

She gunned the Beetle forward onto the rutted surface, tyres slewing through fresh heaps of fallen leaves. She no longer had concerns about trying to pretend that she wasn't following them – on an isolated route like this, the moment they spotted her headlights they'd know what she was up to. She thus roared along, the unmade track rising and falling in undulating humps. More leafy grit flew as she careered around ever-sharper bends. And now, at last, she spotted them again. She depressed the pedal, steadily closing the gap between them.

The rear of the van ballooned towards her, a dingy brown, smeared with oil and grime. It wasn't exactly flying, but it was travelling at a good fifty, which on this road was pretty perilous. Lucy slowed a little so as not to collide with it, but there was now only thirty yards between them. This certainly seemed to have distracted the van driver. At the next tight bend, he skidded along the verge, his nearside wheels threshing leaves and twigs. There was an open stretch after that, the dim ribbon of the road extending for several hundred yards.

A veteran of several chases, Lucy expected her opponent to floor it.

But he didn't. He maintained his current pace, and then she realised why. These guys were supposed to be the police. Openly running would be the last thing they'd do, especially if they now thought they were being followed by one of Tammy's friends. Trying to maintain their pretence would be the most obvious tactic – but that would suit her, because ideally she wanted to follow them rather than tackle them. On which subject, realising that she'd made another turn since she'd last spoken to Des, she grabbed at her phone again . . . only for the van driver to suddenly lurch his vehicle left onto an even narrower track.

Lucy dropped the phone onto the passenger seat as she swung after it. This thoroughfare was equally rutted and muddy, but now she could see that it was actually a driveway rather than a road. It curved away through the woodland, terminating on the forecourt of what looked like a derelict house.

119

The van pulled up sharply. Lucy braked too, slithering to a halt about twenty yards at the rear of it, though from the exhaust pumping out of its tailpipe, its engine was still running. Before she could decide what to do next, one of the van's rear doors clunked open and a figure sprang out. It was the beanpole with the blond hair and the snarl. He slammed the door closed behind him, and came quickly towards her.

She noticed that he was pulling on a pair of black leather gloves.

'Christ . . .' she breathed.

Her heart thumped her ribs as she braced herself. She could hardly expect to speak with authority here and yet *not* reveal who she was. Even if she did reveal it, it wouldn't be easy laying the law down in thigh-boots and fishnets. The only option was to try and rough it, just bullock her way through as if she was an ordinary outraged citizen. Meanwhile, the guy, even though young, looked meaner the closer he came. He might be tall and thin, but there was something lithe about him – the way he walked, the way his arms swung at his sides – as if he was actually quite athletic.

She cast around for a weapon. She had her rape alarm and Mace in her shoulder bag, but that was down in the passenger-side footwell. She wouldn't be able to reach it in time. Instead, her left hand scuttled along the dash and into the glovebox, which, typically for Des Barton, was crammed with grotty bits and pieces. As the blond guy rounded the front of her car towards the driver's side, her fingers rooted amid broken pens, half-eaten sweets, wads of paperwork – and then alighted on an aerosol canister. She yanked it out, but it wasn't especially heavy in her hand. When she gazed down at it, she saw nothing more useful than a tin of de-icer.

The guy leaned down at her window.

Swallowing her nervousness, Lucy lowered the pane to speak with him.

'And what the fuck do you think you're doing?' he wondered, his gaze creeping down to her fishnet-clad thighs. He seemed amused by the sight. 'You want to get arrested too . . . you slutty little bitch?'

'I need to see your ID,' she said.

'You need to see my ID?' He stuck his ferrety face right into hers, and dangled a pair of handcuffs alongside it. 'How's this? Now get out the fucking car, like the good little cock-sucking slapper you no doubt are.'

'Wait,' she replied. 'Here's my ID.'

'Your . . .?' Puzzled, he leaned even closer.

And she ejected the aerosol's contents into his face.

He tottered backwards with a screech, cupping both hands to his eyes. At the same time his feet slid in the mud and he thudded down onto his back. Lucy kicked the driver's door open and leapt out. She landed the toe of her left boot in his groin as he writhed there, at which he gagged and curled into a ball. With no time to actually stop and think about what she was doing, she ran towards the van, swerving through its plume of exhaust to its offside. The driver's window was already wound down. The driver turned a startled face towards her. It wasn't the younger guy she'd expected, which meant there was more than two of them. This one looked older than the beanpole, with fatter cheeks, a mop of greasy hair, piggy eyes and a wispy moustache under his fat, flat nose.

It was the nose she aimed for, banging her right fist into it. Lucy wasn't the kind of copper who indulged in this sort of behaviour often, but the crunch of cartilage was strangely satisfying. With chicken-like squawks, the driver groped at his face, blood geysering through his grubby, ring-cluttered fingers.

'Wanker!' she spat, before backing toward the rear of the van, shaking her hand hard to ease the sting out of her knuckles. It hurt so much when you actually hit someone; the movies never got that bit right.

She yanked down on the lever of the van's rear doors, and with an echoing *CLUNG*, they sprang open. She assumed the combat posture as the glow of her own headlights permeated the dank interior, fully expecting the next bastard to jump right out at her. However, he didn't. This was the younger one, the teenager with the narrow shoulders. He cowered at the far end, crushing himself against the partition wall. His face was written with panic, his eyes glinting with tears. His hands had clawed in front of him, but only as if to ward her off.

Alongside him, Tammy lay bound and gagged, lengths of washing line knotting her wrists together in the small of her back, strips of silver duct tape plastered across her mouth and around the back of her head.

'Come on, love, we're going home,' Lucy said, taking the girl by the ankles and lugging her forward.

Re-energised by Lucy's arrival, Tammy scrabbled the rest of the way on her bottom and ankles, and jumped outside, audibly roaring under the duct tape. She needed no assistance as she pulled and yanked at the clothesline, finally releasing her own hands. When she tore off the gag, she coughed and choked, a stream of rancid vomit spilling out. It was anyone's guess how long it had been percolating in the back of her throat.

'You soppy little bastards!' Lucy told the kid in the van. He still pressed himself into the wooden partition, eyes wide with terror. 'You picked the wrong night to come out and play, didn't you? I ever see you trying to abduct girls around here again . . . I'll follow you home afterwards and slit your throat while you're in bed! And your bloody mates! You getting me . . . you little toad, you fucking little shithouse! *I SAID DO YOU GET ME?*'

He nodded and whimpered, a bubble of green snot appearing at the end of his nose.

Lucy took Tammy by the elbow and steered her back towards the Beetle. The girl yammered incoherently, sobbing and trying to speak at the same time.

'It's alright,' Lucy said. 'It's over now.'

They reached the front offside of their ride, where the tall, thin blond was still lying scrunched into a foetal ball. It struck Lucy that she might have inflicted more damage than she'd intended with that kick. But the devil if she cared now. Tammy clearly felt the same, because she kicked him too, savagely – in the back and the head, before stepping around to the front and landing another couple in his face, to which he could do no more than groan aloud, eyes screwing shut as his head flirted backwards and sideways.

'Enough!' Lucy said, grabbing her elbow again, hastening her to the front passenger seat and pushing her inside. If nothing else, Lucy wanted to get them away from here now, before any police units arrived; that would save a shedload of awkward explanations. She slammed the door closed, rounded back to the driving seat and leaned down one more time to the injured blond.

'You and your mates are lucky you're still alive,' she hissed. 'But don't be reassured by that. I've clocked your registration mark. That means every person I know will be looking out for it. So you'd better stay at home from now on, sonny. Or move cities, or change your life and become a fucking monk. Because I'll tell you now, you're not going to be safe doing anything else.'

Chapter 11

'Listen, it's no biggie,' Tammy said, sniffling over her coffee. 'We get raped from time to time. There's nothing we can do about it. It goes with the territory.'

Lucy regarded her askance from the other side of the café table. Even given the mess Tammy was in – her hair a frenzy, her eyes red and bleary, cheeks streaked with clotted mascara – this was an astounding comment.

'How can you talk like that?' Lucy finally asked.

'You're in the lifestyle too,' Tammy said defensively. 'You telling me you'd never let them take it for free if they were trying to muscle you?'

'I think that was a bit more than people muscling you, love. God knows what those three losers had in mind. I'm not sure it would've stopped at rape.'

'It would have.' Tammy wiped her nose with a tissue. Despite the fact she was still sniffling, her usual bravado was already returning. 'They were just kids.'

'So how come you're still crying?'

Tammy shrugged. 'Had a scare, but that's all.'

Yet more bravado, Lucy realised.

'But that doesn't mean I'm not grateful,' Tammy added hastily.

124

'I'm more grateful than I can say. I don't know any other girl who'd do what you did tonight. I owe you one big time.'

That was one thing Lucy could at least relax about. It had crossed her mind that merely helping Tammy the way she had might have threatened her cover, but the girl seemed happy to accept that it had simply been a generous act from a fellow lost soul.

'I couldn't let it happen.' Lucy sipped her own coffee. 'You've been friendly to me since I showed up here. And while I could do something, I thought I should. I'm a bit handy.'

'Yeah, I saw . . .' Tammy cackled. 'Where did you learn all that stuff?'

'Saltbridge.'

'What . . . over in Crowley?'

Lucy nodded warily. She hoped she wasn't saying too much. But her elaborate and carefully memorised cover-story had needed to accommodate her Crowley accent, which in the ears of a foreigner might only be slightly different to that of an inner-Mancunian, but to a native of the north-west would easily be detectable, and telling easily detectable lies was never a good way to start when you were going undercover.

'Rough area, Saltbridge?' Tammy asked.

'Roughish,' Lucy said. 'How about you?'

'Harpurhey, originally.'

'Bloody hell, *you* ought to have developed some street-smarts too.'

'I *have*.' Tammy straightened in her seat as though attempting to puff herself up, which was pretty laughable given her bedraggled state. 'Hey . . . I'm alright, me. Just took my eye off the ball for a sec.' She glanced furtively around, and seeing that the counter staff's attention was elsewhere, lowered her cup beneath the table, at which point there was a noticeable *glug-glug-glug* as she flavoured her coffee with vodka.

'Your problem is you've got too much of a taste for that

125

stuff,' Lucy commented. 'Half the time you can't see what's going on under your nose.'

'Whatever gets us through the night, isn't it? Anyway, just helping me out doesn't give you a right to lecture me. You're not my mum.'

'You sure you're alright?'

'I'm fine.' Tammy rubbed at the welts where the clothesline had bitten into her wrists. 'Where'd you get the car, anyway?'

'Oh, that.' Lucy glanced through the cafeteria window to where the Beetle was parked next to a hedge. She hadn't driven Tammy back to the lorry park for the simple reason that Des would still be there, probably hopping from foot to foot by now, which would have been something of a give-away. 'I nicked it.'

'You nicked it?' Tammy gawked at her. 'You fucking serious?'

'Took the first wheels I could find, didn't I?'

'And you just left it out front like that?'

That might have been a mistake, Lucy now realised. The car was next to a hedge, but close to the slip road. It could easily be clocked by passing traffic, especially if that traffic happened to be police officers looking for a recently stolen motor. And okay, it wasn't exactly stolen, but this was the lie she was trying to sell.

'Perhaps we'd better get going,' she said, standing up.

Tammy looked hesitant. 'If we get caught in a stolen car, Digby'll be all over me with that belt of his. I'll look like raw meat when he's finished.'

'You let *him* push you around too much as well.'

'It's easy for you to say that. You being so . . . what's the word you used, "handy"?'

Lucy went to the counter to pay. When she'd finished, Tammy was done with her coffee/vodka, and they went outside together.

'I know a chop shop where you could drop this off,' Tammy said as they climbed into the Beetle. 'But I doubt they'd touch it. Right bloody dustbin.'

Lucy said nothing as she slid behind the wheel. Now that her passenger was alert to the fact they were in a hot car, and looking it over more carefully, she hoped there was nothing lying in plain view that might indicate its owner was a policeman. Not that it would be easy to spot anything specifically in Des's scruffy interior, especially when the doors were closed and the lights off.

'You ever thought of getting out of it?' Lucy asked, as she drove back to the East Lancs.

'What . . . this life?' Tammy sounded amused. 'And waste the gifts God's given me?'

'I don't think he intended you to use them this way.'

'You're doing the same thing.'

'Yeah. Wish I wasn't.'

'Well . . . how do you think I feel? I mean deep down?' Tammy sniffled again.

Lucy glanced sideways and saw fresh tears sparkling in the girl's lashes. As before, the 'tough chick' routine had proved wafer-thin, especially now the adrenaline was flagging and a fuller understanding of what had nearly happened was dawning on her.

'Sodding bastards,' she said, swallowing hard.

'If it's any consolation, they won't try it again.'

'I only hope they do. With any luck, they'll run into Lotta.'

'Who?'

Tammy remained tearful, but gave a crooked grin. 'They won't know what's hit 'em then.'

'Who's Lotta?' Lucy asked.

'Top beauty, she is . . . hottest ticket in town. But you wouldn't mess with her.'

'Hardcase?'

'Put it this way, Keira, love . . . she'd make *you* look like a nursery teacher.'

'Good to know girls can look after themselves.'

'It's more than looking after herself. Lotta once told me that if she ever got the chance, she'd collect the dicks and ball sacks of every bastard who ever stuck it to her and put them on shields on the wall in her flat.'

Lucy nearly lost control of the car. They were back on the East Lancs by now, and at ten o'clock on a Friday night it was almost bare of traffic, but she still skidded from one lane to the next.'

'What's up?' Tammy asked, grabbing the dashboard with fright.

'Nothing . . . oil slick on the road. We're fine, but what's that you just said . . . your mate collects dicks and ball sacks?'

'Nah.' Tammy waved it away. 'Lotta was just talking. When you get to know her, she's lovely. You wouldn't want to cross her though. Big strapping lass, built like one of them wrestling babes. And just as sexy.'

'And Lotta works the streets?'

'You're joking, aren't you? Way too classy for that. Back in the day, I was . . .' She halted mid-flow, as if unsure whether or not to continue. Was it possible there was something that even the brash, indecorous Tammy could be embarrassed about? 'Well . . . there's this club in Cheetham Hill. Don't know if you've ever heard of it. SugaBabes?'

Lucy shrugged. 'When I say I'm new to the game, I mean it.'

'It's the crème de la crème. Dead posh inside, dead well paid. Only the best-looking girls work there, but Lotta's the star attraction. I'm telling you, Keira, it's amazing. The only punters who come in are loaded. You don't get toe-rags staggering in at the end of piss-ups.'

128

'And you used to work there?' Lucy tried not to sound too sceptical that an alcoholic street-girl like Tammy could find work in such a cultured establishment.

'Yeaaaah,' Tammy said, again defensive. 'When I started out.' She took another swig of vodka. 'Suppose you're wondering how I finished up out here?'

'I'm not actually,' Lucy replied. 'But if this is as classy a place as you say, I'm wondering what the chances are of me getting a gig there?'

Tammy pondered this. 'Well, you look good enough. You're clean . . . I *presume* you're clean?'

'Yeah, course.'

'Because they'll give you a raft of medical checks.'

'I'm clean.'

'There'll probably be a try-out session.'

Lucy glanced sidelong at her. 'Try-out session?'

'Course. Someone'll try you out first. See if you're any good. That always happens.'

'I see . . .'

'But I wouldn't bother if I were you.'

'No?'

'You never heard of the Twisted Sisters? Jayne and Suzy McIvar?'

Lucy considered. Those names *did* ring a bell, though she couldn't quite place them. In any case, she didn't want to let on that she had any kind of inside knowledge. She shook her head.

'They run the place,' Tammy explained. 'And trust me, if you don't want to get on the wrong side of Lotta, you really don't want to get on the wrong side of those two.'

'Lotta still works there then?'

'Far as I know.' Tammy swilled more vodka. 'Nothing higher you can aim for round here if you're intent on staying in. Good dosh, no skanks putting their hands all over you, stinking of Kentucky Fried, grease and engine oil under their fucking fingernails . . .'

When she put it like that, Lucy had to admit – a berth at SugaBabes, try-out session or not, almost sounded desirable.

*

'And what on Earth are *you* supposed to be?' Cora Clayburn wondered.

Lucy spun around from the kettle, shocked. It wasn't yet five o'clock in the morning. The very last thing she'd expected was that her mother would already be awake. Cora stood in the kitchen doorway in a house-robe and slippers. Her hair was tousled, and she was sallow-cheeked, but clearly, like mothers the world over when their offspring are out and about in the early hours, she hadn't been deeply asleep. Most likely, the sound of her daughter returning home unexpectedly early had disturbed her.

That said, she looked wide awake now. In fact, she was goggle-eyed as she advanced into the kitchen. And with more than a little reason, given that Lucy was standing making herself a brew while wearing her camisole, hot pants and thigh-boots.

'What are you doing up?' Lucy asked.

'I asked first.' Cora sat unsteadily at the kitchen table, eyes fixed on her daughter's attire as if it was the worst thing she'd ever seen.

'I guess you already know the answer to that,' Lucy said, finishing off the tea. She'd deliberately withheld from her mother the actual details of her new role, to avoid scaring her. But Cora wasn't dim.

'You're not on one of these awful undercover operations . . . when you go out all night dressed as a prostitute?'

'It's nothing to worry about. We're not actually getting picked up.'

Cora didn't look in any way reassured. 'That's hardly the point! What if someone we know spots you?'

'It's not happening around here.'

'So let me get this straight . . . they've actually got you standing on street-corners to try and catch this maniac?'

'Mum . . .' Lucy bustled across the room and kissed her on the forehead. 'I understand your concern, but the murderer's not looking for female victims. We're genuinely not in danger.'

'Okay, so what happened to your hand?'

'Oh . . .' Lucy had forgotten that she'd notched a couple of knuckles. In fact, the whole of that part of her right hand was enflamed and throbbing. 'It's nothing.'

Cora fished a pair of glasses from her house-robe pocket. 'Let me have a look.'

Reluctantly, Lucy offered her sore paw.

Cora examined it, and then stood up and moved to the medicine cabinet, taking out some antiseptic wipes, a tube of ointment and a roll of wraparound sticking-plaster. 'Who did you punch?' she asked.

'That's no concern of yours.'

Very delicately, Cora cleansed the bruised and swollen flesh. 'I suppose I should just be grateful it wasn't the other way around.'

'I told you. We're not in danger . . . we *are* the danger.'

'I hope you know what you're doing, my girl.'

'I ought to after ten years.'

'There are some very, very bad people out there.'

'Yeah, well . . . if I get my way, there'll soon be one less.'

Chapter 12

'So what do we know about this Tammy Nethercot?' DSU Nehwal asked.

She sat on the desk at the front of the Ripper Chicks office, fidgeting with a pen. Slater stood to one side.

'She's in the system, ma'am,' Lucy said from her own desk, stifling a yawn. It was mid-afternoon and she hadn't long been back on duty, but as usual she hadn't slept well during the interim period. 'Form for tomming obviously, but also for shoplifting, drunk and disorderly, possession . . .'

'Not the most reliable witness then?'

'She's been on the game a long time. Probably since she was well underage. I'd be inclined to trust her on this, though . . . at least a little bit. Plus, that thing I helped her out with last night. She reckons she owes me one. And those are her words, not mine.'

'On which subject,' Slater said, 'I traced the VRM of that van, as you requested in your report. Belongs to a certain Gavin Longton, apprentice diesel-fitter from Little Hulton. He and his associate, Jamie Hargreaves, have been done twice in the past for indecent assault against prostitutes. Basically, they want the works but don't like paying for it. The third one, the kid . . . we've no name for him yet, but it shouldn't be difficult pinching all three of them if that's how you'd like to proceed. Though given the extreme methods you yourself employed, I don't think that'd be a very good idea.'

'It certainly bloody wouldn't,' Nehwal chipped in.

Lucy pondered. It had never occurred to her that the attack on Tammy might have any direct relevance to the enquiry. She *had* considered that it may indicate an escalation in violence against working girls in general as retaliation for the murders, though there wasn't broad evidence of that as yet. Now it sounded as if the three bastards involved had been nothing more than a scummy-arsed rape-team on the look-out for action.

'I don't think it'd be practical to pull them in this time, sir,' she said. 'Tammy would never cooperate anyway – she's too frightened of her pimp. Plus it'd blow my cover. But at the very least we need to watch those three.'

'Already taken care of,' Slater replied. 'I've forwarded their details to Salford Robbery. They've got the resources to sit on them for a few weeks.'

'The main thing from our perspective,' Lucy added, 'is that it's given me a real *in* with Tammy. She's now desperate to do me a favour.'

There was a pause, before Nehwal glanced at Slater. 'SugaBabes? What do you think?'

He shrugged. 'I think it's the best lead we've had so far. I mean, there are other lines of enquiry, but none of them seem to be going anywhere.'

'The real problem here is the McIvar sisters,' Nehwal said 'They're not small-time.'

'It's not really them we're after, though, ma'am,' Lucy replied. 'It's someone on their books.'

'You're certain this Lotta still works at the SugaBabes Club?' Slater asked.

'Tammy doesn't know that for sure,' Lucy said. 'And I can't press her too hard on it, because she'd get suspicious. But the truth is we won't know until we get inside.'

He looked discomforted by the mere thought. 'Wouldn't it just be easier to send one of the lads as a prospective customer? Get him to ask for Lotta?'

'Possibly,' Lucy said. 'But Tammy reckons Lotta's her real name, not her stage name. One of our grunts goes into that club, starts asking for girls by their real names . . . that'll go down with the McIvars like a lead balloon.'

'Okay, so what's her stage name?' Nehwal asked.

'Tammy doesn't remember.'

Slater looked dubious. 'She doesn't remember?'

Lucy made a helpless gesture. 'False names, stage names . . . whatever you want to call them, sir, they come thick and fast once you get out there. I mean I've already got two and I've only been on the game a fortnight. Some of the girls have a lot more than two – they chop and change them like no one's business. On top of that, Tammy's an alky. She's met that many lasses in this line work over the last few years she struggles to remember most of them by their *real* names. And again, I can't risk questioning her too much.'

The two senior officers glanced at each other uneasily.

'How do you propose to get inside, PC Clayburn?' Nehwal eventually asked. 'You going to offer to turn tricks for them?'

'I've gained Tammy's confidence a little, ma'am,' Lucy replied. 'I've told her my real name now, "Hayley" . . . and she's got me tagged as a reluctant newcomer. She believes I'm only selling myself because I need the cash, and that actually I'd rather do a normal job. She reckons the SugaBabes Club is always looking for barmaids.'

'There are a million barmaids in the north of England. Why would they employ *you*?'

'Well, ma'am, the only girls who'd likely apply are the

ones who know the place is there . . . which cuts the field down a bit. The most trustworthy would be girls who are ex-hookers themselves, in effect girls on the inside already. And Tammy reckons that if I . . . well, if I put my assets on show, that'll catch their eye. It's a brothel after all, not a country club.'

Nehwal frowned. 'I don't like it.'

'Neither do I,' Slater said. 'But I still think it's a good lead.'

Nehwal eyed Lucy carefully. 'You know the Twisted Sisters are suspects in three gangland murders?'

'Yes, ma'am. I've read up on them.'

'Suzy McIvar in particular is a known psychopath with repeated convictions for violence.'

Lucy shrugged. She'd assessed both the McIvars' mugshots, even though they were a little out of date. The twins were thirty-eight now, though the last official police images of them portrayed a pair of Longsight prostitutes in their mid-20s. They weren't identical twins, but looked similar: of mixed-race parentage, lean-faced and mean. Pretty girls possibly if they'd made the effort, but on the occasion of these particular arrests, looking beaten-up and feral.

'They're also affiliated to the Crew,' Nehwal said.

'My understanding is that the Crew don't actually *own* them, ma'am,' Lucy replied.

'The Crew don't own anyone or anything. Not officially. But when they *protect* you, it's as good as. And they protect the McIvars.'

'Hey, whoa . . . I don't suppose these Ripper killings could actually be connected to the McIvars?' Slater suddenly said, thinking aloud. 'Unpaid bills or something?'

'Bit of an OTT reaction,' Nehwal replied, but she looked interested all the same.

'Maybe they were big bills,' he suggested.

Nehwal pursed her lips. 'I'll put a note on the file, but I'd say the odds were against that. Those other homicides the Twisted Sisters are suspected of were double-tap executions. Real professional stuff. On top of that, none of these victims were in the high-roller bracket that SugaBabes normally attracts.'

'What about the Crew themselves?' Slater said. 'If this Lotta *is* Jill the Ripper, could she be a front . . . or a lure? Could these be Crew hits, ma'am?'

But the more Nehwal pondered it, the more visibly sceptical she became.

'Again, the sexual sadism wouldn't fit that pattern. What do they stand to gain by making it look like a serial killer? Jill the Ripper's actually costing the Crew money. It's damping down the demand for girls. But like I say, I'll put it forward at the next conflab.'

'Well, either way,' Lucy said, 'I've got to get in there before we can do anything else.'

Slater still looked uncomfortable with it. 'Whether the Crew are whacking johns or not, they've got a regular involvement with SugaBabes. You've already been made familiar with some of their main players, Lucy. That was on the off chance you'd hear about them while you were on the street. All along we told you there was next to zero chance of actually meeting one of these guys. But you go into that brothel, and the chance increases exponentially.'

'Sir . . . I'm going in purely as a functionary. I mean, if there're no barmaid jobs on offer, I'll volunteer to clean. And whatever happens, I'll only be there long enough to get some names.'

'You realise you'll be outside our help?' Nehwal said. 'I mean we know all about that place, of course . . . we've known about it for years, but for various operational reasons it's suited us to keep it open. But there's still no chance we can send anyone in to watch your back.'

'Ma'am, I've considered all that . . .'

'We can't even risk fitting you with a wire. The likelihood is they'll search you at the start and finish of each shift to check you haven't been pilfering.'

'It's fine,' Lucy said, though this wasn't a pleasing thought.

'The other thing that concerns me,' Nehwal said, 'is your lack of experience.'

'Ma'am, I've been a police officer for ten years . . .'

'We know that. But this situation is all about covert enquiry, and that requires a completely different skill-set . . . as you know perfectly well.'

'Yeah, but it's Lucy who's inveigled her way into Tammy Nethercot's confidence,' Slater argued. 'There's no one else that can take her place at this stage.'

Again, Nehwal looked unhappy. 'How certain are you this Tammy Nethercot can get you a job?'

'That's where it may unravel,' Lucy admitted. 'I'm not one hundred per cent. I'm not even fifty per cent. But I'm meeting her for lunch on Monday, and she's going to make an introduction for me.'

Nehwal arched an eyebrow. 'You're meeting a street whore for lunch?'

'In Tammy's case I suspect it'll be a liquid lunch. I've told her I'm buying, so she's game.'

'What's your cover story going to be for this?'

'Same as before, ma'am. My name's Hayley Gibbs and I'm from Crowley. I was an admin assistant at Bradby & Sons in Clifton until I got caught with my hand in the till, at which point I got my marching orders.'

'Bradby & Sons?' Nehwal glanced at Slater. 'That one of ours?'

'Yeah, it's a good one,' he said. Like all major metropolitan police forces, Greater Manchester operated a range of fake companies, telephone numbers, websites, email accounts and such, all carefully managed by highly trained admin staff, to provide phoney background info for officers engaged in undercover investigations.

'I've also got boyfriend issues,' Lucy added. 'In short, I can't give him any more cash to fuel his gambling habit, and to avoid him beating the shit out of me again I'm living with a friend . . . at least until I get myself back on my feet.'

There was a lull in the conversation, Nehwal's intense brown eyes fixed on Lucy for several seconds longer than was comfortable. 'You sure you know what you're doing here, PC Clayburn? I mean . . . you're *really* sure?'

'I'm ready, ma'am,' Lucy said. 'The only thing that'll stop me is if we catch Jill the Ripper before then.'

Nehwal snorted with unamused laughter. 'Don't hold your breath on that.'

Lucy's shift that Saturday night was uneventful, primarily because a cold autumn wind brought bouts of heavy rain, keeping all but the most desperate punters indoors. She only saw Tammy briefly, though that was sufficient for her to confirm their arrangements for the following week, which, when Lucy arose mid-morning on the Sunday, felt surreal.

Even after shaking off the last vestiges of sleep, Lucy was tired and tense, already worried about the following day. Determined to tough it out, she pulled a sweater over her pyjamas and went downstairs. The house was quiet, the TV switched off, and there was no smell of eggs or bacon from the kitchen, so she assumed that her mother was out. That wasn't unusual on a Sunday morning. Cora wasn't a regular churchgoer, but she attended every so often. Lucy had even teased her about this, commenting that the handsome, recently widowed vicar, Roy Alderton, might have his eye on her, to which Cora, in a curt tone bordering on the disgusted, had replied, 'Stuff and bloody nonsense!'

Seeing advantage in her mum's absence, Lucy made herself some tea and toast, and then went back upstairs and rooted through the deeper recesses of her wardrobe, pulling out a succession of slinky garments: flared skirts, split skirts, miniskirts, crop tops, sheer blouses, skinny leggings and a succession of ridiculously tall, strappy shoes. She hadn't worn any of this gear in quite some time. Even so, she laid it out on her bed and stood there surveying it.

'Going upmarket this week, are we?' her mum asked from behind.

Lucy glanced round, startled. 'You seem to be in the habit of creeping around these days.'

'Or is it just that you're too preoccupied to notice I'm here? Preoccupied with trying to look like a porn star, that is.'

Lucy struggled to conceal her irritation. 'You know, you're reacting to this as if I'm actually on the game.'

Cora assessed the racy wear. 'I think what you're doing is more dangerous than being on the game.'

'You don't know what I'm doing. So if you can't help out, at least stop interfering.'

Cora sighed. 'What help do you need?'

'That stuff I wore before was bought from an adult website . . .'

'God help us.'

'This time I need something a bit classier . . . but not too classy, if you know what I mean.'

'And what've you got?'

Lucy indicated the tasteless array. 'We all dressed to impress back in our clubbing days, didn't we? Trouble is I was a teenager then. Even if I could get into this stuff, I don't think the party girl image is really going to cut it.'

'You need a touch of old-fashioned glam.'

'Well . . . yeah.'

'But something a woman would wear, rather than a kid?'

Lucy looked round at her. 'Exactly.'

'Wait here,' Cora said resignedly.

She disappeared onto the landing and then into her bedroom, leaving Lucy bemused as she heard the sound of her mum rummaging around in her own wardrobe. When Cora returned, she was equipped with an item of clothing Lucy had never seen before: a black, backless pencil-dress with a knee-length skirt and gathered waist.

'This might be a little tight on you, but that won't hurt,' Cora said. 'Black stiletto court shoes and stockings should finish the outfit off, but it'll be easy picking those up.'

Lucy was amazed. 'Where'd you get this?'

'I wasn't always a dowdy middle-aged woman, you know.'

'No one would ever mistake you for dowdy, Mum . . . but this is going some.'

'Felt like a princess in that frock.'

'I'll bet.' Lucy held it up to check the size. 'That bloody worthless bus driver got more than he deserved, that's for sure.'

Cora said nothing, a brief but distant expression on her face.

Chapter 13

Lucy was surprised when Tammy turned up on time that Monday morning. Even more so to see the girl looking presentable: clear of lippy and garish eyeshadow, hair tied in a sensible bun, and without a whiff of alcohol on her. She was wearing a tracksuit, white trainers and a battered old parka. In contrast, Lucy wore the smart, sexy pencil-dress under her beige raincoat, with, as her mum had suggested, a pair of black stockings and black patent stilettos to set it all off. Her make-up was subtle, her dark hair newly cut and styled in a neat, shoulder-length bob.

'Look at you,' Tammy said, scampering across Cross Street from the Royal Exchange to their agreed rendezvous point at the entrance to the Arndale Centre. 'You scrub up special.'

'You don't look so bad yourself,' Lucy replied.

'You mean minus the slap?' Tammy cackled. 'In her moments of weakness, my mam used to say there was a real pretty girl underneath "all that slimy crap". Probably why she smacked me in the face so often, she being an ugly bitch an' all.'

'Mam still around?' Lucy asked as they walked.

'Yeah, somewhere. Probably never die, that one.'

'She know what you do?'

'Who knows, who's bothered? She wouldn't give a shit. I was taken into care when I was five. Only seen her occasionally since. She rarely has a kind word. Anyway, let's not talk about her. The lady you're going to meet is a tad classier.'

They boarded the Metrolink at Market Street, and rode north-east.

'What's her name?' Lucy asked.

Tammy grinned and nudged her with a bony elbow. 'You're in for a treat, I'll tell you. This is the lady herself . . . Jayne McIvar.'

'Jayne McIvar?' Lucy struggled not to show how much of a shock this was.

'Why not? No point talking to someone who can't actually help you.'

'And just out of interest . . . why should she help me?'

'Well . . . you're a mate of mine, and she owes me.'

'She owes you?'

'Yeah.' Tammy gave another of her trademark mischievous grins. 'I know stuff.'

Lucy glanced sidelong at her. 'What're you talking about?'

'Well . . . I used to work at SugaBabes, didn't I? I know stuff that goes on there . . . stuff they wouldn't want me talking about.'

'Tammy, you're not telling me you're going to try and blackmail these people?'

'It's not blackmail. It's a kind of, well . . . you know, an understanding we have.'

Lucy felt even more nervous. 'You're sure Jayne McIvar will share this understanding?'

'It's all about favours. Look . . . someone leaves the company, and that's a security risk. So they like to keep us ex-employees happy. If we need a bit of help now and then, they're the folk to go to.'

142

'It may be a dumb question, but . . .' There was no one sitting anywhere near them in the compartment, but Lucy lowered her voice anyway. 'Wouldn't it be easier for them if you were getting out of line to just . . . well, rub you out?'

Tammy mused. 'If I got out of line, they probably would. I mean Suzy McIvar! Fuck me . . . she's not head of the firm's security for nothing. She's a right demoness, she is! But Jayne believes in carrot as well as stick. And like I say, she owes me. It's not like I'm asking a lot.'

Lucy nodded, but was far from happy with this glib explanation. Just how much potential danger was Tammy walking them into here?

They disembarked from the tram at Queens Road and strolled half a mile north around the edge of Queens Park.

'If Jayne takes you up there today,' Tammy said, 'to the club I mean . . . just be dead grateful. Brown-nose a bit. That never hurts. Oh, and don't ask too many questions.'

'Even if I get the job, it's not going to start today, is it?' Lucy replied. 'Won't she want to do some kind of diligence on me first?'

'Dili-what?'

'Check me out.'

'Maybe,' Tammy said. 'But remember what I said about asking stuff.'

'I'll have to ask questions about the work conditions and that.'

'Well, yeah . . . just so it shows you're not a total numpty. But whatever you do, don't ask about the Taxi Service.'

At first Lucy thought she'd misheard. 'The what?'

'The SugaBabes Taxi Service,' Tammy said. 'I mean that's not what it's officially called, but it's what I always used to call it.'

'What's the SugaBabes Taxi Service?'

Tammy tut-tutted. 'There you go. Failed your first test. I said don't ask about it.'

'I'm asking *you*.'

'Don't ask *anyone*!' Tammy stressed this in all seriousness. 'Pretend it's not even happening. That's what most staff at the club do. Those who know about it.'

'Tammy, what're you talk . . .?'

'Ignorance is bliss, Hayley.' Tammy tapped the side of her nose. 'Trust me.'

Lucy would have questioned her further on this – she didn't like any kind of unexplained loose ends – but they were now approaching a small coffee shop overlooking the edge of the Manchester General Cemetery, which on a drab, grey day in early November looked even more eerie and desolate than usual.

'Almost home,' Tammy said with a wink, though Lucy wasn't sure whether she was referring to the proximity of her birthplace, Harpurhey, or some kind of spiritual commonality she felt with Greater Manchester's most senior whorehouse madam. Oblivious to the increased worry she was causing her friend, Tammy now glanced at her mobile.

'Eleven, bang on. Cool. Jayne always comes here for her mid-morning tea break.'

Before they entered the coffee shop, Lucy noticed a white Audi R8 parked outside it, with a heavily built man slumped behind the wheel. He'd been poring over what looked like a Russian-language newspaper, but broke off briefly to give them the once-over, and then resumed reading. A bell jangled as Tammy pushed the door open. Only one customer was installed in the cosy interior, a woman, and she was seated at the counter on one of five bright blue, goblet-type stools. She had a pen in hand and a leather-bound ledger spread out in front of her. She glanced casually around. An awful lot had changed since the old custody mugshot was taken, but straightaway Lucy recognised Jayne McIvar.

Though she had aged, she had aged well. She had smooth, copper-coloured skin, firm, full lips and bright green eyes somehow enhanced by her tortoiseshell glasses. Her hair was a lively orange-red Afro, currently backcombed and braided in neat parallel rows. She wore a fluffy white jacket, tight white jeans and white cowboy boots. But that was where the pleasant picture ended. This coolly attractive lady might well owe Tammy, as the girl had so brightly and confidently put it, but by the look on her face now, the feeling wasn't totally mutual.

'And what can I do for you, Tamara?' she asked, clearly not even considering the possibility that this meeting might be accidental.

Lucy felt a fleeting surge of panic. So not only had Tammy got no real plan here, she hadn't even prearranged things; in fact she was winging it.

'You remembered who I am!' Tammy exclaimed, delighted. 'How wicked is that?'

'How could I not?' Jayne McIvar replied. 'The one girl of my acquaintance born with a genuinely lovely name, and yet who still insisted on curtailing it so that it made her sound like a scrubber.'

On the subject of how things sounded, Lucy noted, Jayne McIvar did not speak as if she came from inner Manchester. Her accent was noticeably northern, but at the same time refined, its harsh edges sanded off – as if she actually hailed from somewhere in leafy Cheshire. Elocution lessons, most likely. Always the sign of a villain who intended to go places.

'That was the punters,' Tammy protested cheerfully. 'And wasn't it you who taught me the customer's always right?'

Jayne still didn't smile. 'I said what can I do for you?'

'Nothing.' Rather impertinently, Tammy pulled up the next

stool along and perched on it. 'Just thought I'd pop in to say "hi."'

'With a friend?'

'This is Hayley,' Tammy said.

'Ladies?' asked the young, Italian-looking guy behind the counter.

'Cappuccino for me, please?' Tammy replied.

'Latte,' Lucy said.

He nodded and moved away.

'And you both just happened to be in Smedley?' Jayne asked.

'Not really,' Tammy admitted.

'You surprise me.'

'But I wanted a quick chat.'

Jayne laid her pen down. 'Go on.'

'You remember you said to me a bit ago . . .'

'It must have been *years* ago, Tamara.'

'Yeah . . . sure.' Tammy shrugged as if this was unimportant. 'You said that if I ever wanted out of the game, you could fix me up with a barmaid job. At the club, I mean.'

The madam peered long and hard at her. 'You can't be a barmaid *and* a wino, love. That would be something of a problem.'

'It's not for me.' Tammy nudged Lucy. 'It's for Hayley here.'

Thus far, Jayne had given Lucy no more than a cursory glance. Even on hearing this, she remained focused on her former employee. And now, for the first time, she looked annoyed. 'I'm sorry . . . *who's* Hayley? You don't just walk in here and bring us people we don't know, Tamara! You ought to realise that.'

'We *do* know her,' Tammy insisted.

The counter guy returned with their coffees. Carefully, he pushed them over. Tammy nodded and smiled. Jayne nodded at him too, in her case without a smile. Cooperatively, he departed back into the kitchen.

'We *do* know her,' Tammy said again, quietly. 'She's been working with me down on the East Lancs.'

'Oh . . . great.' Jayne sat back on her stool. 'Another piss-artist. That's all we need. Or is she a crackhead? Sorry, sometimes it's difficult to tell the difference.'

'Hey, Miss McIvar,' Lucy interrupted, tired of being spoken about as if she wasn't there. She unfastened the strap of her raincoat and let it fall open on the pencil-dress. 'Do I look like a druggie or pisshead to you?'

The madam appraised her for the first time, eyeing her top to bottom.

'Sorry,' she said, not sounding sorry at all. 'No offence intended, Hayley . . . if that's your actual name. But I don't know you. So how can I form a judgement?'

'I want a job,' Lucy said. 'That's all I'm asking.'

Jayne sized her up again; a tad more attentively this time.

'She's looking for *indoor* work, Jayne,' Tammy added.

'Is she indeed?'

'Yeah, but I'm not bringing her to you as Talent.'

Jayne glanced at Tammy, puzzled. 'In that case why are we having this conversation?'

'I already told you . . . the barmaid job.'

Jayne looked back at Lucy. 'You want to work for us . . . as a barmaid?'

Lucy shrugged. 'Why not?'

'There must be a dozen pubs and bars in central Manchester that are advertising for staff as we speak. Why not just apply there?'

Lucy shifted her feet awkwardly. 'I've got a criminal record.'

'I know plenty pubs where that wouldn't be a problem.'

'And she's got a maniac boyfriend who's always on the

warpath,' Tammy chipped in. 'She needs somewhere to lie low.'

'Plus, I'm in the life already,' Lucy added. 'You know what I'm saying . . . what if I was serving someone in a regular pub, and it turned out to be an old customer?'

All the way through this faltering explanation, Jayne continued to size Lucy up, eyes lingering on her legs, on her bust.

'If we were to take you on,' Jayne said, interrupting Lucy mid-flow, 'you'd make more money on the Talent Team. I mean, you've already been doing that down on the A580.'

'I've told her that, but she won't listen,' Tammy said.

'Why do you want to change now?' Jayne asked.

Lucy shrugged again, awkwardly. 'It's just not for me.'

'There'd be no scallies where we'd put you. We only entertain quality clients.'

'I don't want it anymore, whatever the clients are like.'

Jayne tapped a long, carefully manicured fingernail against her white front teeth. 'Well . . . I'm not saying you wouldn't look good behind our bar. But there's a problem. No vacancies.'

'Ohhh, Jayne!' Tammy protested. 'There's always . . .'

'But we might be short on the coat-check desk.' Jayne watched Lucy with interest. 'Reckon you could do that?'

'Yeah, sure,' Lucy said.

'Pay isn't up to much. Nine quid an hour tops, and you only get to keep half your tips. But then you won't be giving us much in return . . . will you?'

This seemed like a rhetorical question, so Lucy made no response.

'The hours are six nights a week, seven p.m. until five a.m.'

Lucy nodded bravely as if this was just about acceptable, though in truth it wasn't even as long a shift as she was currently working.

'You told me you had a criminal record,' Jayne said. 'What've you been up to?'

This could be the make-or-break moment, of course. Especially if Lucy was now looking to work as a coat-check girl. Despite that, honesty was always the best policy.

'Thieving,' she said.

'Got caught with her hand in the till,' Tammy explained.

'So it's not just thieving,' Jayne said, 'it's thieving from your employers?'

Lucy inclined her head.

'I don't need to tell you what'll happen if that occurs when you're on *our* payroll.' Jayne's green eyes now bored into Lucy like laser beams. 'I must stress this, Hayley. A lot of the people who work for us have a shady past . . . and in some cases a shady present. It goes with the territory, and we are hugely understanding in that regard. But we'd take a very dim view indeed if that generosity of spirit was not repaid in full.'

'I understand that, Miss McIvar.'

'Let's just say this, love. It wouldn't be *me* you'd be answering to.'

Lucy nodded again; it wasn't difficult looking suitably unnerved.

Jayne closed her ledger and slotted it into a large handbag. 'Not that you'll be stricken with temptation. There's a security camera on the coat-check area. But that'll work in your favour too. Someone claims his wallet's suddenly lighter than it should be . . . we can soon find out whether you've been up to your old tricks again or he's just a lying bastard. When can you start?'

'Tomorrow night?' Lucy suggested.

'Okay. Do you know where we are?'

'No.' This wasn't untrue. Lucy had familiarised herself with the area where SugaBabes was located but had learned that, as an establishment with no legal status, it was concealed among ordinary, nondescript buildings. It wouldn't be easy pinpointing it on a map.

'That's okay,' Jayne said. 'I'll meet you right here. Three o'clock sharp.'

'What do you want me to wear, Miss McIvar?'

Jayne stood up, ready to leave. 'You'll be issued with a uniform when you get to the club.'

'Do *I* get anything?' Tammy asked.

Jayne strode to the door, but glanced round. 'You?'

'You always used to say that if I brought something good to the Talent Team there might be a reward in it for me.'

'That was for the Talent Team, Tamara?'

'You might persuade Hayley yet. She didn't half turn over the customers on the East Lancs. Her very first trick was a van-load of navvies, and they drove off hooting.'

Jayne eyed Lucy again, but only briefly. 'Yeah, you'll get something, Tamara.' She raised her voice. 'Marco!'

The young Italian guy reappeared.

'Give 'em both another coffee.' Jayne indicated Tammy. 'Make sure this one gets a couple of extra sugar lumps.'

Chapter 14

Where are you?

The text was signed: *Priya.*

Lucy marvelled. Was she finally on first-name terms with the DSU? But then she remembered that she'd been under-cover today, and just in case, if for any reason at all her mobile phone had finished up in the wrong hands, it wouldn't have looked good if it was found to be carrying messages bearing police insignia.

She keyed in a quick reply:

Metrolink. Heading back to city centre.

Available?

Yes.

Pick you up at Victoria end of Deansgate. 15 mins.

Lucy made it to the rendezvous point on time without difficulty, though it was now five o'clock in the afternoon and central Manchester was embroiled in its daily rush-hour chaos. The pavements thronged with fast-moving pedestrians; the roads were log-jammed with cars, each one of which, thanks to the rapidly falling temperature, belched thick swirls of exhaust into the headlight glare from the vehicle behind. It was dark already of course, and the occasional staccato flashes in the sky, usually followed by distant, booming detonations, reminded her that November 5th was only three days away.

Once she was there, Priya Nehwal pulled up alongside her in a metallic-beige Lexus RX.

Lucy clambered into the front passenger seat, halting only as Nehwal threw an old parka coat into the back. They quickly pulled away from the kerb.

The Lexus was luxuriously warm inside, though as usual, DSU Nehwal was well wrapped in jeans and a tatty, baggy sweatshirt that looked way too large for her.

'At least you're in one piece,' she remarked, not glancing at Lucy as she drove.

'Certainly am, ma'am,' Lucy replied. 'Relatively painless, to be honest.'

'How did it go?'

'Pretty well. I start tomorrow . . . on the coat-check desk.'

Now Nehwal did look round, arching a single eyebrow.

'I'd imagine Jayne McIvar's testing my credentials first,' Lucy added. 'If she finds anything she doesn't like tonight . . . well, I suppose tomorrow'll be a *very* interesting day.'

Nehwal drove on. 'What do you make of her? McIvar?'

'She's no pushover, that's for sure.'

'You got that right . . .' Fleetingly, Nehwal almost sounded impressed. 'She's her own woman, and always has been. Typical of a certain type of criminal, though. I mean she's got the intellect and the drive to turn her hand to anything she wants and make a success of it, but somehow or other she's stuck in this life.'

'I don't get the impression she tolerates fools lightly,' Lucy said.

'No. But to be fair, she's not alone in that.'

There was a brief heavy silence as they headed out of the

centre, following Great Ducie Street until it became Bury New Road, and then driving north through Higher Broughton.

'Thanks for picking me up, by the way,' Lucy said.

Nehwal shrugged. 'No big deal. I happened to be in town. Listen . . .' Her tone changed slightly; softening, though not by a great deal. 'It's been intimated to me by a certain party that I was perhaps a little abrupt with you when you first brought this new information to us. A little on the dubious side, perhaps.'

Her tone might have softened, but her words implied that she herself wasn't entirely convinced.

'And would that certain party be DI Slater?' Lucy wondered.

Nehwal ignored the question. 'I don't want you to think it's anything personal, PC Clayburn. I value any colleague who generates good work. So far, we don't know whether this lead will pan out, but it's interesting and it feels like progress in some shape or form. It was also . . . well, it was also intimated to me that I should be more grateful than I have been for your volunteering to go into the lions' den, so to speak, to see this thing through.'

Lucy was amused, but didn't let it show.

Priya Nehwal had earned her reputation by doing the hard yards; she was certainly the toughest, most hard-bitten police-woman Lucy had ever met. All this soft-soaping – if that was what it was supposed to be – must have been quite a wrench for her.

'I imagine *you've* done plenty of covert enquiries during your own service, ma'am.'

'I have indeed,' Nehwal admitted. 'And it's rarely a cake-walk. I'm not going to go over it all again about how risky this could potentially be for you, PC Clayburn, because that stuff's getting boring now, and it's the last thing you need to hear the night before it all kicks off . . . but don't think I'm dismissive of this work you're doing for us just because I don't slap you on the back now and then.'

'Not a problem, ma'am.'

'Good. So . . . you ready to go home now? I can drop you off.'

Lucy was additionally amused. It sounded as if her boss had actually stage-managed this meeting just to apologise. Either that or to give her a pep talk, though there hadn't been much of that so far. Priya Nehwal might be the ace thief-taker, but she was a bit of a numbskull when it came to close-in man management.

'I should probably go back to the nick,' Lucy said. 'I've barely put in a full shift today.'

'You will tomorrow,' Nehwal replied. 'It's going to be quite a learning curve for you. I'll take you home, and sign you off myself later.'

They were now in Prestwich, and the quickest route from here to Saltbridge lay along the M62 motorway and then down the M60, both of which were still chocka with early-evening traffic. It was almost six o'clock when they finally reached the Crowley West turn-off.

'What about Tammy Nethercot?' Nehwal wondered as they headed into Saltbridge through its outlying housing estates. The traffic here was much thinner. 'Is she a total crackpot, or can we trust her to keep her mouth shut from this point?'

'Well, like I say, she doesn't really know anything. I'm just a mate she did a favour for.'

Nehwal pondered that. 'You know, if this covert op goes west . . . our mate Tammy could end up in a spot of bother.'

'I know that, ma'am.' Lucy was discomforted by the thought of this. 'Whatever happens at SugaBabes, I'm going to have to do my best to emerge at the other side of it with my cover intact. Though I don't suppose there's any guarantee that'll happen.'

'There are no guarantees in this line of work.'

'I took Tammy to a bar afterwards and bought her a drink to thank her. Well, several drinks in her case.'

Nehwal glanced at her again, as if genuinely bemused by such generosity. 'You sure she believes you're a tom? There's no doubt you're a good actor. You've made it this far. But . . .' She appraised Lucy's hair, her flawless make-up, her shapely legs in dark nylon. 'You don't look the part today.'

Lucy shrugged. 'Gone out on a limb today to look good, ma'am. She commented on it, but positively. Overall, I think I'm fulfilling some kind of wish she's got. She's only young, but she's been through the mill, I can tell that. Sounds like her mum was a right old cow, and she never talks about any siblings. Maybe I'm just the big sister she wishes she's always had.'

'Is she a bit dim then?'

It sounded like an unkind question, but Lucy knew it wasn't intended that way. Priya Nehwal was a straight-to-the-point kind of copper, and it was perfectly reasonable for her to enquire into the dependability of a potentially damaged source.

'I think so, yes. But I trust her on *this* . . .'

At which point a figure darted out in front of the car, seemingly from nowhere.

Nehwal shouted a warning as she threw the wheel right, veering the Lexus sharply and dangerously into the opposite carriageway, where it slid to the far kerb, slamming it with its tyres and coming abruptly to a halt. They hadn't struck the figure, but it tottered and fell as they screeched past, falling onto its face in the middle of the tarmac.

Lucy and Nehwal glanced at each other, stunned – and then clambered hurriedly out.

As they did, the figure struggled back to its feet.

It was a bloke, youngish and well built.

'You alright, mate?' Lucy called, rounding the Lexus, but as she encroached on him she saw that he was younger than she'd first thought, no more than nineteen. He was wearing standard outdoor clothing for the time of year: dark canvas trousers, a dark zip-up anorak over a hoodie-top, and black woollen gloves, all set off by an incongruous pair of bright-orange trainers. His hair was a mop of sweaty rat-tails, his face wet, pale and slug-like, though the eyes in the centre of it bulged like duck eggs.

He said nothing, merely backed away towards the opposite pavement.

'We're police officers, sir,' Nehwal called, showing her warrant card. 'You hurt?'

He shook his head; a slight, tight movement.

'What's happened?' Lucy asked him.

He mouthed something inaudible, and then pointed past them, his finger quivering.

They turned to look. Nothing especially stood out. This was Tubbs Road, one of Saltbridge's lesser-used outer thoroughfares. Along this stretch of it there was a row of dingy shops: bicycle repairs, a tanning salon, a pawnbroker's, second-hand odds and sods, all currently closed; and a disused industrial unit, a towering façade of grotty red brick and heavy corrugated iron, scraps of wastepaper dangling from the rusted grille over its front door. No one was there, but between the shops and the factory, a narrow cobbled street led off into icy blackness, and it was towards this that the young bloke had pointed.

Lucy turned back to face him. 'What's going on, mate. . .?'

But he was running again. He reached a corner some thirty yards off, and without a backwards glance, hared around it and was gone.

156

'Incidents like this happen in Crowley all the time?' Nehwal wondered, perplexed.

'Perhaps a bit more regularly than they did before Jill the Ripper, ma'am.' Lucy's unease grew as she assessed the entrance to the narrow street. 'That's Dedman Lane. It leads down to Dedman Delph . . . which is well known round here as a dogging spot.'

'Dogging? This early in the evening?'

'It's already dark, ma'am. What else do they need?'

Nehwal ruminated on this as she trudged back to the Lexus, moving ever more quickly until they were both of them rushing.

'Can we get a car down there?' Nehwal asked, switching the engine on.

'Yes, ma'am. They don't just go there on foot, they park up.'

'This can't be,' the DSU muttered, as she swung the heavy vehicle into the narrow street. 'It just cannot . . . not two miles from the fucking Incident Room!'

The narrow lane dipped quickly downhill, its uneven cobbles providing a bumpy ride, their headlights initially picking out nothing along either verge except fallen leaves and scattered rubbish.

Dedman Delph wasn't a real valley, but man-made. Like everything else on the outskirts of Manchester, it had served industrial purposes sometime in the past. Lucy didn't have a clue what, though the empty, boarded-up ruin at the valley's far end had once been a pump-house of some sort. Most of the Delph's sides, which were steep and crumbly, were clad with weeds and scraggy thorn bushes, while its floor was made from impacted red clay and in some sections flat concrete. Much of that had rotted and split, but it was still excellent for parking.

And for dogging of course. Primarily because at night, as now, it lay in pitch darkness.

They wallowed down onto level ground again, leaving the cobblestones behind, the Lexus tyres sliding on a broken, gluey surface. Nehwal hit 'full-beam', the twin lights spearing out through a black void, finding nothing but rolling, arid emptiness.

'Not much activity tonight,' she commented, driving slowly forward.

'It's not a particularly welcoming place even when there isn't a killer on the prowl,' Lucy responded. 'Wait, ma'am . . . *there!*'

At the far end of the valley floor, maybe a hundred yards away, quite close to where the pump-house stood, they spotted what looked like the interior light of a stationary vehicle. Nehwal slowed them to a halt.

'What's the normal form down here?' she asked.

Lucy shrugged. 'It varies, but generally the doggers wait at the south end of the valley . . . that's behind us, where there's a barbed wire fence. The couples tend to park up at the north end, which is where that one is . . . and turn their internal lights on when they're ready for some action. That's the signal for the doggers to come over.'

'That organised, is it?' Nehwal sounded fascinated. 'Who knew?'

'They like to play it reasonably safe. If a car's doors and windows remain closed, it supposedly means the couples are only interested in putting on a show. But if the windows are open, it's an invitation for the blokes outside to reach in with various of their body-parts. If the doors are open too, it's anything goes.'

Nehwal continued to watch the parked vehicle. It remained motionless, and though it was difficult to be sure from this distance, both their eyes were now adjusting sufficiently to the darkness to distinguish what looked like a single figure in its front passenger seat.

'You seem to know an awful lot about it, PC Clayburn . . .?'

'I've policed this town for the last . . .'

'Ten years, yes.' Nehwal put the Lexus in gear and eased it forward again. Lucy powered her window down. Icy air wafted in, but there was nothing to hear aside from the smoothly purring engine and occasional crackle of distant fireworks.

They stopped again some ten yards short of the motionless vehicle. It was a car, a cream-coloured Ford Fiesta, and it had been parked about five yards to the left of the derelict pump-house, which in the glow of Nehwal's headlights was a scabrous, skullish ruin, the rotted boards having fallen away from its front entrance and the two windows above it.

As they'd already seen, a person occupied the Fiesta's front passenger seat, though the windscreen was so smeary that it was difficult establishing whether it was male or female, or whether it had moved at all since they had first started their approach. Lucy didn't think it had. Nor did she expect that the preponderance of redness she could see all over it could have any kind of benign explanation.

'This isn't good,' she said quietly.

'Agreed.' Nehwal turned her engine off. 'Even so, you have to stay in here.'

Lucy glanced round at her. 'Ma'am?'

'Use your loaf, PC Clayburn. If this is our girl and she's still in the area, we don't want her seeing you the night before you go undercover in a brothel where she might work, do we?'

'If this is our girl you're going to need all the help you can get. She's butchered six men.'

Nehwal grabbed a torch from her glovebox and opened the driver's door. 'I'll call you if I need you.'

Lucy offered her the radio from the dash. 'Take this at least.'

'I checked that out at five this morning. Battery's been dead for the last hour and a half.'

'In that case . . .' Lucy reached behind her. 'Sorry for the disobedience . . .'

Nehwal said nothing but waited outside the Lexus, while Lucy stripped off her raincoat and then wrestled her way into the much heavier parka. Once it was on, she zipped it and then tugged up its stovepipe hood, so that her head and face were almost completely covered.

She jumped out and they approached the Fiesta side-by-side, though Lucy's stilettos were hardly the ideal footwear on the softish clay surface, which broke and shifted under their pinpoint heels. They halted by the vehicle's front-offside corner. In the weak, brownish glow of the interior light, the figure in the front passenger seat was covered by a sheet.

That sheet was dingy and blotched with crimson.

Nehwal dug a pair of disposable latex gloves from her back pocket, and pulled them on. Then she moved forward to the open passenger window, and reached through, catching the edge of the sheet between two fingertips and trying to pull it. Initially, the sheet resisted but then, slowly, it began to slide free, rancid fold after rancid fold passing down over the inert shape beneath, until it dropped into the footwell.

Involuntarily, despite their near half-century of combined experience, the two policewomen grunted with shock.

It was an elderly man – quite elderly in fact, maybe somewhere in his seventies – though actual identification would not be easy. His face hadn't exactly been obliterated, but it was so puffed and bruised and cut, and so much blood had streaked down over it from his dented cranium, that it would have been difficult even for a relative to recognise him. Whoever he was, his trousers had been pushed down to his ankles and his grimy shirt torn open into two flaps; the women didn't need to look too hard at the gory mess exposed between his thighs to guess at the cause of death.

'God almighty,' Lucy breathed.

'There's a spool of crime-scene tape in the boot of my car,' Nehwal said dispassionately, taking her phone from the frontal pouch of her sweat-shirt. 'We want a perimeter ASAP.'

Lucy made to move but then stopped. 'Ma'am . . . what about that idiot we saw running?'

'He's well gone by now, but we need to trace him.' Nehwal tapped in a number.

'A male suspect after all, ma'am?'

'Unlikely. Unless he had his own clever reasons for pointing us in the right direction.'

'A dogger then? Looking for some fun.'

'Probably. Doesn't know how lucky he is he didn't get it, does he? But he's a witness . . . so we need him. Blast it . . . can't get a signal.'

'Lowest part of town. Reception's always poor down here. Ma'am . . . this body looks very fresh.' Though it broke all the rules, Lucy couldn't resist placing a knuckle against the corpse's neck. The banging of her heart steadily increased. 'He's still warm.'

Before Nehwal could respond, there was a clatter of wood-work from inside the pump-house. They swung around together, gazing at the gloomy structure.

Instinctively, Nehwal pocketed the phone so that both her hands were free.

They waited, their smoky breath furling around them.

Aside from a renewed popping and fizzing of distant fireworks, there was silence. Nehwal switched her torch on, its cone of light embossing the mossy, red-brick exterior of the old industrial outbuilding, yet intensifying the blackness behind its apertures. Lucy couldn't help glancing back at the mutilated form slumped in the car. An OAP yes, but the seventh in line, and the others hadn't been even close to that age. One of them had weighed twenty-five stone, for God's sake! Two of them got chopped together at the same time!

Just how physically powerful was this killer? What kind of chance would they realistically stand in a full-on confrontation, even the pair of them together?

'Go round the back,' Nehwal said quietly. 'Cover the rear exit.' Lucy nodded and made to move, only for Nehwal to grip her wrist. 'Go armed.'

'Ma'am, I've been plain clothes all day, I've got no . . .'

'Find something.'

Lucy was initially bewildered by this, but then spotted the way Nehwal was wielding the torch – now like a baton rather than a flashlight. She leaned down and picked up a broken half-brick, before proceeding warily around the exterior, stepping with difficulty through clumps of desiccated weeds and thorns. At the rear, she halted in front of a single narrow doorway, the door itself broken off and lying to one side.

Various stagnant odours leaked through the gap: oil, mildew, rotted rags.

She listened again. Something creaked inside, very faintly – but that could have been Nehwal progressing in from the front.

Unable to believe she was doing this while wearing a skirt, heels and a heavy old coat that wasn't hers, and with a jagged lump of brick in her hand, Lucy edged forward into the darkness – and almost immediately came to another bare brick wall.

From here, she could go either left or right. Theoretically she should have held this point, to ensure no one slipped past. But there was no conceivable way she could allow her boss, who was no more than five-five and in her early fifties, to enter the building alone.

Heart thumping, Lucy went left, turning a corner into open space. Nothing stirred in the inky blackness in front of her. Instinctively, she reached for the phone in her pocket, to switch its light on, only to remember that it was in the pocket of the other coat. Not that she was completely blinded; after so long at the bottom of Dedman Delph, her eyes were readjusting quickly. She spied a row of broken windows further to her left, all covered in wire netting. It gave sufficient illumination to show a floor strewn with boxes and piles of old newspapers, and what looked like masses of wood and timber piled against the walls.

Still there was no movement, neither from Nehwal nor anyone hiding out in here. Even so, Lucy only shuffled forward with caution. 'Ma'am?'

There was no reply. Until a fierce red light seared through the windows, a loud series of *rat-a-tat* bangs accompanying it.

More fireworks . . . but even so Lucy froze.

In that fleeting instant, she'd seen a figure standing in a corner.

Indistinct but tall – taller than she was – and wearing dark clothing, including some kind of hat pulled partly down over its face. It stood very still between an old wardrobe and an upright roll of carpet.

Lucy pivoted slowly towards it. As the firework flashes diminished again, only its outline remained visible – its outline and its face, which, though it was partially concealed, glinted palely, and, she now saw, was garish in the extreme; grotesquely made-up with bright slashes of what in proper lighting would no doubt be lurid colour.

An icy barb went through her as she realised that the figure was wearing a mask.

It could even be a clown mask.

And yet still it didn't move. Its build was difficult to

distinguish, but there was something slightly "off" about it, she now thought: it seemed to sag a little.

Injured maybe? Tired? Or playacting?

Lucy hadn't glimpsed any kind of weapon, neither a blunt instrument nor a blade, but the hunk of brick in her hand suddenly felt ungainly and inadequate.

She faced the figure full on. There was about six yards between them. At any second, she expected it to lurch forward in a blur of speed, maybe silently, maybe screaming.

She lofted the brick as though to throw it.

'Listen . . .' She spoke quietly, calmly. 'I am a police officer, and I am armed . . . and you are going to have to show me both your hands.'

The figure made no move to comply.

'I will tell you one more time . . .'

'Relax,' a voice interrupted.

Lucy jumped as the room filled with brilliant white torchlight.

Nehwal stepped in through a connecting door, which in the dimness Lucy hadn't previously noticed. The DSU's beam focused itself on the shape in the corner.

It wasn't a living person at all, but a mannequin, an effigy suspended between two corroded bolts in the wall by loops of string tied under its armpits, which explained the odd posture. It was made from an old dark suit and a tatty brown sweater. Its head was a crumpled football, with a plastic mask attached to the front, the latter not depicting the face of a clown but the face of a grinning male with a sharp moustache and pointed beard. The broad-brimmed Guy Fawkes hat looked like a fancy dress shop reject.

Nehwal glanced around. 'Lots more firewood in the room next door. Plus several cans of petrol. Someone was planning a big party for Thursday.'

Lucy walked over to the figure anyway, just to be sure. Up

close, it smelled like a pile of unwashed laundry. When she pressed the ragged jersey, it yielded, newspaper crackling underneath. She turned back. 'Ma'am . . . we both heard something.'

Nehwal pointed upward. When Lucy looked, she saw a mass of crisscrossing pipework dangling with cobwebs and crammed with birds' nests. Disturbed by the torchlight, pigeons fluttered back and forth among it.

'There're more of them next door,' Nehwal said. 'Roosting in the firewood, which is all loose. A few bits shifted even while I was poking around.'

Lucy glanced again at the Guy. It sagged on the two bolts, its head cocked to one side as it regarded her with the empty holes of its eyes.

'Ma'am, if you tell anyone about this, well . . . let's just say I'll never live it down . . .'

'PC Clayburn, we've just walked together into what we thought was a murderer's den.' Nehwal scanned the rest of the room. 'We've got a bloke outside who looks more like a pile of dog-meat than a human being. Trust me, I'm not in the mood to be telling funny stories.'

They searched the rest of the place together, but it wasn't large and there was nobody else concealed in there. Eventually, they went outside, where a faint scent of cordite was noticeable, along with traces of smoke settling in the valley from high overhead.

'Going to have to call this in one way or the other.' Nehwal fiddled irritably with her phone. 'And the only way to do that is by finding higher ground. In the meantime . . . I need that perimeter.'

Lucy followed her to the Lexus, though they steered clear of the Fiesta to avoid compromising any telltale footprints or tyre-tracks. Nehwal opened her boot, and handed Lucy a roll of incident tape and several plastic pegs, along with the torch.

'You going to be all right?' she asked. Fleetingly, she looked to be having second thoughts about leaving Lucy here alone. 'I'll be ten minutes max.'

'I'll be fine,' Lucy replied, though in truth she didn't know which to be more unnerved by: the prospect of waiting down here in the blackness of Dedman Delph for ten minutes (or, more likely, half an hour), with a mangled corpse not five or six yards away, or the thought of that eerie, grinning figure inside the pump-house.

Nehwal nodded, and opened the driver's door. 'Whoever our girl is, I'd imagine she's far from here by now.'

Lucy shrugged. 'If she isn't, ma'am . . . well, I can always arrest her.'

Chapter 15

Lucy arrived at Robber's Row late-morning to find that, despite a foul autumn drizzle, the station was under siege. The main road was all but barricaded by press vehicles, their drivers arguing with traffic wardens and uniformed bobbies. Cables snaked everywhere, cameras hovered overhead on cranes, while higher still, a news chopper lofted through the air. Half a dozen live broadcasts were occurring right at this moment, delivered from the station's doorstep.

Word of the latest atrocity had spread like wildfire. Lucy had only got home around midnight, having spent at least three hours getting her statement right, and by then it had already broken across the news networks.

Only because she was on her Ducati was she able to thread her way through this chaos to the personnel car park. It was bedlam indoors as well. Phones trilled, while staff, both police and civilian, dashed along corridors, carting essential paperwork from one office to the next. There seemed to be extra bodies everywhere, more TSGs having been called in to assist with fingertip searches, door-to-door enquiries and so forth.

From what Lucy could gather from the conversations she

earwigged as she ascended the stairways, Jim Cavill and Priya Nehwal had already given two interviews that day, but the Assistant Chief Constable and the Crime Commissioner were now here to hold a conference themselves, so the press room on the ground floor was the main hub of activity. Conversely though, the MIR was largely deserted, the bulk of the team, Cavill and Nehwal included, back at Dedman Delph, assessing the new crime scene. One or two stalwart individuals remained to field communications, and that alone was keeping them busy. They didn't look twice at Lucy, even though she'd been one of the two who'd discovered the new body; not even after she'd come back downstairs having fixed her hair and make-up in the locker-room, and changed from her motorbike leathers into a denim mini-skirt, high heeled shoes, and a sensible but attractive short-sleeved blouse in order to make the correct impression on her debut night at Sugababes.

When the Ripper Chicks had first started appearing in Robber's Row dressed as tarts, there'd been the usual good-natured ribbing, wolf-whistling and ribald cheering. Lucy wasn't exactly tarted up today, but she'd still dressed to eye-catch. However, it made no difference here. It wasn't that the last vestige of good humour had drained out of the taskforce, it was just that those here didn't even have time to notice her – apart from Slater, who showed up a minute later.

'Hell of a bloody morning, this,' he said, yanking at his tie-knot, which was clearly irritating him because he hadn't yet shaved. He spotted her outfit. 'You ready then?'

She nodded.

'Okay . . . upstairs first. Let's have a quick chat.'

Lucy followed him up.

'That dickhead who fled the scene last night turned himself in first thing,' he said as they climbed the stairs. 'Name's

Gordon Worthing. Total plank, but he's out of the frame. He was working overseas when two of the other murders were committed. Reckons he goes dogging down Dedman Delph every chance he gets. Says he never thought there'd be any danger . . . thought Jill the Ripper only whacks blokes who pay for it. Like psycho killers probably make that kind of distinction all the time. Worthing's also given us a name for the old geezer. Mack Reynoldson. He owned the Fiesta. Real member of the dirty raincoat brigade. He's been going down Dedman Delph longer than Worthing.'

'What about the Bonfire Night stuff?' Lucy wondered.

'No sus circs there either.' Slater walked into the Ripper Chicks' office, Lucy following. 'Belongs to the local Scout and Brownie troop, St Bede's. They were only going to build their bommy on Thursday morning in case it rained before then.' He glanced at the droplets streaming down the outside of the window and the turgid grey skies beyond. 'Somewhat prophetic. But it seems they didn't have the first clue about the normal nocturnal activities down there . . . not that I suspect there'll be any more after this. Anyway, fuck all that. Whatever needs doing's being done. We've got other fish to fry today.'

Slater had looked flustered as soon as he'd entered the building, which was hardly surprising. With each new death, the pressure on the team increased tenfold, and it didn't ease one iota as they ran through the plan for that afternoon. There wasn't much that Slater could do other than sit there and listen while Lucy outlined the way she expected it to go and her proposed solutions if problems arose, but at no stage did he look relaxed about it. Even though an undercover unit would park up as close to the SugaBabes Club as feasibly possible, its response capability was going to be limited, especially as Lucy would most likely have her phone taken off her while she was working there. There was no point pretending otherwise; from the moment she left the station today she was going to be alone.

Slater's brow furrowed as the full import of this dawned on him. It was almost as if, in the hectic aftermath of the latest slaying, he hadn't had a chance to seriously contemplate today's operation.

'I need some air,' he said when they'd wrapped up.

He left the office and walked down the passage to a fire-door at the far end, which the smokers in the team usually kept wedged open so that they could nip out for a drag on the top deck of the fire-escape. Thanks to the cold and the wet, there was no one else outside at present, so Slater and Lucy stood there alone.

'I have to tell you, Lucy . . .' He gazed distantly. 'This is one of the most dangerous undercover ops that any officer in a team of mine has ever embarked on. You're going to encounter an awesome degree of villainy.'

'I'm just checking coats, sir . . . I'll be fine.'

'You see someone who might recognise you in that place, anyone at all . . . and you leave at the first opportunity, okay?'

'Sure.'

'I know you're not a central Manchester native, Lucy. I know you've mainly worked in Crowley, but people travel. There are some scumbags who range all across this city. It's not impossible that someone may spot you.'

'I'll only be there long enough to get to know the girls, sir. Just like on the East Lancs. Get them talking, see if I can identify this Lotta. By all accounts, I won't be able to miss her.'

'Don't ask too many probing questions,' he advised.

'I won't ask any questions. I'll let the conversation take me where it does.'

'Seriously, Lucy . . . the Crew are no joke. We've gone

170

extra deep into the backgrounds of the Ripper victims so far, and none of them had any kind of connection with organised crime, not even those two goons fly-tipping. So our best guess is the Crew are *not* behind these murders – that was always unlikely anyway, to be honest. Like Priya said, these deaths aren't their style. But SugaBabes is very much on their radar. They don't just take their cut, two or three of their top men go there for recreation. Now these are bad guys by any standards. If they sense there's a threat to them . . . any at all, they'll rub you out without a qualm.'

'I understand that.'

He looked round at her. 'What time are you meeting Jayne McIvar?'

'Three this afternoon.'

He glanced at his watch. 'Suppose you'd better get going.'

They walked down through the nick. Each floor was a scene of mayhem. Again, despite Lucy's glammed-up look, she didn't draw so much as a furtive glance.

'Jayne McIvar's an unknown quantity to a certain extent,' Slater said. 'She's the brains behind the firm. She's never been in half as much trouble as her sister. But she's still a brothel-keeper, so she's a lowlife despite her flash clothes and urbane attitude. But the point is, she's clever. Much more than Suzy. Suzy's the obvious one to be wary of, but watch Jayne too. I've a feeling she can be a whole lot of trouble.'

Lucy nodded. There was nothing more to be said as they left the building by the personnel door. They exchanged a terse 'speak later', and she walked away around the front of the nick, sidling unnoticed through the press pack and strolling to the nearest bus stop.

By early afternoon she was on board a tram, again bound for Queens Road. The weather had cleared a little, bright but cool sunlight filtering through breaking cloud. Commuters climbed on and off. Those with newspapers were dwelling on Jill the Ripper, perhaps unavoidably as it covered page after page. A succession of ghoulish headlines jumped out.

Madwoman still on prowl

Man-killer going for the record

Jill doesn't just rip; she hacks, slashes, cuts

As before, Lucy walked north from Queens Road, circling around Queens Park to the coffee shop opposite the Victorian-era graveyard, arriving just around three o'clock. The Audi R8 was parked there again, but this time there was no bruiser inside it. Instead, Jayne McIvar sat behind the wheel. She flashed her headlights as Lucy approached, and leaned across to open the front passenger door.

'You're punctual,' she said, as Lucy climbed in. 'That's good.'

She put the car in gear and hit the gas, heading north towards Crumpsall, which if Lucy's recollection was correct, was not the direction in which SugaBabes lay.

'So who are you, Hayley?' Jayne asked. 'What's your background?'

Aware that she was being tested, Lucy again gave the prepared spiel, making sure she changed nothing from last time and trying not to be distracted by the unfamiliar territory they'd now entered. Rows of shops she didn't recognise interchanged with residential districts she'd never visited before. She wasn't overly familiar with north-central Manchester anyway, but she could read signposts, and each new one they passed indicated that they were still heading into Crumpsall, the opposite direction from Cheetham Hill.

She could only assume, or rather hope, that Jayne was taking them to the club by a deliberately circuitous route.

But her muscles were already tensing. She wondered if it could ever be as easy to jump out of a speeding car as it was in the movies.

'All very interesting,' Jayne said, sounding archly sceptical. 'Seems you were telling the truth about Bradby & Sons at least. I gave them a call. You *did* leave them rather abruptly. They weren't terribly forthcoming about why, and I wouldn't expect them to be. But I got the impression it was under a bit of a cloud. Last August, wasn't it?'

Another test.

'June actually,' Lucy said, trying to memorise the route as they started making unexpected turns through ever more drab and depressed-looking neighbourhoods.

'That's right,' Jayne said. 'June. Funny thing though, eh? One minute you're a secretary in a central Manchester firm, presumably pretty well paid. The next you're a coat-check girl.'

'We take what we can get, Miss McIvar.'

'Very philosophical. If that was the height of your ambition, Hayley, I'd be surprised. But I don't think it is . . . is it?' Jayne made another sharp turn; the streets with shops and housing fell behind as they progressed into a completely run-down district of empty lots and boarded flats.

Lucy could feel her blood rushing. Her breathing slowly tightened. On all sides of them now lay acres of sordid dereliction; broken windows, the hulks of abandoned cars. There was nobody around. She made an almighty effort to at least look calm.

'It's not my, erm . . . my long-term plan,' she agreed.

'Give it a rest, Hayley. You're not a coat-check girl.' Jayne swung them sharp left again, this time onto a narrow, litter-strewn backstreet, the terraced housing on either side of which stood in rows of gutted shells. They drove along it at what felt like reckless speed. 'I know what you're *really* coming to us for.'

Lucy kept her mouth firmly shut.

'You're coming to us to lie on your back and make some real money.'

'Miss McIvar . . . I told you I don't want to do that anymore.'

'Pull the other one, love. No one applies to work in a brothel as a barmaid or a coat-check girl.'

'I've already said, I need to keep my head down . . .'

'So you've got a badass ex-boyfriend. Big deal. Haven't we all.' Jayne spoke with an air of world-weary street smarts. 'Jesus, Hayley, I can tell by the way you look, by the way you dress, by the way you carry yourself . . . you're not dumb. So I surely don't need to lay it on the line. You come to work inside an illegal operation, it's got to be worth your while. And yet you're happy to take a pittance?'

'It's my comfort-zone, Miss McIvar. It's the life I'm already inside, and it seemed like an obvious step. And Tammy couldn't speak highly enough of the way you treat your staff.'

Jayne snorted. 'Was she sober at the time?'

'Erm, well . . .'

'And you think I should give you a job on the basis of a drunken slut's recommendation?'

'I thought you *had* done.'

Jayne focused on the road. 'I'll be honest, Hayley . . . I've taken you on because I've got ambitions to put you on the Talent Team.'

Lucy stiffened, feigning discomfort, though in truth feeling slightly happier than one minute ago, when she'd thought they might have worked out who she really was.

'Look, Miss McIvar, if that's the plan, you'd better stop the car now . . .'

'Relax . . . no one's going to force you.' They sped through a pair of rusty iron gates hanging from rotted hinges. 'But think about it. Our Talent Team's the best-earning in the north of England. We've got the hottest girls and the richest clients. The tips alone are phenomenal. You're seriously saying you don't want to be part of that? You can't have a total aversion to it, love . . . you used to sell yourself on the street.'

'That experience wasn't good.'

'Well, put it behind you. This is a different ball game. But like I said, no one's going to make you do anything you don't want to. You can issue cloakroom tickets for us all night, if you'd prefer. But I don't think you'll prefer it for long. A bod like yours needs putting to some real work.' She applied the handbrake and they screeched to a halt.

They were on a cobbled cul-de-sac with a large building on their immediate left, a monstrous, shapeless heap of sooty red-brick. Its roof was steeply sloped and covered in heavy, moss-eaten slate, its piping and ironwork exclusively old and corroded. If it had ever possessed any windows, all were now solidly bricked over. It was impossible to tell what its original use might have been: something utilitarian, a factory or workshop perhaps, though for all Lucy knew it might even have been a legitimate nightclub or a bar. Even the non-industrial buildings in Manchester's inner suburbs tended to have an industrial air. Glancing further afield, Lucy saw that it was only one of several such structures ranged in a horseshoe around the end of the cul-de-sac, warrens of dingy yards and alleys connecting them.

She was then distracted by something touching her bare thigh.

She glanced down. Jayne McIvar's coffee-brown hand, complete with gold-polished nails, a chunky gold bracelet and at least two diamond rings, had settled there. It squeezed the exposed flesh with a warm, firm grip.

'Just for the record . . . you ever done it with a woman?' Jayne asked, now eyeing Lucy with a different kind of interest.

'No, I haven't.'

'It's not such a big deal these days. You should give it a try.'

'Maybe I will, if . . .'

'If it helps your position.' Jayne smiled. 'That's the way it usually goes. But like I say, it'll be your choice.' She moved her hand away. 'I'm sure you'll make the right one when the time comes. For now –' she opened her driver's door '– let's get you suited and booted.'

The sleaziness of the brothel-keeper's approach wasn't exactly matched by the brothel itself, where everything appeared to be brisk and business-like.

The first thing that happened on their climbing from the Audi was that a youngish blond guy, very tanned and muscular, wearing tight jeans and a black sleeveless T-shirt, which hugged his gym-toned torso like a second skin, came outside. He took Jayne McIvar's keys from her and, without a word, drove the car away. Lucy was then led along a narrow entry with a vaulted, glass-covered roof, the panes of which were cracked and thick with greenish grime. The door at the end was a faceless slab of riveted steel, with a retractable slat in the middle, but at present it stood open. Another guy waited there for them. Lucy recognised him from the Audi on her first visit to the coffee shop. He was about fifty years old, and though not especially tall, of bear-like breadth. He at least seemed to be dressed for duty in a shirt, tie and well-pressed, dark-blue suit. But this didn't detract from his menace. His neck was so thick it melded seamlessly into the base of his broad, bullock-like skull, the silver hair on top of which had been shaved to flat bristles. His unsmiling face looked as if it had been hammered out of Russian steel.

'This is Gregor, part of our in-house security team,' Jayne explained as he stood aside and admitted them. 'His assistant,

Vladimir, you just met . . . or "Vlad the Impaler", as he's known to some of our girls who he gets a session with in lieu of pay. She patted Gregor's leathery cheek. 'Gregor here never participates. Even *we've* no idea what floats Gregor's boat, do we, love?'

Gregor said nothing, and still didn't smile.

'Never mind,' Jayne added. 'You won't see much of either of them while you're working . . . they're not intrusive, but anyone gets fresh with you and they'll be there in a flash.'

The club's 'vestibule', as Jayne referred to it, in stark contrast to its grimly functional exterior, was like a grand Victorian entrance hall, complete with black and white tiled flooring, rubber plants, wood-panelled walls adorned with erotic paintings, and, as its centrepiece, a sweeping plantation-house style stairway descending from the upper floor.

Here, another staff member approached them.

'Marissa,' Jayne said. 'This is Hayley, our new coat-check girl. Hayley, this is Marissa, our staff-manager.

Marissa was in her late-thirties, and a willowy, green-eyed blonde, with very pale skin, much of which was on view given that she only wore a filmy nightgown over her skimpy leotard. She had a shapely but sylphlike figure and a wan, near-ethereal beauty.

'Marissa will be your immediate supervisor,' Jayne said. 'You have any problems, she's the one to speak to.'

It all sounded so normal, almost like a real company. Many times in her police career, Lucy had encountered situations wherein legalities and illegalities appeared to blur, as if there was no dividing line. Police officers couldn't afford to think in those terms, yet so many others who existed in this twilit world actually did, that at times it was quite disorienting.

Jayne bustled away leaving her with Marissa, who hadn't yet spoken but beckoned to Lucy with a long, manicured finger, and traipsed away across the hall to the coat-check area itself, a cubbyhole of a cloakroom underneath the staircase. Alongside this, there was a private changing room, which was currently empty.

Once in there, Marissa planted her hands firmly on her hips. 'Okay, babes . . . strip.'

Her voice defied her elfin appearance: it was gratingly harsh, as though she smoked a lot, and had an undiluted Black Country accent.

'Excuse me?' Lucy said.

'Everything. Undies too.'

'I don't understand.'

Marissa looked bored that she was having to explain this again. 'Anyone who works here gets strip-searched when they come in and before they go home. Just to ensure there's nothing on their person that shouldn't be. If you've got a mobile phone, which you doubtless have, you'll have to hand that over to me for the duration of your shift. We can't have anyone here who's got recording or filming devices with them. House rules, sorry . . . and don't bother giving *me* any lip. I didn't make them.'

Uneasily, despite having expected something like this, Lucy commenced undressing.

'Here's what you'll be wearing.' Marissa indicated a scanty uniform hanging from one of the changing room pegs. 'You've already seen where you'll be working. It's next door.'

'Will I . . . I mean . . .?' Lucy feigned alarm. 'Will I not be able to make *any* phone-calls? Not even use a landline?'

'Only in emergencies, which may happen from time to time, but most of the time won't. Everything's regulation here, babes. That means you follow orders to the letter. Understand?'

Lucy nodded dumbly.

'Jayne doesn't run this place with a rod of iron, but it's

got to be shipshape,' Marissa added. 'Any fucking around and there'll be a consequence. What did you do before?'

'I was a secretary.'

Marissa laughed; again it was harsh, unfeeling. 'How fallen are the mighty, eh? Don't worry, you're not alone. I was a professional dancer. A *real* one. Can you believe that?'

'Don't see why not.'

'I was performing Latin and Ballroom before I was nine. Since then, I've been a three-times British Champion and a two-times European Champion. I also appeared in four West End shows. The entertainment world was my oyster. Then I jumped into bed with the wrong junior cabinet minister. The rags were doing a number on him at the time for his philandering ways. I sell them my story, thinking I'm quids in. Next thing, I get a visit from the West End Drugs Squad. They find heroin in my car, coke in my Notting Hill flat. None of which is mine, by the way, but who's going to believe me? The next thing, my name's muck. I can't even get work in burlesque. I come north to see what's going on. The rest is history.'

'I'm sorry,' Lucy said.

'Don't be. I earn more now than I ever did before, and I don't even pay tax on it. Anyway, we've all got sob stories to tell, and I'm not particularly interested in yours. So stop dallying and get them knickers off. Let's check there's nothing hiding where the sun doesn't shine.'

Chapter 16

The overall impression Lucy gained of SugaBabes was that of private gentleman's club combined with old-fashioned bordello.

It comprised six or seven ground-floor rooms, all leading off the vestibule, and all plush: richly carpeted, furnished with couches, divans and armchairs, and yet each with its own theme. There was the Egyptian Room, the Oriental Room, the African Room, the Russian Room. In some ways, Lucy supposed that was reminiscent of London's famously lavish Victorian brothels, but that was the only thing in the entire establishment that leaned towards the tacky. A couple of the rooms had their own bars, but to maintain the classier aura, there were no gaming tables in there, no big TVs screening porn twenty-four/seven.

Though Lucy found that her duty was relatively straight-forward, she shared it with a blonde Polish girl who went by the unlikely name of Delilah. All they had to do was stand behind their counter under the staircase, and take charge of every item of apparel that was handed to them. While their uniforms might consist of black high heels, seamed black nylons, short black tunics trimmed with gold, and black brimless bellhop hats that fastened under the chin with gold straps, this wasn't especially demeaning garb. She'd seen worse in legit establishments like wine-bars and night-clubs. The girls serving – either the barmaids or the waitresses – were similarly dressed, while the Talent Team, as they were called, descended the staircase from about eight o'clock that first evening, looking elegant and glamorous.

Their order of play was evening gowns, expensive hairdos, lots of jewellery and intoxicating perfume. No indecently plunging necklines were on view, likewise no stocking tops. Admittedly, on a couple of occasions the impression was only just this side of slutty – several gowns were perhaps a little too sheer, or maybe if they were backless and split to the waist rather than the thigh, exposed a little more flesh than might be permissible in normal society (though film stars and fashion models did that routinely on the red carpet these days, so what the hell!). But one thing was certain, these girls were the most beautiful and chic that Lucy had ever seen who were actually in the flesh trade. There were no tattoos on show, no pierced belly buttons, no stretchmarks, no varicose veins, much less any needle-tracks or inflamed, coke-reddened nostrils.

Delilah meanwhile, who spoke English well and was pleased to have company, proved immediately to be some-thing of a chatterbox. She named all the girls as they came down from upstairs. Quite a few were Eastern European, but overall they were an ethnic mix. Some were local, from right here in Manchester, but there were girls from much farther afield too – Australia, South Africa, Japan, the Philippines.

'How do they end up *here*?' Lucy asked. 'How does Jayne actually recruit them?'

To this question, Delilah's response was cagier. 'Girls travel, you know. They seek better life. There are many things they

. . . well, they wish to leave behind. At least here they safe, no?'

Well, Lucy thought, *safe-ish*.

She'd already been told that she'd never have reason to go upstairs, and so didn't know what actually went on up there, but nothing unseemly appeared to be happening downstairs. Apparently, according to Delilah, that was another house-rule. As she furtively watched, the girls sat and talked with the customers on couches or at the bars, laughing at their jokes, courteously accepting drinks, though never anything alcoholic – lime and soda was the usual preference. There was no fondling, no groping, no sitting on knees.

The clients themselves were initially an unthreatening group; well-to-do men for the most part – Lucy could tell that from their suits and coats and silken scarves, and from the way they bore themselves and spoke. Most were in middle age – they were probably the only ones who could afford this place – and tended to be clean and polite. Invariably, they were in relaxed and jovial mood when they got here. Letting their hair down, she assumed, after a stressful week CEO'ing their companies or managing their local authority departments, or taking care of whatever else it was they did that put them into this gold-plated category.

Of course such geniality of spirit did not extend right across the board.

That very first night, from about ten o'clock onwards, villains started arriving at SugaBabes. Not in great numbers, but what they lacked in quantity, they made up for in quality. Lucy sucked in a tight breath when she found herself face-to-face with the disfigured visage of Vinny Scott, who was well-known around Manchester as a professional armed robber. She'd never had personal dealings with Scott, so it was unlikely he'd recognise her, but she couldn't fail to place the famously broken nose and the weirdly right-angled razor scar on his left cheek. He barely looked at her as he handed over his black leather overcoat. Underneath it, he wore a string vest and neck-chains, while his muscular arms were covered with tattoos and other cheap bling. He snatched his ticket without a word, and sauntered away into the Egyptian Room, where a couple of the girls immediately attended on him.

Lucy's accelerated heart rate had no sooner begun to slow again when Curtis Laidlaw approached the counter. His racket was importing heroin, speed and skunk cannabis. He was also known as a pimp, as his dyed-blond curls, alligator jacket and brilliant red silk shirt appeared to attest. At least Laidlaw was inclined to be friendlier, or more of a charmer. He responded to Delilah's greeting, by taking her face in his large, dark, jewel-bedecked hands and planting a moist kiss on her lips, before accepting his ticket with gratitude.

Clearly, Laidlaw was here to discuss business with Jayne McIvar, because he then disappeared into her private office.

But more frightening than any of these characters, and more of a loose cannon generally because house-rules just didn't apply to her – as Lucy was imminently to discover – was Jayne McIvar's sister, Suzy, who was official Head of Security at the club. The first Lucy saw of *her* came half an hour after Laidlaw had been admitted to Jayne's office, when Suzy walked quickly downstairs, crossed the vestibule, opened Jayne's door without knocking and slammed it closed behind her.

Similarly beautiful to her sister, but in a wilder, more tigerish way, Suzy wore her orangey-red hair in long dreads bound together at the nape of her neck, and a stud through her left eyebrow. She was slightly taller than Jayne and of a heavier build, as if she worked out, but there was no mistaking her female shape, even though it was currently clad in rocker attire: a tasselled black leather jacket worn over a black

T-shirt bearing a blood-and-thunder metal band logo, tight jeans with a studded black leather belt, and spike-heeled, black leather boots. Her fingernails, which, whether real or false, looked lethally long and sharp, were painted bright green. There was one curiosity: on Suzy's left hand she wore a single, fingerless glove. After she had vanished into the office, Delilah confided in Lucy that this was to conceal a nasty scar.

Apparently, as a rumbustious kid in Longsight, Suzy McIvar had annoyed a local all-male gang by asking to join them. In retaliation, they dragged her into a derelict garage and gang-raped her. She somehow managed to tolerate all that, misguidedly thinking it a kind of initiation test. But afterwards, when one of them produced a carton of battery acid, which he intended to drizzle on her face, she fought back crazily, breaking two of their skulls with an iron bar, and raking another's face – she had claws even then – so severely that his teeth were exposed through his cheeks. Suzy didn't come out of the fight entirely unscathed, having at one point to fend off the acid as it was thrown. It drenched her left hand, rendering it a shrivelled talon for ever more, but at least it missed her face.

All of this tied in with the warnings given about Suzy McIvar beforehand, as did an incident several minutes later when Lucy heard muffled shouting behind the door to the office. It was a voice she hadn't heard previously, almost certainly Suzy's, and it was so sharp and fierce, and rose so rapidly in volume, that she could soon hear every word.

'You think you can badmouth us whenever you fucking feel like it, Curtis! Is that what you're saying?'

There was a mumbled response. It sounded like 'no, no way'.

'You think you can say what you want in this fucking

town?' Despite being clearly audible already, Suzy's voice continued to rise, to steadily intensify. 'You think you've earned that right?'

Unlike her sister, Suzy had evidently taken no elocution lessons, and still spoke – or rather shrieked – with the hard vowels and glottal consonants of inner Manchester.

As before, the response was only semi-coherent.

'Answer the fucking question, you little shit! Do you think you own this fucking city? Tell – the – fucking – truth! Do not make things worse by lying!'

'Course I don't . . .' Lucy heard Laidlaw stammer. 'Suzy, come on . . .'

'*Course you fucking don't! Bang fucking right! So why the fuck . . .*'

Another customer approached the counter, seemingly oblivious to the tirade in the office, briefly distracting Lucy from her eavesdropping. When he'd departed and she had taken care of his coat, it was still going on. It was now echoingly loud in the vestibule, so it must have literally been deafening inside the office.

'So how are you going to fix it?' Suzy wanted to know.

Again, Laidlaw's next response was only semi-audible.

'*Answer the fucking question! How are you going to fucking fix it?*'

Laidlaw gave some meandering, long-winded response.

'What . . . *what did you fucking say? Are you serious? Are you taking the piss, Curtis! Because your life's on the fucking line right now! I'm telling you.*'

Lucy couldn't help eyeing Delilah, who gave a relieved little shrug, as if to say, 'Hey, count your blessings . . . that could be one of us in there.'

'*What's to stop me killing you right now, I hear you ask?*' Suzy ranted on. '*Well . . . nothing! Sweet fuck all!*'

Someone else spoke, presumably Jayne McIvar, as it was

calmer, more controlled, only for Suzy to tear in again before Laidlaw could respond.

'Where're your boys when you need them?' she wondered scornfully. 'I'll tell you, Curtis . . . sitting at home with limp dicks and sweaty faces. You know why? Because they were too fucking frightened to come here . . . and with good fucking reason. But that won't keep them safe, I can promise. Once we've finished with you, we'll come after them! You know why, you treacherous, smart-arsed little shitbag . . .? For the simple reason they're your fucking mates. And when we've done them we'll go after your family . . . and all their fucking families . . .'

There was a further mumble of additional other voices.

'*Shut the fuck up!*' Suzy howled. '*Don't open that slimy yap of yours when Jayne's speaking . . . the only reason not to fucking kill you on the spot – right here, right now – is so you can put this thing right first. So don't get fucking smart, Curtis. You weren't born with the brains of a fucking slug. In fact, get on your fucking knees. Now . . . do it now, you degenerate, scum-sucking prick!*'

Lucy glanced again at Delilah, whose head was down, who would no longer meet her colleague's gaze.

'*ON YOUR KNEES NOW!*'

Lucy swallowed hard, wondering if they were about to hear a gunshot.

'*You little shit! You little bitch faggot. You think you're the fucking man because you know a few names in Afghanistan and Morocco? You think that cuts any fucking ice with us? . . . What? What did you say?*'

'*I'm sorry . . .*' Lucy heard Laidlaw's voice clearly for the first time. He too was shouting, but in desperation, in panic-stricken terror; it was impossible to equate it with the cool dude who'd breezed his way in earlier. '*I said I'm sorry. It won't happen again, I promise . . .*'

'You fucking let us down again, Curtis . . . you wise off when our people come around, and they'll be taking your body home in a fucking bucket! Last fucking chance . . . you hear? *I SAID DO YOU FUCKING HEAR!*'

'Yes, yes, I hear,' he blathered.

'*I CAN'T FUCKING HEAR YOU!*'

And so it went on, for another ten minutes or so, Laidlaw all but begging, Suzy issuing apocalyptic threats, until the door suddenly burst open again and the McIvars' guest tottered out. Gone was the smooth customer, in his place a staggering, goggle-eyed scarecrow of a man, whose shirt hung wetly open on xylophone ribs, whose bleached curls hung on his brow in damp ringlets, and who blundered towards the brothel exit without seeing anything else or any other person.

Suzy McIvar appeared in the office door, and watched him go. A sheen of perspiration gleamed on her own brow, but her mouth was twisted into an angry but satisfied smile. She turned, her eyes briefly locking with Lucy's. Lucy averted her gaze.

With a resounding bang, the heavy office door slammed closed again.

Chapter 17

'Mr Todd, your taxi's here, sir!' Marissa called.

Lucy probably wouldn't have thought anything of this, except that Mr Todd – a tall, balding chap in a purple blazer and tie, both bearing the same serpentine public school crest – who now approached the coat-check counter to reclaim his overcoat and scarf, was someone who had only deposited them there about ten minutes earlier. He said nothing of course; merely smiled at her, and then graciously departed the building.

Even then it might not have seemed curious had it not happened a couple of times already.

Lucy had been working at the brothel for three nights now, and had noticed on various occasions that some of the customers – not many, just a few – seemed to come for the company and a drink rather than the girls. They'd sit at one of the bars, chatting with the other customers, and then, after quarter of an hour or so, Marissa, dolled up to the nines herself in the evening, would call their names out and announce the arrival of their taxi.

In the light of this, it was impossible not to recollect Tammy's cryptic warning about the so-called "SugaBabes

Taxi Service". Whether this had any relevance to that was uncertain – who knew what was going on inside Tammy's head? – but ever since that semi-unintelligible conversation, Lucy had kept half an eye out for anything anomalous involving a taxi.

Not that she had much time to worry about it on this particular evening, because half an hour later she finally encountered members of the Crew.

No one introduced them to her officially, but that wasn't necessary – their mugshots were plastered all over the walls back in the Ripper Chicks office. In addition, they were treated like royalty the second they entered the place, Marissa and even Jayne McIvar busy-bodying around them frenetically.

The first of them was near enough the scariest bloke Lucy had ever seen. Apparently his name was Mick Shallicker, or so Delilah whispered in a consciously awe-stricken voice. Lucy estimated that he stood six foot nine inches tall, in addition to which he was massively framed, and yet he moved with lithe, athletic grace; there was nothing clumsy or awkward about him. Needless to say, his face was terrifying in its own right: square-jawed, heavy browed, with sunken, apelike eyes and a broad mouth full of slabby yellow teeth. It was nicked and scarred aplenty, but not as excessively as these guys' faces usually were. Lucy suspected this was because very few of his opponents had ever been able to throw a punch high enough. His preferred clothing appeared to be a black suit and a thick, black roll-neck sweater. There was something vaguely stylish about that, though the lump of gum he noisily chewed on put paid to any impression it might have given that he was a sophisticated guy.

This was explained when Delilah told Lucy that Shallicker was mainly muscle. Apparently, he only ever appeared as a minder to Crew underboss and – if Lucy remembered rightly – Shakedown merchant, Frank McCracken.

It was McCracken himself who was the first Crew member she actually spoke to.

Like all the others, McCracken brought her his coat, scarf and gloves. Up close, he was every bit as menacing as his reputation, but in his case because he was cruelly handsome: lean-faced, with dark, brooding eyes, diamond-cut features and that razored shock of silver-grey hair. His well-tailored, pale-grey suit had Savile Row written all over it.

Lucy avoided making eye contact as he handed his garb over, but for some reason, during the process, she caught his attention. She sensed him scrutinising her as she tore him a cloakroom ticket and pushed it across the counter.

'We know each other from somewhere, darling?' he wondered.

His accent was 'Albert Finney' Manchester: tough, raw, easily betraying its working class origins, and yet moderated slightly as though from years of mixing with the right people.

Lucy's hapless smile was an attempt to conceal her rising anxiety. Was it possible she'd run into him on the job without realising?

'I don't think so, sir.'

McCracken lingered at the counter, the giant Shallicker hovering behind him, still noisily chewing. 'I'm sure we've met somewhere before.'

'I honestly don't think so.'

'Problem, Frank?' Suzy McIvar asked, approaching.

McCracken shrugged. 'Nah, no problem.' He winked at Lucy. 'Sorry, love . . . ignore me. Getting dizzy in my old age.'

Suzy McCracken gave Lucy a curious once-over, before escorting the gang-boss away.

And that appeared to be that. Up until now, Suzy McIvar hadn't even noticed that a new staff member was present, and McCracken himself didn't seem interested in making an issue of it. In fact, for the next couple of nights the Crew lieutenant mingled easily and comfortably with the other customers, spoke to the girls politely when they came down-stairs, and generally conducted himself like the civilised man he definitely wasn't.

Until Lucy's sixth night working there.

It was around eleven o'clock and she was on her first break of the shift. At the rear of the cloakroom, a narrow fire-exit door connected with a small, walled yard. There was no further egress via this route. The yard had once possessed an outer gate, but that had been bricked up in recent times to provide extra security. The coat-check girls took staggered breaks, so Delilah would go out into the yard for the first hour; she kept a deckchair out there under a stoop, where she could sit and smoke and read a gossip mag by the light from the open door. Lucy didn't smoke, but willingly went out when it was her own turn, slumped into the deckchair, nibbled a butty, sipped from a flask of coffee and tried to get her thoughts in order.

On this particular night, she'd been outside only five minutes when she heard a car screech up on the other side of the wall, a couple of doors bang open and feet come clomping across the cobbled road and up the narrow passage to the club's entrance. More car doors opened and closed, and then there was a grunting, hissing and a subdued but prolonged swearing.

She stood up, ears suddenly straining.

More feet sounded in the entry passage, this time making their way back out to the road, but in leisurely fashion.

'Well, well . . . Pixie,' a voice said. It was Frank McCracken's. 'Seems you've been on the rob again?'

Lucy knew she couldn't let this pass. On one hand, common sense bade her go back into the club and close the fire door behind her, but the hell with that. Thus far she'd gleaned nothing of value from her time at SugaBabes; whether this thing would turn out to be relevant to the case or not, she had to start poking her nose around.

Trying to climb the wall and look down the other side would only attract attention. But there was an older section of brickwork to the right of the point where the gate had once been. Numerous chinks had appeared there where grouting had rotted and bricks had dislodged. She placed her eye at one such and was just able to see the unfolding scene beyond.

Two heavies had climbed from a dark green BMW, and, between them, were restraining a short, thin man with a mop of black curly hair, wearing blue tracksuit pants and a baggy pink sweater, both of which were already stained with blood. He had a youthful face, but even from this restricted angle he struck Lucy as one of those who maybe wasn't quite as young as he appeared. On this occasion, of course, that face was already half-pulverised, its nose broken sideways, gore glutting the nostrils and dripping down over the twisted mouth. This ugly sight didn't faze McCracken, who ambled across the road with hands tucked into the pockets of his suit trousers, Mick Shallicker in tow.

'What stone was he under, Nicko?' McCracken asked one of the beaten man's captors.

'Lying in bed with his bird,' came a grunted reply. 'Like he had nowt to worry about.'

McCracken shook his head. 'Never saw the bigger picture, our Pixie, did he?'

'Please,' the man called Pixie whimpered, fresh blood bubbling from his nose.

'How long you been out, Pixie?' McCracken asked.

'I've not . . . I've not done nothing, Mr McCracken . . .'

'I didn't ask you that, I asked you how long you've been out.'

'Year . . . year and a half.'

192

'A year and a half, and already you're at it again.'

'I said I haven't . . .'

'I heard you the first time, you little twat. But it's a lie, isn't it?' There was no anger in McCracken's voice. He spoke matter-of-factly; only half-interestedly, as if this whole thing had become a tedious routine. 'Everyone *knows* it's a fucking lie. You and your team have been at it again. This year alone . . . two big townhouses down in Wilmslow. Plus a farmhouse out in Delamere Forest . . . way out there in the lovely Cheshire countryside. Every time the same thing. Three blokes wearing ski masks, one pistol each. Occupants battered and tied up. If they aren't forthcoming about the safe and other valuables, one of the burglars gets to work on their toes with a set of pliers. Doesn't usually take long after that, does it, Pixie? Properties get ransacked. High-quality merchandise only. Always a decent haul.'

'It . . . wasn't me,' Pixie stammered. 'I'm keeping my nose clean these days.'

'That's the last lie you'll tell me, you little turd, if you know what's good for you.'

Pixie hung his head, coughing, hawking up blood.

'All together, these three breaks have netted you . . . how much?' McCracken asked.

'Mr McCracken . . . please!'

'According to the newspapers, it's at least three hundred grand's worth.'

'But it's . . . it's not cash,' Pixie stuttered. 'So we can't divi it up that easy.'

'So . . . *what*?' McCracken feigned astonishment. 'We don't get paid?' He chuckled. 'Is that seriously what you're trying to tell us, Pix?'

'It takes time. There's stuff to fence, you know?'

'Ah, so . . . you actually *were* going to pay what you owe, just at some point in the future?'

193

'Yeah, yeah, sure . . . same arrangement as always.'

'Except . . . you didn't tell us you were back in the game.'

'There wasn't time, Mr McCracken.'

'But there was time to lie in bed with that skanky bird of yours.'

'Look . . . I can get the money in a couple of weeks. Soon as we've unloaded enough stuff. The jewellery alone should fetch a hundred grand.'

'Trouble is, Pix . . . it's two hundred.'

Pixie's eyes widened in his blood-spattered face. 'That's two thirds . . .'

McCracken nodded, chuckled again. 'And that's not the end of it, either.'

He signalled to one of the heavies, who came around from the other side of the BMW with a string and brown paper parcel. Cheerfully, McCracken unwrapped it, shaking out what looked like a transparent plastic raincoat, and a pair of transparent plastic gloves.

'Oh, come on, please!' Pixie wailed.

'Now I can see the lads have already given you a seeing-to, Pix,' McCracken said, as he donned the protective clothing, ensuring to button the raincoat all the way to the top. 'But I'm guessing that was because you played hard to get.'

'Mr McCracken, please . . . I'm gonna get you the money.'

'Oh, I know you are, Pix . . . otherwise we wouldn't be having this conversation. But . . .' McCracken ensured the gloves were a comfy fit by flexing his big, knobbly-knuckled hands inside them. 'But, you see . . . I can't just let you walk away with a busted nose. I mean, what would my reputation be worth if I did?'

'Mr McCracken, please!'

Pixie writhed in his captors' gasp, but they held him firm. And as such, he never even saw the right hook that caught him smack-bang in the middle of the face. His nose, which might finally have been congealing from the earlier beating, splattered wide open again. Ruby droplets sprayed over McCracken's plastic coveralls.

Pixie gave a choked gasp of agony.

A left hook followed, slamming into the same spot, the resounding smack of fist on bone echoing across the otherwise empty cul-de-sac. The third blow caught him in the ribs, the fourth under the jaw, the fifth to the left side of the face, the sixth to the right,

Lucy lost count after that. She withdrew from the hole in the wall, heart thundering.

It was the gravest problem any undercover officer could face – what to do in the event of serious criminal offences being committed in your presence. Especially when the overriding priority was to maintain your covert status. On the face of it, if the victim was a criminal himself there was perhaps less of an impulse to intervene . . . but by the sounds of it, this was a savage and protracted beating. Even now it was going on, and the impacts of the blows were deafening. The guy wouldn't die. That was expressly not their aim. But for a police officer to witness such torture, to stand there and do nothing . . . and yet what *could* she do?

And then another voice intervened. Jayne McIvar's. By the sounds of it, she too had emerged onto the road from the club's entry passage.

'Not outside my place, Frank . . . please.'

'*Your* place, Jayney?' McCracken replied, breaking off from his exertions, breathing hard.

'You know what I mean. Anywhere but here, please. It's bad for business.'

Lucy went back to the wall and peeked through.

Jayne, who during the evenings glammed up in make-up, jewellery, an ankle-length cocktail dress and uber-high heels, made an incongruous figure on the grimy backstreet. Pixie meanwhile, still suspended with arms spread between two of McCracken's goons, but now slumped downward, was a bloody wreck; like a man who'd died on a cross. McCracken himself was sprayed crimson, though of course his transparent plastic coating had protected his expensive suit, if not his face.

He took care of the latter by dabbing his cheeks and forehead with a silk handkerchief.

'When I tell you how to package high-class pussy, darling,' he replied, 'you can tell me how to run my end of the operation. Now why don't you be a good girl and go back inside?'

Very reluctantly, Jayne withdrew. McCracken turned back to his victim, from whom there wasn't so much as a twitch, let alone a groan.

'But . . . ultimately, I think we *are* done here.' McCracken lowered his fists. 'Take him to that shithole pad of his. Leave him to the tender mercies of his girlfriend. Let's see if she's worthy of the name. When he comes round, remind him he's got a week and that we're in for two hundred K.'

The goons hauled Pixie's lifeless form around to the rear of the BMW. Someone flipped the boot lid open, and they deposited him inside. McCracken peeled off his gory plastic, handed it to Shallicker, then straightened his tie and headed back indoors.

Lucy backed away from the hole and turned – just as a dark form flashed across the yard towards her from the door; a burly figure, but moving with catlike agility and a frantic clatter of spike-heeled boots. Before Lucy could draw breath, a leather-clad forearm had slammed her backwards against the bricks, and now exerted incredible force as it crushed her windpipe crosswise. In the same blur of speed, a partially gloved hand brought a cigarette lighter to Lucy's face and spurted out a long tongue of flame, which flickered so close to her left cheek that she was certain she could smell her own skin as it singed.

She gagged and whimpered and tried to turn her head away, but her captor was larger and vastly stronger than she was, and held her locked in place.

'Who the fuck are you!' Suzy McIvar demanded in a snakelike hiss. 'And what the fuck do you think you're playing at?'

'Nothing, Miss McIvar,' Lucy stammered. 'Please, I thought I heard . . .'

'*WHO ARE YOU, I SAID?*'

'Hayley Gibbs, Miss McIvar . . . I've only just started here.'

Suzy continued to hiss but now as she breathed, glaring into Lucy's face from point-blank range. Bizarrely, her eyes were odd-coloured, one green, one a muddy brown – another testimony to her violent life, no doubt. Her clenched teeth glinted white between tightly drawn lips. '*What* are you?' she demanded.

'Ex-tom, miss. I work on the coats. Sorry, I just . . .'

'You seem very interested in everything that's going on here for a coat-check girl!'

'I couldn't . . . I couldn't help it. Please . . .'

It wasn't difficult for Lucy to pretend she was so frightened that her words tumbled over one another, because she was. Nor was it purely down to the proximity of that long, wavering flame, which could surely be no more than a centimetre from her flesh. Partly it was due to the craziness imprinted on the face behind the flame. Up close, Suzy McIvar's eyes looked glassy, dead – like they weren't real. The Head of Security resembled her sister, even if she wasn't identical to her, but there was an icy derangement there that even Jayne the brothel-queen lacked. With effort, Jayne

McIvar could pass as a respectable woman, but no matter what fancy feathers this creature donned, she'd always be a street-hoodlum.

'You lie to me, girl, and I'll blowtorch that pretty nose right off your face,' Suzy snarled. 'You'll spend the rest of your life with two bony holes where the snot comes out!'

The lighter-flame felt as if it was performing this task already, Lucy's left cheek flaring heat and pain.

'Just thought I heard something weird,' she stuttered. 'I got curious, that's all . . .'

'I've never seen you around before. Who'd you tom for?'

Before Lucy could blurt out her reply, another voice intruded. 'Don't spoil her face, if you don't mind!'

Over Suzy's shoulder, beyond the tear-inducing glare of the flame, Lucy saw that Jayne McIvar had stepped into the yard. Delilah was loitering worriedly behind her – possibly she'd alerted her mistress to what was happening.

Suzy snapped her lighter closed, the intense heat instantly extinguished, but continued to bore into Lucy's head with her weird, doll-like eyes.

'Did you hire this smackhead bitch?' she replied.

Jayne's heels clicked the flagstones as she approached. 'What's going on?'

Suzy still didn't look round. 'Came out for a smoke and found this one fixing her beady little gaze on Frank and his team.'

'Sorry, Miss McIvar,' Lucy said, addressing Jayne. 'I overheard them . . . I just didn't know what it was . . .'

'This surprises you?' Jayne told her sister. She too was stony-faced with rage, but apparently her ire was aimed elsewhere. 'Right fucking pantomime . . . bang outside our front door! If there was any neighbourhood left here, they'd *all* have been looking!'

'I said did you hire her?' Suzy said.

'She checks out,' Jayne retorted. 'What's the exact problem?'

What seemed like a minute passed, during which Suzy breathed hoarse and heavy like some predatory beast besotted with the scent of blood, her eyes never once leaving Lucy, her prey – until slowly, very slowly, she leaned backwards, dropping her elbow.

Lucy gasped and coughed.

'Maybe there isn't a problem.' Suzy backed off. 'But Hayley Gibbs . . . if I catch you sticking your nose where it isn't wanted again . . .' She gestured with the lighter, before ramming it back into her pocket. 'Well . . . I've told you, haven't I?'

'I know you're pissed off,' Jayne quietly advised her sister. 'We all are. But taking it out on the help won't get us anywhere.'

Suzy chose to ignore that. Instead, she pointed at Lucy one last time before heading back inside, stiff-shouldered and with loud, stumping footfalls.

Lucy could only lean against the wall and gently knead at her bruised trachea. Jayne walked over to her and irritably fingered the chink in the brickwork.

'Not a very good idea, love,' she said. 'Spying on Mr McCracken's business is the last thing that'll win you friends round here.'

Lucy shook her head, struggling to enunciate words that didn't hurt her throat. 'I had no idea that's what I was doing, Miss McIvar . . . honestly. I don't even know who this Mr McCracken is.'

'I believe you, Hayley. You know why? Because if you did –' Jayne placed her fingertips under Lucy's chin and turned her head sideways '– you wouldn't have been doing what Suzy's just caught you doing.'

'I was on my break. I thought I heard something bad, I wasn't sure . . .'

'You'll hear a lot of bad things while you're here, Hayley. If you haven't got the stomach for that, you're in the wrong place.

'Yes . . . erm, yes, miss.'

'It's understandable you're curious, of course.' Jayne frowned, her brows knotting with frustration. 'Bastard gangsters. They lord it over us like kings. We all have to scrape and bow, even me and Suzy. But at present we also have to know what's good for us.' She released Lucy's chin and edged backward. 'No damage done there, at least . . . so you could still make the Talent Team, if ever you've got a mind to. But until then, Hayley, follow my sister's advice . . . get on with what you *are* supposed to be doing, and you'll be fine.'

'Yes, Miss McIvar. Of course.'

Taking it that the interview was over, Lucy scuttled back indoors.

Chapter 18

There were no more dramatic events at SugaBabes over the next few nights, which allowed Lucy to concentrate on what she was supposed to be doing. One by one, she learned and memorised the names of the girls, though it was a time-consuming process as most of them never even came down-stairs until the club officially opened, at which point they immediately began to entertain customers. As far as she could discern there were none working here, at least none she'd yet discovered, who were even casually referred to by the name "Lotta", nor any who matched her statuesque description.

'Mr Billworth!' Marissa called from the vestibule, distracting her from these ruminations. 'Your taxi's here, sir.'

Lucy felt an irresistible prickle of interest, waiting po-faced as a customer ambled into view from the Russian Room. He smiled amiably as he produced his ticket and she handed over his coat and gloves. He was about seventy, with clean-shaved features and long, white, soft-looking hair, and was extremely well-presented in an Armani suit, a pink silk shirt, a pink silk tie and a gold tie-pin. She also noted pearl-studded cufflinks and a Rolex. When she gave him his overcoat she could tell it was richest cashmere.

As soon as Billworth had left the building, Lucy made an excuse to Delilah and wandered out into the yard at the back, where, having ensured there was nobody else hanging around, especially not Suzy McIvar, she warily moved to the chink in the wall. It felt like madness after what had happened last time, but as before, she wasn't making any real ground here and proactivity seemed like the only potential antidote to that.

She didn't know what she expected to see on this occasion – apart from a man climbing into a taxi – or how this might have any connection with the actual case. On the face of it, it felt like it wouldn't. But at the end of the day she was still a cop, and Tammy's weird warning kept echoing through her head. Knowing Tammy, there'd be nothing of great value here – SugaBabes was an illicit operation so, surprise surprise, illicit things were going on – but anything that might at some point give her leverage over the McIvars had to be worth investigating.

When she peered out through the hole in the wall, Mr Billworth was waiting patiently by the roadside while a vehicle swung through a smooth three-point turn in front of him. This vehicle resembled no taxi that Lucy had ever seen. It was more like a limousine – long, dark and sleek, with tinted windows. It certainly carried no roof light nor any sign of a Council licence plate, but none of that was hugely mysterious. Evidently this Billworth was a rich guy. Doubtless he could easily afford this kind of private, five-star service.

But then it took a turn for the strange.

The limousine driver climbed out wearing a grey chauffeur's outfit, including a peaked hat pulled low and dark-lensed spectacles, which, as it was now late at night, could only have been worn to create some kind of disguise.

And then it took a turn for the even stranger.

The chauffeur opened the rear passenger door for Billworth, as one might expect. But before Billworth climbed in, he turned his back on the chauffeur and stood rigidly. The chauffeur, with a near-theatrical flourish, produced a white silk scarf, which he gently tied around his passenger's head, in effect blindfolding him.

Lucy watched in fascination as the chauffeur then assisted Billworth into the back of the car, closed the door behind him, climbed in himself and gunned it swiftly out of the cul-de-sac.

She went back to the coat-check desk in a state of total bemusement.

The blindfold clearly meant that the client was not supposed to know where he was being taken to, so he definitely wasn't being driven home. Was that the case with all of them, these guys who only visited SugaBabes for long enough to buy a single drink, and who were really here to use the SugaBabes Taxi Service – for that was surely what this amounted to?

She wondered where their ultimate destination lay, and why how-to-get-there was a secret kept even from them.

None of this boded well, and though Lucy fully intended to take Tammy's advice and refrain from asking any questions on this front, it was plain that no information was going to be volunteered. Whenever a taxi arrival was announced, no member of staff in the club indicated even by their body language that it was anything out of the ordinary. Delilah, who could talk the hind legs off a donkey, made no reference to it – as if it wasn't even on her radar.

And maybe it shouldn't have been on Lucy's either, even as a police investigator.

Fleetingly, she was furious with herself for showing such indiscipline.

She was here to hunt a killer called Jill the Ripper, not take issue with each and every side-racket the McIvars were perpetrating, ominous though they might appear. So instead of trying to puzzle the taxi business through, she decided that she would make a concerted effort for the rest of that evening to get on with her work, to watch, to keep her ears open, and to discuss inanities with Delilah whenever the opportunity arose. But she wondered how long this could go on for. It was nearly ten days in, and she still didn't appear to be making discernible progress – until another uneventful two hours had passed, and then, rather unexpectedly, there was a development.

Frank McCracken reappeared in the club, again in company with Mick Shallicker, but now with one or two others as well. One of these, Lucy recognised as "Necktie Nicky" Merryweather, while the rest were apparently their personal guests, though all looked to have been cut from similar rough-spun cloth. As usual, once here the gangsters shifted into relaxation mode, cracking jokes and laughing as they handed their coats over the counter.

McCracken turned to Marissa and asked her to 'send Charlie down ASAP'.

Frank McCracken was not one of those curious customers who only came to SugaBabes to make use of the Taxi Service. Whenever he turned up, he tended to spend the entire evening, each time thus far, with a different girl, some of whom he'd simply socialise with at the bar, others of whom – though not many, admittedly – he would eventually take upstairs. However, this was the first time Lucy had heard him ask for a particular girl by name. It was also the first time she'd heard of a girl working here called "Charlie". When the new arrivals had ambled off to the Oriental Room, Delilah, ever the gossip, added a helpful explanation.

'Charlie the most expensive girl in north of England,' she confided. 'She jewel in Jayne McIvar's crown, but she only here two days a week. I think she have private clients too.' Her voice dropped to a whisper. 'She Mr McCracken's favourite. He want her for girlfriend, I think . . . but she always play hard to get.'

When Charlie finally came downstairs, in her own time it seemed, it was easy to understand why she'd be anyone's favourite. With film star looks, flowing white-blonde hair and a voluptuous figure, and wearing a brilliant green, off-the-shoulder evening gown and backless silver slippers with four-inch heels, she looked almost impossibly glamorous. She walked across the vestibule with an easy sensual sway, stopping only briefly to talk with Marissa, before continuing to the Oriental Room, all the way radiating female sexuality.

Along with something else.

Something that interested Lucy even more.

Physical power.

In her heels, Charlie was at least six feet tall, while the rippling green material of her gown revealed strong arms, broad hips, firm thighs. Lucy was reminded of top sports-women; Charlie may have been dressed to kill, but she had a hugely athletic aura.

Lucy had been looking for an Amazon, and here she was. And then there was that name – Charlie. As a rule, it tended to be a derivation of Charlotte. As was Carlotta, of course.

And what was short for Carlotta, if not Lotta?

Lucy slid along the counter to get a better angle on the open door to the Oriental Room. From here, she could see Charlie seated on the bar-stool next to McCracken, her tanned, toned legs neatly exposed through a slit in her skirts, one silver-heeled slipper dangling as she sipped the regulation lime-and-soda. She might be playing hard to get, but she was certainly cosied up to him, reaching out as they spoke, running a teasing finger down the side of his jaw.

'Who *is* Charlie?' Lucy casually asked Delilah. 'I mean, what's her story?'

'Ahhh . . .' The Polish girl gestured vaguely. 'No one know. Only come to Talent Team four year ago. Most people think she porn star in America, but something go wrong and she come home.'

'She's English?'

'London, I think.'

'Surely a girl in that league doesn't need to do this for a living?'

'She like it. She have cash.' Delilah's eyes bulged, as if she was massively impressed by the info she was imparting. 'She come in wearing fur, dripping jewels . . . when she bother to come in.'

'How do Jayne and Suzy tolerate that?'

'They not control her . . . like you say, she not need this job. But when she here, I guess they see her as asset. Like I tell you, Mr McCracken's favourite. Spend all night with him when she here.'

'Suppose *that* empowers her,' Lucy said. 'Means she can do what she wants.'

'No one say "no" to Charlie.'

'Kind of a boring name, though . . . isn't it? I mean . . . Charlie?'

Delilah shrugged. 'We pick and choose names. When you look so good you not need fancy one, uh?'

It was tempting to ask if Charlie had ever gone by any other name. But that might seem like one question too many. Thanks to Delilah's penchant for chatter, there'd be other opportunities to learn about Charlie without seeming overly nosy. But one thing was certain, in Lucy's eyes at least: Charlie – the most expensive girl in the Twisted Sisters' high-class establishment – now qualified as something else: one of those ever-elusive 'major lines of enquiry'.

On the surface it might seem ridiculous. Here was this highly paid prostitute. That in itself was a rare enough thing.

Would she really want to muddy those waters with a string of pointless murders just because men had been unkind to her in the past? But then again, such thinking didn't allow for psychosis, for bloodlust, for an unstoppable compulsion to kill. Jill the Ripper was a serial killer. That meant killing wasn't her hobby; it was her vocation.

Killing was what she did. Whether she liked it or not.

That night, Charlie left the club in McCracken's company. It was one o'clock in the morning when the goddess of the house sashayed back upstairs to gather her personals, while the mob lieutenant and his towering, ox-like sidekick came to collect their coats.

'Been working hard tonight, darling,' McCracken told Lucy. 'Take this for your trouble.' He handed her two folded twenties. She thanked him profusely as she accepted it.

Again, his eyes lingered on her as though he knew her from somewhere.

'Anything else I can do for you, sir?' she asked.

'Nah, it's fine.' He shrugged his coat on. Charlie came back downstairs, now wearing a mink and carrying her handbag.

'Ready, love?' he asked.

'Always ready for you, Frankie,' Charlie replied in a chirpy Cockney voice.

They linked arms and left the building together, Shallicker ambling at the rear, his shovel-like hands thrust deep into his pockets, his big jaw working his latest lump of gum.

'Looks like she's not playing hard to get *tonight*,' Lucy said to Delilah.

Delilah waved that away. 'She go home with him sometime. I think he have more work to do to make honest woman of her.'

Lucy was impressed even by that. It said a great deal about

Charlie that she would keep a major player in the local underworld on tenterhooks. How often did guys like Frank McCracken get strung along by the women in their lives?

As she pondered this, she noticed Suzy McIvar crossing the vestibule, Gregor close behind her. The two of them halted half-way over, Suzy glaring at the door that had just closed behind McCracken and his party. It was written in the murderous frown on Suzy's face that there was no love lost there.

Lucy watched carefully. It was easy enough to work out what was going on here.

Jayne McIvar, as the diplomat, was more tolerant; she recognised that the Crew were top dogs and that playing their game was the only solution to what otherwise could become a messy problem. Suzy, the more elemental of the two, was clearly less happy to accept this. Suddenly she noticed the coat-check girls watching her. Her frown became a snarl.

'You two got nothing better to do than fucking gawk?'

Abashed, Delilah withdrew into the cloakroom. But before Lucy could follow, Suzy called her back, stalking across to the counter.

'Hayley Gibbs!'

Lucy turned round.

Suzy's odd-eyed gaze penetrated her like a spear. 'What is it with you and Frank McCracken? He thought he knew you from somewhere, didn't he?'

Lucy's thoughts raced as she shook her head. 'I don't know, Miss McIvar . . . he seemed to think that before, but I've never met him in my life.'

Lucy felt scared again, not to mention helpless.

Suzy continued to glare at her. 'You're sure there's nothing you're not telling us?'

'He was just tipping me, Miss McIvar.'

'Do *not* lie to me, cutie! If it turns out you're not who you say you are, I fucking swear . . .'

'Now what?' another voice interrupted.

It was Jayne, finally drawn from her office by the angry tones. She took things in immediately, and made swift eye-contact with her sister before glancing at the ceiling, indicating that Necktie Nicky and a couple of other Crew associates were still on the premises. 'You talking trash again?' she said with quiet intensity.

'Just trying to establish a few facts,' Suzy retorted.

'Really? Didn't we long ago establish the fact that your temper is one day going to get us into it deeper than whale shit unless you learn to rein things in?'

Suzy pointed at Lucy. 'This one's got something going on, I'm telling you.'

'No one has got *anything* going on here!' Jayne stressed. It was a strangely meaningful statement, Lucy thought – and its import was not lost on Suzy, who slowly and grudgingly lowered her finger of accusation.

'Haven't we agreed that we really don't want any scenes *inside* the club?' Jayne asked, though it wasn't really a question. Again, her tone implied that Suzy's outburst might have consequences. She threw another pertinent glance at the ceiling. 'We don't want anyone thinking we might – just *might* – end up being a source of embarrassment, do we? Not for *any* reason.'

Suzy said nothing. She glowered at Lucy one more time, but clamped her mouth shut.

'Why don't you cool off, eh?' Jayne suggested. 'Go and find a leather bar you can have a drink in.'

Suzy switched that icy, odd-coloured gaze to her sister, but only for the briefest time. And then she turned on her heel and strode to the main entrance, slamming the door behind her.

Chapter 19

'I'm telling you, ma'am,' Lucy said, 'this Charlie's a good fit for the profile.'

She'd found Nehwal and Slater in a corner of the cramped and noisy snug of the Aspinall Arms, the old-fashioned red-brick local at the rear of Robber's Row.

With police shifts starting and ending at unusual times, the Aspinall tended to be busy at all hours, but today, with the addition of journalists as well, it was literally packed to its outer doors. Groups of lunchtime drinkers stood shoulder-to-shoulder around them, shouting and guffawing.

'The trouble is,' Nehwal said, 'you're supposed to be looking for someone called Lotta.'

Lucy shrugged. 'Charlie . . . Charlotte . . . Carlotta . . . Lotta. They're all horns on the same goat, and this is *some* goat, I'll tell you!'

Slater rubbed at his neck. His cheeks were sallow, his brow creased. 'I hear what you're saying, Lucy, but this sounds tenuous.'

'It *is* tenuous,' Nehwal agreed, before Lucy could reply. 'But I *do* see the link.' She gave it more thought. 'I take it there's no one else working there called Lotta?'

'Not as I've been able to discover, ma'am,' Lucy replied. 'Not yet. The trouble is I can't probe too much. The intel's got to come to me rather than me go looking for it.'

'You've at least learned some of the other girls' names?' Slater asked.

'Oh yeah. We've got a Silvie, a Silky, a Danielle. We've got a Marguerite, we've got a Jezebel, we've got a Courtney, we've got a Celeste . . .'

'But no Lotta?'

'Not so far.'

'When you say she fits the profile, presumably you're going on more than just the two names sharing an etymological root?' Nehwal said.

'Totally, ma'am. Charlie's a looker. On top of that, she's tall, she's shapely and she's blonde . . . she ticks all those boxes. And she's powerful, I mean physically. I can tell that just by looking at her.'

'But there's no smoking gun?' Slater said.

'Not so far, sir . . . no.'

He sipped at his beer. 'There's no way you can engineer some kind of meeting between Tammy and this Charlie, so you can confirm afterwards that it's the same person?'

'I don't see how that'd be possible, sir. Not without arousing even more suspicion. The way I see it, what we really need to know next is who Charlie is. I mean her true identity, where she lives, what her other life's all about . . .'

'You've checked the database?' Nehwal asked.

'Been on it all morning, ma'am. No one matches.'

'And nobody else at SugaBabes is in a position to fill you in?'

'I'm not sure anyone there knows her that well. But again, I don't want to risk asking too many questions. I've already been warned to keep my head down.'

'I suppose uncovering her real ID would help us build a

proper picture,' Slater said. 'Trouble is, short of tailing her from the brothel – which is always problematic, as they'll have spotters everywhere – I don't see how we can do that.'

'I do,' Lucy replied.

Nehwal glanced up at her. 'Okay . . .?'

Lucy leaned forward to speak in confidence. 'We need to put an obbo on Frank McCracken.'

The two senior officers regarded her askance.

'Excuse me?' Nehwal finally said.

'You want to put the Shakedown captain of the Crew under surveillance?' Slater asked in a tone that suggested he needed clarity, that he'd obviously misheard what she'd just said.

'Only his home address,' Lucy confirmed. 'That way we can spot Charlie whenever she arrives. And when she leaves again, we put a tail on her.'

There was a protracted silence at the hemmed-in table.

'She's his on/off girlfriend . . . at least that's my information,' Lucy explained. 'So she's bound to be there some of the time. Look . . . I know we're already pushing the boat out having me at SugaBabes. It's a high-risk environment – at times it feels very high risk. It'll be no different at McCracken's home address. But there ought to be more places to conceal a vantage point around there, plus Charlie's going to be less on her guard, isn't she? She comes out of his front door in the morning, on some quiet suburban housing estate . . . is she really going to be looking over her shoulder when she heads for home? And we might not need to sit on the place for too long . . . sometimes Charlie and McCracken leave the club together. All I'd need to do in those circs is alert the surveillance team soon as I get off shift, and they can watch out for the first girl who exits McCracken's pad the next day.'

Nehwal said nothing, but by her expression the idea was growing on her.

'We ought to consider this, ma'am,' Lucy urged her. 'It surely can't hurt.'

Eventually, the DSU nodded. 'I guess it's what you call lateral thinking. Which is all we can really ask for in this situation.' She glanced at Slater. 'Any resources you can divert from the Intel Unit for this?'

The shock of Lucy's suggestion seemed to be fading from his face too. 'Don't see why not. We aren't getting any other results.'

That wasn't entirely true, but they weren't the results the taskforce needed. Only the previous day, Ripper Chick enquiries had led to the arrest of a couple of suspects: two female addicts from Stockport, who, in the guise of turning tricks, had rolled a number of drunks at knifepoint, though their motive had always been robbery rather than murder. Only one person had actually been stabbed, and that had been superficial. The arrest team had obtained the blade, which was nothing like the sort of weapon required to saw off a penis and scrotum. In any case, the two prisoners were human scarecrows on whom the slutty street-gear had hung like rags on wire frames; neither of them had even closely resembled the buxom suspect on the CCTV footage. They'd both now been charged with other offences, but were no longer implicated in the Lay-by Murders.

'If I put in an action request, ma'am, can *you* okay it?' Slater said.

'Gimme a break!' Nehwal replied. 'This is Frank McCracken we're talking about. The SIO can okay it, or no one does.'

'You really sure about this?' Slater asked Lucy.

'I'm not sure of anything, boss,' she replied. 'But I went to SugaBabes looking for their top girl, and I found her. Whether she likes collecting male sex organs, or just says she does, is another question.'

Nehwal deliberated. 'McCracken lives in Didsbury, doesn't he?'

'Like a king,' Lucy said. 'I've been checking him on the system today, too.'

'Didsbury . . .' Nehwal thumbed her chin. 'I'm sure we can find an observation point round there somewhere. Okay . . . assuming the boss has it, it's an obbo for Mr Shakedown.'

'Whoever it is, ma'am, just make sure they keep their heads down,' Lucy said. 'I've seen these fellas in action, and I'm telling you, it isn't pretty.'

Nehwal gave her a frank stare. 'It's *you* who'll have to keep your head down.'

'Ma'am?'

'*You'll* be on the obbo too.'

'Me?'

'Frank McCracken may be the smoothest gangster in Manchester,' Nehwal explained, 'but he's also Jack-the-Lad. Yeah, some nights Charlie will go home with him and that'll give us an advantage, but overall, how many bimbos are likely to visit that palatial residence of his? Probably more than a few. And thus far there's only *you* can really identify the main suspect.'

'But I'm working for the Twisted Sisters, ma'am . . . it's not like I can just take time off.'

Nehwal considered this. 'Well . . . it's too early for you to resign from SugaBabes. How about you working there nights and manning the OP during the day?'

'And when's she going to get some kip?' Slater wondered.

Nehwal sighed. 'Well . . . you'll need to be on the OP now and then, PC Clayburn. We can't have this thing dragging on. We have to find this girl, Charlie, and either bring her in or dismiss her from the enquiry.'

'I'm sure we can sort something out,' Slater said.

'Send me the forms, Geoff,' Nehwal told him. 'And I'll

prioritise them. In the meantime, sort out your surveillance team . . . quickly.'

A couple of minutes later, Lucy and Slater were heading back up the stairs in Robber's Row, the DI having wolfed his pint and his pie and chips.

'Someone needs to get onto Cheshire CID too, sir,' Lucy said. 'Seems there've been three aggravated burglaries down there in the last few months, two in Wilmslow, one in Delamere Forest. Townhouses and a farm. Occupants badly assaulted. I've no actual details, but tell the investigation teams they need to look at a guy called Pixie. It's obviously a street name, but I'm sure they'll have it listed.'

'This undercover stint's proving useful,' Slater remarked.

She shrugged.

'How you finding it?' he asked. 'I mean day to day.'

'I won't pretend it isn't a challenge. There's something about that Suzy McIvar. She's not a full shilling.'

'You're telling me.'

'If she was blonde and white, I'd have her down as a suspect.'

'Wouldn't be a bad call.'

'And I don't think she's overly fond of the Crew.'

'She likes to take care of business personally . . . but the Crew have rules and the McIvars are signed up to them.'

They entered the Intel Unit, which at present was empty, the rest of the girls having not yet mustered for duty, and trekked into Slater's office. While the DI booted his desktop up, Lucy slumped into a chair. The night shifts weren't a problem for her in themselves – so long as she didn't have to come to work during the day as well, but at the moment there was no other way she could have conflabs with supervision. She yawned and stretched.

'What does your gut tell you about this lass, Charlie?' Slater asked as he typed.

'You mean do I think she's the killer?'

'You've been in this job long enough to let your nose lead you.'

Lucy pondered. 'I find her suspicious, sir. Even in that company, she stands out.'

'And yet don't serial killers supposedly like to hide?'

'Suppose that depends on how narcissistic they are?'

He nodded and continued typing.

Like most wannabe detectives, Lucy had read extensively on serial murderers. A rare breed among criminals, they often had unique psychological characteristics, not least an over-whelming desire to remain central to the story. For most repeat killers, it wasn't simply a sexual thrill; it was a power game. And that wasn't just the power they wielded over their victims, but the power they could exert over entire terrorised communities. You didn't hear about bank robbers writing cryptic letters to newspapers, or drugs couriers taunting the police with complex clues. In their twisted fantasies, serial killers were the most dominant personality around, and yet to make that fantasy real they needed to impose themselves constantly, even if such self-promotion ultimately compro-mised their anonymity.

'This Charlie is so narcissistic she even prick-teases the mob,' Lucy said. 'No one gets what they want from her unless they pay.'

'Perhaps she's just a hard businesswoman,' Slater said.

'She's still on the meat-rack. Either way you cut it, boss, it's odd.'

'Okay.' He typed on. 'That's good enough for me.'

Chapter 20

Frank McCracken's private residence was located at 17 Yellowbrook Close, Didsbury.

This was a swish suburb by almost any standards. Formerly a prosperous township in its own right, Didsbury had been absorbed by Manchester during the Industrial Revolution, but was now famous for the quality of the restaurants and boutiques on its high streets, and for its leafy residential avenues. It would never have surprised the police to find a major league criminal living here. Their home addresses were rarely located in districts where dealers and prostitutes plied their trade, where there was aggro in the pubs, or where underworld rent-collectors spent each crack-of-dawn kicking down shabby front doors.

Seventeen Yellowbrook was a particular case in point. Frank McCracken might have risen through the criminal ranks after his misspent youth on a Salford council estate, but these days he occupied a luxury, five-bedroom villa, detached from the equally affluent properties on either side of it and standing at the end of a long, block-paved drive. Thanks to a preponderance of trees and shrubbery around its boundary, it was heavily secluded from its neighbours, but the cops were fortunate enough to find a spot in the adjacent Leatherwood Road; a house that was currently between owners and whose upper-rear bedroom window gave reasonable vantage over the premises in question.

Basing the OP on Leatherwood Road wasn't ideal, but it had some advantages.

By necessity, the surveillance team had to leave the blinds on their window half-closed, mainly because it served as a useful shield, though this obviously restricted things a little. At the same time, the two houses were about seventy yards apart, and 17 Yellowbrook could only be viewed through the gap between two other properties, but if you had a telephoto lens handy – which the team did – a clear visual could still be had of its electronically operated front gates, the whole of its front drive and its front door. Another perk of being in the next street was that it meant the team could come and go without attracting suspicion. McCracken's people wouldn't even see them, while to prevent the occupants of Leatherwood Road getting curious, they dressed in paint-stained overalls and used vehicles mocked-up as decorators' vans.

But from Lucy's point of view, this whole thing was far from easy.

Her initial hope that Charlie would simply leave the club with McCracken one night and all she'd need to do was call the team and let them know the target twosome were en route, was thwarted by the rareness of these occasions. It seemed that Charlie didn't go home with Frank McCracken as regularly as he might have liked. (What was it Delilah had said . . . about the brothel's top girl playing hard to get?) As such, Lucy, the only one – as Nehwal had said – who could identify the suspect, had to play her full part in the obbo, which was scheduled to operate around the clock, rotating staff.

And in reality this was pretty impractical.

Lucy was still working at SugaBabes, and that was already a thirteen-hour day. More to the point, Didsbury, which was in south Manchester, was a good half hour's drive from the centre of operations, even on her Ducati Monster. Initially, she attempted to manage this, heading straight home after finishing at the club, grabbing five hours sleep, then biking down to Didsbury for about one in the afternoon, from where she could participate in the surveillance until about five, which left her two hours to bike it back to Robber's Row, get herself ready and then use public transport to head into work at SugaBabes. When she wasn't at the OP, the team would photograph all comers and goers at 17 Yellowbrook, and Lucy would assess them on the iPad at the next opportunity.

As it was, for the first three days no one Lucy recognised visited McCracken's house, either when she saw them herself in the flesh or later on film – apart from McCracken himself, Shallicker, who seemed to live there, and a few other lackeys from their firm.

Ultimately, this frenetic schedule left Lucy agog with exhaustion, which affected her performance at SugaBabes. Four nights into the surveillance, she'd only been on duty at the coat-check counter for about fifteen minutes when Jayne McIvar, glammed up as usual, stopped in her tracks while perambulating past.

'Fuck's sake, Hayley!' she hissed. 'You look like a bag of shit this evening!'

'Oh . . .' Lucy came abruptly awake. 'Sorry, Miss McIvar. Erm . . . they're digging the street up. I've not had much kip recently.'

'Don't give me excuses, give me solutions. If you can't get your beauty sleep at home, find a bed somewhere else. And when did you last launder that uniform?'

'Erm . . . sorry, Miss McIvar?'

'It's your uniform, love, so *you* keep it clean. Now for Christ's sake, smarten your act up!'

After that shift, Lucy rang Slater to try and modify her itinerary, which she felt was leaving her exposed. His response was to have a camp bed put into the bedroom at Leatherwood Road, where Lucy, on arrival each afternoon, could sleep until such time as a face arrived at McCracken's door, at which point the other members of the team would summon her to try and put a name to it. This only happened intermittently, perhaps once every two or three hours, but she still had to come wearily to the window and look. A couple of times, when it was plainly obvious the person at Frank McCracken's front door could not be Charlie, the glamorous hooker – like when it was an elderly lady collecting for charity, for example, or on another occasion, when it was a rotund middle-aged woman who'd arrived in a delivery van – she almost lost it.

On the fifth day, she finally did.

Fortuitously, she only had Des Barton for company that afternoon, Des already knowing her well and therefore proving more tolerant when she exploded with anger.

'Jesus Christ, Des!' she snapped, drawing back from the viewfinder. 'I mean Jesus H. Christ!' She pointed through the window at the distant figure coming back down McCracken's drive. 'That's not even a sodding woman!'

'What?' Des said. She stepped away from the tripod, and he put himself forward to look again. 'Ahhh . . . you're right.'

Now that he was face-on to the OP, it was plain that the latest visitor to no. 17 was actually a young man who happened to have longish, fair hair. Though perhaps the gas company logo on his beige jacket ought to have been something of a giveaway, not to mention the clipboard he was carrying.

Lucy slumped wearily onto the camp bed. It was hardly the most comfortable berth anyway. She had a single quilt on it, which was rucked and dingy-looking in the grey autumn daylight, and a pillow that was basically a ball of sponge and did little to support her head. The rest of the room was littered with a sordid detritus: newspapers, magazines, toffee wrappers, fast food cartons, empty Coke tins. In addition, because they couldn't open the window, it stank: chips, ketchup, human sweat.

She scrubbed a hand through her unruly mop of hair, and rubbed at her face. 'I'm sorry, love,' she mumbled. 'I'm just out on my feet.'

'All we need is one sighting,' he said in attempted consolation. 'Just one clear shot of this bird's face, and you're done. You can sleep for a week.'

'Yeah, until I have to go back to . . .'

'Best not tell me that, chuck.'

'No, no . . . you're right, sorry.'

Lucy's presence at SugaBabes was still at the highest level of classification. The rest of the surveillance team were well aware they'd been posted at Frank McCracken's house, which was a biggie in itself. But all they knew about this girl Charlie was that she was an associate of McCracken's and a viable suspect in the Jill the Ripper crimes, and that Lucy could identify her – and frankly, that was all they wanted to know. You felt extra pressure when an investigation led to the highest levels of criminality. At that stage, the less you knew the less you could accidentally tell.

Des offered her a bottle of water. 'Drink?'

'No, thanks. That'll only make me want to pee . . . which'll also keep me awake.'

'Something to eat then?'

She glanced across the room at him. 'Does that mean *you* want something to eat?'

'Well . . . I haven't had any scran since brekky, and it's nearly three.' He grinned; his clear desire that she respond with a helpful suggestion was almost boyish.

'Why don't you scoot round to the shops and get us both a McDonald's, eh?' she said. 'I'll hold the fort here.'

'Really?' He jumped to his feet.

'Yeah, go on.'

'Good, I'm famished.' He pulled a donkey jacket over his white, emulsion-spattered overalls. 'Oh . . . my treat by the way.'

'Damn right it's your treat.'

'What do you want?'

'Just get me a cheeseburger.'

'Any fries with that?'

'No.'

'Coke, milkshake?'

'For Christ's sake, Des, you sound like you work there. Just go. And don't take forever.'

He grinned again and left. Lucy estimated that she'd be alone on the OP for the next twenty minutes or so, during which it would be a wrestling match just to stay awake. In truth, the thought of food repulsed her, though eating might also help gee her up.

She remained dutifully by the window, hoping and praying that Charlie wouldn't show up until Des had got back. As well as her own motorbike and the scruffy decorators' van, she also had the keys to an unmarked Datsun that was parked at the side of the house. But the last thing she wanted to do was tail a suspect on her own. It was difficult enough doing that with only one vehicle, but in her current bog-eyed state she'd seriously struggle.

However, when, five minutes later, someone did actually appear at the front of Frank McCracken's drive and press the gatepost buzzer, it woke Lucy up more fully and abruptly than if she'd stepped barefoot onto a live cable.

At first there was nothing outstanding about the figure. Lucy only saw whoever it was from behind. Though clearly female, she was dressed dowdily in jeans, flat shoes and a shapeless blue anorak. Most likely it was a cleaner, or some other functionary. But she *was* fair-haired, and that had to be worth a second glance. Lucy got onto the telephoto camera, adjusting the lens and positioning one finger over the button. The woman was now more clearly visible, though her back remained turned as she introduced herself via intercom. A second passed before the electronic gates swung open to admit her. By this time it was clear that she wasn't Charlie, not even in disguise – she wasn't tall enough. Lucy relaxed again.

But then the woman looked furtively round, and Lucy saw her face.

Her first feeling was numbing bewilderment, followed in short order by that bizarre process your brain goes through when, stricken by complete and utter disbelief, it tries to compensate by assuring you that this must be an error, a simple mistake, that there'll be a perfectly rational explanation which, in your momentary shock, you've overlooked.

And yet, when all that was done – and it lasted no more than a second – and the woman walked up McCracken's drive and entered the house via the front door, the dumbfounding realisation kicked in that, whatever else, there was *no* mistake here.

And it continued to kick in, harder and harder, until Lucy felt physically sick, until she was suddenly so certain she was about to swoon that she had to grab hold of the windowsill. Her mouth was dry as sandpaper. She couldn't feel a speck of saliva on her tongue.

Because despite there being no explanation for this, she could already see the implications of it – and they were very far-reaching indeed.

Des got back sooner than Lucy had expected, in just under fifteen minutes. She remained by the window, saying nothing when he handed over her burger.

'You okay keeping point while I sort this lot out?' he said, brushing a load of paperwork from a trestle-table and laying out his own quarter-pounder with cheese, his Big Mac, his large cola and his double helping of extra-large fries.

She didn't respond.

'Lucy?'

'What? . . . yeah, that's fine.'

She was still reeling from what she'd just seen. But because it made no sense to her, because there was no logic in it from whichever perspective she looked at it, she still didn't know how to react. She couldn't even show bemusement.

Internally, a voice kept trying to say things to her like: *You've obviously just missed something. The answer will be right under your nose.*

But no matter how hard she tried, she couldn't.

'You alright?' Des asked, his mouth full.

'Erm . . . yeah.'

'Not hungry after all, then?'

'What . . . oh.' She glanced down, still not having torn the greasy wrapper from her cheeseburger. 'No. Do you want it?'

'Well . . . never like to see things go to waste.'

She crossed the room, put it down on the table next to him and went back to the window.

'You sure you're okay?'

'Like I say, Des, I'm just tired.'

'Give us two mins to scoff this lot, then you can get your head down again.'

'No, it's alright,' she said firmly. 'You take your time.'

It was now very important to Lucy – imperative in fact – that she be the only person looking when the most recent caller to Frank McCracken's house re-appeared. Firstly, because she had to be absolutely sure about what she'd seen and that her overwrought imagination was not playing tricks on her. Secondly, so she could ensure that no one took a photograph. She herself had made certain the woman wasn't photographed going in, and she needed to be equally certain that she wouldn't be photographed on the way out.

Even so, Des had polished off his lunch a good twenty minutes before the woman finally re-emerged, walked down the drive and vanished from sight along the road. Fortunately, it hadn't been difficult to get him to extend his break by an extra half-hour. All Lucy had needed to do was offer him a daily paper and tell him to make sure he got a proper rest, as it wasn't fair given that she'd spent a lot of that day asleep.

He'd gleefully complied and so missed the female visitor completely.

Just before five o'clock, Lucy pulled her waxed combat jacket over her paint-stained jumper and jeans, grabbed her motorbike helmet, and with only a few words of farewell, departed the building. Outside, her Ducati waited alongside the decorators' van. An unlikely police vehicle, she'd been permitted to bring the bike to the OP – it wasn't as if she had much choice anyway thanks to her rapid-fire schedule; she now saddled up and tore off the estate, heading north as fast as the M60 evening traffic would allow. But, half an hour later, instead of veering off at the Crowley East junction and heading for Robber's Row, she proceeded another six miles to Crowley West. From here, it was a matter of minutes to Saltbridge. Lucy was well aware that going home now might make her late for her seven o'clock start at SugaBabes, but at present this was a secondary issue.

She *had* to go home, very urgently indeed.

Chapter 21

When Lucy wheeled her bike into the back yard of her mother's house, it looked like there were no lights inside. Rather than stowing the machine in the shed, she leaned it on its kickstand and gazed up at the rear of the terraced building. She hadn't been mistaken; it stood in total darkness.

She glanced at her watch. It was just six o'clock.

Her mother would normally be home by now. Even if she hadn't been to work for some reason, she'd usually be in at this time, putting the tea on. Admittedly, if she wasn't, it wouldn't be completely unprecedented. She could easily have been diverted: making a delivery or something, visiting a friend, even calling at a pub with some colleagues, though that would be unusual on a Wednesday evening.

Testing the back door, Lucy found it locked. She took out her key, inserted it and pushed her way inside. There was no smell of cooking in the kitchen, suggesting that no one had been in there for most of the day.

Lucy stood still and listened, but heard nothing.

She walked through into the lounge, her eyes gradually attuning to the gloom. Everything was as it should be: the coffee table cleared of that morning's breakfast things, all cushions arranged neatly on the sofa and armchair, newspapers and periodicals stuffed into the rack.

Yet when she reached for the light-switch, she did so warily – she'd learned from experience that if an enemy was close by, the moment you shed light on them was the moment they attacked. But when she flipped the switch, there was no one else present.

She glanced from the front window to see if her mother's yellow Honda was parked outside. It wasn't, but that proved nothing as their garage was located in a freestanding row of garages at the end of the street, and it could already have been put away for the night.

Despite zero evidence there was anything abnormal here, her heart rate slowly increased as she stepped through into the hall. She *so* wanted normality – *so* yearned for it. But she knew what she'd seen that afternoon. Things could never be normal here again.

Stopping by the foot of the staircase, she stared into the silent darkness at the top.

Fleetingly, Lucy felt dazed. These last few days had been difficult verging on the impossible. So hectic had the turnover of jobs and duties been that half the time it was a blur. On some occasions she'd found herself sleepwalking through it, quite literally. She half-wondered if today's astonishing development might owe less to reality and more to fatigue-induced fantasy. Likewise, the absence of her mother from this house; in usual circumstances Lucy wouldn't think twice about it – there'd be some mundane reason. While the growing sense of menace in here – her own home for God's sake! – had to be down to exhausted paranoia. There was no reason to assume her mother was anywhere other than heading back here from work right at this moment.

Except . . . Lucy *knew* that that could not be the case.

Somewhere overhead, a floorboard creaked.

Followed by silence.

'Mum!' she hesitantly called. 'You up there?'

There was no reply, so Lucy ascended. Padding stealthily, hair prickling in that old familiar way from whenever she was entering the danger zone. Not that she felt especially vulnerable. She had a spare set of appointments in her bedroom wardrobe – another baton, more body-armour, an extra pair of cuffs. But it might be a matter of reaching them before the intruder could strike . . . if it *was* an intruder.

She halted at the top.

The doors to the bathroom and her own bedroom stood open. Dimness lay beyond them, but the door to her mother's room was closed – and that seemed odd considering that no one else was supposed to be here. Quickfire thoughts raced through Lucy's mind. There'd been no signs of forced entry downstairs, but that was no guarantee of anything; she'd hardly made a forensic recce of the doors and windows.

There was nothing else for it.

As quietly as she could, she edged into her room, opened the wardrobe, drew the Autolock Baton from the harness hanging inside and snapped it out to full length. Then she crept back to her mother's bedroom door.

It was only polite to knock, to let them know you were coming.

Yeah . . . right.

She kicked the door open and barged in, baton to shoulder as per the manual.

'Whoever the fuck you are, stay . . .'

But no one else was in there.

She snapped the light on and scanned the bedroom, bewildered. It wasn't much larger than her own; there were no niches or hiding places she couldn't see from the doorway. Unless . . . inexorably, Lucy's eyes were drawn to her mother's wardrobe. She listened again, and fancied there was faint movement inside it: a rustle, as of clothing, another low creak.

'What the hell . . .?' Lucy crossed the room at speed, yanking the wardrobe open.

Inside it, her mother – her sweet, elegant, ever dignified, always ladylike mother – was curled up at the bottom, regardless of the shoes she was crammed on top of or the garments draped over her from above. Her arms were wrapped around her knees; her shoulders trembled.

Slowly, almost painfully, she turned an ashen face up to her daughter, its cheeks wet and smeared with mascara. She attempted a sad smile.

'I knew it would be you.' Cora's voice was feeble, tearful. 'I knew you weren't supposed to come home tonight, I knew you were on duty till late . . . but I still knew it'd be you. You're so much smarter than people think, you coppers, aren't you . . . love?'

'What's . . .?' Lucy felt her world cavorting around her. For a second she could barely speak. 'What's . . . what's going on, Mum?'

'I am so . . . so sorry,' Cora said.

Lucy reached down and, with some difficulty, helped her mother climb out.

Yet once she was back on her own two feet, the older woman didn't even look shamefaced to have been found the way she had. She sniffled again and dabbed at her face with a scrunched, sodden tissue – clearly she had been crying for some time – which she then tucked into her cardigan sleeve. With the swift eye of a professional, Lucy checked her top to toe. Cora was in her normal clothes. They hadn't been damaged or disarrayed in any way, though Lucy hadn't expected that they would. Her mother had *not* been attacked.

'Who were you hiding from?' she asked quietly.

'Oh . . .' Cora sat on the bed. 'You.'

'*Me?*' Despite everything, Lucy was genuinely taken aback.

'Don't pretend you didn't come home early to look for trouble, Lucy.' Cora's tears hadn't dried yet, but the look she now threw at her daughter was almost accusatory. 'That's why you've got that horrible club in your hand, isn't it? Why you've got a face like thunder.'

Suddenly self-conscious that she was armed in her parent's presence, Lucy laid the baton on the sideboard. 'I thought we might have an intruder.'

'I don't blame you for that, I suppose,' Cora sighed. '*I* don't know what to expect now either, if I'm honest.'

'Mum, you need to start making sense.'

'On reflection that might be easier said than done.'

'Look . . .' Lucy struggled to give voice to her confusion. 'At this moment I have a very perplexing picture in my mind. Of someone approaching a certain house in Didsbury this afternoon . . .'

Cora nodded, raised her tissue again and blew her nose.

'And that person then looking furtively over her shoulder just as I was about to take a surveillance shot of her. But, I mean . . .' Lucy laughed without humour. 'I must've been dreaming that bit. Mustn't I, Mum? Mustn't I?'

Very delicately, Cora wrapped her tissue and reinserted it into her sleeve. 'You weren't dreaming, and you know you weren't.'

'Yes, I *know* I wasn't.' Lucy's tone stiffened. 'What I don't know is what the devil you were doing there. Frank McCracken is Manchester's top gangster, or one of them. And you're my mother. *What in Christ's name were you doing there?*'

'I knew you'd think I'd betrayed your trust,' Cora said from the lounge armchair.

She'd regained her composure somewhat, but now clung tenaciously to another twist of tissue, into which she continually sniffled. Her eyes were bright with unshed tears. Lucy stared at her from the middle of the room. She'd met enough people in her time who'd gone through trauma to know delayed shock when she saw it. But on this occasion, any sympathy she might feel – even for her own mother – had to be tempered by a hard-headed determination to find out what the Goddamn hell had been going on. For the life of her, she couldn't imagine how her mother might have finished up on Frank McCracken's doorstep, unless she herself had left some classified paperwork lying around. Lucy knew that she hadn't, but even if she had, it was surely inconceivable that her mother would pick it up and do something with it.

'That's why I felt so awful, so torn in my loyalties,' Cora added. 'That's why I was hiding when you came home. But I was only half-hiding, wasn't I, Lucy? I wasn't actually frightened. It was more a case of me not thinking I could face you. Plus I wasn't really sure what it was I'd done . . . by that I mean how it might work out. I just hoped it would somehow be for the best.'

'Mum . . . what's going on?'

'I knew you'd find out, love . . . like I say, you coppers are cleverer than people think. So I just knew the moment I did that thing today . . . I could feel it in my bones that you'd find out . . . that you'd come back here already knowing about it. But even if you didn't, I was going to own up . . . I couldn't do what I did today, Lucy, and not tell you . . .'

'Okay . . .' Lucy tried to remain calm. 'So tell me.'

Cora's voice became a plea. 'Do you have any idea how much I worry about you, darling? I hate you being a police officer, literally hate it.'

'I'm well aware of that.'

'It's a dangerous world out there and I'm terrified of you getting hurt.'

'The trouble is, Mum, I'm an adult and I make my own decisions.'

'After what happened last time . . . that horrible incident in Borsdane Wood . . .'

Lucy finally lost patience. 'We're not talking about last time, Mum!' She couldn't keep the whip-crack from her voice. '*We're talking about this afternoon.*'

'But that's what this is all about. Don't you get it?' Cora remained seated, but was visibly tensing up again. Fresh tears seeped onto her cheeks. 'Look . . . two days ago I was doing the laundry . . . when I found this indecently short little black-and-gold number.'

'Yes, it's mine . . .'

'I know it's yours. I also happen to know that it comes from the SugaBabes Club.'

In the midst of everything else, this was a cannon ball to Lucy. It almost took the legs from under her.

'Mum . . .?' It barely came out a whisper. 'How . . . how on Earth is it possible you know anything about SugaBabes?'

'Because, my dear, I used to work there.'

Cora said this simply, straightforwardly. As if it was the most obvious thing in the world. But for the next few heart-beats Lucy fancied the room was tilting upright. 'Mum, if this is some . . . some kind of . . .'

'Yes, I always joke about things like this!'

'*You* worked at SugaBabes?'

Cora held her daughter's gaze. She suddenly seemed stronger than before, more in control. 'This was the early 1980s, before you were born. But I wasn't a prostitute, Lucy. SugaBabes was different in those days. It was a strip club.'

'Oh well . . . that's a load off . . .'

'They are very different things.' Now there was defiance in Cora's voice.

Lucy was still incredulous. 'You're telling me you were a stripper?'

'I suppose you find that difficult to believe?'

At first, Lucy didn't know how to react. Being pragmatic, it would certainly explain a few things: her mother's air of faded glamour, her mother's dancer's figure – which she still kept trim and shapely despite burying it in frumpish clothes; and on the subject of clothes, that neat little cocktail frock she'd produced out of thin air. It might also explain why she'd expressed such a lack of empathy for the kerb-crawlers killed by Jill the Ripper, but conversely, why she also found Lucy's jokes about her flirting with the local vicar disgusting – not because she thought him unattractive, but maybe because she didn't think herself worthy.

'Yes. I was a stripper,' Cora confirmed, still defiant. 'And I used to work at SugaBabes. It wasn't exactly respectable. But back in those days there was a strict no-interaction with the audience rule. It wasn't like one of these awful lap-dancing places you get now. We got up on stage, we did our bit, we went off again. We were proper dancers too. We gave them a real show . . .'

'*Good God almighty!*' Lucy exploded. '*What in hell am I listening to here?*'

'I'm trying to explain!' Cora jumped to her feet. 'This is tough for me too . . . so you'll just have to soldier on and listen, alright?' She took a deep breath. 'I was a young woman at the time. I had various problems in those days, which I've now put behind me . . . but I didn't see eye to eye with your grandparents much. So after I left home, which was all pretty acrimonious and unpleasant, I took any job I could get.'

'And where the devil does Frank McCracken fit into this?'

'SugaBabes was a bit dodgy even then,' Cora confessed.

'Not as dodgy as it is now. It had a front door for one thing. It was an official licensed premises. It wasn't so bad a place. But there *was* an underworld presence, and Frank worked there as . . . well, I suppose you'd call him a low-level enforcer.'

'An enforcer?' Just hearing her mother use such technical jargon felt as if it would knock Lucy off her feet.

'He wasn't even *that* important. A bouncer, really. Lucy . . . you have to understand, we were just cogs in a machine. We had no status. So we used to chat. We became friends.'

'And you've stayed friends? Is that what you're trying to tell me? After all this time?'

'I've had no contact with him at all since I left. The instant you were born, I walked away from that sordid existence. Has there been a single hint during your life of anything improper? Have we lived any way other than respectably?'

Lucy couldn't reply; she didn't think they had, but now she was wondering.

'But . . .' Cora sighed again, 'there are some things that can come back to haunt you. I might be a boring middle-aged woman now, who spends all day loading supermarket shelves, Lucy . . . but I'm not blind. I read the papers. I've seen Frank's name mentioned from time to time. It's plain as mustard that he's gone up in the world.'

'If you can call it that,' Lucy scoffed. 'You know what I saw him do the other night?'

'I don't need to hear because I saw him do it plenty of times myself. We got rough customers back in the day. Drunks, football hooligans. It was Frank's job to sort them out, and he used to . . . boy, did he used to.'

'Jesus, mother, you almost sound impressed.'

'What young girl wouldn't have her head turned by that kind of thing? A bloke who's handsome, who's always smartly turned out, who can deal with the bad guys . . .'

'*Jesus Christ!*' Lucy shouted. '*He's not James Bond!*'

'I'm well aware of that,' Cora shouted back. 'That's why I've kept him at arm's length all this time. I had no idea SugaBabes was still operating. But when I saw that uniform in the wash, I recognised it immediately. The waitresses used to wear that same livery back in my day . . . and I know you've been working undercover and I know you've been rubbing shoulders with ladies of the night. It wasn't difficult putting two and two together, Lucy. So . . . well, I made a couple of enquiries.'

'Enquiries?'

'With a few old friends.'

'Old friends, I see.' Lucy chuckled bitterly. 'So when you just said you'd put that life behind you . . . it was basically a downright lie?'

'Lucy, you can't just *un-know* people. You don't lose touch with folk who were close friends during bad times, no matter how pious you might feel about what you did back then. Anyway, they confirmed my worst fears – that SugaBabes was still going but that now it was a high-class brothel. And . . .' Cora's emotions began to overwhelm her again. Yet more tears flowed. 'I . . . just couldn't stand the thought of you being in there . . . with those kinds of people, who'll now be much worse than they ever were back in my day.'

They'd had this sort of conversation before, of course. And Lucy had no reason to believe that her mother wasn't being truthful when she brought the same argument up again. But now, it seemed, there were other factors to consider; perhaps less wholesome reasons why Cora might not want her daughter to be a policewoman.

'So what exactly did you go to see McCracken about?' she asked.

This was the crunch question. It was actually a bone-chilling moment. Everything that occurred in Lucy's life from this second on might depend on the next answer her mother gave.

'I went to see him about you,' Cora said simply.

'About *me*?'

Cora stared boldly at her. 'To exact a promise from him that should your investigation at the club cause any problems for his firm, he'd be merciful to you.'

'My investigation at the club?'

'Into the Lay-by Murders.'

'You told him *that*?'

'Why should it upset you? He doesn't want this murderess on the prowl any more than you do.'

'Why! Seriously, Mum . . . *why!*' A chill like white ice sped through Lucy's body. 'Because . . . because you've blown my cover? Just casually and totally blown it all to Hell?'

'Lucy, I had to protect you . . .'

'*Protect me!*' Lucy didn't want to shout again, but suddenly she couldn't help herself. 'You've probably killed me. What do you think would have happened if I'd gone back there tonight?'

Cora shook her head. 'Frank's not like that.'

'Frank's exactly like that, Mum! He's a thug and a maniac, and I'm sure you know that deep down, because that's why you were crying when I came in here . . . because it suddenly struck you what you'd damn well done!'

'Lucy . . .'

'You've just thrown God knows how many hours of police surveillance right down the sodding drain! You've exposed the entire bloody operation!'

'At least you'll be safe.'

Despite the heated atmosphere, this last comment was delivered with a certain degree of frozen calm, as if this one factor alone outweighed all other considerations.

'Ohhh,' Lucy said slowly. 'So that was your real plan? To

make *certain* I couldn't go back there? I mean, that *must* be it. Because if you're really such a worldly person, mother, that you used to rip your knickers off in front of a baying crowd, you're not seriously going to believe that a hardcase mobster like Frank McCracken would tolerate me being in that club purely for old time's sake! I mean, you're not that fucking dim, are you!'

'Lucy . . . how dare you speak to me like that!'

'Oh, pardon my language . . . bloody hell.'

'Lucy!'

Lucy stormed to the kitchen door. 'Don't bother. I can't talk to you right now.'

'Where are you going?'

'You think I'll tell *you*? That'll be the next fucking thing Frank McCracken knows.'

'For God's sake, you don't understand . . .'

Lucy tottered through the kitchen, but spun round at the back door. 'I understand that you just demolished the very best chance I've had to get back into my bosses' good books. In revealing your past to me the way you have tonight . . . in a way I can't ignore and will now have no choice but to report, you've just ensured that I will *never* get promoted. That I will *never* get a transfer that's beneficial to me. That there'll *never* be a whisper behind my back that isn't hostile. So thanks, Mum! You weren't just a star back in the good old days . . . you're a bloody star now as well!'

Ignoring all further protests, she stalked out into the yard, snatched her helmet and climbed onto her bike.

Chapter 22

'Hello, this is Tammy. Or Tamara, if you like . . . if you think that's sexier, if it tickles your fancy.' A girlish giggle. 'Anyway, I'm working at the moment. Busy girl, me. But please leave a message and I'll get back to you . . .'

Lucy took another sip of brandy and coke and cut the call. This wasn't something she could do by answerphone. However, the next time she called, a few seconds later, Tammy's real voice came chirping through.

'Hi Hayley!' It was almost nine o'clock in the evening, but she didn't sound drunk as yet.

'Tammy, thank God you're alright,' Lucy said. 'Where are you?'

'Where I usually am, on the East Lancs. Business is slow tonight. This murdering bitch is keeping all the johns indoors. Anyway, where are *you*?'

'Never mind where I am. Listen, love . . . you've got to drop out of sight for a while.'

'What?'

Lucy glanced along the bar. It was some fleapit in the middle of Crowley, but given that this was a Wednesday evening, it was virtually empty. Only a couple of other customers, a boy and a girl, sat facing each other in a seating bay near the front door, while the barmaid was at the far end, fiddling with her iPhone.

'You've got to disappear,' she said again.

Tammy chuckled as if this was all some daft misunderstanding. 'I don't follow.'

'Get off the streets. Go home . . . right now.'

'Hayley, what're you talking about?' Finally, there was a hint of concern in Tammy's voice.

Lucy swilled more brandy and coke. 'You're in trouble, love . . . and it's my fault.'

'What do you mean?'

'Firstly, my name's not Hayley, it's Lucy.' She took a deep breath. 'Secondly, I'm a cop.'

A long, disbelieving silence followed, and then came a harsh but whispered: 'Fucking bitch . . . you absolute fucking bitch!'

'Listen to me, please . . .'

But Tammy hung up. Lucy sagged on her stool. She was tempted to bang her half-empty glass on the bar-top and signal for another, but drunkenness was no solution at a time like this. Besides, it was already her second and she still had to ride her bike across town. Instead, she tapped Tammy's number in again. It went straight to voicemail. So she tried again, and again, until at last, very abruptly, it was answered.

'*What do you want, you cow?*' Tammy demanded.

'You've got to get off the streets!' Lucy asserted. 'And I'm not joking when I say that!'

'Have you set me up, or something? Are you here to nab Digby, is that it?'

Lucy almost laughed. 'Nothing so bloody mundane, love . . .'

'You bitch! I trusted you, I was a friend of yours when you didn't have anyone! I even stopped you getting knifed!'

Lucy didn't quite remember the knife incident that way, but this was no time to split hairs. 'Tammy, listen . . .'

'So, are they going to lock *me* up too? I mean, my understanding is that it's not even a crime to be on the game these days. All I'm trying to do is make a living . . .'

'For God's sake, shut up and listen! This is a lot more serious than you and Digby getting banged up for lowering the tone of the neighbourhood. *A lot more.*'

There was another long silence, this time broken by heavy, nervous breathing.

'Seeing as you haven't got the guts to tell me face to face,' Tammy eventually said, 'I suppose you'd better tell me now.'

'Tammy –' Lucy drained her glass '– it was *you* who put me into SugaBabes, remember? *You* were the one who got me the job there?'

'Oh . . . oh my God!' Tammy whispered, as the meaning of this finally dawned on her.

'They've sussed me,' Lucy added. 'And I can't go back.'

'*Oh, Jesus wept!* You telling me Suzy McIvar knows? You've got to call them! You've got to call and tell them I didn't know what I was doing!'

'You think they'll listen?'

'Oh, Jesus. And they're protected by the Crew.' Tammy sounded tearful. 'That means the heavy mob know about me as well! They'll all think I'm in on it!'

'That's why you've got to disappear.'

'Just going home won't be enough. There're people who know where I live . . .'

'Is there anywhere else you can go?'

'What does it matter to you, you bitch? You've slaughtered me, you've ruined my life!'

Lucy would have liked to reassure her at this point, to advise her that it would only be temporary, that pretty soon all the bad guys would be inside, but that would be yet another bare-faced lie. 'Where exactly are you?' she asked.

'I'm not telling *you*, am I? Talk about a fucking security risk.'

'Just disappear, Tammy. I doubt they'll waste too much time looking for you.'

'How am I going to live, eh? What's Digby going to say when I stop earning for him?'

Lucy shook her head. It was truly amazing, given every other problem facing Tammy at this moment and in general, that what Digby thought could ever be a priority. How the girl had ever become so enthralled to that cowboy-booted loser was beyond understanding. But there was no constructive advice she could seriously offer. Lucy had known so many prostitutes attempt to make it on the straight and narrow – sometimes because they'd had a kid, or because they'd had a health scare, or perhaps because it had always been their long-term plan. And yet almost none of them had ever succeeded. There was too much against them and too little in their favour.

'The best thing is to relocate,' she said bluntly.

'Relocate!' Tammy retorted. 'To where? I've never lived outside Manchester.' Now it sounded as if real tears were flowing. 'You vicious, venomous cow . . .'

'Tammy, it wasn't intentional.'

'No, it never is with you coppers. You don't set out to stitch us up, you just use us and discard us, don't you? And whatever happens to us after that, tough shit, that's our fucking problem.'

'All I can do is give you this heads-up.'

'Thanks for nothing.'

'You're going to do it, though? You're getting off the street?'

'I don't have a clue where I'm going to go. But I'll tell you this, Hayley – or whatever your fucking name is – you'd better hope I don't find you there.'

And she hung up.

There was clearly no point calling her back this time, so Lucy finished her drink and, again resisting the urge to order another, exited the bar through the rear to where her bike

241

sat alone on the pub car park. This whole thing was a nightmare that she still couldn't believe. Beforehand, while things hadn't exactly been under control, at least they'd been running smoothly. This part of the investigation had been moving towards an outcome, which, while it might not necessarily have netted them Jill the Ripper, would have been some kind of result, and then – *POW!* – the whole thing had blown up in their faces.

She slid her helmet on, kicked the Ducati to life and cruised back out onto the road.

The worst part of all this was that she didn't know how much her mother had confided in Frank McCracken. Cora knew very little in truth. But she'd divulged to him that Lucy was involved in Operation Clearway, which would almost certainly have set the mob boss's alarm bells ringing. It was impossible to imagine that he wouldn't have made SugaBabes his next port of call, and wouldn't immediately have asked some searching questions.

What kind of info was the undercover cop looking for? Who did she make friends with? Was there anyone on staff she showed particular interest in? And there was only one response to that last question, which they'd no doubt put to Delilah with maximum force.

It was Charlie. She'd been asking questions about Charlie.

What would happen after that, Lucy could only surmise. At the very least, Charlie would be warned that she was in the police crosshairs. She would surely disappear, drop out of sight. It wouldn't be hard for her. She was a mystery woman as it was.

Lucy's despondency grew as she headed across town. She finally banked onto the Brenner estate, and then onto Cuthbertson Court, drawing to a halt at the end of the drive attached to her bungalow. She took off her helmet, but remained astride her bike, head hanging. Once again, the awful predicament ate through her.

'Mum,' she muttered. 'What have you done?'

She'd have no choice but to go straight to the MIR in the morning and hold her hand up. And she couldn't leave anything out. To do that would be the biggest risk of all. Police officers who told lies to their own supervision were walking the highest tightrope imaginable. But seriously, it would hardly look good . . . that Lucy Clayburn, the eager beaver young copper who specialised in getting her own gaffers shot, also happened to have a really garrulous mum, who, bizarrely beyond belief, was a friend of the underworld!

Okay, you couldn't blame children for their parents. But why had Lucy said anything to her mum at all? That was the question Slater and Nehwal would want answering, no doubt while they fast-tracked the paperwork consigning her back to Division – if she was lucky.

She slumped over the handlebars. The first big job she'd been involved with since Michael Haygarth, and she'd bolloxed this one too.

Only after several minutes was she able to climb off the machine. For a moment, her legs were too whackery to stand on. She could only hope and pray that Jill the Ripper was someone else, that Charlie would turn out to be nothing more than a red herring, and that the enquiry would not be damaged in any significant way.

She took her helmet off, shook out her hair and turned to face the bungalow. Her home. Even though she viewed it more as an investment, as a long-term project; somewhere to do up as and when she could, while living much more comfortably with her mother. Though by the looks of things, that plan would now need revising, and pretty damn quickly.

It was a pleasant enough structure: small and detached; lace curtains in the windows; grass on the front lawn; a wrought iron side-gate, with fir trees hemming the paved path behind it. Typical suburbia. But indoors it was a horror show. There were no carpets down, there was minimal furnishing, the decorating was only half completed – and there was no phone or computer link, she realised with a groan. But if nothing else, at least there was a bed with a mattress on it, and a linen box containing some sheets. It would suffice. It would *have* to, as she was going nowhere near Saltbridge for the foreseeable.

The mobile bleeped in her pocket. When she checked, it was a text from her mother.

Call me. Please.

Lucy deleted the message and tucked the device back into her pocket. And then heard a noise, like a scuffling of feet – which drew her attention to the side-gate and the dimly visible passage beyond. The gate was still closed, but Lucy could have sworn the dark outline of a man had just ducked away down the side of the house.

A chill ran through her. Several times she'd wondered if leaving the bungalow unoccupied for so long might attract problems: vandals, burglars, addicts. She'd always then managed to dismiss this possibility, mainly because it was too discomforting to dwell on. But that didn't mean it wasn't something she could damn well deal with if she had to.

On the other hand, of course, it might token something much more serious.

Lucy stuck her helmet on the handlebars of the bike and hurried to the gate. The whole side-passage was visible through its bars, the evergreens on the left and gable wall of the bungalow on the right. She could even see the rectangular pall of street lighting where it opened into the back garden. No one was standing there. Nothing moved.

Only vaguely reassured, she opened the gate and walked warily down to the far end. She stopped at the corner and peeked around. Again, the small back-garden was typically suburban: a square lawn perhaps twenty yards by twenty; a flowerbed on the left, a rockery on the right; neatly hedged on both those sides, while at the back a wooden fence stood to about six feet. Beyond that lay a belt of trees. Lucy pivoted as she ventured forward, scanning all corners, but only after several seconds noticing a problem: a section of the wooden trim that formed the upper part of the rear fence had broken loose and was hanging free.

It could be anything. Kids might have done it weeks ago, for all she knew. But instinct advised that this had only happened recently – as in some time in the last minute. As if to confirm this, there was a scrabbling of undergrowth on the other side of the fence.

'Hey!' she shouted, dashing over there.

The scrabbling changed to a *thrashing*. It sounded frantic.

Lucy vaulted onto the top of the fence, though, with its frame weakened, it wobbled and cracked down the middle, throwing her forward, depositing her on hands and knees in damp tangles of bracken. She glanced up, squinting though the thickets. This wasn't an actual wood; it was ninety yards deep at most, ending at Halpin Road, the main thoroughfare between Crowley and Urmston. Her vision now attuned itself, and she spotted the intruder – a silhouetted shape cavorting around tree-trunks as he tried to distance himself from her.

Lucy jumped up and hurtled in pursuit. 'I'm a police officer . . . stay where you are!'

But before she could cover any ground, he danced out of sight.

'Shit!' she hissed, staggering in mulch and falling over a root, landing on her face again.

When she got up, there was still no sign of him, though she didn't think he could have made it as far as the road just yet, which meant he had to be somewhere close by. She advanced stealthily, listening but hearing nothing except the dull patter of dripping dew and a distant hum of night traffic.

And then a *CRACK*, as if a weight had impressed on a twig – behind her.

Lucy spun round – as a gigantic black shape loomed through the leafless branches from about ten yards away; an enormous, featureless figure, which, now that she'd seen it, made no secret of its presence, advancing towards her with hefty, crunching footfalls. Lucy fumbled with her phone as she backed away. The figure came steadily on, already less than eight yards off, now less than six, now five.

When she'd first seen the prowler, her police instincts to chase had kicked in. But this was quite clearly not the same guy, by the looks of it several inches taller and broader, and several stones heavier. Moreover, by the way he came on apace, he intended to break her into pieces with his bare hands.

Almost involuntarily, Lucy turned and fled towards the orange glow of the streetlights. With thudding impacts, the figure behind started running.

It was a short distance to Halpin Road, but the woodland floor was still slippery, still uneven. She fell again, plunging down through a mass of fungus and other forest rubble, but dragging herself up and staggering forward. Only for a second figure to step in front of her, this one smaller than the other but no less menacing: solidly built and wearing a hood.

Lucy changed course, careering through rhododendrons, twigs and other meshed leafage, finally fighting her way out onto the pavement – where a car was waiting by the kerb, its engine rumbling. She skidded to a halt, sweating, wreathed in smoky breath.

She glanced right. The figure that had blocked her way had also emerged onto the pavement and now walked slowly towards her, hands deep in his hoodie pockets. He was black, well-built but with a grizzled beard, pockmarked features and one eye pale and milky. Like herself, his rough clothing was covered with moss and bits of leaves.

Thunderous feet clomped stone as another person stepped onto the pavement, this time behind her. Lucy twisted round. As she'd half expected, it was Mick Shallicker.

He wore his customary black suit and black roll-neck sweater. Even though he too had been lying in wait, he was less bedraggled: streetlight reflected from his brightly polished brogues; there wasn't a speck of green stuff anywhere on his person. But his Neanderthal face was etched with a horrific grin, spade-like teeth splitting him ear to ear as he chomped on yet another ball of gum.

Lucy backed slowly away from him – she backed away from the pair of them, even though this took her to the pavement's edge and the waiting car.

'There's a good girl,' came a familiar voice from inside it. 'Hop in.'

She glanced over her shoulder.

The car was a sleek, black Bentley Continental saloon; off the top of her head, one hundred and fifty big ones to drive from the showroom. Its rear passenger door hung open.

'Come on, darling, we haven't got all night,' the voice added.

She glanced again at Shallicker and the other Crew operative. They were still encroaching, slowly – no longer overtly menacing, but making it clear with their body language that if she didn't comply they'd simply muscle her.

Lucy had no choice. She bent down and climbed in.

Chapter 23

'Hi, Lucy,' Charlie said from the driver's seat. She looked as beautiful as ever, kittenish but sensual: bright pink lippy, grey shadow to enhance her blue eyes, pale blonde hair flowing from under a brown leather cowboy hat, the statuesque torso accentuated by a tight silk blouse and black suede waistcoat.

Frank McCracken was in there too, smartly suited as ever, but with his collar unfastened and tie hanging loose. He was seated at the far end of the back seat, smiling pleasantly as he patted the empty space alongside him. Lucy tried not to sit quite that close, but Shallicker folded his colossal body in behind her, which had the effect of pushing her along until she was sandwiched between the two of them. Shallicker grinned again as he leaned over her, still chewing on his gum, which from this unpleasant proximity smelled of peppermint.

It was all Lucy could do not to shudder with revulsion, but she fought down the temptation in case it would be construed as fear – not that she wasn't genuinely frightened.

'You know Carlotta, I take it?' McCracken asked her.

'Carlotta?' Lucy said.

She looked at Charlie, who beamed again, brightly, as if they were two old friends rediscovering each other after years apart. It almost appeared genuine, Charlie, or Carlotta or whatever her real name was, seemingly thrilled that the police officer in their presence knew who she was – which was all the more unnerving because it was so bewildering.

'Charlie's my street name,' Carlotta said, twisting a platinum lock around her right forefinger. 'Like yours is Hayley. Nice name, that, Hayley.' She still sounded sincere. 'Wish I'd thought of it.'

The other heavy who'd accosted Lucy in the woods, the black guy with the beard and milky-white eye, now slid into the front passenger seat. He closed the door behind him and turned to face them, his one good eye riveted on Lucy.

'You know Mick, don't you?' McCracken said, nodding at Shallicker, who put a muscle-thick arm around the back of her shoulders, to squash her all the more. 'Meanwhile, the handsome devil in the front is Tyson. Not his real name, but that's what we call him . . . used to be a tasty light-heavyweight until he met someone better, as that manky right eye of his will attest. But he can still mix it when the mood's on him, can't you, lad?'

'Whenever and whoever you want, boss?' Tyson replied coolly. 'Just say the word.'

'No need for the rough stuff tonight, Tysie,' McCracken said. 'Babes, just drive around for a bit, eh?'

Carlotta shifted gears and hit the gas, and the Bentley pulled smoothly from the kerb.

It wasn't especially late at night, but it was midweek and there was little traffic. So they drove unhindered, taking turns at random but noticeably sticking to the main roads. It was several minutes before McCracken spoke again.

249

'So . . . *Detective* Lucy Clayburn. How honoured am I?'

'Not as much as you may think, Mr McCracken,' she said. 'I'm a plain old constable.'

He almost looked affronted. 'They sent a woodentop to keep an eye on *me*?'

'Needs must, I'm afraid. We're short-handed.'

He chuckled. 'So are we. Good people are hard to find these days.'

'You need to know something, Mr McCracken.' Lucy tried to speak boldly, but was doing her level best to stop her voice from shaking. 'Even if I walk away from this in one piece, abducting a police officer is likely to get you twenty years in prison.'

'Aww!' Carlotta glanced at her through the rear-view mirror. 'She thinks she's in danger.'

Lucy glowered in response, to which the blonde beauty winked.

'We're not abducting anyone,' McCracken said airily. 'You got into this car of your own free will, and I've got three witnesses here who'll say exactly that.'

'You turned up at my house late at night, uninvited, a whole bunch of you,' Lucy replied. 'That's threatening enough. And you could only have found your way there by following me from my mother's . . .'

'We did tail you, I must admit,' McCracken said. 'But relax, constable . . . seriously. Like I say, all we're doing is going for a drive.' He regarded her with interest. For all this debonair charm, his stare was coldly penetrating. 'You think if I was going to kill you, I'd come to get you in my own motor? First off, I'm actually quite impressed that you managed to get into SugaBabes. Impressed with *you*, that is. I'm not so impressed with Jayne and Suzy McIvar, but that's between me and them.'

He glanced away again, as if seeking his next words carefully. Lucy looked through the windows. She supposed it was vaguely comforting that they were still in Crowley, apparently content to keep navigating its complex system of highways and byways.

'Up until now, we've kind of coexisted with you Manchester coppers, haven't we?' McCracken said. It wasn't posed as a question so much as a casual observation.

'Not through any desire on our part,' Lucy replied.

'That's what you think. Oh, you take bits of our operation down whenever you can. That's what the law does. Inconsequential stuff usually and it's up and running again the next day somewhere else, so it doesn't make much difference. But it looks good in the papers. Everyone's happy. But the one thing we can't have, Constable Clayburn, is . . . well, *this*.'

Shallicker's monstrous arm tightened around her shoulders. He leaned on her all the harder. The reek of his peppermint breath was almost overwhelming.

'I like you,' McCracken said. 'I honestly do. You can't be no scaredy-cat doing what you did. But it's a liberty too, and people don't take liberties with us. And yet that isn't the worst of it, is it?' He glanced round at her again. 'I mean, you were actually trying to fit us up.'

'We don't fit people up, Mr McCracken . . .'

'Well, *you* may not, *Constable* Clayburn . . . when you're pounding the beat, when you're swapping stories about those good old days you don't even remember with some nice old dear, and all for a cup of lukewarm tea in a sheltered accommodation at the back end of nowhere.'

'There are bigger fish in your pond, are there?' she said. 'Fine, good. So why talk to *me*?'

'I'll tell you why, Constable Clayburn. Because I'm in a good mood. And because I want it to end *here*. Yeah, that's right.' McCracken nodded. 'I want this whole thing to go

251

away tonight, and I reckon you're just the person to sort that out for me.'

'It's already gone away,' she replied.

'Has it?'

'I can hardly go back to SugaBabes now, can I?'

'You certainly wouldn't be advised to. You wouldn't be advised to go anywhere near Cheetham Hill, knowing Suzy McIvar. But what are we really talking about here, Constable Clayburn? I mean, let's not mince our words. It's Carlotta, isn't it . . . that bit of hot stuff there in the driving seat? My girlfriend.'

'Hah!' Carlotta hooted. 'You wish.'

McCracken sighed. 'She winds me up so much she might as well be my wife. But let's not go there for the time-being, eh?'

'Definitely not,' Carlotta agreed.

'You reckon she's Jill the Ripper, don't you?' McCracken said.

'Do I?' Lucy remained resolutely noncommittal.

'I can't think of any other reason why Operation Clearway would be so interested in her. But what's intrigued me is how you came to develop that interest? I mean, Carlotta here's the Lady Gaga of hookers. She's sexy, she's mysterious, she's aloof. She's totally dominant. No one pushes her around.'

Carlotta nodded approvingly to hear herself so described.

'Look at her,' McCracken said, awed. 'How together she is. How relaxed. You really think she has a side-line where she gets her jollies butchering lorry drivers?'

'I don't think anything on the matter,' Lucy said.

'Well . . . I reckon I'd know about it if she did, but I don't expect you to take *my* word for that.' McCracken addressed Carlotta. 'What do *you* think the reason is, love? I mean, *you're* the one looking at life in prison if we let the constable walk. Surely you have an opinion?'

'I reckon they don't like strong women, Frank,' Carlotta replied. 'We have to be shrinking violets, you see. If not that, we can only be deranged killers.'

Lucy knew she was being baited here, that this was a ruse to lull her into revealing sensitive information. And despite that, it almost worked. It was so tempting to shout that this was bunkum; that they'd been led to Carlotta through evidence – circumstantial, but evidence all the same. Of course, it might be that Lucy's life would depend on her giving them something at some point, but until then she was determined to resist.

'Nah. Can't be that.' McCracken shook his head. 'I mean look at Constable Clayburn here. *She's* a strong woman . . . and they gave her a job.'

'Yeah, but I think Constable Clayburn probably knows when to keep her opinions to herself.' Carlotta again locked gazes with Lucy through the mirror. 'That's not me, and never has been. Back in the day, Lucy, when I was anyone's, I had a right temper. I'd say things I didn't mean . . . about cutting fellas up if they pissed me off. About fucking 'em and murdering 'em because they were no longer any use to me . . . just like they do with us. About cutting their dicks and balls off and decorating my hallway with them.'

Lucy tried not to react. This was still the part no one outside the taskforce knew anything about; the severing of the victims' genitals.

'This what Jill the Ripper's doing, Constable Clayburn?' McCracken asked with fascination. 'I can tell by the look on your mush that we're getting close. Imagine that, eh? Collecting John Thomases. Bit naughty, or what? That'll be the bit you withhold from the public, yeah? So you can suss out all the fruit-loops who troop into your nick every day with delusions of grandeur? Well, don't worry . . . you don't have to confirm or deny. We're only making an educated

253

guess based on unwise things the babe may have said in the past. And we won't say anything either way. We don't want to hinder your investigation. In fact, this is what tonight's ride-along is all about, Constable Clayburn. Believe it or not, we want to help you . . . by dismissing certain suspects from your enquiries. Again, I don't expect you to take my word for that. So . . .' He nodded at Shallicker. 'Would you do the honours, Mick?'

Shallicker reached into his jacket and handed over a wad of colour photographs. McCracken flipped through them before selecting one.

'Check this out, Constable Clayburn.' He showed it to Lucy; it depicted himself in evening dress, complete with tuxedo and bowtie, and Carlotta in another glamorous evening-gown, her tresses done up Madame Pompadour style, as they stood one to either side of a short, stocky but handsome man with a rich brown beard and shoulder-length hair. Above them hung the glittering canopy of a tall, theatrical building.

'Now,' McCracken said, 'what's that place?'

'*The Opera House*,' Lucy answered. 'Quay Street.'

'That's right. And who's that, do you think, between me and the babe?'

'Alfie Boe.'

'Correct again. Another cracking Lancashire lad. Now, you are aware that Alfie did a one-off charity concert for the RAF at *The Opera House* a few weeks back?'

'I think I heard about that,' Lucy said, already suspecting where this was leading.

'Guess what night it was?'

'I'm sure you're about to tell me.'

'October 6th ring a bell?'

'Yes,' Lucy said.

'Go on,' McCracken urged her. 'Don't keep us in suspense.'

'That was the night Ronnie Ford was murdered.'

'That's right.' McCracken laughed. 'That was the night Jill the Ripper sliced up that Warrington lad. And fucking shit, there's Carlotta with me and Alfie Boe at *The Opera House* on the same evening. He didn't know who we were, of course . . . but it was a charity do, and everyone was chucking into the pot for the honour of a pic. Anyway, the point is . . . it couldn't have been Carlotta, could it? You see that show ran from half-seven until just after ten, but we all had to get there for six for the photo-call. You can check those times if you want, but I'm sure there's no need. When did your man die again?'

'Between seven and nine.'

McCracken smiled. 'How cool is photographic evidence?' He pushed the photo into her hand. 'Especially when it's yours to keep. Now, what else have we got down here? Oh, how about this?'

He flashed several more glossies. Variously, they depicted McCracken and Carlotta on loungers alongside a swimming pool, posing during dinner on a balcony overlooking a magnificent seascape, at the far horizon of which the sun melted in a crimson haze, and then standing at the prow of a yacht as it progressed across rippling blue waves towards a soaring, boulder-strewn shoreline.

'That's Santorini,' McCracken said. 'Fab place. You ever been?'

'No,' Lucy said.

'That's me and Carlotta again . . . having lunch in the hotel restaurant. Look at that view. That's us on the volcano trip. That's us by the pool. Amazing place . . . you ought to visit. If you want to check the bookings, we went there last September. You know where I'm going with this, don't you?'

'Yes,' she said. 'Graham Cummins.'

'That's right,' McCracken chuckled again; it was fast becoming his phrase of choice. 'He was killed over in Southport, wasn't he, on September 17th? Smack in the middle of our trip to Santorini. Which kind of means Carlotta couldn't have done that one either.' He pushed these other photographs into Lucy's grasp. 'And if that's not enough, try using the old noggin. Seriously, Constable Clayburn . . . why would I be lying if my favourite lady of the night was doing this nasty thing? Why would I cover for her? I want you to catch Jill the Ripper. I'm sure you've been hearing this disgustingly materialistic phrase till you want to puke, but she's *really, really bad for business*. Oh . . .' He glanced from the window. 'Looks like we're home.'

Lucy looked around too. She hadn't noticed, but they'd entered Cuthbertson Court, and in fact were pulling up at the foot of her drive, alongside her Ducati.

McCracken sat back. 'Now . . . wasn't that a useful exercise?'

'Can I get out?' Lucy asked.

'Course you can. Mick . . .?'

Shallicker opened the door and clambered out, standing back to make room. Before Lucy could climb out after him, Carlotta turned and put a hand on her arm.

'You got off lightly, babe,' the blonde said, this time only half smiling. 'Think about that.'

'Well *you* haven't got off at all,' Lucy replied. 'You want to know why, Lotta? Because you keep some very poor company, and one of these days that's going to bite you right in your shapely rear-end.'

Carlotta's smile faded completely but she said nothing else.

Lucy levered herself out and stood on the pavement, watching as the Bentley swung quietly away. She was out of her depth in so many ways on this case. But the whole thing overall had deflated her. It was true what she'd said about Carlotta not having got away with anything – but in reality that was because she hadn't done anything.

Quite patently, Carlotta was not Jill the Ripper.

Chapter 24

'So let me get this straight,' Priya Nehwal said, studying the photographs with disbelief. 'Frank McCracken turned up at your house and offered you a ride in his Bentley?'

Lucy knuckled at her brow, but the ache behind it didn't ease. DI Slater's office, which was poky at the best of times, seemed even smaller and stuffier with the three of them crammed inside it. On top of that, she felt scummy and tired, and was still wearing the paint-caked stakeout clothes that she'd been stuck in yesterday, having had nothing else to change into.

'PC Clayburn, I asked you a question,' Nehwal said.

'Yes, ma'am . . . that's about the strength of it.'

'And you went?'

'Well . . .' Lucy smiled to herself, 'yeah.'

Slater looked stunned. 'He didn't coerce you in any way?'

'He didn't need to,' Lucy said. 'I volunteered. He'd obviously recognised me at SugaBabes, so I thought I'd salvage anything from the job I could before we called a halt to it.'

'So he didn't actually put a hand on you?'

'Not as such.'

'What about that big lunatic he always has in tow?' Nehwal asked.

'Mick Shallicker,' Slater said.

'Shallicker, yeah,' Lucy grunted. 'He didn't touch me either. I won't say he didn't put the wind up me though.'

'That's what he's there for,' Slater commented.

'So they took you for a ride and told you they know everything?' Nehwal still sounded as if she didn't totally believe it.

'Not quite everything, ma'am,' Lucy replied.

Even now she was holding certain things back. She'd studiously avoided mentioning her mother's role in the affair. Previously, that had looked like it would be impossible but McCracken's intervention had changed everything. She could now claim the surveillance at the club had been compromised simply because the gangster had personally revealed to her that he knew about it. There was no need to add anything else. In one way it was a get-out-of-jail card, but it was still discomforting. Not only did she feel guilty about betraying her gaffers, but the truth still might leak out at some point in the future.

'I didn't confirm that Carlotta was our chief suspect,' Lucy said. 'McCracken's only guessing that she is.'

Nehwal still looked unimpressed. 'I just don't see how he got from sussing an undercover cop in the McIvars' brothel to assuming that his girlfriend is a murder suspect. For all McCracken knew, you could have been there working Vice.'

Lucy shrugged offhandedly. Even in Nehwal's fearsome presence, it was difficult not to show how stressed and irritable she felt. She'd barely slept the previous night, of course – which didn't help, and hadn't even been able to wash properly as there was no hot water in the bungalow.

'I can only assume, ma'am, that as soon as he sensed I was a cop, he asked around at the club and Delilah – she's the girl I worked with – revealed that I'd shown some degree of interest in Carlotta. It may also be, if he felt there was a threat to him, that he had his boys sweep the neighbourhood surrounding his house and they detected the observation point.'

'They're nothing if not efficient,' Slater said.

'Which is more than can be said for our surveillance team,' Nehwal retorted.

'Come on, ma'am.' Now Slater himself looked peeved. 'These guys live in a permanent state of paranoia. They plan a blag, and if there're more cars than usual parked outside the local nick on the day in question they'll cancel it.'

'Either way, it means the Didsbury obbo's gone west,' Nehwal said, 'as well as the obbo at SugaBabes.'

'No point in it now, anyway,' Slater replied. 'I mean, whether this lass Carlotta's guilty or not, she'll go to ground like a frightened rabbit.'

'She didn't seem *that* frightened,' Lucy remarked.

Nehwal waved the photographs. 'And this is the proof McCracken offered of her innocence?'

Lucy nodded. 'I haven't had much chance to assess it, ma'am, but I suspect the dates will check out.'

'Could these pics have been mocked up?' Nehwal wondered.

'Anything's possible these days,' Slater said. 'But why go to that trouble? We can check bookings with the theatre, the hotel, the airline, the holiday company. Knowing McCracken, it'll all be watertight.'

'So . . . where does that leave us, apart from Nowhereville?' Nehwal switched her attention back to Lucy. 'Especially *you*, PC Clayburn. You can't go back to SugaBabes and you can't go back on the streets. I doubt it's safe for any of the girls to go back on the streets now.'

Lucy had to concur. 'I'm not sure how much McCracken's firm will have guessed about the Intel Unit, ma'am . . . but they'll almost certainly assume there are others out there like me.'

'Especially if this kid, Tammy, tells them, eh?'

'All Tammy can tell them, assuming they ask her, is that she first met me at the lorry park. She doesn't know any more than that.'

'Where's Tammy now?' Slater asked.

'In hiding, I hope.'

'You tipped her off?' By her tone, Nehwal disapproved.

'Of course I tipped her off.' Lucy struggled to keep the heat out of her voice. 'Ma'am, I *had* to. I mean we could put her into protection, but what could she give us in return? And how long could we keep her for? I mean, this is the Crew, who've supposedly got longer memories than the Foreign Legion . . .' She left the point hanging.

There was a brief silence as the three of them pondered the impasse.

'Well . . . thanks for your input, PC Clayburn.' Nehwal stood up.

She flipped through the photos again, at some length, before laying them on Slater's desk.

And that's it? Lucy thought. *That's all the reward I get . . . before you bin me back to Division?* But of course she bit her tongue. She had no right to imagine she occupied the moral high ground here. She was deceiving her own bosses; not being straight with the people who were supposed to be on her side. Plus it was her own wretched mother who'd blown the gaff.

But it still seemed unfair – that it should end like this. Not that Lucy didn't have one or two items left in her armoury.

'Ma'am, there's something else,' she said. 'Something we could look into.'

Nehwal, who'd been about to leave, glanced back.

'Its unofficial title is the SugaBabes Taxi Service.'

Nehwal gazed blankly at Slater, then back at Lucy. 'Sorry, what're you talking about?'

'The normal form when punters turn up at SugaBabes is they have a drink and then they pair off with a girl or two, and eventually head upstairs. They settle their "bar-bill", as they call it, before they go home. But one or two of them every night, they just sit at the bar and, half an hour later, this no-mark middle-manager called Marissa calls their names out. "Taxi's here!" . . . and off they toddle. Only it's not a real taxi. I looked through a gap in the back wall once, and it's something like a limo.'

Nehwal shrugged. 'Makes sense. A comfy ride home. They pay enough to be there.'

'No, ma'am. They're given a blindfold to wear before they get into it. On top of that, Tammy warned me about this thing beforehand . . . not in any detail, but she said it was a more-than-touchy subject. Sounds like it's bad news even to ask questions about it.'

'A blindfold?' Nehwal queried.

'Yeah. But it's worn voluntarily. It's like they're being taken somewhere they want to go, but part of the deal is they're not supposed to know how to get there.'

'And what do *you* think it is?' Slater asked Lucy.

'I don't know, boss. And something tells me I should. Or at least that *we* should.'

'You think some of the customers are looking for something a little different?' he said.

Lucy nodded. 'What else?'

'Well, it's certainly interesting,' Nehwal said thoughtfully. 'But I don't see how it's relevant to our case.'

'I'm not saying it is, ma'am,' Lucy replied. 'But if anyone ever fancies getting into the guts of the Crew . . . that might be a way.'

'Getting into the guts of the Crew, eh?' Nehwal smirked. 'That's one of those difficult areas, I'm afraid. For various reasons we don't need to go into.'

Lucy understood what she meant. It wasn't always practical for police forces to confront organised crime head-on. Some syndicates, like the Crew, were legally elusive – it cost a lot to take them down, and then someone else, maybe someone worse, would only fill the void. In certain cases, it might even be desirable to keep them. They could have imposed a stranglehold on the local underworld that was beneficial to wider society rather than damaging. This definitely applied to the Crew, whose controlling presence had hugely reduced the gangland wars that had once devastated the north-west of England. Other crime groups might even cooperate with law enforcement at various levels, mainly to wipe out their competition but also to keep the police sweet – establishing a mutually advantageous relationship.

But even if several of these criteria applied to the Crew, Lucy suspected there'd be someone somewhere in Britain's legal establishment who was keen to put the knuckle on this remarkably powerful cartel, and in any case, she was damn sure there were some rackets so unsavoury that no civilised society would tolerate them.

Almost as though she'd mind-read Lucy, Nehwal added: 'However, I agree this is something we may want to look into. Not us personally . . . we have a murderer to catch. But there are others. Geoff, can you pass PC Clayburn's intel on to someone who can process it and maybe take action accordingly, please?'

'Course, ma'am.'

Nehwal left the room, and Slater slumped back into his chair. He threw Lucy a raised eyebrow. 'So . . . how do you think McCracken clocked you?'

She shook her head, guilt again gnawing at her insides. 'I thought with SugaBabes being in Cheetham Hill and me having spent my entire ten years in Crowley, that would be all the cover I needed. Seems I was wrong. Sorry about that, sir.'

'Can't be helped. Going to have to get the rest of the team in early today for a briefing.'

'So are we all going back to Division?' she wondered.

He made a helpless gesture. 'It's always good to have spare bodies. But I can't justify hanging onto you all when the Intel Unit's been closed.'

'We're definitely closing it?'

'Priya's going to discuss it with Cavill. Until then I won't have a clue. You look shot, by the way. Last night shook you up more than you're letting on, I'm guessing?'

Lucy half-smiled. 'If I say "no, I'm tough as nails and don't give a shit about idle threats from cheap gangsters" is that more likely to glue me to the enquiry?'

Slater smiled back. 'You know the way things stand. I agree, though. Going back to uniform now won't be much return for your efforts. But things being as they are . . .'

'Sir, you did say that you and DSU Nehwal might be able to get me back into CID.'

'I also said we had to catch the killer first. And that seems farther away now than ever, don't you agree?' She had no option but to nod and shrug. 'But as I say . . . this decision rests with their high and mightinesses. Until we hear something, you might as well get yourself a coffee, and get your statement sorted. I know you had a rough night so maybe have a shower too, try to relax a bit. Hopefully we'll know something by three o'clock. We'll set the briefing for then.'

It was actually four in the afternoon before the briefing commenced, because it took Slater that long to drag everyone in. It gave Lucy more time, at least. As the DI had suggested, she completed her paperwork, got showered and finally, thankfully, found the time to change into some clean scruffs – jeans and a hoodie top – which she kept in her locker for just such an occasion.

The briefing, when it finally went ahead, didn't go quite as Lucy had anticipated, though the outcome was still far from ideal. Slater, who took charge of it alone, didn't waste words on explanations, simply announcing that they'd been compromised, certain underworld figures having identified that female police officers were out on the streets, posing as prostitutes.

'Firstly, all you CID officers,' he said. 'As from tomorrow, you'll be re-attached to the main investigation team. Report for duty at eight. You ladies – you Ripper Chicks, as I know you've revelled in being called – we've reached the decision that it isn't going to be sensible to cut you all loose from the enquiry. Several of you, eight in fact, have developed genuine suspicions about certain street-girls you've become aware of, so it would be lunacy to send you home now. That said, none of you are going back out there in the guise of prostitutes. Instead, you eight will be redeployed as under-cover surveillance – in other words, you'll join the TSG lads in unmarked cars and the backs of camper vans and the like, and you'll watch your targets covertly, even following them when they drive off with their clients, on the off-chance you may need to intercept the killer while she's actually in the act.'

He read out a list of names, the eight women who were to be reassigned in this capacity. Inevitably, Lucy wasn't one of them.

'We're also going to take some volunteers to perform the same duty,' Slater added. 'Another eight preferably.'

Every girl in the room put her hand up. Slater studied them, his eyes finally coming to rest on Lucy. 'Put your hand down, PC Clayburn. I'll talk to you in my office afterwards.'

Lucy lowered her arm. It was from the remainder that Slater selected his eight.

'You ladies who are staying with us,' he concluded, 'go

with DS Clark. She'll give you the nuts and bolts of your new assignments, but duty calls . . . so shake your backsides.'

With no need now to change from their casuals to their tarty street-gear, the new surveillance team trooped eagerly out, the girls chattering brightly, relieved they were no longer on the streets but glad they were still part of the enquiry.

Slater turned to the others. 'The rest of you . . . clear your desks and whatnot, and DS Bryant will sign you off. As from tomorrow morning, you're back on Division. But in the meantime, if, say in twenty minutes, you'd all like to reconvene at the Aspinall Arms, we'll have a goodbye drink together . . . and I'm buying.'

The girls complied, heading out. Only Lucy remained in her seat. She was still there when the rest had gone. Slater beckoned to her as he headed into his office. She sloped in after him and stood stiffly as he sat at his desk.

'I'd have done anything to keep you on board, Lucy,' he said. 'Firstly, because I think you've been a more-than-competent plain-clothes officer. In fact you were thrown in at the deep end, and you've been exceptional. Secondly, because I know how keen you are. You've put in some seriously long hours without any complaint. But the situation is that you're too exposed. What happened with McCracken means that the Crew are *very* aware of you. We can't possibly send you out in a similar capacity to last time.' He gave her an apologetic smile. 'I'm really sorry it's ended this way, but looking on the bright side . . . you've got a stack of overtime out of it. You'll probably be able to go on holiday or something, won't you?'

Lucy made no response.

'And at the very least,' he said, 'I'm hoping you'll pop round to the pub so I can buy you a drink.'

'A drink?' she replied slowly.

'Yeah, you know . . . join the other girls.'

'Seriously, sir? I was in that brothel fifteen days without any kind of cover. I was strip-searched twice a day, cavity-searched a couple of times. It was threatened I'd get my nose blowtorched off, constantly hinted to me I was about to get *tried-out*. And then I went and had my bloody home invaded! And in return I get one drink?'

'Look, Lucy . . . it's all about risk assessment.'

'If I'm sat in an unmarked van, I'm not going to be any more at risk than the others.'

Slater shrugged. 'Who are you going to watch, Lucy? You had one suspect, and even if she *is* our girl – which she obviously isn't – she's not going to strike again now, knowing we're sitting on her.'

Lucy shook her head. Suddenly, it was a struggle to keep the tears in, which infuriated her as much as it shocked her – she couldn't remember the last time she'd actually cried. Maybe it had *never* happened during her adult years. Until now.

'Sir . . . I can't believe you're doing this to me.'

'You're going back to do your job. You're a police officer, Lucy . . . no more, no less.'

'And a fuck-up, yeah?'

'What?'

She opened his office door. 'I finished Mandy Doyle's career and now I've screwed up this job too! Is that what you're bloody saying?'

'You conceited little . . .' Slater jumped to his feet. 'Shut that damn door and sit down!'

Grudgingly, Lucy obeyed.

'What makes you think this is all about you?' he demanded, lowering his voice.

She *so* wanted to tell him at that moment. About her mother's involvement. About how, having learned the things she'd learned, her role in this enquiry could never be less

267

than personal. About how she *had* to participate for the sake of her own sanity, *had* to prove that she was on the right side. Of course, even if she *did* tell him, it wouldn't work in her favour. Then he'd have no choice but to show her the door.

'I just want to get into these people,' she said, rather lamely.

'Who?' he asked.

'The Crew.'

'Why?' He wasn't scoffing; it was a genuine question. 'Because they gave you a scare last night? Join the club. They scare me too. But in truth, they've done us a favour. We had a good suspect. But thanks to Frank McCracken – and I never thought I'd see the day when I was saying that – she's now been dismissed from the enquiry. Now we concentrate on real possibilities. And anyway . . .' He sat down again, heavily, tiredly, 'what's wrong with going back to uniform? You're bloody good at it!'

'Mickey Mouse stuff,' she retorted.

'Mickey Mouse! Last month you locked someone up for robbery and kidnapping. You want to know the last time I felt a collar that good?'

'I got lucky, that's all.'

'We all need a bit of luck. Besides, even if you spent every day showing kids across the road, uniform's still the most vital part of the job, and you know it.'

Lucy knuckled the tears from her cheeks. Fleetingly, she was helpless. How could she articulate without sounding egocentric that what this was really about was proving herself at a higher level, was making up for what had happened last time – to herself if no one else?

'I'm sorry, sir,' she muttered. 'I'm just disappointed.'

'I get that. You reporting back to Division tomorrow?'

'Suppose so. My relief's on lates.'

'Well, *you're* not.' He scribbled something on a piece of paper. 'Today's Thursday. Go back on Monday. Until then, I'm writing you off sick.'

Lucy felt a new sense of panic. 'Why?'

'Because you're stressed, and after what happened last night it's hardly surprising.'

'No disrespect, sir, but that's even worse.'

He glanced up, puzzled.

'That'll make it look like I'm wussing out! You know what they'll say . . . typical bird, can't handle the pressure.'

'Give over,' he said. 'I know blokes who've been in this job twenty years who take every opportunity they can. I've seen 'em take a week because they've stubbed a toe.'

'Yeah, but they're blokes.'

As soon as she left the office, Lucy regretted that final comment – mainly because it was cheap and unbecoming, and irrelevant to the issue at hand, but also because she found Priya Nehwal sorting through paperwork in the briefing room, and as the connecting door was only flimsy, the DSU had most likely heard everything that had just occurred.

Without glancing round from the filing cabinet, Nehwal beckoned Lucy over.

Lucy approached nervously.

'Is this a common thing with you, PC Clayburn?' The DSU slid the drawer closed. 'Playing the gender card?'

'No, ma'am.'

'Until today, you mean?'

'I didn't mean it that way,' Lucy said. 'It's just that I don't want to look weak or incompetent. I'm neither of those things.'

'Then take it on the chin.' Nehwal regarded her carefully, watching her every move and reaction. 'If you think it's hard to get on as a policewoman now, you should have tried it when I joined the job . . . when every day I paraded for duty and the section sergeant announced to the entire relief: "This morning's big question is whether WPC Nehwal is wearing tights or stockings." When my tutor constable would offer to take care of my paperwork for me if I spent half of each night-shift in the station kitchen making him a slap-up curry.'

Lucy said nothing. She knew she'd had it relatively easy compared to previous generations of women who'd joined the police, but none of that was much consolation at present.

'Now look . . . you're in the job for the right reasons,' Nehwal said in an easier tone. 'You wouldn't have lasted ten tough years if you weren't. But don't spoil all that now with this self-pity routine.'

She handed Lucy a tissue. Lucy took it, shocked to realise that she was crying again.

'It isn't self-pity, ma'am. I just want to prove myself. I'm a copper. It's all I've ever wanted to be.' She sniffled. 'Shit . . . sorry, ma'am! This is all I bloody need.'

'You clearly *are* upset after last night,' Nehwal said. 'However it actually went down, it's had an effect on you. I've been in the job twenty years longer than you. I've seen every kind of PTS there is. You're not exactly shaking like a leaf. But that's because you've internalised it. And that's never good. So let it out now while there's no one else here. And don't beat yourself up so much. It's not like you haven't contributed to this enquiry.'

'All I managed to do was dismiss a suspect. Was it worth it?'

'Depends how you look at it. You also got to know some of the worst villains in Manchester. And now they've got to know you. For a copper that's not always a bad thing.'

Lucy wasn't completely sure whether she agreed, but she nodded anyway and after the DSU had left, went to her desk and locker and cleared them of the few bits and pieces they contained. The office phone then rang. Lucy had no option but to answer it.

'Incident Room, Intelligence Unit.'

'PC Clayburn, please,' came a muffled male voice.

'Speaking,' she replied. 'How can I help you?'

'Okay, erm . . .' The caller seemed surprised to have reached her so quickly. 'Erm . . . you don't know me, right?'

Lucy hit the record-and-trace switch, at the same time deducing what she could from his accent, which, though he was clearly holding a cloth over his mouth, told her that he was a native Mancunian. 'If you say so, sir.'

'I understand you're trying to find this Jill the Ripper?'

'That's right, sir.'

'Well . . . it's a bit embarrassing, this, but I think I can help.'

'Why's that embarrassing?'

'Because she tried to kill me too . . . but I managed to get away.'

Lucy straightened up. 'Who are you please?'

'I can't . . . can't tell you that.' The voice was suddenly hurried, panicky. But then it calmed a little. 'I'm not saying it over the phone. I'll meet you in private though.'

'Whoa, wait . . .' Lucy glanced round, but no one else had come into the room. 'Are you saying you know who the murderer is?'

'No. I can give you a good description though. And . . . I've got a photo.'

Lucy's spine tingled. 'A photo?'

'Snapped a shot of her on my phone, just before she attacked me. I don't think she realised. Otherwise I'm sure she'd have finished me off.'

'Were you injured, sir?'

'No. As I say, I got away.'

'When did this happen?'

'Look, I can give you all the details if you'll meet me. But I need you to come alone.'

Which suddenly sounded a little bit fishy.

'Why's that?' Lucy asked.

'I need assurances this'll be kept quiet.'

'Sir . . . we're not concerned about the morality or immorality of men who use prostitutes. All we're interested in . . .'

'You're not listening!' Abruptly, he'd turned aggressive. 'I want to make sure my name's kept out of it. I mean *totally* out of it . . . even if you catch her because of what I tell you.'

'That's okay. We use confidential informants all the time.'

'I don't even want to be classified as an informant. I want this meeting never to have happened. Okay?'

'I'm sure we can come an arrangement.'

He paused, breathing hard. 'Okay, here's the deal . . .'

'Before we discuss anything,' Lucy interrupted, not ready to let this unknown person make *all* the running. 'I've got one question for you . . . which you're going to *have* to answer.'

Another pause. More heavy breathing. 'Go on . . .?'

'Why've you called *me*?'

'What?'

'Why did you ask for me by name? Do we know each other?'

More silence. And then a thud and a click, and the line went dead.

'Shit!' she hissed. 'Damn it to sodding, bloody hell!'

When Des Barton finally dared to poke his head in, Lucy had pulled her combat jacket on and was now poring with biro in hand over a Greater Manchester A-Z.

'Hiya, chuck,' he said, approaching.

She glanced up. 'Des, just the man . . .'

'You alright?'

'What? Oh yeah, sure.' She flipped another page of the map-book, tracing across it with the nib of her pen.

'Thought you'd have gone round the corner for a couple of cold ones?' he said.

'Thought *you* would have.'

'Yeah . . . first chance I've had in yonks to get home in time for tea. That'd go down well.' He paused. 'Why I'm really here is to say sorry about what happened. I know you wanted to stay on.'

'It's nothing,' she replied.

'It is?' He looked puzzled, but shrugged. 'Fair enough. Anyway, there *is* some news . . . I chased the VRMs of all the red sports cars clocked at that roundabout near the scene of the Ronnie Ford murder, like I promised. Not too many of them. Five in total.'

Lucy glanced up again. 'Five? Over the whole period?'

'Yeah. I've had one of our researchers check 'em, and none of their owners have form.'

'Well . . . we tried.'

'However, in an effort to be thorough – because we only had that chippie bloke's word that it was a sports car – I've now had them extend the search a little wider. To *all* red cars.'

'Cool.' Preoccupied, she flipped another page.

'I thought you'd be pleased.'

'I am.'

'So . . . what're you doing now?'

She tapped her teeth with her pen, then slammed the book closed, shoved it into her jacket pocket and headed for the door. 'I'll tell you on the way.'

'Hang about!' Des didn't follow. 'On the way where?'

She glanced back. 'A lead's just come in, and I could really use a wing man.'

273

He folded his arms. 'I'll bet you could, but first . . . out of due consideration for the fact I'm just about to go off duty, you're going to tell me what it is, aren't you?'

Lucy glanced at her watch. It was six-thirty. Time was running out, but Des was right; if she wanted his cooperation the very least she could do was cooperate back. So she explained, telling him about the call she'd just received, how it had been directed to her personally, how the caller had claimed to have a photographic image of Jill the Ripper, and how she'd now traced his call to a public phone-box on St Clement's Avenue over on the east side of town.

Des rubbed his jaw. 'You're going to log it obviously? You're going to tell the boss?'

'I want to make sure it's kosher first.'

'Any idea who this guy is?'

'None. He wouldn't give a name. He's not even arranged to meet me. But I want to look the call-box over. See what's what before I cordon it off.'

'Most likely there'll be nothing.'

She shrugged. 'I can also check if there's a camera in the area that might've filmed him. Or ask around, see if someone was looking out of a bedroom window or something. I just need someone riding shotgun. Make sure I don't get jumped.'

'I don't know, Lucy. I promised Yvonne I'd be home on time tonight.'

'We'll be ten minutes tops.'

'Erm, we *won't* be ten minutes,' he stated. 'St. Clement's Avenue's the other side of the borough. And if we start asking around . . .'

'There won't be any of that,' she promised him. 'If there's anything that spikes my interest, I'll call it in straight away. But I don't want to go live on this yet in case it turns out to be nothing. Look Des, you've probably guessed from what Slater said that I'm the one who got rumbled. I'm already on the verge of looking a plonker . . . so I want to get this right.'

Though clearly torn with indecision, Des finally, reluctantly, nodded.

'Great,' she said. 'Look, I'll take my bike; you take your car. Then you can shoot straight off after if there's nothing in it. You won't even need to come back here.'

'This had better not turn out to be a ball-acher,' he said, following her from the room.

'As if I'd do that to you.'

Chapter 25

Lucy rode ahead of Des's juddery old Beetle, crossing the benighted centre of Crowley, which, with rush hour behind them, was rapidly emptying of traffic and pedestrians.

St Clement's Avenue was towards the eastern end of the borough, on one of its old industrial parks. They reached it by taking Adolphus Road, which dipped down under a couple of railway bridges and then passed through several hundred acres of derelict land. Once there'd been lines of terraced streets here and, no doubt, sometime in the future, car showrooms and warehouse DIY stores would spring up to replace them, but at present it was disused. Beyond it stood Penrose Mill, a square-shouldered Victorian colossus whose chimneys hadn't smoked in decades and whose parallel rows of oblong windows looked in on dust-filled emptiness.

Lucy circled around the Gothic structure via a series of cobbled side-streets, eventually swerving into St Clement's Avenue and proceeding along it at pace. The phone-box from which the call had been made sat in the glow of a single streetlight at the junction with Sawberry Lane, another identically bleak and underused thoroughfare.

Lucy parked up some twenty yards away, Des slowing to a halt behind her. She took her helmet off and walked warily forward. The box was empty, but already she could see a white envelope lying on top of the telephone. She glanced around before entering. The crossroads was hemmed in by tall fences of corrugated metal, but no one else was in sight.

There wasn't a sound, until Des slammed the door to his Beetle, the impact of which echoed across the decrepit neighbourhood.

Glaring back at him, to which he mouthed a bewildered 'What?', Lucy dug a pair of disposable gloves from her pocket and snapped them in place before entering the phone-box.

The envelope, which had been neatly sealed, was typewritten:

PC CLAYBURN

Holding it by its corner, she took it outside, where she opened it, going in from the bottom end rather than the top so as not to disturb any DNA-loaded saliva. She extricated a single typewritten sheet:

YOU WANT TO KNOW MORE
MEET ME AT 8
THE PLAYGROUND, MULBERRY CRES
COME ALONE
NOBODY ELSE OR WE DON'T TALK

'What do you think this is?' Lucy wondered, slipping the note into a sterile evidence sack.

'A bollocking,' Des replied. 'If you don't take it straight to the boss.'

'Yeah, but it's addressed to me.'

'And who are *you*? No disrespect, Lucy . . . but you're no

one.' He set off back to his car. 'That makes this a bit too weird.'

'Whoa . . . Des, we have to go over there now. We've got twenty minutes or this deal's off.'

He glanced back, clearly unhappy. 'At the very least we should call it in.'

'He said I have to go alone. The fact he's taking me across town means he's probably going to be watching me. If the whole taskforce turns up, we'll not see him for dust.'

'He's typewritten this note, chuck. You know what that means? This is pre-planned.'

'Yeah, I get that, but like I say . . . we do nothing and we lose it all. We've now got *less* than twenty minutes.'

Des dallied by his car. 'You seriously want to go over there?'

'What choice have we got?'

'But if I follow you . . . which someone has to, he might leg it then too.'

'Not if you stay back a little and try to keep out of sight.'

'You'd better not be glory-hunting here, Lucy.'

'Des, I didn't ask for this.'

'Look . . .' He tried to sound sympathetic. 'I don't know why you're not part of the team anymore. You say you're the one who got rumbled. But it was always likely to happen, you being an old hand – there was always more chance you'd get clocked than most of the other girls. But whatever it was, even if it was your fault, *this* is not going to make up for it.'

'Des . . .' Lucy held her ground. 'We need to check this lead before it fizzles out. So are you coming or not? We haven't got time for you to think about it, to go asking for permission, to hang fire till we get some back-up . . . we've got to act on it *now!*'

He glanced again at the plastic-wrapped note. 'You know

there'll probably be another one of these when we get there, sending you somewhere else. It's the oldest trick in the book.'

'All the more reason for us to play it canny.' She stowed the evidence in the inside pocket of her combat jacket, boarded her bike and hefted her helmet. 'So don't crowd me.'

'And I *really* wanted to get home for tea tonight.'

She pulled her helmet on and lifted its visor. 'Do you want to get your tea, or do you want to be the guy who turns in a photograph of Jill the Ripper?'

'Just get going!' Des opened his car. 'And don't hit the gas. I know I'm supposed to be hanging back, but in this donkey-wagon that won't be a problem at all.'

The second location was somewhat less intimidating than the first: a middle-class housing estate on the edge of Crowley Golf Course. Though it was only mid-evening, plunging temperatures and November damp was keeping the locals indoors. Light still showed through most downstairs windows, but only via drawn curtains. All was quiet.

Mulberry Crescent was in the very centre, and near enough identical to all the other roads on the estate, distinctive only for the fenced-off kiddies' sandpit and playground at the south end of it. Lucy and Des had agreed beforehand that he wouldn't actually follow her there, but would park in Dunwood Avenue, which stood adjacent, and sit with his headlights turned off but his engine running. As they were both officially off-duty and not equipped with radios, they'd agreed to maintain an open line to each other via their mobiles. Des had expressed dissatisfaction with the idea when he'd realised it meant she'd be out of his sight. That seemed to defeat the point of the whole exercise, but as Lucy argued, it was surely a mistake to risk calling this guy's bluff when they hadn't gleaned anything useful from him yet.

Subsequently, Lucy cruised down Mulberry Crescent alone. She constantly checked over her shoulder. No one was ever in sight, but there were countless parked cars, low walls and shadowy places concealed amid suburban shrubbery, where someone could hide while they watched her. And given the quirkiness of this whole situation it seemed highly likely that someone would be.

She drew to a halt at the kerb beside the gate to the playground. Beyond its waist-high mesh fence lay the sandpit, and beyond that a row of benches facing the swings. Though obscured by dimness, a lone figure looked to be seated on one of those benches.

Whoever it was, his back was towards Lucy, and he was hunched forward so that she couldn't determine any distinguishing features.

She dismounted, removed her helmet and tucked it under her arm, and quietly explained the situation to Des as she approached the playground gate. His tinny response, which she could barely hear because she couldn't risk taking the phone from her pocket, went something like: *'Take it slow and easy.'*

Lucy did so, opting to cross the sandpit rather than follow the flagged path around it, as that would hush her footsteps – though of course, on reflection it felt like a pointless safeguard. Whoever this guy was, he'd know that a motorbike had pulled up behind him.

Lucy halted when she reached the grass again. The slumped figure was ten yards in front.

'Hello?' she said. 'Can I ask what you're doing here?'

The figure didn't move, let alone reply.

Lucy advanced, warily. 'I should advise you I'm a police officer.'

Still no response.

'Careful chuck!' came Des's tinny voice.

280

'I'm actually *the* police officer,' Lucy said. 'The one you've been wanting to speak to.'

The figure was now only five yards away, yet in the absence of light he was still only vaguely discernible. She recalled that disguised voice on the phone. Was it possible . . . was it conceivable that he was actually a *she*?

Wild thoughts flashed through her mind: crime scene photos of mutilated male faces; healthy skulls hammered out of shape; hair matted with blood and bone fragments.

'I don't appreciate the way you've gone about this,' she said, every muscle tightening. 'But given that this is a serious issue I'm prepared to give you the benefit of the doubt . . .'

She was three yards short of him when a motion-sensitive arc-light at the top of a pole in the middle of the play-ground exploded to life. Lucy jumped, and spun halfway around.

Belatedly, she glanced back to the bench.

What she'd thought had been someone sitting there was nothing more than a bin-liner tied at the neck with twine and, by the looks of it, packed with rubbish.

'Shit!' she said under her breath.

'*What's happening?*' Des asked from her pocket.

'Nothing.' Inadvertently, she spoke aloud. 'Misidentification.'

'*Where are you, chuck?*'

She lowered her voice again. 'Where I'm supposed to be. On the playground.'

'*I'm coming round there.*'

'Negative, Des. Stand by . . . he may not be done with me yet.'

She pivoted three hundred and sixty degrees, but thanks to the safety light saw nobody else there. However, as she walked back towards the gate, her eyes fell on the pillar box across the road – and the white envelope lying on top of it.

She hurried over there.

As before, the front of the envelope was inscribed:

PC CLAYBURN

When she opened it, it contained a single sheet, printed:

8.30
EMPORIA SUBWAYS
COME ALONE OR NO DICE

Again, this gave her approximately twenty minutes to get back to the town centre. She could only imagine what Des's view would be, and she received it with both barrels when they next had a conflab, though as before they had to do this under a pretence of not knowing each other, Lucy sitting astride her bike alongside his open driver's window while they waited at a red light.

'So it's back across the borough again,' he said in a tone of deep dissatisfaction.

'He obviously wants to make certain I'm coming alone,' she replied.

'Lucy . . . he's a witness who doesn't want his name in the papers. This is a hell of a lot of trouble to go to for that.'

'Well, what do *you* think he's up to?'

'Either he's got a bit more in mind than giving you a statement. Or . . .'

'Or what?'

'Or it's someone ripping the piss.'

She almost glanced round. 'Why would someone do that?'

'You tell me . . . you're the one who's made enemies in CID in the past.'

She was stunned. 'You don't mean one of our lot?'

'Who else knows you're on the taskforce?'

'Someone would send me all the way round town to even a score for something that happened four years ago?' she said. 'Seriously?'

'More likely to have a laugh,' he replied.

'I thought Operation Clearway was strictly for grown-ups.'

'Tell that to the guy who christened you "the Ripper Chicks". I know plenty fellas in this job who've never grown up, and so do you.'

'So what do you propose?'

'Bag that letter along with the other one, take them both back and log them into evidence. If it is someone fucking about, let them shit themselves, wondering whether forensics'll turn up their dabs.'

'Can I make an alternative suggestion?'

He rolled his eyes. 'Go on.'

'That we proceed to the Subways, check out this one last lead, and if that's a load of cobblers too, we do exactly what you've just said. Des . . . suspicious though this is, we can't *not* try to see what's going on here? How would we sleep tonight?'

The light changed and they proceeded side-by-side to the next intersection, where another red brought them to a temporary halt. Lucy wasn't actually convinced that this was cover enough. If someone *was* watching, he'd see that she was interacting with the car next to her. But in all honesty, if this guy was for real and a genuine witness, it shouldn't really matter to him if more than one police officer showed up. Okay, he might be a nervous sort who'd gone to inordinate lengths to avoid a complex police entanglement, but ultimately he couldn't seriously have expected an officer to fly solo on this given the potential risks.

'How do you want to play this?' Des asked. 'There's a lot of subway space under the precinct and he didn't give you a specific spot . . . which is another thing I don't like about it.'

'Been thinking about that,' she said. 'I can leave my bike anywhere, but I'm gonna park at the south end, near the bus station, and walk through from that side.'

'And what about me?'

'Perhaps you can park on the taxi rank at the north end and walk through from that side? Meet me in the middle. That way, if he realises I'm not alone and legs it, you'll be in a good position to head him off. And if he attacks me . . . well, you'll be there in a minute or two, won't you?'

They drove on together through the intersection, Des still far from happy.

Chapter 26

Crowley shopping precinct had been improved significantly in modern times.

Formerly a concrete Stalinist monstrosity, which had appeared overnight circa 1970 like a carbuncle on the already grim industrial landscape, it had now been completely rebuilt and re-named 'the Crowley Emporia'. Whereas in its former incarnation the precinct had mainly occupied ground-level, with living space overhead – tiers of dismal grey flats rising above a labyrinth of bleak passages off which cubbyhole shops mostly sold cigarettes, booze, girlie mags or second-hand junk – it was now an art-deco retail palace boasting a variety of interconnecting floors and galleries, all airy and spacious and covered against the rain by stained, sound-proofed glass, and as such it was filled with traditional high street names.

No one could argue that in a depressed backwater of a town, which had suffered from its 'Manchester satellite' status rather than benefitted, the Crowley Emporia wasn't a rare success story. But beneath it, the old subway system remained, even if it was little more now than a shabby relic of a forgotten past.

When first built at the end of the 1960s, Crowley shopping precinct had covered about a square mile and a half of the town centre. Major roads encircled it on three sides, and so the local authority had seen fit to install a complex of underground car parks and walk-throughs, only accessible by steep stone staircases. In addition to this, permanently faulty wiring had ensured they were ill lit. The net-result, even back then when the subways were used regularly and by necessity, was lots of graffiti, lots of litter and lots of unsavoury characters loitering in the gloom. Especially at night.

In modern times, the pedestrianisation of most of the above-ground area, and the addition of surface-parking and unloading bays for the retailers, plus new clean toilets and cafeterias, meant that this lower section was completely defunct. Certainly that was Lucy's view. No one she knew used it any more unless they were up to no good. At least three times, she'd made juicy arrests down there: indecent assault, robbery, and possession with intent to supply. In truth, there was nowhere more ominous where this unknown letter-writer could have asked to meet her, but Lucy was increasingly determined that she wasn't walking away from this thing empty-handed.

She and Des split up when they were a couple of streets away, and so when she arrived at her destination, Crowley Central Bus Station, at 8.35pm, she wasn't quite sure whether she'd got there first or second. Not that it mattered. She halted her bike close to the entrance to the gents toilets, and lowered the kickstand. The bus station rolled away in a south-easterly direction, sliced into regimented rows by lines of lamp posts and steel-roofed shelters. One or two buses were idling at their terminals, the drivers behind their wheels reading evening papers. There was no sign of any passengers, but then it was now almost nine o'clock on a Thursday evening.

Lucy clasped her helmet under her arm as she walked west along a row of closed and grilled shopfronts, eventually coming to an entry-point, where a flight of wet stone steps dropped down a white-tiled stairwell. She shoved her hand into her pocket and cut the open line to Des. There was no point in it now. Once they were underground, all reception would cease.

Despite stepping lightly, her trainer-clad feet resounded as she descended, the only light above her already flickering on and off. At the bottom, some twenty feet down, she turned left. Here the white-tiled wall gave out and she was into the subways proper, a bare grey passage dwindling ahead of her, occasional patches of it blotted out where yet more lighting had failed. Lucy wrinkled her nostrils at the usual fetor of stale urine. She strained her ears for anything unusual, but heard only dripping water and the occasional muffled mumble of vehicles. When she started forward, she trod softly, glancing repeatedly over her shoulder to ensure that no one came down the stairway behind, but all she saw was the foot of that stairway gradually retreating into the twilight.

Des had been right: there'd been nothing specific in the last letter about where this guy expected to meet her, which didn't bode well. There was no focal point to the Emporia Subways. It was a windswept maze of barren concrete tunnels. It was also a succession of tight corners, behind any one of which an assailant could be waiting.

She glanced around the first. Another passage trailed off. Most of the lights down that way were broken, so it led eventually into complete darkness. Meanwhile, an opening on the right connected with a cavernous space that had once been used for parking. It was strewn with litter and autumn leaves, water dripping from the brick arches forming its ceiling. At its far side, a large, barred gate blocked the slip road leading down from above. Lucy wandered in there anyway. The corroded hulks of two abandoned vehicles occupied a far corner, but there was nothing else.

Frustrated, she moved back to the junction. There were several more openings ahead, but increasingly this whole thing felt like a wild goose chase. She wondered if she should shout out to Des – he couldn't be too far away – and then they could hook up and call it a night.

But some elusive sixth sense forbade this.

It was that old hunch thing again.

Perhaps Lucy's was better honed than she'd thought, because half a second later she spied a figure crossing the passage about sixty yards ahead. She halted, but already the figure had vanished from view. Due to another faltering light bulb she'd only caught a glimpse of it, and that was insufficient to show whether or not it possessed the dumpy, raincoat-clad physique of Des Barton.

Again, instinct prevented her calling out. But she hurried forward.

The figure had walked across the passage from right to left, and when Lucy got there, it looked to have headed down a short flight of steps, at the foot of which another barred gate stood ajar. Beyond this lay some kind of darkened basement area.

Lucy hesitated. What actually was *below* the Emporia Subways?

Though she'd been a cop in this town for ten years, she didn't know. Even during routine patrols of the Subways, Lucy had never descended to that level. Usually, it was closed off.

She sidled down the steps to the gate and peered through, though she wasn't able to see much. It would have been nice at this moment to have her baton or CS spray with her, but of course she was in plain clothes and off-duty. She didn't even have her handcuffs or torch. Despite this, she pushed at the gate. It was heavy and stiff, but it creaked sufficiently open for her to slide past it. She could just about discern a steel footway trailing away in front, steam rising through it. As her eyes attuned further, she saw pipes and valves on either side, and twists of leaky, foil-wrapped conduit snaking overhead.

She took her mobile out and activated the light, though it didn't bring a great deal extra into view. Training it ahead, she progressed forward, feet clanking on the grille.

The route ran straight for maybe fifty yards before ending at a T-junction. Lucy stopped, more palls of steam drifting past. Five yards to the right stood a closed door made of heavy, riveted steel, with no handle visible. On the left, the passage led past a row of massive, churning cisterns. She opted for that direction, still training the light in front. But every additional step now felt like folly. There was no good reason why this informant, if that's what he genuinely was, would be all the way down here. Despite these misgivings, she turned another corner.

More of the same faced her: conduit lining the ceiling, liquid gurgling through horizontal pipes. However, at least this next passage appeared to be doubling back towards the entrance. She followed it, occasionally getting caught in gusts of steam as they burst through meshed vents. However, a few yards further on, the path veered sharply to the right, terminating at a bank of wheels and dials. At which point, from somewhere in the dim recesses of this complex place, there was a short, thin squeal.

Lucy froze. It had not been a squeal that some human or animal might make, but metallic.

Try though she may, it was impossible not to picture a knifepoint creeping along metal.

Glancing behind her, she was confronted by a wall of steam so dense that it was more like moorland mist. Even her phone light failed to penetrate, turning it an iridescent white.

Another squeal sounded, this one closer – and accompanied by a loud *clatter*.

Still that terrible knife, but now a blunt instrument too.

Instinctively, Lucy felt again for her own weapons, which of course were hanging in her locker back at the station. Her ears strained for further sounds, only for the steam to actually envelope her, billowing up from below. Coughing and wafting, she lurched forward, trying to fight through it – and didn't notice the figure standing in her way until she collided with it.

'Hey!' she shouted, jumping back, assuming the combat position.

Just as quickly, the steam evaporated, to reveal Des rubbing his thigh and glaring at her reproachfully. 'You're all knees and bloody elbows,' he complained.

'God almighty, Des . . . you scared the crap out of me!'

'What're you doing down here?'

'I thought I saw . . . someone.' She glanced past him, but saw only more steam. 'I thought someone came down here. Was that you?'

'I came down here because I couldn't find you and the gate was open.'

That didn't rule Des out, she supposed, but whoever she'd seen had looked taller.

'You weren't kicking things around?' she asked. 'Weren't hammering pipes by any chance?'

He looked baffled. 'Not as I noticed.'

'Did you hear anything like that?'

'I heard something, not sure what. I assumed it was you.'

'The last one was like half a minute ago. Des . . . he's got to be down here now.'

'Unless *that* was what you heard.' Des pointed up past her shoulder.

Lucy turned, and now that her eyes were fully adjusted, gazed through another mass of dust-shrouded pipework to a high, mesh-fenced balcony, accessible by a switchback steel stair and on top of which what looked like an exterior door stood open.

'You mean he was making a quick exit?' she said.

'Yeah. He's had his fun, he's dragged us down here, and now he's gone home.'

Lucy's heart sank. Suddenly, it all seemed incredibly likely. The squealing she'd heard was the sound of unoiled hinges, the clattering the sound of the outer door being lugged open.

Irritated, she commenced walking.

Des limped in pursuit. 'So where we going now?'

'Out.'

'That's the first thing I've heard all evening that I like.'

They worked their way through the maze of pipes and conduit, at last locating the foot of the stairs and climbing to the top, where Lucy halted and looked down. From this height, it was impossible to make out any detail of the subfloor level they'd just wandered around.

'Someone's got nothing better to do, love, that's all,' Des said.

She shook her head, unsure what to think. They re-emerged into the outer world through a maintenance door that Lucy had previously only ever seen locked. It was located about fifty yards to the right of where she'd parked her bike.

'I feel like a right pillock,' she muttered.

Des shrugged. 'Ultimately, it wasn't too bad a call. You're right in that we didn't have much time to decide what to do, and it was a lead of sorts . . . there wasn't too much scope for doing anything different.'

'I dunno. We could have gone straight to the boss with it. That's what you'd have done.'

'And who's to say I'd be right? You think Jim Cavill would

have been happy with me if *he'd* been the one trekking all over town. It's a bag of shit, chuck. These things happen.'

But Des was bouncing from foot to foot as he uttered these words of comfort, and Lucy knew why. It was nine o'clock, and he *had* to get home.

'Okay,' she said. 'You shoot off. I'll book the evidence in.'

He nodded, looking relieved, but just as quickly frowned. 'I'd like to say "see you tomorrow", but I won't, will I?'

'You don't get rid of me that easily,' she replied. 'I'm back in uniform from Monday, and I'll still be working out of Robber's Row. We'll see each other plenty.'

He slapped her on the shoulder, before turning and heading for the nearest corner. Lucy climbed onto her bike, but before she put her helmet on, glanced again at the black doorway leading to the subterranean level.

Anyway you cut it, this didn't *feel* like a piss-take. She'd allowed herself to think that it was possibly because the whole thing was so elaborate. But for the very same reason she now had doubts. Hadn't it all been just a bit *too* intricate? Especially when the most you were going to get out of it was a couple of sniggers. Especially when seven people had been brutally slain and what this really amounted to was an obstruction of that investigation.

Despite Des's logic, it really didn't compute that this was just a silly game.

Des checked his watch as he walked quickly along the pavement.

There were no two ways about it; Yvonne would go spare – especially as on this occasion he hadn't even phoned ahead to warn her that he'd be late. It wasn't like he could blame her either; not after twenty-five years of this kind of thing. When he'd first told her he was joining the Intel Unit and would be working a solid four-till-four, she'd initially been pleased. Though it had meant that he wouldn't be around in the evening, which she wasn't overly keen on, it had also meant that he'd be in by the time she woke up in the morning and would be with her for most of each day. It also meant the hours would be regular. There'd be no unexpected over-time. Somewhat typically though, this acceptable arrangement hadn't lasted long, and they were already back in the realms of uncertain starts and even less certain finishes.

Des sighed and walked faster.

Yvonne had never really got used to him being a copper. They'd first begun dating at middle school. They were engaged when they were nineteen, and married by the time they were twenty-one. She'd then been stunned when, at the age of twenty-three, he'd announced that he was packing in his job as a trainee plumber and applying to join the police. It would be better money and better prospects, or that was how he'd tried to sell it to her, but it had still come as a hell of a shock. Because back in those days, kids from their part of Manchester, especially kids of mixed race, didn't join the cops; not in the numbers they joined now. But she'd stuck with him – of course she had – through all the thick and thin that had followed, for which he was supremely grateful as well as still being madly in love with her.

Even all these years later, Des came over warm and fuzzy when he thought about this: the girl of his dreams, the perfect wife and the ideal mum, who'd not only kept a beautiful home for him but had gone on to bear him six children. Lord knew, that was hard enough in this day and age, but when the father was nearly always at work it would chal-lenge anyone's relationship. It was less warm and fuzzifying to ponder that, he supposed – especially when he had so little to show for all this time on the job. He earned thirty-six grand a year, which wasn't too bad, but for a lifetime of unsocial hours it wasn't a great pay-off.

Something that Yvonne was less than delighted about, along with her fears for his safety, of course, which never went away.

The main problem here was that Yvonne was superstitious. She got that from her late grandma, who'd been born in St Kitts, and who'd reckoned that just being a policeman was asking for trouble because it challenged the forces of chaos. Those forces didn't forgive, Grandma had said, so being a copper would get steadily more dangerous the longer Des stayed in. Each new day, the evil stacked against him would increase, and the chance that something bad would happen grew ever greater. Now, in his third decade in the job, he thought, he must be walking very thin ice indeed.

That was when he saw the figure standing in the recessed doorway.

The west side of the Emporia was a relic of the old precinct, an immense monolithic structure, mostly bare concrete, with exceedingly narrow, castle-like windows. Apparently it was now in use by the local authority as the Tax Office. It had a single-glazed entrance door set at the back of a shadowy, rectangular cave, which no doubt would be the sort of place you'd find homeless people sleeping, though there was no one roughing it there now – just this single figure standing with back turned, staring in through the frosted glass.

Des slowed as he walked past, and then, reluctantly, stopped.

Even if he hadn't been on the lookout for someone who might have been leading Lucy a merry dance, as a police officer he couldn't just stroll away from this; not without making at least a basic enquiry. He glanced round, to check if he was alone. No one else was in sight. The only vehicle nearby was a blue Renault van parked on the other side of the main road. He glanced back to the dim shape in the recess.

'Hey mate . . . you alright?'

The figure didn't move.

Des made a rapid assessment of what he was facing here. Five foot eight, this guy, tops. Pretty solidly built. Wearing a black anorak over a hoodie, with the hood pulled up.

'Hey, pal?' Des ambled towards him. 'What are you up to? And don't give me attitude . . . I'm a copper.'

In a sudden, sharp movement, the figure drew its right hand from its jacket pocket, revealing a tight, leather-gloved fist, which even as Des watched, balled itself even tighter.

Des halted, and as he did he heard one of the doors to the Renault van on the other side of the road bang open. Feet clobbered the tarmac as they came rapidly across.

Oh . . . Yvonne, love, he thought. *I am so . . . so sorry.*

Chapter 27

Lucy contemplated the perplexing situation for several minutes before opting to take a final turn around the exterior of the Emporia, this time on her bike.

She kicked the Ducati to life and rode across the bus station, banking east onto Langley Street, passing the Post Office sorting centre and heading north-east along Pearlman Road, where the micro-pubs and fast food outlets were. She glanced into each alley and doorway as she passed, but saw no one. Finally, she emerged onto the pedestrianised section at Brunton Way. There still wasn't a soul in sight, but she decelerated and traversed it slowly. At the corner of Brunton and Brick Kiln Terrace stood the red-brick façade of Crowley Indoor Market. Here, she swung a left and headed west along Bakerfield Lane, where the taxi rank was located. She expected to find one or two individuals there, even if it was only cabbies standing chatting while awaiting customers. But this too was a dead zone. Thursday evening, she reminded herself. Crowley was yet another provincial town which these days relied on its nocturnal economy, though in truth it only came alive at weekends, when the town centre in particular swarmed dusk till dawn with drunken, brawling revellers.

But then, spotting something peculiar, she slowed to a halt.

Des's Volkswagen Beetle was parked at the back end of the taxi rank. The cabbies wouldn't have liked it, had there been any here to object, but he'd simply have flashed his warrant card. The curious thing was that the Beetle was still here.

Though stationary in the middle of the carriageway, Lucy remained astride her bike, staring at the parked car. He ought to have collected it and headed home by now. With a pang of unease, she throttled up to the next junction, where she swung left, cutting through a red light and speeding south down Kenyon Lane, in effect back towards the bus station. He would have come this way on foot, and she was hopeful that even now she'd see his short, rain-coated figure stumping happily along. But this was dashed almost immediately when she passed the entry to the Tax Office, and just in front of it spotted Des's body lying face down in the gutter.

Lucy braked so hard that she skidded along the kerb, but that didn't stop her jumping off the machine and throwing her helmet aside.

'Des! Des, it's Lucy!' She slid to her knees beside him, hurriedly checking for vital signs. To her relief, he groaned, but it was a horrifying shock to then note the multiple red trickles twisting away over the tarmac. 'Oh, Jesus . . .'

She probed around his neck and the base of his skull. A slow throb in his carotid revealed a regular pulse, but God knew how much damage had been done. Even more was threatened when she reached under his body and lifted him slightly, but she *had* to do this – it was crucial she check underneath him to ensure that *nothing* had been hacked away.

Miraculously, it seemed, nothing had. The front of his trousers were intact and dry.

Relieved, she glanced round the empty street, belatedly

wondering if the attacker was still lurking nearby, perhaps half-concealed. But there was no trace of anyone. Not so much as a parked vehicle.

Des now responded to her presence by groggily turning his head. He croaked in agony.

'Don't move, Des!' she shouted. 'Lie still, for God's sake!'

'Knathered . . .' Des burbled through a mouth that had literally been mangled. His lips were ribbons, his teeth broken. It was from this gruesome wound that most of the blood was streaming, though in addition his nose had been flattened – that too was pumping gore – and his eyes, which were both swollen closed, resembled ripe plums. 'Tho knather . . .'

'Des, it's Lucy. Can you hear me?'

'Luthy . . . too lathe, babe . . .' He chuckled and choked. 'Didn't thee him . . .'

'Stay conscious, okay! And don't bloody move! I mean it. Especially not your head.' She jumped back to her feet, digging out her phone.

'My neck'th hurting . . .'

'That's what I mean, you dipstick! Just stay put!'

The call to the MIR was answered by a DS Clubb, who was on night-cover.

'This is PC Clayburn!' Lucy shouted. 'Listen, sarge, I'm off-duty at present, so I've no radio . . . but you've got to get onto Crowley Comms. I'm on Kenyon Lane with DC Barton. He's been seriously assaulted. I mean *badly* . . . extensive head, neck and facial injuries, heavy bleeding. He's conscious but he doesn't have the first clue where he is. I need backup, supervision and an ambulance. And I need them right bloody now!'

As always in times of emergency, it seemed to take an age for support to arrive.

Like all police officers, Lucy had been through extensive first-aid training. But so often that went out of the window when you were confronted by a grisly horror like this. You weren't a doctor, you weren't a nurse. You didn't *really* know what to do.

As she dropped back to her knees, she was sufficiently knowledgeable to check again for Des's vital signs, but she now worried about where to put her hands for fear of making things worse, while his open wounds were so located that she could hardly apply padding to them. As a panicky after-thought, she stripped her combat jacket off and laid it over him to try and keep him warm.

While she did all this, she stared again down the street. Still there was no one.

She continually spoke to Des. That was important too. You had to keep talking to them, try to keep them preoccupied, maintain their conscious state.

'What happened?' she asked, to which she got no response. As Des couldn't open his eyes, it was difficult telling whether he was still conscious or had drifted into oblivion. 'Des, it's Lucy . . . tell me what happened!'

'I, erm . . .' He coughed and spat out a fragment of tooth. 'My neckth hurting . . .'

'I know your neck's hurting, love. You've probably got whiplash. Someone gave you a pasting. Now tell me who it was.'

'Didn't . . . thee any . . . fathes . . .'

'Okay. How many were there? One bloke or more?'

'Erm . . . thoo . . .'

'Two of them, okay. What happened . . . did they jump you for no reason?'

Des screwed up his face as he tried to think, which brought another groan of agony. 'Luthy . . . can't thee . . . Jeethuth . . . I can't thee . . .' He began to panic, tremors of fear passing through his rigidified body.

'It's alright,' she said, putting gentle hands on his shoulders. She perhaps shouldn't, but it was anything to calm him down.

299

'You've got two black eyes, that's all . . . two real shiners. It'll be alright in a day or so.'

Good God, she hoped that was true. Thanks to the raw, puffy state of his brows and lids, she couldn't see his actual eyes to estimate how much real damage had been done.

He stuttered again and coughed. More glutinous blood splurged out into the gutter.

'Keep bithing mi tongue . . .'

'Yeah, well you're gonna need a dentist too, but that's all. Des, you're gonna be fine.'

'Tath . . . Tath Offith . . .'

She glanced across the pavement towards the recessed entry to the Tax Office. When she'd walked a beat here as a young PC, she'd always though that an ominous spot at night. At least one mugger she knew had lain in wait there for a victim. She'd also found an OD in there one morning, syringes hanging from both his bruised and perforated elbow-pits.

Shimmering blue lights now swept over her as the first support vehicle ground to a halt a few yards away. Another followed immediately afterwards. Then came the ambulance.

Gently but firmly, the paramedics eased Lucy aside. One of them handed her jacket to her.

'What happened?' Ken Brady asked; he was the section sergeant on night turn.

Lucy shook her head, helpless to give an explanation. Deducing that she was partly in shock, Brady didn't press it. He turned as more uniformed patrols arrived, and commenced supervising them, having them lay out cones and visi-flashers to close the road.

'Is he going to live?' one of the PCs asked. His name was Luke Morton, and he too was a black lad from central Manchester. He'd only transferred into Crowley a couple of years ago and had known Des previously. Maybe they came from the same Moss Side neighbourhood.

'He's alive,' Lucy confirmed. She glanced over her shoulder, scanning the street. 'But there's someone else round here who won't be for much longer . . .'

However, this growing sense of belligerence extinguished itself quickly when a metallic-beige Lexus RX pulled up, and not only did Priya Nehwal climb out of it, but Detective Chief Superintendent Cavill did as well. It was no surprise to see them. They didn't know what was happening here – they didn't have the first clue whether it was connected to the case – but with one of their own taskforce officers injured, they'd responded instantaneously.

Cavill was a tall, lean man, with sandy hair, pale-blue eyes and buck teeth. As SIO on Operation Clearway and with so many officers at his command, the chances were that he wouldn't know who Lucy was, though no doubt Nehwal had briefed him on the way here. Cavill spoke first to the senior paramedic, who updated him as best he could. All Lucy could glean from this was that Des was stable but in a bad way. He had undetermined injuries, possible multiple fractures around the facial area and some trauma to his neck . . . but his vital signs were strong. There was no indication that he had been stabbed or shot, so they were going to remove him to Casualty at St Winifred's Hospital.

Cavill nodded. Then he and Nehwal turned to Lucy.

For the first time, irrelevant as it seemed, she noticed how they were dressed. Cavill, as ever, wore an immaculate three-piece suit complete with crisply folded pocket handkerchief. Nehawl, equally characteristically, was tousled and scruffy, wearing a tracksuit over what Lucy suspected were pyjamas, and wellingtons.

'Is this connected to Clearway, PC Clayburn?' the latter asked, eyeing her carefully. 'Or is it something else?'

'I think it's Clearway, ma'am,' Lucy replied.

'Okay. So what happened?'

'We were following a lead . . . I'm not sure . . .'

'Get your thoughts in order, and focus,' Nehwal said. 'Don't think about DC Barton, don't think about anything else. Just tell us what happened.'

'It was a lead . . . yeah.'

'What lead?'

Before Lucy could elaborate, her name was called from the ambulance. She spun around.

Des had been belted onto a gurney, his head and neck immobilised and a blanket laid over him. But despite the junior paramedic's best efforts, he was waving his left arm, trying to catch her attention.

'Luthy!' he called, cringing with pain and effort.

She rushed across the pavement. 'I'm here, Des.'

'Luth . . .' His left eye had now partly opened. It was deeply bloodshot underneath, almost crimson. 'The one who dith me . . .'

'Yeah, don't talk now, love. You're going to hospital.'

'No, you gotha lithen . . .' If he hadn't been so groggy from his wounds, not to mention the sedative they'd shot into him, he'd have been even more animated, but he still made sharp, jerking motions with his free hand, stressing the importance of what he was trying to say. 'Ren . . . Renaulth van. Blue.'

'A blue Renault van?' she said.

'Yeah . . . a bith guy.'

'A big guy?'

'Yeah . . . thtank . . .'

'I didn't get that, Des.'

'We've got to take him now,' the senior medic advised.

'You've gotta go, Des,' Lucy said, leaning over, clutching his hand just once. 'I'll follow you down to the hospital.'

He shook his head, cringing again.

'I'm sorry, we can't wait,' the medic said.

'Thtank . . .' Des gasped. 'Pepperminth . . .'

'Peppermint?' Lucy said slowly. 'You're saying he stank of peppermint?'

'Enough,' Cavill interjected. 'He can give us a full statement when he's fit.'

Lucy stepped backwards and allowed them to place Des in the rear of the ambulance. Despite his incoherent protests, the doors closed on him. But she barely saw any of this. She barely even noticed as the ambulance lurched from the kerb, weaving through the new array of lights and cones and rocketing off in the direction of the hospital.

Lucy's blood had initially run cold when she'd heard the word 'peppermint'. But in the short time since, it had started seething again, and now, as the spinning blue beacon dwindled into the distance, it came very rapidly to the boil.

'Does that means something to you, PC Clayburn?' someone asked.

Lucy was aware it was Nehwal, but suddenly that didn't matter.

'Sorry, ma'am,' she mumbled. 'I'm on the sick, remember. That means there's somewhere else I need to be.'

'PC Clayburn . . .?'

Lucy ignored her, turning and walking stiffly along the pavement, swooping for her motorbike helmet en route. As she reached her Ducati, a grey Nissan Altima grumbled to a halt in front of it, and Geoff Slater tumbled out, still pulling on a jacket and tie.

'What's happened?' he asked her, breathless.

'Sorry, sir,' she said, saddling up and sliding her helmet on. 'Gotta go.'

She kicked her machine to life, and before anyone could ask further questions, arced around in the middle of the road, threading through the cones, and hitting the throttle hard as she headed for the M60 motorway.

Chapter 28

When Lucy reached 17 Yellowbrook Close, Didsbury, it was just before ten.

There was no sign of a blue Renault van, but unusually, especially given the lateness of the hour, the electronically controlled gates to Frank McCracken's property stood wide open, and all the exterior lights were switched on. McCracken's Bentley Continental was parked at the front end of the drive. Its bonnet had been raised and a guy in green overalls with an open steel toolbox on the floor alongside him was fiddling underneath it.

Mick Shallicker stood halfway along the drive, speaking on his mobile. Behind him, the front door to the house was also open, warm evening lamplight spilling out. Shallicker didn't initially notice that Lucy had arrived. His back was half turned and he seemed engrossed in his conversation. Only by chance did he happen to glance down the drive as she dismounted from her bike and threw off her helmet.

'Anyone ever tell you that chewing gum's a filthy habit?' she shouted, walking towards him.

A look of bewilderment etched itself on Shallicker's apelike face. He cut the call, pocketed the phone and came down the drive. It was the usual thing: casual aggression; airy confidence in his own physical superiority.

'You'd better get your boss out here,' Lucy added. 'Or I'll go and get him for you.'

'You're trespassing, love,' he said with a nasty smirk. 'So get your cute arse off this fucking property! Right fucking now!'

Lucy didn't even break stride as she approached, which seemed to surprise him – even more so when she reached down and snatched up a wrench from the startled mechanic's toolbox. For the first time, the big minder hesitated.

'You're overstepping the mark, copper,' he advised her. 'Don't push your luck.'

'It's you who's overstepped the mark . . . *big time!*'

Shallicker spread his arms, looking to stop her sidling past, but instead she swept down with the heavy lump of steel, smacking it across the side of his kneecap.

'Fuck!' he gasped, tottering sideways against the Bentley. Lucy threw herself into him, crushing her body onto his massive frame, driving the wrench handle crosswise against his neck, crooking his big caveman head sideways.

'You're under arrest, Shallicker . . . for assaulting a police officer!' she hissed. 'You don't have to say anything, but it may harm your defence if you don't mention when questioned something you later rely on in court. Anything you do say may be given in fucking evidence! Now get the fuck down!'

She smacked his knee again, this time on the other side, his entire leg buckling out of shape. He squealed as he slumped to the ground, where she kicked him in the guts.

'Stay there, you bastard . . . so I can find you again when I'm done with your boss.'

She turned back to the house. Perhaps it was no surprise that McCracken had now appeared. He stood in the doorway, stripped to his shirt-sleeves, drink in hand. Smiling.

'PC Clayburn,' he said, 'what a surprise . . . or maybe not.'

'Put that glass down,' she instructed him, approaching. 'And keep your hands where I can see them.'

'Certainly.' McCracken leaned around the inside of the doorjamb, possibly to place the drink on a shelf, but maybe to reach for something else.

Lucy darted forward. 'Hands were I can see 'em, you jumped-up little shit!'

'Or?' McCracken wondered as he showed empty palms. 'You going to beat me up too? On my own front doorstep?'

'That depends how cooperative you intend to be!' She grabbed him by his collar, dragged him out onto the path and rammed him back against the wall of the house. 'But if you feel like trying something, be my guest!'

He smiled throughout this hard treatment. 'I think you're making a mistake here.'

She spun him around, pressing him face-first into the brickwork as she twisted his left arm behind his back and bent it into a wrist-lock. 'You're the one who's made a mistake.'

'This is pretty rough stuff . . .'

'You've been around long enough to remember the old unwritten rule of the anti-gang units, Mr McCracken . . . you do one of ours, we do *two* of yours.'

He chuckled as she wheeled him down the drive. 'I'm not quite sure *you* remember that, *Constable* Clayburn.'

'You can stop playing the mockery card, too,' she spat into his ear. 'I've still got more rank than you.'

'That is true, I won't deny it.'

'And I can handle your goons blindfolded, as I've just proved. You're under arrest by the way, in case you hadn't realised.'

'Under suspicion of what?'

'In your case, conspiracy to assault a police officer.'

'Conspiracy? Sounds heavy.'

'What else? You don't get your own lily-white hands dirty these days, do you? You leave that to brainless fall-guys like Shallicker.'

'Well, you certainly *felled* him,' McCracken said as they passed his groaning minder.

Other police cars screeched to a halt at the end of the drive, presumably having followed her from Crowley. The first was Geoff Slater's Altima. Slater himself jumped out; his jaw dropped when he saw who Lucy had in custody.

'Detective Inspector Slater,' she said, determined to get the first word in. 'These two men are both under arrest in connection with the attack on DC Barton earlier this evening. I propose to take them down to the Custody Suite at Wythenshawe Police Station, and interview them straight away.'

Slater glanced at Shallicker, white-faced. 'You'll probably need to take that one to Wythenshawe A&E.'

'I'm booking them both into Custody first, sir.'

Behind them, uniform patrols were now arriving, including a sub-divisional van. The local lads knew full well who Frank McCracken and Mick Shallicker were, and looked bemused when Lucy told them that both mobsters were under arrest. They handled the twosome with something like kid gloves as they placed them in the rear of the van, especially Shallicker, whose melodramatic limp was deserving of an Oscar – or so Lucy scathingly advised him.

'You know, Lucy,' Slater said quietly, once the prisoners had been removed. 'No matter how worthy the cause, acting on impulse is rarely the right decision.'

'They nearly killed Des Barton tonight, sir,' she replied. 'He could be crippled, blinded, we don't know. They're not just walking away.'

'Well . . . let's hope *you* do.'

Lucy regarded the house as the uniformed search team prepared to enter it. A figure was visible in one of its bedroom windows. It was Carlotta, wrapped only in a bath-towel. She waved and gave Lucy a bright, cheerful smile.

Lucy's next exchange with DI Slater was more heated. It occurred in the Wythenshawe Custody Office at three in the morning, both of them now frazzled with fatigue.

'Your determination to get justice for a colleague is understandable, but it's a non-starter,' Slater snapped.

'The peppermint gum!' Lucy protested. 'The fact Des said a big guy attacked him . . . they don't come much bigger than Mick Shallicker.'

'There are lots of big guys, and there was no peppermint gum on Shallicker when you locked him up. There wasn't any trace of it on his breath, for that matter.'

'A glass of whiskey would take care of his breath,' Lucy said.

'Uniform have searched his room at McCracken's house. There's none there either. Nor is there any clothing that looks mussed or dirty, or anything with blood on it.'

'He's a professional, boss. He'll know how to clean up.'

'His hands aren't nicked either.'

'He'll have worn heavy-duty gloves, or used a cosh.'

'The trouble is, Lucy . . . these flip answers won't cut it in court. All that matters at present is that we haven't got very much. In fact it's a big bloody zero.'

'At least let's put him on an ID parade,' she said. 'See if Des can pick him out.'

Slater ripped his tie off. 'Des is in no condition to pick anyone out. His vision's impaired; he's severely concussed. Even if he did manage it, the Defence would have an absolute field day. Then there's the not insignificant matter of the witnesses.'

'Witnesses?' Lucy scoffed. 'A prozzy who also happens to

be McCracken's girlfriend, and a bloke who works for the Crew.'

'He's a mechanic.'

'He works for the Crew, otherwise he wouldn't have been anywhere near the place.'

But for all her ranting and raving, Lucy understood the basic reality of the situation.

She and Slater had interviewed both suspects for two hours, and naturally they'd denied any involvement in the attack, claiming they'd been present at Yellowbrook Close all the previous evening. Moreover, uniformed officers had taken statements from Carlotta Powell and the mechanic, Ted Hope, and both supported this claim – they too had been at the house all evening, and at no stage, they said, had either Frank McCracken or Mick Shallicker left the premises. Lucy didn't believe a word of it – especially not where Shallicker was concerned; she was one hundred per cent certain that he'd been Des's main assailant. Of course, proving it was always another matter.

Throughout this intense discussion, the custody sergeant and his young clerk watched po-faced but fascinated. They were used to all sorts here at Wythenshawe nick, but they'd never had celebrity internees like Frank McCracken and Mick Shallicker before. It was anyone's guess how all this was going to end, but it was all very entertaining.

'Try and discredit Hope all you want,' Slater said tiredly. 'But you won't succeed. Because the Crew don't officially exist. And even if by some miracle you can prove they do and that he's contracted to them, it still doesn't mean he's telling lies.'

'This is a damn stitch-up!' Lucy said.

'Congratulations. You're finally getting there. And guess *who's* been stitched!'

Other voices now intruded, Priya Nehwal emerging from

the front office in company with McCracken's solicitor, a certain Jonah Gladbrook. As usual, Nehwal, though she'd managed to dispense with the pyjamas, was a scruffy mess; in contrast, Gladbook, a tall, surprisingly young and handsome chap, looked sharp and well-groomed in pinstripes.

'You can cut the crap, Jonah,' Nehwal was in the process of saying. 'We know your clients are gangsters, and you know we know it . . . so spare us the victimisation line.'

'So you're refusing to accept culpability?' Gladbrook replied.

'No, we are not, because there isn't any. A police officer was very severely injured earlier this evening . . .'

'Not by either of my clients.'

'Well, that's a moot point, frankly. PC Clayburn thought she had sufficient evidence to make an arrest, and I'm not entirely convinced she was wrong. However, I accept that ultimately it proved to be a bad call. Sorry, but this stuff happens.'

Gladbrook placed his briefcase on the charge-counter. '"Sorry"? That's all we get, Priya? Mr Shallicker is lucky he hasn't got a broken kneecap.'

'That too was an error by PC Clayburn.'

'An error? It was police brutality, plain and simple.'

The DSU glanced irritably at Lucy, whose cheeks reddened. Even if there'd been much more evidence in their favour, it was increasingly plain that the extreme force she'd exerted during the arrest would alone ensure that this case could never make it to court. She ought to have realised that at the time, but she'd been completely overwhelmed by rage. The main question now, she supposed, was might she herself finish up on charges?

'I'm not sure how the general public would view a police brutality claim,' Nehwal replied. 'If you were to push it, I mean really make an issue of it . . . it'd be interesting to see how it panned out. Shallicker's nearly seven feet tall, built like a gorilla and specialises in hurting people. While PC Clayburn's not six feet, female and was clearly trying to defend herself.'

Gladbrook looked unmoved. 'There is at least going to be an internal investigation?'

'PC Clayburn will be subjected to full disciplinary measures. If nothing else, she's broken several of our own protocols, which we don't take lightly.'

'And my clients?'

'Will both be released without charge.'

'And they'll receive a full and unconditional apology?'

'I think I can safely guarantee that.' Nehwal looked at Lucy again, daring her to say otherwise.

Gladbrook pursed his lips. 'I'm not sure this is good enough, you know, Priya. I really should take Mr Shallicker's complaint to the IPCC.'

'Do so.' Nehwal folded her arms. 'And let the rest of the underworld know what a pussy he is for letting a slip of a girl get the drop on him.'

Gladbrook picked his briefcase up and signalled to the Custody clerk, who collected some keys and headed down the cell corridor.

'I like you, Priya . . . I always have,' the solicitor said over his shoulder as he followed. 'But you probably haven't heard the last of this.'

Nehwal made to go after him, but pointed at Lucy first. 'And neither have *you*, my dear. The duty-officer has kindly vacated his office for the next hour, which is the very least we're going to need. Wait in there for me.'

Lucy looked at Slater, who arched a sympathetic eyebrow.

Glumly, she made her way through the station to the inspector's office, which, as promised, stood open and empty. She entered and waited there. As an officer with ten years' experience, Lucy wasn't unused to bollockings, but Priya Nehwal's were legendary. The only uncertainty now was whether the DSU would open proceedings by formally cautioning her and then writing everything down, or whether she'd be content to give her a monstrous tongue-lashing. Senior officers were bound by duty to record and investigate complaints of assault made by members of the public against their cops, regardless of the circumstances. But something Nehwal had said – about Shallicker not wanting to lose face – gave Lucy hope. Thus far at least, his legal rep hadn't sounded as if he was insisting on this course of action, and there had to be a reason for that, which the astute-as-ever DSU had figured straight away. Not that Lucy's future would necessarily rest with Priya Nehwal. There were much higher authorities, and if McCracken's people opted to go all the way with this, a far more cold-blooded decision could be reached.

Then, rather to Lucy's surprise, her mobile started to ring.

She looked at the clock on the wall. It was almost four in the morning. When she fished the phone from her pocket, the name indicated was 'Andy Clegg'.

Puzzled, she put the phone to her ear. 'Andy? Everything alright?'

'Oh . . . Lucy,' he said, sounding surprised. 'Sorry, expected to be leaving you a message. Yeah, everything's fine. Apart from the fact I'm still out here on the East Lancs.'

'Crap work, mate, but someone's got to do it.'

'At least we're not on our own these days. I've got Annabelle with me.' He referred to Annabelle Arkwright, who was one of the Ripper Chicks Slater had kept on. 'She's got a couple of marks we're interested in.'

'I'd like to say rather you than me,' Lucy replied. 'But at present that wouldn't be true.'

'Listen, Lucy . . . glad I've caught you. That little tart you were friends with? What was her name?'

'Tammy?'

'Yeah, that's right, Tammy. You circulated an email about her yesterday morning, yeah?'

'Yeah, but you won't see her, Andy. She's gone to ground.'

'Not so,' Clegg replied.

'What?'

'That's what I'm ringing you for. I knew she was supposed to be keeping a low profile. But I've just seen her at that lorry caf on the East Lancs. She's off her face. Pissed as a rat, I suppose, or stoned . . . giving grief to all the punters, making a right show of herself.'

Slowly, Lucy's worn-out muscles knitted up again. 'Andy, you've got to tell me this is a wind-up.'

'Why would it be a wind-up?'

'You saying she's out there now?'

'Yeah.'

'Out in public, making a scene?'

'Yeah.'

'How long's this been going on?'

'We weren't watching the caf. I just happened to park up there for a leak, and saw her. She might've been there all night.'

'Is there anyone else with her?'

'No, she's alone.'

'She won't be for long. Andy . . . you're a prince, but I've got to go.'

'Glad to help, Lucy . . . see you later.'

Lucy cut the call, and peeped out into the corridor. There was no sign of Nehwal yet. Doubtless, she was still trying to smooth things over with McCracken and his solicitor. Lucy rubbed nervously at her jaw. The way she saw it, she was already so deep in it that no rational person could expect her to find an easy way back – and all for the sake of some undeserving toe-rag's kneecap. The hell with that, she decided. She might as well give them a real reason to sack her.

Scribbling a quick note on a Post-it and sticking it on the duty-officer's door, she hurried back to Custody, grabbed her motorbike helmet from the peg and dashed out through the personnel exit.

Chapter 29

It was half-past-four when Lucy found Tammy inside the café on the East Lancashire Road.

The girl was slumped at a corner table on her own, a near-empty bottle of vodka in one hand and another, fully empty, lying in front of her. Lucy had seen for herself how well this particular establishment did for night-custom; truckers, taxi-drivers, travelling salesmen and other shift-workers kept it busy until breakfast time, when the next wave of hungry blokes would pile in through its doors, rubbing their hands in anticipation of a fry-up. But on this occasion it was noticeable that all the tables immediately encircling Tammy were empty, even though there were half-eaten meals and half-finished drinks on some of them.

'All you fucking bastards can just stop gawking!' Tammy shouted hoarsely, glowering around even though no one actually *was* looking at her. The few customers remaining stared pointedly in different directions. 'I don't care what you fucking think,' she added. 'To me this is an *honest* living.' She was as garishly made-up as usual, but clearly at the back-end of another rough night: lipstick smudged; mascara staining her cheeks; hair hanging in a lank, streaky mess.

'This is an *honest* living . . . you hear me? And yet no one likes us, no one wants us. Till they need a shag of course. And now that other lot . . . them fucking bastards. They made me into this, and they won't even let me earn a living from it anymore! Absolute bastards!'

'Tammy!' Lucy hissed, moving quickly down the aisle. 'What the hell do you think you're doing?'

Tammy glanced up at her, confused. Her eyes half-crossed as she tried to focus. 'And who . . . who the diddly-fuck are you?'

Lucy realised that this was the first time the young prostitute had seen her in anything approximating normal everyday clothing. She sat down at the table.

'You don't recognise me?' She eyed the two bottles. 'How much have you drunk?'

'Hayley . . .?' Tammy half smiled, but then her mouth twisted into a snarl. 'Hateful Hayley . . . the fucking traitor! You fucked me up! Fucking killed me!'

'You've as good as killed yourself coming out here. How long have you been hanging around the East Lancs?'

'All night . . . and no takers.' Tammy made a grand but meaningless gesture. 'Is that because *they've* been told too? That I'm a grass, a snitch. Is that what you've been doing, Hateful Hayley? Getting on the blower, spreading your poison about me . . .'

'You stupid, foolish child!' Lucy tried to keep her voice down, but her tone was taut. 'Do you have half a clue what'll happen if one of the other girls out here is connected to the McIvars? If she hears that they're looking for you? Do you think these pathetic friendships you people have formed in this nowhere place will stop tongues wagging the moment there's some money on the table?'

'They *all* have that connection, the bitches! Every fucking one. Whereas *you* . . .' Tammy leaned over the tabletop and prodded a finger into Lucy's breastbone. 'You know fucking no one. You ain't connected nowhere. And you're the one I was dumb enough to trust. Same old fuck-up Tammy! Tammy the fuck-up!'

'For God's sake, shut it. Stop making a spectacle of yourself.'

Tammy tried to swill more vodka, only to find the bottle empty. She tossed it away in disgust. It clattered on the tiled floor. 'Bit bloody late for that, Hayles.' She belched foully. 'They've *all* seen me.'

Lucy glanced over her shoulder. None of the other customers were paying open attention. With luck, they were genuine punters and though they were doubtless earwigging, would most likely be living in hope that Lucy was a friend whose timely arrival would now remove the offensive personality from their presence.

Of course, you never knew.

Lucy looked at the serving-counter, from where the two ladies currently on duty watched with expressions of deep concern.

She leaned towards Tammy. 'We've got to get out of here now.' She spoke quietly but intently. 'Don't give me a hard time, or I'll be forced to arrest you. Do you understand?'

'You'll arrest me?' Briefly, Tammy's eyes glazed over. She almost toppled from her chair. 'You'll arrest . . . after everything I've done for you? Some mate you fucking are!'

'At the moment, love, I'm the only mate you've got in the world. Now get up and let's skidaddle out of here . . . quietly.'

Lucy stood first, turning to scan behind her again.

And went rigid.

Two figures had appeared on the other side of the café's smeary front window. It was Gregor and Vlad from SugaBabes. They peered through the glass at her, their faces blank. Both wore black gloves and heavy black coats, and

317

that didn't bode well. Heavy coats in late autumn were perfectly normal, but that didn't mean they couldn't also conceal a wealth of high-calibre sins.

For half a second Lucy turned numb.

As Priya Nehwal had said, the McIvars had ordered at least three assassinations in the past, all by shooting – and one of those had apparently occurred in a kebab shop queue, so the public nature of this place would be no protection.

In fact, a public execution served an extra purpose: it sent out a message.

Tammy meanwhile had not noticed the two men. At present, she couldn't see much past the end of her nose, but she stood up anyway and circled round the table into the aisle, where she tottered against Lucy.

Lucy grabbed her elbow with an eagle-like talon. 'Okay, listen,' she whispered harshly. 'We're still leaving, but we're not going through the front. We'll go the back way.'

'The back way . . .?'

Lucy glanced at the window again. Gregor was on the move, walking to the café door. Vlad remained where he was, quite close to where she'd left her Ducati. Whether or not he'd recognised it as belonging to her she didn't know, but exiting through the rear of the café would still draw him away from there, and that gave them a chance. He was one guy, and if she could get him to run around the café's exterior to try and cut them off, they might be able to nip back the other way. Tammy would have to ride pillion of course, drunk as she was, but that was a small risk compared to staying here.

'We go *now*,' Lucy said, ambling towards the counter, steering Tammy alongside her.

The two women behind it watched apprehensively. The older one cracked half a smile, perhaps assuming that Lucy was coming to apologise for her friend's behaviour. But that

318

smile faded when Lucy suddenly veered towards the hatch at the counter's end.

Behind them, the café bell rang as its front door banged open.

'*When I say run, you run like the bloody clappers!*' Lucy hissed.

Tammy mumbled something inaudible.

'Sorry about this, ladies,' Lucy said brightly, addressing the counter women.

The older one half-smiled again, but then shouted as Lucy lunged for the hatch, lifting it and pushing Tammy through into the *Staff Only* area. There was a furious kicking of tables and chairs behind them, and shouts of outrage as customers were unseated. Lucy shoved Tammy through an open doorway on the right, which led into the café kitchen, and then turned back. Gregor was only halfway across the room. The other diners, for the most part blue-collar men, were hampering him more than he'd expected, refusing to be pushed out of his way easily.

The next thing to hamper him was Lucy's motorbike helmet, which she bowled overarm as hard as she could. It flew across the café interior, hitting him clean in the face.

The impact was deafening, and even Gregor, no doubt used to all kinds of obscene violence, toppled sideways, clutching at the tattered, bloodied mass that had once been his nose. Lucy charged into the kitchen in pursuit of Tammy, only to find that she hadn't got very far. In fact she was leaning on a worktop, vomiting onto the bread and butter.

'Jesus wept!' Lucy grabbed her by the collar of her fleece, and yanked her down the length of the galley-like room. An exit door loomed in front of them. Lucy slammed the bar down and rammed the door open with her shoulder, pulling Tammy outside after her.

The dank night air embraced them, but they were now

319

on the opposite side of the café from her bike. By sheer instinct, Lucy dragged Tammy left towards the building's rear corner. The alley running along the back connected first with the semi-derelict toilets and the heap of broken auto parts. But it would also take them back to the main lorry park, where there might be other rides available if the Ducati remained out of reach. Unfortunately, halfway along the alley, with Lucy struggling to keep her companion upright, a silhouetted form cavorted into view at the far end, arms spread like a wrestler's. It was shorter and leaner than Gregor, but it was also lithe and athletic. Without doubt, it was Vlad the bloody Impaler.

Lucy made an about-turn, still lugging the stumbling Tammy.

As they rounded the previous corner again, the kitchen door came back in sight, now in the process of opening. There was much shouting and swearing on the other side. Gregor, no doubt. Lucy spun left. A plastic bin stood nearby – it would suffice. She grabbed it under its slimy rim and hurled it. It spilled detritus along the path, but still rolled in front of the door and as Gregor came kicking his way outside, wedged itself under his shins.

He fell forward full-length, slamming his already wounded face on the concrete, which elicited a massive grunt from him. Though he tried to get up again as the girls approached, he now looked stupefied by pain. Just to be on the safe side, Lucy kicked him a good one in the jawbone as they staggered past – and he crumpled back down, this time apparently lifeless.

Hand in hand, they scrambled around the building's front corner, hoping for a clear run to the Ducati. But no sooner had they spotted it than Vlad, having raced back around the other side of the building, loomed into view again. He was thirty yards away on the far side of the bike. He might not get to it before they did, but he'd make it well before they were able to mount up and hit the ignition.

Lucy backed away, turning. Only one other option was open to them.

If they headed northward from the café, they could cut across its overspill car park and into the copse of roadside woods which ran parallel with the East Lancs for who knew how long, but mainly comprised thick evergreens and so might provide some kind of cover.

Barely aware what was happening, Tammy swore as Lucy lugged her in that direction. The girl was wearing ridiculous platform soles, which made running fast all but impossible even on flat tarmac. As such, she lagged behind, a dead weight on Lucy's arm. Halfway across the overspill, Lucy considered telling her to kick the wretched shoes off, but they were fastened by buckled ankle-straps, which would take vital seconds to loosen.

Instead, Lucy glanced back, and saw Gregor lying prone beside the café's rear door, now with Vlad kneeling alongside him. As she watched, the younger enforcer glanced up after them, and then jumped to his feet.

'Shit!' Lucy lurched on, still dragging her moaning passenger.

At the end of the overspill, a waist-high net fence separated it from the evergreens. Lucy didn't hesitate, but quickly pushed Tammy over the top of it.

'For Christ's sake!' the girl complained.

Lucy clambered over herself, and they stumbled on side-by-side through a much deeper darkness as the nighttime firs engulfed them.

The next few moments were almost surreal. They travelled side-on to the East Lancs, so they could see it through the trunks on their right: the yellow-lit strip of tarmac, the pairs of headlights flickering past in either direction. Their own progress was more difficult, their feet tangling with thorns and fallen branches. They skidded, tripped, barked their shins. Lucy looked constantly over her shoulder. There was no visible sign of pursuit, but it was impossible to know for sure – the firs had closed behind them, blotting out any lights from the café. But that only meant it was so dark that Vlad could be within reaching distance and they wouldn't realise it.

'*You dizzy mare!*' she hissed more loudly than she'd intended when Tammy suddenly dropped to her knees.

She tried to haul her back up. Tammy half-resisted, muttering belligerently, creating a pointless, fumbling struggle in the darkness. It only ended when Lucy dragged the girl violently upright and drove her on by clamping one hand on the nape of her neck. As she did, she filched the mobile from her combat jacket – she might just have time to make a call. But then she heard a crackle of undergrowth immediately to their rear. She tucked the phone away again – she'd have had to speak loudly enough for whoever she rang to hear her message, which would surely alert Vlad if that was him behind, and to get a coherent text out could take vital seconds.

She pressed on determinedly, still propelling Tammy along-side her, and now at last the trees opened in front of them like curtains, and just beyond those stood another fence. They blundered up to it. On the other side of that lay what looked like a siding filled with roadworks. It was still open to the A580 on their right, occasional cars roaring past, but otherwise was little more than a vast apron of dirt and gravel, which extended over a fairly large area, finally terminating on its left-hand side, about one hundred yards from the road, at a huddle of buildings which were just about distinguish-able in the dull glow from the streetlamps.

Lucy made a quick calculation, briefly ignoring Tammy who'd slumped thankfully down again and whimpered as she tended to the cuts and bruises on her shins.

It seemed unlikely that Vlad, or even Gregor if he was back on his feet by now, would keep following them indefinitely. They'd both be under strict orders to rub Tammy out, but they'd have to trade that off against the possibility of getting pinched, and it seemed a near-certainty the staff back at the café would have called the police by now. Help had to be on its way.

Lucy decided to go for it. Finding a hiding place and lying low for just a little longer was their best option. She reached down, grabbing Tammy by a knot of hair.

'Ow . . . *Ouch!*'

'Up! Quickly!'

'You're tearing my bloody hair out, you bitch!'

Mercilessly, Lucy yanked her up and over the next fence onto the dirt ground beyond.

'What the fuck're you doing?' the prostitute snapped, this time struggling back to her feet under her own steam. 'You've torn half my scalp off . . .'

If nothing else, at least the pain of that appeared to have sobered her slightly.

But just in case it hadn't, Lucy slapped her face. Very hard.

'What part of this have you missed, Tammy!' she spat. 'One of the McIvars' assassins is back in those bloody woods! He may not yet be aware which way we've gone, but if you keep screaming and shouting, he won't need to see us, will he! You fucking little idiot!'

Tammy's shock was such that she merely stared at Lucy, putting fingers to her stinging cheek. Now she looked to have sobered up significantly. Even so, Lucy knocked her hand down, grabbed her by the collar again and pulled her at a stumbling-run across the open ground, veering towards the distant buildings.

No sooner had they done this than a dark-coloured Vauxhall Corsa pulled into view. Unlike the other passing traffic, it wasn't flying along the East Lancs. In fact, it wasn't on the East Lancs at all, but prowling northward on the hard shoulder. It hadn't gone a dozen yards, before its engine began revving and it swerved left into the siding.

'Shit!' Lucy shouted. 'Run, Tammy, damn it . . . *RUN!*'

The Corsa didn't make it too far, ploughing a muddy trail through the grit, and having to smash its way past cone-and-ribbon fencing before it got near them. Even then it bounced into and out of a ditch, only just managing to land on its shocks, at which point it slid to a halt. Lucy glanced back and saw its driver's door burst open and Vlad emerge.

As he did, he drew a pistol from under his coat.

Now she didn't hesitate to put the phone to her lips, placing a direct call to Foxtrot Comms and delivering her message as loudly and urgently as she could.

'This is PC 1485 Lucy Clayburn, November Division . . . off duty at present, but with a vital witness under my protection. *Armed felon in pursuit!* I'm currently trying to find cover in a roadworks siding, which I don't have an exact location for . . . but it's somewhere off the East Lancashire Road just north of the Boothstown lorry park. *Repeat, I have an armed felon in pursuit!* Request immediate support, including firearms.'

There was an echoing boom and something invisible whipped past them from behind.

'Shots fired!' Lucy shouted. 'Repeat . . . *shots fired!*'

Chapter 30

As Lucy and Tammy ran, a line of tall steel-mesh fencing loomed in front of them, beyond which lay a temporary slip road made from stones and clay. Lucy broke free of her charge and threw herself at it shoulder-first.

The fence was freestanding, so it collapsed immediately, falling flat. Lucy fell too, and rolled across it. Tammy tripped but kept her feet, and then Lucy was back up, dragging her on across the slip road. On the far side of that, increasingly evident as their eyes adjusted to the poor light, stood various pieces of heavy equipment: wheelbarrows; cement mixers; stacks of cones; several sections of concrete sewer pipe yet to be laid. They wove through this clutter and veered across more open ground towards the buildings, which up close were no more than a row of workmen's cabins standing in darkness.

Another shot was fired.

It roared, the slug again whipping by with inches to spare, smashing a fist-sized hole in the nearest of the cabin doors. Whether this disabled the lock in some way, Lucy wasn't sure, but she flung herself forward and the door banged open on impact. She toppled through into a black interior. Tammy whined with terror as she tumbled in behind. Lucy jumped back up and slammed the door closed, but even as she did, a second bullet-hole exploded in the middle of it, a shaft of yellow light spearing through.

Lucy gasped and ducked away, hitting the light on her phone and spinning round to find anything that might assist. It was the usual thing – plywood walls, a tarpaper floor, the combined smells of mud, oil, asphalt. But aside from a side-desk spread with paperwork and a row of hooks on which safety helmets and hi-viz jackets hung, the room was empty.

Meanwhile, a pair of heavy feet came pounding up to the door on the other side.

'*Hayley!*' Tammy scrabbled with the handle of an internal door.

Lucy dashed over. They barged through it and hared down a short passage from which various other offices opened, all tiny and bare, finally entering a more spacious room at the end. Extra hi-viz jackets and hardhats hung in here. There was a table in one corner, a filing cabinet, and a row of tools propped against the far wall.

Lucy lurched first to the tools, and snatched up a spade. It could be used as a weapon, she supposed, but it would be heavy and cumbersome. Besides, it might serve another purpose. She whirled back to the open internal door and glanced down the corridor. Yellow street lighting glimmered from the room at the far end, but then a male silhouette stepped into view, gun still in hand.

Lucy slammed the door and braced the spade against the inside of it, ramming its hilt under the door-handle and, tearing up a wedge of tarpaper flooring, jamming the blade against that. It wasn't much of a barricade, but it might buy them a little time.

'What're we going to do?' Tammy wailed. 'We can't stay here!'

Lucy glanced over her shoulder. There was a window behind her with mesh across it, and another external door. That was their way out. But there was no guarantee that safety really lay outside. From here they probably had a choice of running across open farmland or back to the East Lancs and along the hard shoulder. None of those options would offer much protection from gunfire.

A massive impact crashed through the room. The internal door shook in its frame, but the spade held it fast. Lucy backed away and jumped aside. It was pure instinct but it saved her life, as two more shots punched massive holes in the woodwork.

'*Jesus Christ help us!*' Tammy wept.

'Just get out of here!' Lucy yelled. 'Get outside!'

Tammy attempted to comply, but could only shriek in dismay. Astonishingly, given that the others were all open, the outer door appeared to be locked.

Another massive shoulder-impact struck the internal door. Its frame shook; the jamb split. Only by a miracle was the spade still in place, but it wouldn't last much longer – it was already sliding underneath the tarpaper.

Lucy again surveyed the tools: shovel, spade, a big rubber sledgehammer, spirit level, pickaxe . . .

Pickaxe.

She grabbed and hefted it.

It was heavy, not to mention awkward: an arc of thick but tapered steel on the end of a solid hickory handle.

Again it would be heavy and clumsy, but it would do in a crisis like this.

She spun back to the internal door. Vlad launched himself against it repeatedly, battering it slowly inward. The spade slid deeper under the tarpaper.

Lucy rushed forward, threw the pickaxe back over her shoulder and, giving it everything she had, swung it down, punching it through the wood at just about neck-height – a blow that coincided perfectly and deliberately with Vlad's next shoulder-charge.

There was a muffled squawk on the other side, and then a bizarre silence, which lingered for several seconds. Briefly, and with some considerable effort – because its blade was lodged in place – Lucy had to strain all her gym-toned muscles to wrench the pickaxe head free. When she did, she blinked in shock; its bottom six inches of steel were dark with blood.

She certainly hadn't killed the bastard – she could now hear him again on the other side of the door; what sounded like a low, pathetic keening, followed by a drunken stumbling of feet as he moved away. Was this total victory, she wondered, or just a breathing space?

She hurried across the room to where Tammy cowered by the locked outer door.

'Out the way!' Lucy instructed her.

Tammy scrabbled aside as Lucy swung the pickaxe again, mightily, sundering the lock with a single blow. The door broke open when she yanked at it, and then they were out into the night air. They were now at the rear of the cabins, another plain of grit and rubble stretching into the darkness ahead of them. It was anyone's guess what lay in that direction. But Lucy had no intention of finding out. Dropping the pick and taking Tammy by the wrist, she circled warily back around the flimsy structures towards the front.

The ribbon of the East Lancs came into view.

Predictably, no police support had arrived as yet. But maybe it wouldn't be needed. Only a hundred yards away, the Corsa sat skew-whiff where it had ground to a halt.

It would be a risk. There was a lot of open ground to cover before then, but skulking inside those wooden buildings was no guarantee of safety, especially as the wounded hoodlum was still in there too. Lucy jerked forward, walking quickly but quietly, refusing to relinquish her grip on Tammy's arm, her eyes fixed on the cabins as they bypassed them and crossed the slip road – only to hit a nail-biting halt when the main cabin's mangled front door burst open and Vlad the Impaler came see-sawing out, pistol hanging low.

It was like watching a broken marionette. His head lolled exaggeratedly; his legs wobbled like rubber. He barely seemed aware of Lucy and Tammy as he tottered for several yards and fell against the drum of a cement mixer, before slumping down to the ground, where he lay on his face.

The two women waited, hardly daring to breathe.

The prone form was approximately thirty yards to their right. That was close enough for them to see that he'd dropped his pistol – it lay beside his left hand – and to distinguish the extent of his wound: by the looks of it, the pickaxe had pierced him at the point where his neck met his left shoulder. Even from here it was plain that this was more than a mere gash. As Vlad had fallen, his black coat had flapped open and, though he was wearing a white muscle shirt underneath, it was darkly and wetly stained all down its left hand side.

'Head for the car,' Lucy whispered, pushing Tammy towards the Corsa.

'And what're *you* doing?' Tammy asked, as Lucy edged towards the body.

'We need the keys, don't we?'

'For Christ's sake, we can hotwire it!'

'No, Tammy . . . it's a modern motor. It won't be anything like as easy as that. And keep your voice down.'

'He might not be dead . . .'

'I'm hoping he's bloody not!'

Lucy continued forward, only to hesitate again – this seemed like madness. What if the bastard was faking it? The temptation was suddenly to retreat, to turn, to run, to keep running. But no . . . head had to rule heart here. Even if this

329

guy was out of the fight for good, there could be others of his ilk around. There was no argument: Lucy and Tammy needed those damn keys to make a clean getaway. It might also help if they got hold of Vlad's gun.

'Go to the car,' Lucy said again, sidling forward.

Tammy did as she was told, walking over there but constantly glancing back.

Lucy stepped as lightly as she could, but cringed with each crunch of grit. The fallen Russian was now about fifteen yards away and evidently still alive; he shuddered as tendrils of pale steam wafted up from him. But the claret-coloured pool forming under his torso meant that he was losing blood profusely. It occurred to her that she ought to do something about that. Staunch the flow if nothing else. But then, the son of a bitch had been trying to *kill* them. It would be difficult playing doctor after that. The divisional support units she'd asked for might be struggling to locate them, but they'd get here eventually. He'd have to take his chances until then. Besides, she was more worried about herself. It would be bad enough having to search through pockets sodden with blood, but the bastard's left hand still lay close to that pistol. Unconscious though he seemed to be, he was easily in reach of it. Even if she managed to nab it first, it wouldn't be hard for him to snatch her wrist in the process.

She crossed the final few yards with extreme stealth.

Vlad shuddered again, and groaned.

Lucy halted, but told herself that it had been a nervous reaction.

She took another hesitant step forward. And then . . .

Putta . . . putta . . . putta . . .

In truth, she barely heard this automatic gunfire because it had been silenced. Even so, she glimpsed the stroboscopic flash in the corner of her eye.

330

When she spun round, another gun-toting figure had appeared, rising up on the other side of the Corsa. And though this newcomer wore a full head ski mask made from black leather, from its female outline it clearly wasn't Gregor.

There hadn't been two of them. There'd been three.

And Tammy – twenty yards from the car, with nothing to shield her – was still the main target. The unexpected fusillade, fired from what looked like a machine-pistol with a black tubular sound-suppressor extending its muzzle, raked her clean across the midriff.

She went down like a sack of meal.

Lucy went down too, diving and rolling, and in the process grabbing hold of Vlad's pistol. She wasn't an authorised firearms officer; she'd never carried guns on duty, though she had been trained to handle and disarm them. But this was a Glock 9mm, very common to police officers and ridiculously easy to use. As she came to rest on her front, she took aim with both hands at the masked figure advancing round the Corsa.

Lucy's brow was slick with sweat. She already had a good idea who this new player was, though it was impossible to be certain. Either way, the machine-pistol, which had a massive magazine inserted into its underside, was still levelled on the curled-up shape of Tammy.

With no choice, Lucy squeezed off three quick shots.

The range was about sixty yards and she was untrained to shoot, so she missed, but each slug struck the Corsa, the first two taking out a window each, the third punching through its bonnet and caroming up from the chassis, either the ricochet itself or slivers of shrapnel ripping across the assassin's neck, slicing open the ski mask so that braided orange tresses fell out.

There was no question now; it was Suzy McIvar.

She likes to take care of business personally, Geoff Slater had commented.

She was even wearing her trademark spike-heeled boots and tasselled leather jacket.

The murderess scrambled back around the Corsa to take cover, and maybe nurse her wound – though that could only be minor. Lucy fired again. Two more quick shots, each tearing holes through the Corsa's bodywork. Then she jumped to her feet, pumping the trigger more as she dashed forward. The Glock's standard magazine capacity was seventeen rounds; she knew that much. She didn't know how full this particular weapon's clip had been to start with, but there was no stopping now; she had to keep the bitch pinned down, at least until she could check on Tammy. So she kept firing as she advanced, hitting the car over and over.

The fallen girl was heavily bloodied, but made no sound as she lay in a ball, clutching her abdomen. It already looked horrific, and normally would require a professional and delicate response. But none of the usual protocols of first aid applied here. Lucy had to get the casualty out of range any way she could. But even as she slid to her knees alongside Tammy, the machine-pistol reappeared, periscope-style, above the Corsa's bonnet, and another burst of strobe-like fire dazzled the night.

Fortunately, because Suzy wasn't looking, the shots went wide. But there was still no time for an on-the-spot diagnosis.

The fireman's lift was always the easiest way to carry an injured party out of a combat zone. It had been tried and tested in every battle in history. But it could only ever be a last resort. Even so, this was exactly the situation Lucy now faced. Ignoring Tammy's gasps, she grabbed the wounded girl by the armpits, and, thankful that she was small and relatively light, threw her up and over her shoulder, clamping her in place by looping her left arm around the back of Tammy's thighs. The prostitute squealed as her perforated midriff took all the weight. But Lucy couldn't afford to respond to that. She might not just be hurting the girl, she might be killing her. But they would both of them die if they stayed here.

She turned and tottered away, struggling not to overbalance.

Another blast of stroboscopic light threw their combined shadows across the open ground. A frenzy of dirt was ploughed up around them, the floor erupting beneath Lucy's right foot and tearing away the entire sole of that training shoe – leaving her with no grip on her right side. Subsequently, almost immediately, she slipped in the mud and fell forward, taking Tammy down with her.

Tammy hit the ground first, whimpering like a child as the wind wheezed from her lungs, but as she landed, trapping and twisting Lucy's left arm underneath her.

Something *cracked*.

The pain was immense, sickening. It was centred in Lucy's left forearm, but swiftly ran the entire length of her body, even into her head, where it popped like a light bulb.

Dizzied by the intensity of it, Lucy knew instinctively that she'd fractured a bone, probably her left wrist. But at present she was operating on pure adrenaline. More an automaton than a thinking being, she scrambled back to her feet, grabbing Tammy's collar with her right hand and dragging her behind as she stumbled on, the sole of her damaged trainer flapping wild and loose.

She veered first towards the workmen's cabins, but now heard Suzy McIvar's feet come thudding in pursuit. There was another strobe-like burst, which raked the cabins from top to bottom, pummelling them full of holes, turning them to Swiss cheese, making it quite clear that there was no refuge to be had there.

Lucy released Tammy as she pivoted back around. She didn't know how many shots she had left in the Glock – it couldn't be many. But Suzy, about forty yards away, made a perfect target. Again, Lucy aimed and fired. She hadn't expected to hit, and she didn't – but Suzy went to ground, ducking and rolling fast, more and more of her braided hair flying loose.

Lucy jammed the Glock into the back of her jeans and staggered on, dragging Tammy behind her again as she swerved away over ground now strewn with wire and rubble. In the midst of it, protruding up at an angle was the concrete rim of a sewer pipe. She tottered towards it, panting. It was only about three feet in diameter and she had no idea how far it led underground, but in these circumstances any kind of cover was desirable. On reaching it, she lugged Tammy up into a sitting posture, hunkered down and, hooking her arm underneath the girl's bottom, levered her a foot or so into the air. Though it was agonisingly difficult one-handed, she inserted Tammy over the pipe's rim feet-first, gripped her under her right armpit and then let her go – so that she slid downward out of sight.

It was anyone's guess what lay below. But it couldn't be any worse than staying here.

Lucy grappled with her injured arm as she glanced quickly back. She'd thought it had gone numb below the elbow, but merely touching it lanced pain to the ends of her fingers.

Suzy was about thirty yards away, but on one knee. She'd dispensed entirely with her ruined ski mask and was in the process of cracking one clip loose from her machine-pistol and replacing it with another. Lucy didn't wait to see more. She vaulted over the rim herself, and slid down the interior of the pipe. The worst possible outcome here would be if it was blocked a few yards down – perhaps with building or demolition rubble. Both she and Tammy would literally be rats in a barrel.

But in fact she continued to descend, bouncing over joints

and repeatedly jarring her arm. She was about twenty feet down and feeling faint, when she dropped through another circular opening into a horizontal pipe, landing on top of Tammy, who now lay face up and perfectly still. Breath rasping through a throat turned raw, Lucy rolled sideways off the girl, to find the pipe filled to several inches with sludge and icy ditch water. She groped in total darkness, feeling first at the casualty's neck – and almost choking with relief when she detected a pulse. Tammy moaned, but it was impossible to tell how badly she'd been hurt. Next, Lucy played her fingertips across the girl's lower midsection. It was a mess of torn, slimy material. Tammy moaned again, this time with faltering breath.

'Good God!' Lucy muttered. She glanced overhead. At the top of the upper pipe, a disc of night sky was distantly visible. No silhouetted head was framed there, but it wouldn't be long before Suzy appeared, pointed her weapon down and unloaded another clip. She wouldn't even need to be a good shot; they were directly in the firing line.

Grunting anew, Lucy crawled away from the aperture, dragging Tammy by her feet into ever-deeper darkness. With thin squeaks, two loathsome furry bodies scampered off, their tales whiplashing Lucy's face. She didn't care, only coming to a rest when they were at least a dozen yards from the foot of the upper pipe. She dug into her pocket again, pulled out her phone and, though she couldn't get a signal, hit the light, the milky glow of which shimmered along the cylindrical concrete passage in both directions,

As she did, she heard a faint scuffling behind her.

She glanced over her shoulder, wondering if this indicated more rats scurrying away into the depths, or feet descending from above. Dust trickled downward from the entrance to the upper pipe. For several taut seconds, Lucy was frozen rigid, wondering how much further she could drag the wounded girl, wondering if the pipe would run continuously straight so that bullets could pass easily along its entire length – but then the scuffles began to diminish, the plumes of dust to settle. She waited tensely, listening hard.

The urge was still to press on, but where to . . . into the bowels of the Earth?

She risked glancing down at Tammy.

The phone-light illuminated a face that was still as death and pale as ice.

Tammy's eyes were lidded but motionless; clots of half-congealed blood trailed from either side of her mouth.

Further down her body, it was even worse.

Still with half an ear cocked to the passage behind, Lucy made a quick, cursory examination of the girl's midsection, now with the aid of the light, and though she didn't want to rummage too much through torn, gore-slick clothing, she rifled it sufficiently to spot at least two puckered, coin-sized bullet-holes several inches apart in the middle of the girl's abdomen, from which, even as she watched, more and more blood was pulsing.

A slow realisation dawned that her part-time friend was not going to make it. No basic first aid would fix this.

Lucy did her best, finding a packet of clean tissues in her pocket and screwing them into the wounds, but there was nothing she could do about damaged internal organs. Gently as she could, she mopped stringy, copper-red hair from the girl's sunken eyes, at the same time looking back along the pipe again.

There was still no sign of that bitch, Suzy. Whatever the delay was, it at least gave them a chance . . . but Lucy was increasingly hesitant to clamber on into the opaque black-ness. Hauling the ailing casualty through God knew how much more bricks, filth and sewage would only cause her an awful lot of suffering.

'Tammy?' Lucy said quietly. 'Can you hear me? Tammy . . . it's me.'

'Dunno . . .' Tammy murmured. 'Dunno . . .'

'Tammy, it's Hayley,' Lucy said. 'But my real name's Lucy. I'm a cop, if you remember.'

'Lucy . . . yeah.'

'Tammy, listen . . . you're pretty banged up.'

'Feel sick, Lucy . . .'

'That'll pass soon, love. Look . . . I'm so, *so* sorry I brought you to this. It was never my intention to see you hurt.'

'Suzy . . . did this . . .'

Lucy put fingers to her lips, shushing her.

She listened intently, ears pinned back. Fleetingly, she'd again thought she'd heard a scuffle of boots on concrete. It might not have been that of course. Another rat possibly?

As before, the sounds faded quickly. In fact, the silence was suddenly ear-splitting. Was it possible, she wondered . . . could it conceivably be that Suzy McIvar had opted *not* to venture down here, but to flee the scene instead?

Lucy hardly dared to hope.

'No one screws with the Twisted Sisters, eh?' she said, still keeping her voice down.

'Should'a known . . . should'a . . .' But the mere act of mumbling words brought pain to Tammy's tortured, blood-less features. 'I messed . . . up . . .'

'You've done nothing wrong, love,' Lucy said. 'In fact, you've been great. You almost helped us crack a really serious murder case . . .'

Tammy's lids inched open, the eyes underneath filmy and unfocused.

'I did good . . .?' she stuttered.

'You did brilliantly.' Lucy took her hand, and kept it in a firm grip.

'Can do good . . .'

'Just lie here, rest. Help's on its way.'

'Wanna . . . do good. Do'n wanna die . . . drunk . . .'

'You're not going to die.'

Though it almost choked Lucy to say this. It might have been her imagination, but the young prostitute seemed to be shrivelling up in front of her. And yet, almost imperceptibly, Tammy's grasp on Lucy's hand tightened until she held it in a near-fist.

'K . . . kids,' Tammy stammered. 'Lucy . . . they're selling kids.'

'What . . . what's that?'

'In the brothel.'

'No, love . . . you're mistaken.' Lucy shook her head. 'I was undercover at SugaBabes for two weeks. There were no kids working there. Not even collecting glasses . . .'

'No' there . . . listen!' Though it took effort, Tammy's eyes widened until they were bright, bloody orbs. Wracked, she reached up her other hand and clutched the lapel of Lucy's combat jacket. 'Lucy, there's . . . another place.'

'Another place?' Despite her exhaustion, Lucy felt a tremor of anticipation, a swift revival of her policewoman's instinct.

The McIvars had another place.

Accessible, no doubt . . . via the SugaBabes Taxi Service.

Lucy checked one more time over her shoulder, but she was finally starting to relax on that front. Suzy had left them alone down here for so long now that it surely meant she wasn't coming. Besides, what Tammy was now stammering was too important to put on hold.

In fact, it was so important that Lucy activated both the camera and the microphone on her mobile so that she could make an audible and visual record of it.

No cop ever wanted to be in a position where he or she was taking some kind of final statement or dying declaration. But what was necessary was necessary.

'Tammy, I'm recording this . . . okay?'

'Sure . . . wanna . . . help.'

'Who do you think shot you tonight, love?'

'Suzy . . . Suzy McIvar . . .'

'I think it was Suzy McIvar too, but why would she do that?'

'Protect . . .' Tammy's eyes fluttered closed.

'Protect what, Tammy? What was Suzy trying to protect?'

The eyes opened again, perhaps by half a centimetre. 'The other place . . .'

'And what's the other place, Tammy?'

'Taxi takes you . . . from SugaBabes.'

'Is it another brothel?'

'Child brothel . . .' Tammy coughed and struggled to breathe. With a glottal gurgle, more thick blood spewed from her lips.

'A child brothel?'

'Uh . . .'

Lucy glanced backwards one more time. Still there was no sign of pursuit.

'Tell us more if you can,' she urged her. 'Tammy?'

'They run . . .'

'Who's they, love?'

'Jayne . . . Suzy McIvar. They run . . . taxi.'

'A taxi?'

'Not real . . . SugaBabes Taxi . . .'

'Tammy . . . how do you know about this?'

'Was . . . part of it.'

'You mean you were a prostitute at this other place?'

'Yeah . . . when I started . . .' Tammy gave a deep groan. 'Oh, Lucy . . . so sick . . .'

'Try and concentrate, love . . . tell us everything you can.'

'Not . . . not all customers. Just some. High payers . . .

pervs, paedos. Check in . . . at SugaBabes, then . . . taxi. Blindfold . . . so they never know where . . .'

'But *you* know where, don't you?' Lucy trained the phone-cam on the girl's haggard face.

Tammy gave a vague nod. 'Ordinary house. But . . . feels bigger on inside.' Bizarrely, even in the midst of her pain, she chuckled at that.

'And what's the address?' Lucy asked.

'41 . . .'

'41 . . .?'

'Trestlehorn Avenue . . . Whitefield.'

'Okay, 41, Trestlehorn Avenue, Whitefield. And let's just be clear, Tammy. . . that's a brothel where underage prostitutes are working?'

Another vague, barely perceptible nod. 'Kiddies . . .'

'And you were there, you say?'

'Nine years old . . .'

'You were working as a prostitute for the McIvar sisters at the age of nine?'

'Others too. How they make . . . big money . . . right?'

'How long were you there for, Tammy?'

'Kicked me out when I . . . sixteen. Too old . . .' She tried to chuckle again, only for additional blood and foam to spatter from her mouth. 'Put me in SugaBabes . . . only 'bout a year. But . . . like a drink. Not impressed. Bitches . . . alright plying me wi' booze when I was . . . nipper, eh? Keep me docile, suppose. But . . . doesn't suit 'em later . . .'

'Let's be quite clear about this, Tammy. You were a child prostitute, working for the McIvar sisters in an underage brothel located at 41, Trestlehorn Avenue, Whitefield. And as far as you're aware, that place is still in operation?'

Tammy nodded again, but grimaced. More blood oozed out. Thicker this time, darker.

Lucy cut the interview and glanced again at Tammy's

wounds. The temporary dressings were already sodden crimson. It was a horrendous sensation, knowing there was nothing else she could do – but now, very abruptly, she noticed something else, namely that the light in the sewer had changed. As well as the pale glow cast by her phone, a faint blue iridescence came flickering along the pipe. By the looks of it, as she craned her neck to peer backwards, it was filtering down from the upper world.

Lucy could have shouted with delight. After many years of tough scrapes and close calls, she'd learned to appreciate the arrival of the blues and twos.

'Okay, Tammy,' she said urgently. 'You just sit tight. Believe it or not, help's finally got here. And not before time. Just hang on, you hear me, girl?'

Tammy tried to say something, but it was inaudible. Her eyes had closed again. The steamy breath from her bloodied lips was thinner, weaker, but at least it was still visible.

'I promise I'll be as quick as I can,' Lucy added.

She scrabbled back until she was underneath the upper pipe. If it had been difficult coming down, ascending back to the surface was murderous. It wasn't too steep, but there were no grips, no footholds. The only way she could manage it was by working her way upward with her knees pressed into the facing wall and her back braced against the one behind. Again and again, she caught her left arm on the concrete. The jolts were frightful, like electric shocks; they knocked her giddy, almost sent her tumbling back down. But she persevered, because this wasn't just a case of escaping the subterranean realm – now someone's life depended on it.

When she reached the top, of course, she had to exercise additional care. There were likely to be firearms men on the plot, and she didn't want her head blowing off by accident. So she peeked cautiously over the rim rather than climbed straight out.

Amid a flood of swirling blue light, several mobile units were parked along the hard shoulder of the East Lancashire Road. All looked like uniform cars, though there was no sign yet of an ambulance. Then she spotted the upright oblongs erected between them. Ballistics shields, she realised. The figures moving frenetically around behind these looked to be wearing helmets with visors. That was the shots. By the looks of it, they'd got here before the medical personnel, which wasn't ideal but it was better than nothing. What was noticeably absent was the Vauxhall Corsa. Lucy wouldn't have thought it driveable after the number of slugs she'd put into it, but Suzy McIvar had clearly got it going – and when Lucy glanced towards the workmen's cabins and saw that the prone shape of Vlad was also missing, she realised that the queen-bitch had even managed to take her wounded sidekick with her.

That also was less than ideal. But just having survived this was something of a result.

As Lucy's left wrist was the injured one, she anchored herself at the top of the pipe by hooking her upper left arm over the rim, and used her right to fish her phone from her pocket, flick its light on again and wave it from side to side. At the same time, she shouted: 'Over here, but don't shoot! I'm a police officer.'

There was a flurry of movement behind the shields. Lucy called out again.

'Police officer! I have a civilian casualty with severe gunshot wounds. We need an ambulance quickly!'

More frantic movement. No one advanced to meet her, but strong torch-beams swept the rubble-strewn siding.

'For Christ's sake!' she shouted. 'Shake your bloody arses!'

'PC Clayburn?' came the tinny-toned voice of a loud-hailer.

'Over here!' she cried, now hoarse. 'Surely you can bloody see me!'

342

'PC Clayburn! Are there any other armed persons here, to your knowledge?'

'I don't think so, or at least not any more,' she called. 'But it's full body armour, okay? And keep those bloody guns handy, or whatever it is you do. But for God's sake, do it fast. We need medical assistance!'

When the next response came in the affirmative, Lucy scrabbled back down the pipe. It was an even bumpier ride than before. Again and again, she struck her arm on the side – until she was ready to throw up from the pain. But at last she came to the bottom, where she hunkered onto her hands and knees, and splashed back through the silt towards Tammy.

'It's alright, love,' she said. 'If you can just hang on a bit longer, help's coming.'

But Tammy made no reply, and when Lucy turned her light on again, the girl's eyes had glazed. Sluggish blood no longer ran from her mouth and no breath issued from her cold, dead lips.

Chapter 31

The remainder of that night was something of a blur to Lucy. They insisted on taking her to hospital, which she steadfastly maintained she didn't need – only to remember, somewhat belatedly, that in actual fact she did need it, because she had a broken arm.

While she waited to see a Casualty doctor and then waited for a late-night X-ray and then for the diagnosis, which was a hairline fracture to the ulna, and lastly, as she waited for treatment in the Fracture Clinic, she gave innumerable statements to various officers of different rank and from different departments. But it was increasingly difficult to work out who these people were or why she was talking to them – not just because of shock and fatigue, but because she was also by this time on a heavy dosage of painkillers and antibiotics. All the while she remained in a bedraggled, bloodstained state, until at some point in the night one of her colleagues brought her a change of clothes: a black GMP tracksuit with white piping, which was neat enough to look at but too large for her, and a clean pair of trainers. She wasn't really aware who was responsible for this or at what time it happened, but was vaguely cognisant that her own clothing had to be taken away for forensic analysis, as she too had fired shots during the roadside battle.

It was confirmed to her repeatedly that Tammy Nethercot had been pronounced dead at the scene, having suffered fatal gunshot wounds. Each time, Lucy received the news dully and without further comment. Deep in the stew of her thoughts, she was already one hundred per cent certain about this, because she'd been there and had seen it for herself. But during the few occasions that long torturous night when she was able to snatch some sleep, usually while propped up in one of those uncomfortable, plastic waiting-room chairs, she relived the incident in vivid if disjointed fashion: stroboscopic flashes of gunfire; wooden workmen's cabins flying to pieces; broken, gritty ground hitting her in the face; the smell of blood and cordite; and then a terrible tunnel, a long concrete tube filled with refuse and ditch-water and rats, and then Tammy's face, bluish/white and yet peacefully reposed as if she was asleep, and improbably beautiful, not a speck of dirt to mar her girlish looks aside from a tiny droplet of red at the left corner of her mouth.

But of course that hadn't been right at all; it had been much, much worse than that. And so Lucy would always wake in a state of grogginess and confusion, and would ask the first person she saw: 'What happened? Did Tammy survive?'

This was a repeating, seemingly endless pattern, thanks to which she barely noticed the hours creep by or the changes of staff in the hospital, or the return of gloomy November daylight to the car park outside. She actually managed to sleep properly, or so she thought, while they were working on her in the clinic. If not, it was a mystery why she had no recollection afterwards of who was responsible for encasing her lower left arm from the elbow downward in plaster and gauze, and suspending it across her chest in a sling. However, when she finally emerged into the waiting room, which, as it was now almost noon, was buzzing with the next batch of patients, she felt a little bit fresher even if still deeply tired.

In that regard, the first person she saw was probably the last person she particularly wanted to converse with, but the look on Priya Nehwal's face as she came down the central aisle between the rows of occupied seats was less truculent than usual.

'So . . . what exactly am I supposed to do with you?' was the DSU's opening gambit. But she still didn't look vexed. If anything, her tone bordered on the affable.

'Sorry, ma'am?' Lucy replied.

'Let's chat.' Nehwal indicated a far corner where most of the seats were still empty.

Wearily, Lucy limped over there and slumped down. Nehwal sat on the seat next to her.

'In the last couple of days, PC Clayburn,' she said, staring directly ahead, 'you've broken just about every rule that British police officers are supposed to abide by. Including disobeying a direct order from me, which is the one I'm really narked about. But –' Nehwal shrugged, as if it were all now beyond her control '– you've also displayed remarkable courage and tenacity, and have cleaned out a whole nest of villains in the process; a bunch of lowlifes whom most of the rest of us thought were immune to any serious charges. So I repeat . . . what am I supposed to do with you? How exactly do I reprimand the woman of the moment?'

'I . . .' Lucy struggled to find an answer. 'I don't know what's been going on, ma'am. I mean while I've been in here.'

'Well . . .' Nehwal lowered her voice. 'To start with, Suzy McIvar has been arrested on suspicion of murdering Tammy Nethercot and of attempting to murder you.'

'Already?'

'You said it yourself. These people are good. We had to move fast.'

'Pity no one moved fast enough to save Tammy.' Lucy felt like crying, though no tears seeped from her tired eyes.

'Suzy McIvar's not having it, obviously,' Nehwal added. 'But the evidence we've got seems pretty conclusive. Your statement wouldn't serve on its own, but we also found the ski mask she dropped at the scene, which has blood and saliva on it. It's currently being tested, but the DNA will almost certainly turn out to be hers. You said she shot at you with some kind of machine-pistol?'

Lucy nodded. 'I think so, yeah.'

'Well, the spent magazine that we recovered indicates that it was a Shipka, a Bulgarian-made 9mm submachinegun. Particularly deadly at close quarters. We haven't found the weapon itself, but after arresting McIvar a couple of hours ago, we searched her apartment and found the same kind of clothing you described. Again, it's a bit early to say for sure, but forensics already reckon there's firearms residue on it. The Corsa was reported stolen a few days ago of course.'

'Of course.'

'That's been found too. Dumped and burning.'

'Great,' Lucy groaned.

'But not completely incinerated. There's still plenty evidence of the shots you fired at it, and there are even a couple of bloodspots on the bonnet.'

Lucy looked round. 'That'll be Suzy's too. She got hurt . . .'

'And that's the other thing,' Nehwal said. 'You mentioned in your statement that the gun-woman was wounded in the side of the neck.'

'Yes . . .?'

'Well, Suzy McIvar has a fresh graze on her neck. It's only slight, but I think it'll be more than enough to send her down for life.'

'Even without the gun, ma'am?'

'We'll find the gun, don't worry. Or what's left of it. We'll also find those two Russians, though we're having trouble putting hands on them at present.'

'They're probably illegals,' Lucy said.

Nehwal shrugged. 'Unless they run home to Mother Russia, it won't matter. The whole of the McIvars' firm is unravelling, and everyone involved is now looking to make a deal . . . that's chiefly because they've actually got a much bigger problem hanging over their heads.'

'Trestlehorn Avenue?'

Nehwal nodded. 'That address was raided a few hours ago by the NCG's Organised Crime Division. There were no customers there. The warning had already gone out.'

'But is it what Tammy said it was?'

'You really don't want me to go into the detail of what they found there,' Nehwal said, her expression briefly distant. 'Put it this way, a significant number of children were removed to places of safety. Some British, some foreign. All the usual sorts – runaways, street kids . . . They'd been trafficked, groomed, plied with drugs and drink, you name it. Several arrests have followed, and unsurprisingly, quite a few McIvar underlings are suddenly being very cooperative indeed. Particularly this girl, Marissa Cudworth. You know her?'

'Yeah.' Lucy snorted as she remembered the ex-dancer's hard-ass routine. 'She'll be talking for her life – she was an active participant in the Taxi Service.'

'She plays her cards right, she could end up being a star witness.'

'Against Jayne McIvar as well as Suzy, I hope?'

Again, Nehwal nodded. 'The Twisted Sisters are the main object of interest. At present, both are locked up. But, good news though all this is, none of it really helps *us*, does it?'

'No, ma'am. I suppose not.'

'The Lay-by Murderer is still on the loose.'

'I'm sorry about that.'

'You know, Lucy . . .' This was the first time Nehwal had ever called Lucy by her first name, and it wasn't at all unpleasant; it almost felt like a verbal thumbs-up. 'I have a reputation in this job for being a toughie. But after your sterling efforts of the last few days, somewhat wayward though they were, even I would struggle to live with myself if I decided that Jill the Ripper's ongoing liberty was *your* fault. Don't you think?'

'I really thought we were onto her.'

'We are.' Nehwal stood up. 'Whoever she is, she's not that clever. Oh, she's choosing her targets carefully, she's scoping out her ambush points before she lures them there, but she's still riding her luck. Even if we don't catch her, at some point one of these blokes is going to turn round and plant her on her backside.'

Lucy stood up too. 'I just hope my interest in Carlotta Powell didn't divert vital resources from real lines of enquiry.'

'Even if they had done, it wouldn't look very good if I made a song and dance about it . . . you with an arm shattered in the line of duty and most likely heading for a commendation, not to mention a promotion, I suspect.' She eyed Lucy sidelong. 'If you want one.'

'I'd rather have a transfer,' Lucy replied.

'You still hankering after detective work?' Nehwal sounded surprised. 'After all this?'

'Especially after all this. It's something I'm good at, I think.'

'You're a bit of a wrecking-ball, Lucy.'

'Yeah, but this time it's the underworld that's come tumbling down, isn't it, ma'am. Or at least a good chunk of it.'

A shadow of a smile touched Nehwal's lips. 'I'll see what I can do.'

'How's Des, by the way?'

'Concussion, fractured cheekbone, two fractured eye-sockets. But otherwise fine.' They walked out into the main corridor. 'See for yourself, if you want. He's in the next block. Wallingford Ward.'

'I will, thanks.'

'You're going home after that, I take it?' Nehwal said, though it sounded less like a question and more like an order.

'I'm on sick leave, ma'am . . . so unless someone needs me for something, yeah.'

'If someone needs you, they'll knock on your door, don't worry. By the way, Traffic brought your bike back to Robber's Row. They even recovered your helmet. But it'll all be safe there until you're fit for duty again. Get yourself a taxi home from here. Charge it to us.'

'I will, ma'am.'

They prepared to part ways, Lucy heading off to the Wallingford Ward while Nehwal exited into the car park. But briefly, they faced each other across the corridor. For an absurd moment, Lucy thought the DSU was going to embrace her. Needless to say, that didn't happen, but Nehwal had never seemed as amiable as she did at present; no doubt this was down to members of her team having secured an unlooked-for but pretty decent result. Of course, Nehwal couldn't have reached the level of respect she enjoyed in the service now if she'd been all snarl and aggression. You had to be tough, that went without saying; you had to be extra tough if you were a woman. But no one liked a personality with no give in it whatsoever. Lucy had always surmised that she'd have to *earn* DSU Nehwal's friendship, and diverting from the established protocols had hardly been a short cut to that. But now at last, thanks to having put her body on the line, some kind of happy juncture seemed to have been reached.

'Go home, Lucy,' Nehwal said again. 'I mean it. Go home and put your feet up.'

Lucy nodded. Only to glance back when they were a few yards apart. 'Ma'am?'

Nehwal looked round from the exit door.

'Thanks,' Lucy said.

'For what?'

'For not launching me off the front step. We haven't worked together that long, but I've given you half a dozen reasons why you could and maybe why you should.'

Nehwal looked briefly thoughtful. 'Everyone makes mistakes, Lucy. Even professionals. It's human nature, and there are various degrees of seriousness within that – there are some foul-ups that simply can't go unpunished. But the only people I don't want in this job are the people who aren't actually coppers. People who are playing at it, people who are only here for career advancement, people who'd rather be anywhere than on duty. No one could accuse *you* of that. Now, like I say . . . go home and get some rest. You need it.'

Lucy didn't enter the private room that Des was located in, because when she glanced through the glass panel in the door, she saw that his wife, Yvonne, was already in there, alongside his two youngest children, a pair of cute pre-school girls wearing pigtails and, despite the autumn bleakness outside, bright, flowery dresses.

Des, for his part, though bandaged around the head, with his neck in a brace, lint looped under his chin, lots of stitching visible and one eye still firmly closed, was sitting up in bed in a hospital gown, grinning broadly as they showed him colouring books they'd recently filled in. An enormous bunch of grapes sat on a dish on the cabinet alongside him. There was also a preponderance of flowers, cards and boxes of chocolates.

Yvonne Barton was perched at the far end of the bed, while her daughters did all the talking. Lucy had never met her, nor had even been shown a picture of her until now, but was unsurprised to see a beautiful lady in her mid-forties, elegantly dressed in a dark skirt-suit and heels, her hair done up in a luxurious beehive. In comparison, Lucy felt like a scruffy urchin, her own hair still dripping dirt and leaf-mould, her face and hands grubby, her plastered arm zipped up inside a tracksuit top that barely fitted her. Quite a change from the 'glam' attire she'd adopted for SugaBabes. No one could say this case hadn't brought out the chameleon in her. But none of this was why she decided not to intrude. The plain fact was that Des looked happy. He was with his family, those who totally and unconditionally loved him. Whatever he remembered about the beating he'd received, if he remembered anything at all, this was the perfect antidote to it. It hardly seemed fair crashing in on the cheery reunion like some brutal reminder of the nasty world waiting outside.

So she turned and walked away, exiting the hospital on its side where the taxi rank stood.

As soon as Lucy stepped outdoors, the cold embraced her viciously. She stumbled to the crash barrier, lightheaded. She was already in thrall to that curious physical weakness that always seems to kick in after hospital treatment. Despite the painkillers, her arm was hurting and her fatigue running bone-deep.

There were no taxis at present. So she leaned on the metal barrier and gazed bleary-eyed across the car park. In her addled state, it seemed to elongate, to telescope outward in length and breadth, acres and acres of damp, leaf-strewn tarmac. Lucy rubbed at the back of her neck, suddenly suspecting that she was going to be sick. She retched, but it was so long since she'd eaten that nothing came out. And then someone spoke to her.

'Lucy?'

Lucy looked round – to spy her mother, coated and gloved

against the chill, coming cautiously along the crash barrier. A padded anorak, one of Lucy's own, was folded over Cora's arm. Her face wore a deep frown of motherly concern.

'How are you?' she asked.

'It's nothing,' Lucy stuttered. 'Nothing a . . . a six-month luxury cruise wouldn't put right.'

'Lucy . . . you need to come home now, so I can look after you.'

'Yeah, course, Mum . . .'

'I'm serious, darling. You need to stop this foolishness . . . and come home.'

Lucy straightened up. Stiffly, defiantly.

And yet despite the anger of recent days, not to mention the sense of betrayal still nagging at her, it was difficult in her bruised and battered state to continue feeling hostile towards her parent; she was the sole stable fixture in Lucy's life, the one person who'd always been there, who she'd always been able to turn to whether with a cut knee or a broken heart, the person who'd offered comfort and control in equal measure.

'You know, Mum,' Lucy stammered. 'Because of your friends . . . a girl who never had a chance in life died last night . . . in a sodding sewer.'

'I'm aware what happened,' Cora said sadly. 'And I'm aware there's some culpability on my part.'

'*Some* culpability!' Lucy did her best to bristle. 'This wonderful guy you once knew signed Tammy's death warrant the instant you gobbed off to him about me!'

'We can talk about that later. First, you've got to come home.'

'I don't have to do any such thing. Quite clearly, me and you live in different worlds . . . only you don't seem to have realised it.'

'I can't help the past, darling.' Cora imbued the word 'darling' with absolute sincerity. This was Lucy's mother at her sympathetic, soft-hearted best, and yet Lucy still wondered if she knew the woman anymore.

'The past, yeah,' Lucy said. 'But now you've brought it to the present. And someone's dead because of it. I'm lucky *I'm* not dead. You know they shot my bloody shoe off!'

'Look,' Cora said. 'You've got a serious injury. It's patched up, but you can't go back to that half-furnished bungalow, where there's probably no hot water, no central heating . . .'

Lucy shook her head, which effort alone toppled her against the barrier. 'Aren't you even sorry?'

'Of course I'm sorry.' Cora put an arm around her shoulders. 'But I did what I did for the best . . . or so I thought. I realised almost immediately afterwards that it was a mistake, but I can't do anything about that now.'

'You really don't know these old friends of yours at all, do you?'

'Again, we'll talk about that later. Look at you, love . . . you can barely stand up.'

'This is nothing.' Lucy shook herself free, and tottered again. 'Just . . . just tired.'

'When did you last have something to eat?'

'I could've had something last night when they brought me in, but they advised against in case I needed surgery . . . which I didn't. So I'm fine.'

'You still have to come home, Lucy. I told your superintendent that's where you'd be if she needed you. Yes, that's right . . .' Cora nodded, bright-eyed; an effort to infuse some stern motherly humour into the conversation. 'She called me at home to let me know you'd been hurt, and I chatted with her for quite some time while we were waiting for you to get your arm fixed. I got to know her pretty well.'

'I hope you were careful,' Lucy snorted. 'It's not quite as easy to pull the wool over Priya Nehwal's eyes as it was mine.'

Cora remained determined. 'Is this the way it's going to be? Every time I say anything, you try to get the better of me with some smart-arse reply? Fine, I accept. It's the price I'll pay for what happened. In the meantime, you need to come home.' She draped the spare anorak over Lucy's shoulders and looped a scarf around her neck. 'And as your mother, I have to be there to supervise it . . . so that cold, dreary bungalow of yours is not an option. Do you understand?'

Lucy didn't argue further. She'd already decided that she couldn't go back to Cuthbertson Court; not at present. The thought of a warm drink, a warm bed and someone to assist if she needed help was just too seductive.

'One thing you did right, Mum,' Lucy said as they trudged across the car park, leaning on each other. 'You made me realise how hard this job can be. I had no idea before. But whatever you think, tough . . . I'm staying in it.'

'Fine,' Cora said. 'But one thing at a time, eh?'

Chapter 32

On arriving home, Lucy had as thorough a wash as she could with one arm immobilised, accepted a bowl of chicken soup and a mug of milk, and then, as her mother instructed, limped upstairs, lay on the quilt in her bedroom and dropped her head into a soft pillow.

She'd often found at the end of unpleasant shifts that she didn't slide into sleep easily, despite being physically and emotionally drained. Some police officers could hit an internal switch and it all went away. Lucy had never possessed this gift, though she was good at putting on a front. Now that she was alone, with no one to impress, she had no choice but to lie there and relive it. And though it wouldn't be true to say that she didn't sleep at all – she certainly dozed – she tossed and turned constantly, her mind awash with half-formed memories trawled from the difficult hours that had recently passed, snippets of reality inter-woven with fantasies and imaginings. None were in any way relaxing.

'Why are you so wedded to this awful job, Lucy?' Tammy asked from the end of the bed, where she stood with a cup of tea clasped in her hands.

Lucy mumbled in response. There was no energy left in her body with which to wake up and tackle this thorny issue. Besides, somewhere deep down, she knew that it wasn't Tammy; it was her mother.

'What are you trying to prove? Who are you trying to prove it to? You ride that terrible motorbike, you get shot at for a living. I'm at my wits' end every day you go on duty.'

Lucy couldn't respond to that either. In fact, she *wouldn't*. They'd had this conversation so often before that it was no longer worth a reply, especially as it was clear that her mother now had other, less admirable reasons for not wanting her daughter to remain a police officer.

Of course, that didn't stop Cora talking. Mumbling in fact, continually as Lucy tried to sleep. No longer conversing with her daughter as such, but with someone somewhere else in the house – for what seemed like hours.

At first Lucy fancied she was dreaming this too. But gradually, as her room swam properly back into focus, and she squinted at the digital clock on her sideboard and saw that it was now two-thirty in the afternoon, she understood that it was reality; that her mother was discussing matters with someone downstairs. They weren't talking loudly, but their voices were intense and animated. Whoever the visitor was, it was a man – she could tell that from his masculine tone. The words were inaudible, or so Lucy thought – until she levered herself upright on her one good arm, to listen.

'So what are we going to do about this, Cora?' the man asked.

'At some point she'll have to listen to me,' Lucy's mother replied.

'Why would she?' he said. 'She's on a mission.'

'A mission? To do what?'

'To be the man of the house. What else?'

'That's a very sexist point of view.'

'Oh, for Christ's sake . . . with all this crap coming down, you're giving me PC bullshit!'

And now Lucy realised who was speaking – at last the voice was familiar to her, horribly so – and she could scarcely believe it.

'There are reasons behind everything *everyone* does,' the man said. 'Would I have got to the top of the tree if I hadn't been desperate to put my abysmal childhood behind me? Not very likely. She's grown up with a mum who's a perfect lady. But she needed some of the other stuff too, to counterbalance . . . someone who'd raise his voice now and then, who'd throw a punch if the family was threatened. She needed a dad. So now she's fulfilled that role, herself. She's opted for the most macho career she could find. And that's not a criticism, by the way . . . I think it's praiseworthy. But it still gives the rest of us a big, big problem.'

Lucy almost tripped in her haste to get downstairs, where she burst into the lounge, kicking the door open so hard that it slammed on the wall, shaking the ornaments in her mother's display cabinet.

'*What the hell is this maniac doing here?*' she bellowed.

Cora was seated on the couch, hands joined on her lap as though in prayer. On the other side of the room, Frank McCracken – now 'dressed down' in a sweater, slacks and deck-shoes, slouched in the armchair. Before Cora could reply, Lucy rounded on the gangster.

'*Get your arse out of here!*' She jabbed a vicious finger at him. '*Right now, or I'll beat your sodding brains out!*'

McCracken shrugged at Cora. 'Told you she reminded me of me.'

Cora, suddenly flustered, opened her mouth to reply but nothing came out.

Glaring at her with accusation, Lucy stormed across the room to the front window to see how many goons he had waiting outside. But the terraced street was deserted.

And then, belatedly, his last comment struck home. She turned stiffly back to look at him.

'What did you say?'

He arched an eyebrow. 'You mean you haven't worked it out yet?'

Lucy's spine crawled as she stared from McCracken to her mother. It more than panicked her when the latter hung her head, refusing to meet her gaze.

'Mum . . . what is he talking about?'

Cora still said nothing.

'I said what the hell is this bastard talking about?'

'Sorry I wasn't around much, pet,' McCracken replied on Cora's behalf. 'But I suspect you'd have preferred it that way . . . wouldn't you?'

'I'd prefer to get a straight answer!' Lucy snapped, though she determinedly didn't look at him. 'Mum, what's happening here? You've got to tell me!'

Cora analysed the carpet. 'All I ever wanted was what was best for you . . .'

'Don't give me that Saint Cora crap!' Lucy shouted. 'What's going on? Why the hell is he *here*?'

Cora finally glanced up. Her eyes glinted with moisture. 'All those years ago, me and Frank . . . we weren't just friends.'

'You're not . . .?' Lucy shook her head. 'You're not . . . telling me what I think you're . . .? No!' She shook her head again, violently. '*This is a lie!* This is a total fabrication! He's got you onside somehow, he's made you think you're actually part of his team and that I'm the enemy. Mum, he's a career criminal, a murderer . . .'

'He's also your father.' Cora said this in a calm but firm

voice, as though there was no soft way to do it. But she'd turned white as a sheet in the process.

'This is a lie,' Lucy whispered harshly. 'This *has* to be a lie.'

'I know it's a shock,' McCracken chipped in; the only one in the room who looked unfazed by the situation. 'It was a shock to me to learn my daughter was in the fuzz. But why else do you think I thought I recognised you in SugaBabes that first time?'

Lucy looked round at him, unable to form words, barely hearing what he was saying. She rubbed at the tears of rage blurring her vision.

'Your mum sent me a photo of you when you were sixteen,' he explained. 'At my request. I'd finally got curious. I admit I probably haven't looked at it for a decade or more. So when I saw you in the club that night, I didn't make the immediate connection . . . but something about you seemed familiar. Your mum confirmed it when she came to see me last Wednesday.'

This had to be rubbish, Lucy told herself. It had to be. Rubbish of the vilest, most disgusting kind. But *was* it? Hadn't she perhaps suspected something like this? Why on Earth would her mother have even gone to see McCracken? Just a friend, she'd said. But it was a strange thing, staying in touch with a friend when he'd morphed into one of the deadliest criminals in Britain. What kind of friend did you ask favours of, who, with a click of his fingers, could and would have people killed?

She gazed at her mother again, wet-eyed. 'What . . . what about the likeable rogue bus driver? All that guff you filled my head with when I was a girl!'

'It wasn't total guff,' Cora said. She at least had the good grace to look embarrassed by this part of it. 'He was real. The only difference was, I was seventeen at the time and he was twenty-four. That day he turned up at our house in his bus, when he was supposed to be delivering passengers, my dad sent him off with a flea in his ear. I never saw him again, much less slept with him.'

'Always been a sore point with me, that story,' McCracken said chattily, fingers steepled. 'I mean, I've never minded not getting any credit for producing a fine specimen like you, Lucy. But the thought of some prat with a big plastic badge on his lapel and a stupid hat. Probably fancied himself a regular Reg Varney . . .'

'Shut up!' Lucy howled. After all the violence and terror he and his kind were responsible for! After what had happened to Des Barton! Just sitting here in their living room like . . . like he *belonged*. 'Just don't talk again in this house!'

McCracken smiled blandly, and made a zip-fastener motion across his lips.

Lucy looked at her mother again. 'And you never told me? Not even before I decided I was joining the police . . . you never once told me the truth?'

'I didn't want you in any way connected with that life,' Cora replied. 'Lucy, I experienced it for myself, and I wanted so much better for you. And Frank agreed.'

'Oh, Frank agreed, did he? Very bloody big of him!'

'He stepped back,' Cora said. 'Agreed to respect my independence and keep out of it. He even offered me money to help me through, but I refused . . .'

'That's money he now spends on high-class whores!' Lucy blurted.

'We went our separate ways by choice,' Cora said. 'I'm not going to criticise him for finding other girlfriends later on.'

'No, but don't you go thinking he ever regretted that decision.'

'Oh now, fair's fair,' McCracken complained. 'I *did* wonder from time to time how you were getting on.'

'And he offered me money more than once,' Cora added.

'Blood money,' Lucy scoffed. 'Mob money. He robs other criminals, Mum . . . and if they refuse to pay up, he tortures and kills them. That's what he does. That's his job.'

Cora remained pale-faced, but apparently wasn't shocked.

'You don't even look surprised,' Lucy said.

'What was I supposed to do, Lucy?' Cora said. 'Get rid of you . . . on the off-chance my evil boyfriend had planted some kind of demon seed in my womb? To protect you from someday making a discovery like this?' She paused to let her words sink in. 'What was done was done. I did the best I could to try and fix it, and your father did too.'

'Don't call him that!'

'It's only a biological term, love,' McCracken commented.

'And don't give me "love"!' Lucy spat at him.

'Frank's here now because he'd heard you got shot,' Cora said.

'Incorrectly, as it turned out,' McCracken added.

Lucy laughed bitterly. 'I bet that was disappointing for you.'

'Lucy,' Cora said, 'you don't know Frank.'

'I know him better than you do! For God's sake, mother, he's probably here to finish me off. He'll have been the one behind the original attack.'

'Uh-uh,' McCracken said in a firmer, sterner tone, as if this was one point he quite categorically wanted to make. 'I was *not*. And if you don't believe me, officer, you can pat me down right now.'

'Wild accusations won't resolve this, Lucy,' Cora said with a hint of reproof.

'Wild accusations?' Lucy jabbed another finger at

362

McCracken. 'This so-called man is the exact opposite of everything I stand for. And you've got the nerve to . . .'

'I didn't choose your career for you!' Cora's tone had finally toughened, as if the time for tantrums was over. 'I always told you I'd much rather you became a teacher or a nurse or a librarian or even a shop girl . . . anything to keep you from sliding back into that world I left behind.'

'So that's why you've always hated me being a cop?' Lucy said scornfully. 'Because you were afraid it might one day expose your dirty little secret.'

'It's not unproblematic for *any* of us,' McCracken opined.

'Yeah, but she had me thinking she was actually *worried* about me.' Immediately, Lucy felt like kicking herself. She couldn't believe she was actually talking to this guy.

'Of course, I was worried about you,' Cora said. 'Every day you went on duty, I worried. Because I've seen it from the other side. I know what can happen when things turn ugly.'

'Yeah, well, they're *really* going to turn ugly now.' Lucy chuckled harshly. 'In fact, you'd better kiss this fella goodbye while you've still got the chance, mum. The Twisted Sisters are facing imminent annihilation, and he's going down with them.'

'And maybe not.' McCracken smiled at her; again blandly, with that infuriating air of easy confidence. 'Sorry to burst that balloon, pet.'

'Are you on some kind of fantasy kick?' Lucy wondered, genuinely flabbergasted by his manner. 'Your whole attitude since I walked in is that at some point I'm going to start liking you . . . that whatever I say now, I'll eventually be your mate. Are you for real, McCracken? I've had ten years of cleaning up the messes in this town that people like you leave behind. The ruined lives, the bereaved parties . . . you may be my father in the dictionary definition of the term, but I'm never going to pay that more than lip service. Because you see, I'm a police officer and I uphold the law . . . while you mug people, and arrange assassinations, and run child prostitutes . . .'

'I wouldn't get your hopes up about making that latter charge stick,' he replied. 'My associates and I knew absolutely nothing about that underage brothel.'

'Yeah . . . tell it to a judge.'

'I won't need to.' His tone was now tolerant, as though he was imparting a difficult lesson. 'It'll never get to a judge. I mean, the McIvars will, but they're a busted flush. No doubt your colleagues are trying to pitch a deal to the pair of them as we speak, hoping to net themselves some bigger fish. Am I right?'

'Like I'd tell you,' Lucy sneered.

'I'm right. I know I am. But it won't work.'

'McCracken . . . you're a fucking nonce.'

The smile on his lips tightened a little. 'I wouldn't push your luck too far . . .'

'Luck won't come into it. You're going down.'

'You say you've been a copper ten years, Lucy. If so, you ought to have learned by now not to listen to the assurances of solicitors. They're professional liars. Especially when they're-representing clients facing life imprisonment.'

'We'll see.' Lucy strode to the door.

'Where are you going?' Cora demanded.

'Where do you think? Home.'

'*This* is your home.'

'Not as long as *he's* here! And not as long as *you're* here, either. My own mother . . . a gangster's bloody moll!'

Lucy raced back up the stairs, still in a state of horrified bewilderment. She almost diverted into the bathroom so that she could vomit into the toilet bowl, but, determined to remain strong, she barged into her bedroom instead, where she unzipped her tracksuit top and ripped her sling off. If there was any pain to be had, the fresh-flowing adrenaline accounted for it. Besides, she needed something warmer if she was getting out of here. She pulled on a thick, fleece-lined hoodie, grimacing a little as she gingerly fed her plaster-sheathed arm through its sleeve, and then threw the padded anorak over the top of that. As an afterthought, she tugged the trackie bottoms off and climbed into a fresh pair of jeans and trainers, before grabbing her personals, which the hospital had given her in a small plastic bag: her keys, her wallet, her warrant card, her phone and such.

When she got back downstairs, her mother and McCracken stood by the lounge door.

'Lucy, you're not thinking of telling anyone about this?' Cora said.

'Course I am,' Lucy mocked her. 'I'm always looking for new ways to hammer nails into the coffin of my career. Mind you –' she smiled coldly at McCracken '– it'd be the end of *your* career too, wouldn't it? Might be worth it just for that.'

'We'd *both* have an awful lot to lose,' he agreed.

Lucy headed to the front door. 'Be thinking about that when you make your next move.'

'One other thing I came to tell you,' McCracken said; she glanced back. 'Mick Shallicker's legal rep won't be pressing any further claims against you.'

Lucy shrugged. 'What's that, an attempted bribe?'

'A statement of fact. No one on our side considers there was any police brutality during the course of Mick's arrest.'

'Next time I'll try harder.'

Lucy banged out through the front door, but halted on the step. It was only mid-afternoon, but already a dank autumn dimness lay along the street, through which the dull glow of the streetlights barely seemed to penetrate. Fat, icy droplets spat from a sky as heavy and grey as concrete. She'd never seen less promising conditions for a brisk outdoor walk. But she didn't have much choice. Behind her, she heard them move back into the living room. Their voices were muffled, but as long as the door was open she could hear.

'She's a real piece of work,' McCracken remarked.

'Her father's daughter,' Cora said tearfully. 'And don't smile like that, Frank. This has ruined my life.'

'You were living a lie anyway, love.'

'It was a lie I liked.'

'I can sort this out.'

'So long as it doesn't involve killing anyone.'

'Lucy was exaggerating about that.'

'I hope so.' Cora's tone turned harsh. 'I mean . . . I'd really hate to think that you *were* the one who tried to have our daughter shot last night.'

'Do you think that's even vaguely possible? Given that I came here incognito, unarmed, unaccompanied . . .?'

Lucy couldn't bear to listen to any more and struck out on foot into the rain, which, by the time she'd reached the end of the street was pouring heavily. With no option and nowhere else to go, she grabbed the first bus that came along. It was bound for the town centre, but conveniently, one of its stops was close to Robber's Row.

When Lucy entered the nick, it was a quarter-to-four. She'd hoped to sneak in unnoticed through the rear personnel door, creep upstairs, grab her motorbike helmet, which with luck had been left somewhere where she could easily find it, and then quietly leave again, reclaiming her bike en route and heading over to Cuthbertson Court.

It didn't quite work out that way.

Almost immediately, she met people she knew, both coppers and civvy staff, and a succession of shoulder-slaps followed. If anyone felt peeved with her for getting yet another of her colleagues injured, it was forgotten, at least for today. Word of the previous night's incident had got around quickly, and congratulations were heaped on her both for her bravery and her quick thinking, along with commiserations for the loss of her witness. Some she met, mainly CID officers who'd been filled in on the bigger picture, wanted to shake her hand for the damage she'd done to the McIvars' firm and because her exposure of the child brothel in Whitefield was going to send several scrotey characters down for some lengthy stretches.

It was all very enjoyable, but it was a hollow victory too, because internally she was still raw. Lucy's home life as she knew it was over; the agony of that burned her like acid, and she had no idea how she was going to make such pain go away. At the same time, no amount of heroic do-gooding would secure her future in the police when she harboured a damaging secret like this. At some point, inevitably, the truth would come out.

Despite all this, Lucy kept a brave face, insisting that she'd just been doing her job. When someone enquired how she was feeling, expressing surprise and admiration that she was even here after being gunned down herself, she tried to correct this, assuring them that she hadn't taken a bullet even though she had been slightly hurt – though this only elicited further questions and answers.

In one way, these delays worked in Lucy's favour. They prevented her going straight upstairs, so by the time she finally did, moving past the door to the MIR on cat-like feet in case she ran into Nehwal, the rest of the Ripper Chicks had already gone out. The office was empty and, even better, the crimson globe of her helmet sat on her desk, awaiting collection. She didn't rush straight in to reclaim it, but glanced first into Geoff Slater's office. This too was empty. His laptop was closed, which implied that, wherever he was, he wasn't about to return imminently.

Relieved, Lucy went into the main office. But she'd no sooner reached her desk than one of the civilian researchers from downstairs entered the room behind her.

'Sorry . . . can you help me?'

Lucy glanced back awkwardly. 'Erm, yeah . . . if I can.'

The girl was young and rather gawky, wearing ill-fitting jeans and an open-collared shirt, with unruly orange locks and large-framed glasses. Her staff-badge indicated that her name was Tara Rutherford. 'I'm looking for a DC Barton. I was told he works on this floor, but all these offices are empty.'

'Des is off sick,' Lucy said. 'He won't be in for a few weeks, at least.'

'Ah . . . right. He requested this lot, you see.' Tara presented a thin sheaf of printouts, which she clearly hoped Lucy was going to take off her hands.

Lucy didn't, but glanced down. It looked like a bunch of intelligence sheets.

'Apparently, DC Barton requested some info concerning the owners of several cars he'd developed suspicions about?' Tara said.

'Oh yeah, that,' Lucy replied. 'Red cars going through the Rake and Harrow roundabout near Abram, wasn't it?'

'That's right, but there were over three hundred, which he'd kind of expected . . . so he asked me to refine it further.' Tara now all but shoved the sheaf into Lucy's grasp. 'These are the ones whose owners have got criminals records. There are ten in total.'

Lucy's interest was only half-pricked. In the light of recent calamitous events, this minor lead she'd generated over three weeks ago seemed completely unimportant. It had been the

368

longest of long shots anyway, according to Des, and he was probably right. However, if all she had to do was check out ten names, it could hardly hurt.

She flipped quickly through them, immediately seeing that the vast majority were unrelated to the case: drugs offences; TWOC; assault; drunk and disorderly.

And then prostitution.

This one was right at the end, and it stopped Lucy in her tracks. Not just because of the nature of the offence, but because it was the only female rap sheet in the pile.

Her interest somewhat more kindled, she read the accompanying notes.

The name of the offender was Darla Maycroft. She'd been born in Kersal, Salford, on June 23rd 1980, which made her thirty-five years old. She had five convictions for soliciting in public places – all between 2006 and 2012. She'd been in her late twenties and early thirties at the time, so it wasn't just a bad patch she'd gone through when she was a kid. However, no offences of any sort had been recorded since then. The last known address for Darla Maycroft was 16 Moorhill Close, Lostock, Bolton – a fairly well-heeled district, if Lucy remembered correctly, and only five or six miles from the border with Crowley.

A grainy black and white image depicted a young, blonde-haired woman, though it wasn't great quality. But again . . . *blonde* hair.

Lucy lowered the notes in order to think.

'Will you make sure DC Barton gets this stuff when he's next in?' Tara Rutherford asked, clearly impatient to be dismissed.

'Don't worry, I'll take care of it.'

Tara nodded and left the room. Lucy barely noticed as she flipped more pages concerning Darla Maycroft, her attention now caught by a biro notation in the margin, which indicated that she was the owner of a red Volkswagen CC. Lucy was familiar with the CC; it was famous among motoring buffs as the family sedan that resembled a sports car. Which would explain both the chippie man's mistake and the reason why it hadn't been flagged up during the first search.

Again Lucy pondered.

Was it possible?

Was this Darla Maycroft, a known former prostitute, the same woman who'd made a quick recce of the fatal woodland only a few days before Ronald Ford died there?

She knew that she ought to go straight down to the MIR and hand this lot over. If not to Priya Nehwal herself, to DI Dawson, who was Action Manager for the taskforce.

But again, on the surface it still seemed unlikely. By the chippie man's own admission, hundreds of people came and went in that place. It proved nothing.

Okay, it was probably worth looking into . . . but it could hardly be a priority.

And yet Lucy was even more agonised by that, wondering if all she was doing now was trying to find reasons for *not* pushing this intel up the chain, if deep down what she really wanted to do was to check the lead herself.

There was no doubt that after the trauma of Tammy's death, or maybe *because* of it – the kid had died as a direct result of Lucy's enquiries – she still felt attached to this case. And with that awful new truth currently wrecking her life at home, she had nothing else anyway. That alone had to be sufficient motivation for cranking out some kind of result here.

Her own mother and father, for Christ's sake!

If those lowlife bastards thought they were going to take her down with them, they had another thing coming. Lucy Clayburn wasn't just a cop, she was one of the best cops going. And she'd damn well prove it. Whatever it took. *Sodding bastards . . .*

Priya Nehwal would understand. Not that she wouldn't still go ballistic of course. She might now have decided that Lucy was her kind of copper, but she'd still be absolutely furious. And she'd have every reason to be.

Or then again she might not.

On reflection, it couldn't really hurt if Lucy made a few discreet enquiries before sharing this lead. If she mooched around first and it led to nothing, fine . . . it wouldn't matter; no one would be any the wiser. While on the other hand, if it *did* lead to something – like Jill the Ripper! – Nehwal would hardly be in a position to complain.

But really, seriously . . . Darla Maycroft, who drove a pricey motor and now lived in the middle-class suburb of Lostock, was the Lay-by Murderer?

Lucy had to be kidding herself. These psychopathic freaks usually demonstrated a pattern of antisocial behaviour and violent offending long before they switched to killing. Plus they tended to come from the most abusive backgrounds. All that said, just because there was no such detail on Darla's sheet, that didn't mean she hadn't had issues.

The printout was frustratingly sketchy, but Lucy scanned it again for anything that might help persuade her she wasn't barking up the wrong tree. Her eyes finally fell on a physical description of the subject. This had been taken at the time of her last arrest, which was in 2012, when she'd been thirty-two years old.

One passage in particular caught Lucy's attention:

> *Blue eyes. Natural blonde hair.*
> *Sturdy, athletic build.*

And more important still:

> *5ft11ins tall.*

Chapter 33

Grantwood Gardens in Lostock wasn't the epitome of middle-class Greater Manchester, but it was a good approximation for that. A grid-work of orderly, tree-lined suburban streets, it boasted detached and semi-detached houses, front lawns with pruned shrubbery, and drives with more than one car on them. It was neither as grand nor as showy as the swanky corner of Didsbury where Frank McCracken lived, but it was prosperous all the same in a quieter, more down-to-earth fashion.

No cop would ever argue that prosperity was a reason for crime not to happen, though most would agree that in suburbia it tended to lie behind closed doors. Not that such knowledge made this place seem any the less sinister to Lucy as she rode slowly along its affluent avenues. It was now 4.30 in the afternoon, so though occasional clusters of school kids were still sauntering home, their mothers and fathers mostly hadn't returned yet. House lights were coming on as dusk deepened, but only here and there. At least the rain had eased off, but it was a typical late afternoon in November: very cold, very damp, very misty.

As a rule, Lucy enjoyed plain-clothes work. That was one

of the things that attracted her to CID. She understood the power and authority of the police uniform, and she appreciated the reassurance it gave to those in need. But if what you really wanted to do as a copper was snag criminals, you couldn't beat a pair of jeans and a scruffy old anorak. That enabled you to get right into their faces before they even knew you were there. But on this occasion, especially as she banked left onto Moorhill Close, she felt more than a little bit self-conscious. The combination of scruffs *and* motorbike would undoubtedly make her stand out here.

Moorhill Close was a cul-de-sac, so when she coasted to a halt a couple of houses down from number 16, she wasn't far from the turning-zone at its far end. She switched her engine off, lowered her kickstand and sat astride the Ducati for several seconds, flexing her left hand. The plaster cast only encased her up to the knuckles, allowing sufficient dexterity in her fingers to manipulate the bike's clutch, but it hadn't been easy – there'd been a lot of stiffness there, and while the whole of her lower arm, the hand included, had previously felt numb, the sheer effort of handling the powerful machine, even at relatively low speeds, had created a throbbing ache just below her elbow.

But there was no point dwelling on this when she had other stuff to attend to.

She removed her helmet and regarded the house in question.

It was pretty well identical to all those around it, with a front wall that came to about waist-height, a small front lawn, and slatted fencing separating it from the neighbours on either side. The house wasn't exactly a new-build, but it wasn't far off, constructed in the attractive cottage style from off-brown brick, with diamond-paned front windows and a bright yellow front door with a black, wrought iron knocker and hanging plants on either side. Again, Lucy found it difficult to imagine that this could really be the place where a degenerate killer lived. So often those creatures had been dragged up in vileness and hate, and knew no emotion other than the joy they derived from inflicting on others the same misery they themselves had suffered. It was the ever-downward spiral of violence, dirt and degradation. But of course there had been other culprits too, who, as part of their darker purpose, had managed to overcome this, at least superficially; who had affected a front of wholesome normality in order to hunt more effectively.

So thinking, Lucy dismounted and walked towards the foot of the drive to no. 16, which currently was empty. No car was present on it, nor under the lean-to carport on the left side of the house. However, a red Volkswagen CC was parked on the road at the front.

This still didn't mean anything. She already knew that the owner of this property possessed a Volkswagen CC; it was a hardly a smoking gun. She threw another glance up the drive. Despite the presence of the vehicle, all the lights inside the house were switched off, its windows like blank eyes in the evening gloom.

She looked back towards the cul-de-sac entrance. No one was in sight, either out on the street or standing at an open door. The issue now was whether anything she did from this point on could be construed an illegal search. She certainly couldn't justify a warrant as yet. It was all too circumstantial. Even to sniff around the exterior of the house might be deemed questionable, and anything she uncovered inadmissible.

But the CC was on the road – and that was a public place.

As casually as she could, she circled the car. Nothing noteworthy caught her eye inside it: a dog-eared map-book jammed beside the driver's seat; a tin of cola in the circular drinks-holder attached to the dash. But then on the back seat – a black beret. A black knitted beret, very similar to the type the chief suspect had been wearing when filmed climbing into Ronnie Ford's car near the petrol station in Atherton.

It was several seconds before Lucy realised that the heavy breathing she could hear was her own. She leaned as close as she could to the window, dug out her mobile, activated its light and shone it through the glass.

There was no question about what she was seeing.

She backed away, glancing along the cul-de-sac again and then at the house. Its windows remained dark – which was good. It meant she could poke around a little more. She knew that she shouldn't, of course. Possibly she could justify a warrant now, but the way the brass would respond if they learned that she was still on the case, she needed to be one hundred per cent sure of her facts.

She walked up the drive, the silent façade of the property looming towards her. From what she could see, there was plenty of access to its rear. On the right side, a narrow passage, only barred by a wooden gate with a latch, led round to the back, while the carport on the left was wide open at the front, empty inside, and then opened again at the other end via a normal-sized doorway. She opted for the carport.

Once under its slanted roof, she halted, activating her phone light again to scan the darkened interior, though there wasn't much to see: a floor of oily concrete, a few scruffy boxes in the corners. The left-hand wall was lined with shelves bearing cobweb-covered tools, bottles of weed-killer and such, while overhead the ceiling was underhung by a few rotted rafters laden with planks, fence-posts and the like. It was all very mundane.

She prowled on, passing through the open door at the back and into the rear garden, where, as before, nothing untoward met her eyes.

It was encircled by clipped hedges, and consisted of a patio, a lawn, a rockery and a flowerbed, all of it littered with autumn leaves. A few non-seasonal bits and pieces were also scattered around: a hosepipe on a reel, a couple of sun-loungers. Four colour-coded wheelie bins were lined neatly under the kitchen window.

Lucy ventured past these to the larger French window. When she shone her light through it, it revealed a tidy little lounge containing armchairs, a settee, a flat-screen TV and ornaments on the mantel. Absolutely nothing in any way mysterious. When she glanced up, she saw two bedroom windows, a satellite dish and a burglar alarm box.

Standard suburbia. It could not have been less suspicious.

But the trail of clues that had led her here was not fanciful, with the beret in the car the strongest evidence yet – though even that was to change half a second later, when Lucy spotted something else.

Beyond the French window, drawn up against the wall of the house, was a garden table made from wrought iron and with a glass top; the sort of thing you ate your barbecues off on summer bank holiday afternoons. But it was not the table as much as what was underneath it: a pair of black wellingtons. And it was not the wellingtons as much as what they were coated with. Lucy approached and squatted down. Again, she shone her light close-up.

Lumps of dry, reddish grit were clustered all over the boots' lower parts.

She knew exactly what this was.

Clay.

She also knew where it came from, because she'd had to scour the same gummy material from that non-too-cheap pair of stiletto court shoes she'd bought for her undercover op.

Dedman Delph.

'Well, girl,' she muttered, vaguely dazed. 'You wanted a smoking gun . . .'

But there was a problem here. As she remained crouched, she was increasingly convinced that she was missing something. Something obvious perhaps.

So obvious that abruptly, without any real prompting, it struck her.

These wellingtons were rather large; she estimated size eleven at least. And yet the high-heeled footprint they'd found close to Ronnie Ford's corpse had been no more than a size seven. Lucy rose slowly to her feet, flesh tingling.

She thought about the CC parked on the road in front of the house, rather than on the drive – that was the sort of thing you did when you had another car. She glanced over her shoulder onto the lawn – there were *two* sun-loungers.

'Jesus Christ,' she breathed.

The 'tag-team from Hell' theory held good after all.

Suddenly it didn't feel like a cool idea to be hanging around here.

She walked quickly back across the garden, all the way telling herself that this should be no surprise. That big lorry driver, Larry Pupper, had been dragged a hundred yards; much easier with two of you than with one. While so many of the other killings had been ambush attacks, the victims lured to secluded spots where, no doubt, the second murderer was lying in wait. She entered the carport through its rear entrance, fiddling with her phone. Nehwal was the obvious person to call, or, failing her, anyone at the MIR.

But halfway through the interior, she slid to a halt.

Through the carport's open front, she saw that a vehicle, a silver Mondeo, had pulled onto the drive. It could only have arrived in the last minute or so, but already it was parked. Its headlights were switched off and there was nobody inside.

377

The blood thumped in Lucy's ears as she stared bewilderedly out at it. She hadn't heard anything: no voices, no thudding of car doors. And no lights had come on inside the house. As her eyes roved across the Mondeo, she noted what looked like several bulging shopping bags sitting on the drive on its nearside. So they'd come home all innocent-like; another average day. And then they'd spotted her Ducati . . .

Lucy stayed exactly where she was, raising the phone to key in the number – at which point, in a black blur, something swept down from the darkness on her right, something heavy, made both from wood and steel. It smacked the mobile phone from her grasp, and sent it skittering across the floor of the carport. Lucy's fingers were only struck a glancing blow, but even so the pain of that was blinding.

Yelping in agony, she tottered backwards.

Her assailant stepped into view in front of her, blocking all access to the drive. At first the figure was silhouetted. No details were distinguishable, except that whoever this was, they were tall and athletically built, and wearing what looked like a hooded running top and jeans. A split-second later, they adjusted their position and Lucy saw two additional things: street-light glinting on blonde locks hanging out from under a woolly hat, and the weapon with which she'd been attacked, which was a garden fork.

She held her ground, breathing hard.

'I should warn you that I'm a police officer,' she said, 'and that you will only make this situation a lot worse for yourself by resisting arrest.'

The blonde woman said nothing, merely lowered the fork the way a soldier would a bayonet, and advanced.

Lucy turned to run, thinking that if she could get back into the rear garden, she could circle the house via the passage on its other side. But this escape route was also blocked, a second figure, a male, now standing in the rear doorway. In the dim moonlight, she glimpsed an anorak, dark hair, a pencil-thin moustache. He didn't appear to be armed and wasn't much taller than the woman, but he was of broader, stockier build, and the chances were he'd be the stronger of the two.

She twirled back to face her former opponent.

The prongs of the fork were perhaps two feet away when Lucy jumped upwards, reaching with her right hand for one of those decayed wooden rafters and yanking down on it, using all her weight. With a shuddering *CRACK*, the rafter collapsed and a mass of planks and fence slats followed, cascading down between them in a cacophonous, splintering deluge, partially covering the woman. Crying out, she raised her arms to protect herself, dropping to her knees in the process, almost losing her grip on the garden fork. But before Lucy could take advantage and scramble forward, the man had jumped onto her from behind.

He was as strong as she'd suspected, his arms like iron bands as they wrapped around her.

'Meddling bitch!' he hissed into her ear. 'You just made the biggest fucking mistake of your . . .'

Lucy lashed up and back with her plaster-encased left arm. It *clunked* on his temple with what had to be the force of a hammer-blow.

He grunted in shock, his bear hug grip slackening.

The jolt of pain lanced not just the full length of Lucy's arm, but through her shoulder and deep into her torso. But this was life or death. She struck again with her cast, hitting him a second time in exactly the same place.

This time the grip was broken, and he staggered sideways.

Lucy lunged forward, kicking through the wreckage. The woman was halfway back to her feet, coughing, wafting at dust. Lucy dodged around her, only for her own feet to catch in the clutter, which sent her sprawling – though this turned out to be a good thing as she landed alongside her phone. Snatching it and jumping back up, she sensed the woman coming at her from the left. More by instinct than design, she ducked – just managing to evade a massive, two-handed blow from the garden fork.

This set the woman off-balance, and allowed Lucy to scamper out onto the drive. As she did, she speed-dialled the Comms Suite at Robber's Row. The call was answered by PC Adam Martindale, normally one of the operators when her own shift was on duty.

'Adam, it's Lucy Clayburn!' she jabbered as she stumbled away. 'Urgent need of assistance. PC under attack outside 16 Moorhill Close in Lostock, on the Kilo Division. Two suspects, one male, one female, both connected to the Jill the Ripper enq . . .'

Before she could say more, a hefty weight struck her in the middle of the back, clobbering her spine and kidneys. She staggered forward, gagging, dropping the phone and falling to her knees beside the Mondeo's front nearside corner. The garden fork landed next to her with a clatter. Winded and sickened, but at least conscious, she clambered over the shopping bags and crawled on, following the car's nearside. From behind came a gabble of semi-hysteria.

'Get up, you useless shit!' the woman shrieked. 'Do the fucking bitch!'

'You stupid cow!' the man replied. 'She's made a call. I fucking heard her!'

'Shit . . . we can still do her!'

'Just fucking move it!'

Two pairs of feet came hammering down the drive. Lucy curled into a ball next to the wheel-arch, in an effort to protect her head – but the twosome bypassed her, circling around the Mondeo's offside. A split-second later, she heard car doors slam open and closed, and then an engine rumble to life. She climbed shakily to her feet as the red Volkswagen CC spun through a manic three-point turn and sped away along the cul-de-sac.

Exhausted and wracked with pain, Lucy searched around for her mobile, finally locating it by the foot of the nearby fence. It was dented and scuffed, its screen cracked, but still functioning even if the earlier call had been cut. As she stood up with it, an elderly man in shirtsleeves appeared at the front door of the house beyond the fence. Evidently having heard the commotion, he looked both curious and alarmed.

'Police officer, sir,' Lucy called to him. 'Go inside please. Lock your door.'

She hit re-dial as she limped down the drive.

'Adam, it's Lucy,' she said, climbing astride her bike.

'Lucy!' He sounded relieved. 'Local units are en route, but what's going on?'

'I was sitting on a couple of suspects in the Jill the Ripper case, and I repeat a *couple*, as in two of them, not one. The female is Darla Maycroft, IC1, blonde . . . of the address I gave you before. She's already known to us. The male, who's also IC1, is unknown to me, but probably her live-in boyfriend. As well as divisional support, I need you to message Operation Clearway. Tell them exactly what I've just told you. Advise them we need a search-warrant and CSIs.'

'Lucy, aren't you supposed to be off sick?'

'Adam, listen . . . both suspects are now mobile, driving a red Volkswagen CC, index Bravo-Foxtrot-six something or other. Any Bolton patrols to stop on sight and detain. Listen, mate . . . I've no radio and have a fractured left wrist. In other words, I'm not going to be able to give you a running commentary. In pursuit, nevertheless. Over and out.'

Chapter 34

If it had been testing enough at an easy pace using one hand to steer her powerful 900cc sports bike across Crowley and Bolton, Lucy knew that pursuing a pair of suspects at high speed would be much more of a challenge, especially as that one good hand was still smarting from where she'd been hit across the fingers.

But that wasn't the only problem. First of all, she had to catch up with her targets. She powered across the Grantwood Gardens estate to its nearest entrance, which was on Beaumont Road. This in itself was a gamble. There were likely to be several other exits from the estate which the fugitives might have used, but Beaumont Road was a major artery in the district and the most likely to facilitate an escape. Even so, Lucy hesitated before pulling out into it. Did she go left or right?

Greater Manchester was now in the midst of rush hour, vehicles bottled up in both directions. Had they opted to go right from here, in effect turning across two lanes, it would have taken them longer to make good their flight. So most likely they'd gone left. Even then, the slow-moving traffic would hinder them, though it would hinder Lucy as well.

By necessity, she decided, the niceties of road behaviour could not be a consideration this evening.

She turned her machine left, but instead of forcing her way in among the sluggish, exhaust-pumping cars, she mounted the kerb and proceeded along the pavement. She didn't screw the throttle for fear of pedestrians stepping out in front of her, but by the time she'd reached twenty-five she was already overtaking the traffic on the road. A couple more hundred yards – that was surely all it would take before she spotted them, but now, even at this low speed, her left arm was giving her problems. The increased throb of the Ducati's v-twin engine sent painful vibrations along the fractured bone, and while the clutch wasn't heavy, the fingers on that hand were stiff and restricted by her cast.

She gritted her teeth and pressed on, passing more and more slow-moving cars, many of their drivers and passengers glaring at her as she shot by, assuming her some lout attempting an illegal short-cut. And then, only a minute or so later, she spotted the Volkswagen CC.

It was about fifty yards ahead, and as she'd hoped, mired in the same jam.

She quickly decelerated and, when the first gap came along, veered out into the traffic to fall in place about five cars behind it.

Her thinking on this was twofold: firstly, because of the felons' sedate pace, they clearly thought they'd eluded any pursuit and so were not risking mindless stunts like dangerous overtaking or heading the wrong way down one-way streets – but if they suddenly became aware of her now, she might panic them into doing precisely that; secondly, she was in no position to take these crazies down by herself, and so the best policy was to sit on their tail, hopefully without being noticed, and guide the support units in.

She filched her phone from her pocket, activating its speaker.

'Adam, I'm on the A58, heading south. You've got to get someone along here, mate . . . everything's cool at present, but these bastards are going to throw me off at some point.'

Apparently oblivious to her, the CC now swung casually north onto Wigan Road. This was a less congested route, and so the car slowly accelerated away. Lucy had to weave around a couple of the vehicles in front in order to make the turn herself, catching several angry toots, but determined to stay in touch. When the CC then veered onto Hulton Lane, Lucy banked in pursuit. This was an even more open road, so the target accelerated again. There were still a couple of cars between them, but now Lucy suspected that the duo had spotted her after all. She throttled up, trying discreetly to close the gap, and at the same time wondering what the endgame here was going to be.

She had no clue where the fugitives thought they were running to. They might have pre-prepared a bolthole for themselves, in the event of an emergency abandoning everything, including their house and their old lives, in order to stay at liberty. But that couldn't be easy in this day and age. And if they'd noticed that she was tailing them, they were hardly likely to make it happen now. Not without trying to get rid of her first.

She dug her phone out again, but it was increasingly difficult. It meant she had to hold course with her left hand, and that limb wasn't just agony now, it was dead wood in terms of the control she could affect through it.

'Adam!' she shouted. 'I'm still sitting on these bastards. Where are you all?'

'Lucy the whole network's gridlocked. Everyone's struggling . . .'

'Enough excuses, Adam . . . we're approaching St Helens Road, but I think they've clocked me and I expect we'll have rabbits very, very soon. *I need that support!*'

Ahead, another line of traffic waited at the junction with St Helens Road.

The CC decelerated again, so Lucy decelerated too. The lights changed and they proceeded, St Helens Road dipping under the M61 motorway, after which the CC swung onto Plodder Lane, now heading east towards Farnworth. The aptly named Plodder was basically a B road and largely empty of other cars, and Lucy found herself directly behind the target. There was about forty yards between them, but it was now a certainty that she'd been spotted. Slowly but noticeably, the CC sped ahead, effortlessly accelerating to fifty. Lucy did the same, increasingly tense though at least feeling good that they were veering towards the border with the N Division, as that was where most backup was likely to come from.

But then, at Glynne Street, the suspects broke for it.

The CC made a sudden crazy swerve, swinging out into Albert Road, cutting across two entire lanes of oncoming traffic, causing much screeching of tyres and shunting of vehicles, its driver then flooring his pedal as the southward route opened up in front of him.

Lucy threaded through the resulting chaos as fast as she could, which wasn't very.

By the time she'd hit Albert Road, there was no sign of the CC. She zipped forward, looping around a sharp bend and only just avoiding an elderly couple in the act of crossing. The male of the two shook his walking stick at her as she blistered past.

The Volkswagen CC was fast, but the Ducati Monster was faster still, and nippier on the turn. When the target swam back into view, Lucy swiftly gained on it – only for its driver to make another unexpected manoeuvre, swerving right and vanishing onto the Collingbourne council estate. Lucy was horrified. There were still likely to be school kids around here. Despite the cold and dark, there might even be younger children playing out.

There was certainly lots of double-parking, which massively narrowed the thoroughfares they were now chasing through.

Again, she was perplexed as to where the fugitives thought they were running to. They'd reached the boundary between the K Division and the N, but this estate was a huge cul-de-sac in its own right. Still the CC attempted to shake her off, screeching around concrete islands, bulleting through unmarked crossroads. Unsuccessful with that, it hit the side streets and back alleys, wheelie bins flying everywhere, trash exploding in fountains. Hot breath fogged the inside of Lucy's visor as she clung on behind; the pain in her arm now penetrated her entire left side. She was almost dizzy with it; only by focusing on the tail lights in front to the exclusion of all else, did she hold the course.

On the far edge of the estate, they spun onto a narrow lane called Chorlton Green. It ran between a row of drab maisonettes on one side and a tall hawthorn hedge on the other. Beyond the hawthorns lay the Barcroft playing fields, which were currently hidden in darkness. Lucy didn't think that Chorlton Green led anywhere else, just swung right at its southp-east end and curved back among the council houses – which meant that if she could get some support units here, these maniacs were finally trapped.

She attempted to call Comms again, but almost lost control in the process, skidding along the gutter and nearly crashing headlong into a concrete waste bin, which some stupid kids had toppled over. She swerved past it so sharply that she smashed through a flimsy garden fence, and ploughed across two overgrown front lawns before regaining the road.

'Adam!' she panted. 'I'm on the Collingbourne, on Chorlton Green . . .'

'Lucy, it's difficult keeping track of you . . .'

'Just send me anyone you've got!'

She cut the call and revved forward, catching up with the CC more quickly this time. A shabby old van was in the process of making a three-point turn, and the CC had been forced to slow as it approached, its driver hitting his horn repeatedly. A burly looking guy in a vest and overalls pants emerged from one of the maisonettes, outside of which the pavement was cluttered with furniture; he gestured with a V-sign and shouted obscenities. But the CC driver, spotting Lucy in his rear-view mirror, swung his wheel right, hit the gas and mounted the pavement. The guy in the vest dived to safety as the car bullocked by, clouting a ratty-looking couch out of its way and inadvertently clearing a path for Lucy too.

She almost bucked from the saddle as she leapt over the kerb, but fishtailed through the wreckage of furniture and hit the road surface again, still upright.

The CC accelerated ahead of her, now tearing up the narrow street at sixty-plus. Lucy throttled up too, but not quickly enough to prevent his next bizarre tactic: a sharp turn through a gap in the hawthorn hedge. Lucy screeched in pursuit, almost ditching as she did, the stink of burnt rubber filling in her nostrils – and found herself jolting along a muddy track lined on both sides by more dense hawthorns. They were heading onto the playing fields, she realised. Somewhere on the left up here there was a small clubhouse – little more than a changing shed really – and on the right a bunch of rugby and football pitches. Beyond all that, there was woodland where the fleeing twosome might duck out of sight, but the CC wouldn't be able to go much further. She screwed the throttle harder. The route curved and twisted, but the Ducati handled the leaf-cluttered quagmires with ease, and she constantly glimpsed the CC's tail lights, especially when it skidded to a sudden, ear-rending halt.

It had no choice, she now remembered. This access road was only a few hundred yards in length, and then there was a pair of concrete bollards.

'Gotcha!' she whooped.

But even as Lucy swept up from behind, the CC's two front doors burst open and a figure emerged one on either side, the pair of them sprinting past the bollards into the darkness.

Lucy throttled after them, skimming through the gap between the hedge and the car, passing the concrete obelisks and racing along what was now little more than a footpath. Her arm throbbed as the bike bounced and slid, but the running shapes were only forty yards in front. Her headlamp picked them out cleanly: the man was in surplus army trousers, boots and a black anorak; Darla Maycroft's hooded running top was bright blue with white piping. She'd lost her woolly cap, her fair hair streaming out behind her.

They were clearly in good condition; pounding along with hard, heavy strides. But for all their strength and stamina, Lucy was on wheels. She gained steadily, engine roaring – only for the duo to suddenly diverge, breaking apart in opposite directions.

Briefly, she was thrown. She'd no idea where the woman had gone – the fair-haired form had literally just vanished into the darkness on their left. But the man had veered onto the actual pitches, which lay spread out to her right, their level grassy surfaces and the white structures of football and rugby posts clearly discernible in the yellow streetlight filtering through the hawthorns.

The woman was the main target, officially. But the man was still in sight.

Lucy swerved after him, her back wheel slewing amid heaps of muddy autumn leaves, but quickly regaining traction and propelling her forward again. He was going full pelt, like a lunatic, throwing a single glance back towards her as he went. She caught a half-glimpse of his pale, sweat-slick face. Then he veered left, heading across the first pitch from its east side to its west. Lucy powered after him, throttling hard. In some ways it was almost too easy. How she was going to physically restrain him when she dismounted, she didn't know, but simply pursuing him was no problem.

And then he too disappeared.

Just dropped out of view . . . directly in front of her.

Lucy was stumped – but only realised the truth when it was too late.

One of the pitches was much lower than the others, and the next thing she knew, she was skidding down a terrifying gradient. The shape of the man flipped blurrily past in her left-hand vision as he rolled away sideways.

Leaving Lucy entirely alone.

There was no time to effect a controlled crash. The flat surface of the lower pitch rushed up and hit her at a one-twenty-degree angle. The jolt was colossal, Lucy almost thrown over the handlebars. She clung on, but the bike went wildly out of control, zigzagging across the slick grass and heading straight for a set of rugby uprights, the tall steel shaft of the nearest post a brilliant white in her headlight.

She bailed off, hitting the ground with a brutal impact, which hammered through her entire body. Miraculously, her broken left arm was spared as she cradled it tightly across her chest, even managing to shield it when, through sheer momentum, she found herself rolling pell-mell through leaves and muck.

In the background meanwhile, the collision between the bike and the post was huge, a booming *CRUMP!* of steel and a rending of magnesium alloy.

Moments of uncertainty passed, during which Lucy lay half-insensible. Only slowly did she become aware of the world around her, first as a cold dampness seeped through her clothes from the well-trampled pitch, and then from the distant shouts of laughter.

Laughter?

Someone thought this was funny.

Gradually, in the sluggish mix of her thoughts, she remembered.

They'd got the drop on her pretty completely: wrecked her bike, broken her body . . .

And they thought this was funny?

In which case she was damned if she was leaving it here. Not after coming *this* far, getting *this* close . . .

But Lucy was so groggy that just climbing back to her feet was an ordeal. Every part of her body hurt: joints were twisted; limbs felt like putty they were so battered. She grunted with pain as she pulled her helmet off and dropped it, her head swimming as she tottered back towards the upward slope. And yet she could still hear them. Some way distant, but hooting with laughter. Clearly they'd found each other again in the darkness, and now felt they were onto a winner.

If nothing else, *that* galvanized her, giving her new strength.

Which she was clearly going to need.

When she reached the darkened slope, she was still so dazed that it reared above her like the south face of Everest. But she knew she couldn't afford to dally. All they needed to do was get back to their CC. Lucy had their address, but they surely didn't intend to return home. More likely they'd just disappear. That wasn't impossible. Other killers had done it – certainly for long enough to claim more victims.

She whimpered for breath as she laboured up the muddy, tussocky incline. When she clambered onto the flat at the top, it was all she could do not to flop down onto her face.

It was impossible to see very far in the darkness, but those two lunatics had to be back at their motor by now. If they reversed it to the main road, they were away. It was that simple.

She limped on regardless, heading roughly towards where she thought the playing fields entrance was, but so physically beaten, so shaken from the crash that her eyes struggled to attune to the dimness and any real sense of direction eluded her.

At which point she heard their jeering laughter change in timbre.

Suddenly, without any obvious explanation, their scorn had gone. Instead, there was anger and shock there. It rose in intensity. Even though they must still have been eighty to ninety yards away, she could hear them clearly.

'*Fuck!*' the man shouted. '*What the actual fuck!*'

'*You stupid bastard!*' the woman shrieked. '*Didn't you even look?*'

'*There's no fucking glass here, you dumb bitch! Check it yourself!*'

Lucy stumbled forward faster. It was all grey murk, all fog and pain, nothing but grassy emptiness on every side of her. She thought she was crossing the final pitch, but if it turned out not to be that she'd have no hope of collaring them, whatever their problem was.

But then, a squat, boarded structure emerged through the gloom in front, with a black rectangular aperture in the middle of it. The changing shed – for the local football and rugby teams. If nothing else, that nailed Lucy's location. She was slightly off course, but swerving left, she put herself back on the path to the bollards.

Fifty or so yards along it, she found the CC. There was no sign of the two fugitives – she couldn't even hear them anymore. But the car was exactly where they'd left it.

Up close to it, she tottered to a halt, wreathed in breath and sweat, amazed.

Ribbons of rubber and ply cord hung where the CC's front tyres had once been. No wonder the duo were so furious, but it was mystifying all the same. There was a hefty dint in the car's front bumper, from where it had caromed past the old sofa, but that minor impact could not have been sufficient to blow out the front tyres. Likewise, there was no broken glass lying around. As Lucy hurried past the vehicle, she saw that its rear tyres hung in tatters too – and still there were no fragments of glass to explain it.

Whatever had caused this, it was an unlooked-for boon, but even though the fugitives were now on foot, they could still vanish back onto the Collingbourne if they got far enough ahead. She dashed on down the track, fumbling for her phone – only to find that her pockets were empty. She must have lost it in the crash – her last link to her colleagues gone.

But there was no time to go back and search.

Panting, she rounded the corner onto Chorlton Green, and saw them again: about a hundred yards away on her left. Possibly feeling the exertion themselves, they'd now slowed to a walk, albeit a fast one – which might still be enough to get them away.

Directly ahead of them, a right-hand turn led back onto the estate.

Lucy blundered in pursuit, still clutching her arm to her chest, briefly imbalanced and as such half-tripping over a kerb, which caught their attention. They were still far ahead when they glanced back, but immediately they started running again, perhaps sensing that they were close to eluding her, that one final effort was all it would require.

At which very inopportune moment, a police van cruised around the corner into their path, and instantly applied its brakes.

As did the two fugitives.

'*Yes!*' Lucy ran all the harder, again finding new strength. '*Yes, yes!*'

It got better. The uniformed bobby who climbed from the van was a very familiar sight.

PC Malcolm Peabody had clearly been despatched by Comms to the edge of the division in response to her calls. He looked stern-faced and suspicious as he pulled on his hi-viz anorak.

'Malcolm!' Lucy shouted.

He glanced along the road towards her.

'Grab those two!' she hollered. 'They're murder suspects!'

Lucy lengthened her stride. Despite Peabody standing right in front of them, she expected the duo to dart away or take some kind of evasive action. After all this effort to escape, there was no chance they'd just hang around and let an ordinary patrol officer put his hands on them. But fleetingly, showing his inexperience, Peabody was inert, torn by indecision.

'*MALCOLM!*' she shouted in warning.

Peabody reached one hand under his anorak to clutch the hilt of his baton. But to both his and Lucy's surprise, the female suspect's reaction was neither to run nor fight, but to burst into loud, hysterical tears.

'We've . . . we've not done anything,' Lucy heard Darla Maycroft sob. 'All we did . . . went shopping, came home . . . found this, this crazy woman at our house . . . thought she was a burglar. She caused damage there! She assaulted Peter! We ran for it . . . she chased us . . .'

The performance clearly threw Peabody. He glanced agitatedly back towards Lucy, who was now only thirty or so yards away. The fugitives turned to look too. It was difficult to read their faces in the yellow street lighting, but though Darla's cheeks were genuinely wet with tears, there was no sorrow there, no anguish. She was blank, devoid of emotion.

Peabody stepped around them. 'You sure you've got the right people, Luce . . .?'

'*Bloody fool!*' Lucy hissed.

'Not to worry, love,' the man called Peter told his woman, putting one arm around her.

His face was *not* blank – but twisting slowly into a mask of demented rage.

'*OUT THE WAY!*' Lucy barged headlong into Peabody, buffeting him aside and aiming a furious kick at the male suspect's crotch.

The impact of toe in groin was bone-crunching.

The man called Peter gave a shrill, pig-like squeal as he toppled sideways onto the road, hands clasping his crushed gonads.

Darla Maycroft screamed too, but in her case with outrage.

'You bitch!' Lucy rounded on her, grabbing the lapels of her running top and head-butting her right on her pretty little nose.

'*Lucy, what the hell . . .?*' Peabody protested.

Lucy spun the stunned woman around, kicking her wobbling legs from underneath her and knocking her down to her knees. Peabody's mouth slackened open even further when she dug her hand into Darla's hood, which now hung suspiciously low on her back, and gingerly withdrew two implements.

The first was a large, heavy knife, its hilt bound with duct-tape, its thick steel blade at least fifteen inches long, the edge honed until it glinted, though for half its length it was also serrated – so that it might serve as a hand-saw.

The second was a ball-peen hammer.

Lucy dropped them to the ground, before twisting the suspect's wrist behind her back, causing her to wince and cry out. It had only struck Lucy over the final few yards why the fugitives had come here, and what it was the man called Peter might have kept hidden in the local changing shed. Meanwhile, Peabody pulled his cuffs from their pouch and dropped to one knee alongside the groaning male.

'In the States, Malcolm,' Lucy said, breathing hard, 'they call what that bastard was in the process of doing "reaching". It's something you'll have to learn to spot . . . hopefully a lot quicker than I did.'

Epilogue

Even Blackpool tended to be quiet in mid-December. Its seafront, the world-famous Golden Mile, was lined with garish festive lights, the Tower glittered and shone like a five-hundred foot, wrought-iron Christmas tree, and there was some activity in the various bars, clubs and cafés tucked away down its side-streets, but the bulk of the resort's attractions were closed.

It was getting dark when Lucy crossed the tramlines to the Queen's Promenade.

She huddled inside her fleece and muffler, her gloved hands buried in her pockets, even her left one, which was still fixed in a cast of dingy, crumbling plaster.

Everything was wet; it had been raining all afternoon, but now it was too cold for that. Instead, a bitter north-westerly brought squalls of sleet across the Irish Sea, setting the multi-coloured bulbs dancing on the overhead cables. It was high tide, so dark, grey waves boomed and foamed beyond the parapet railing.

Despite all this, a solitary male figure waited on a bench, peering out into the tumult.

Lucy approached him warily, but before she drew close,

a towering shape stepped into her path. She glanced up at the scowling ape-face of Mick Shallicker. He gestured, and grudgingly, she held her arms out so that he could pat her down for a wire.

'We going through this rigmarole every time I have to speak to him?' Lucy asked.

'Frank thought you never wanted to talk to him again,' Shallicker said. 'Now suddenly you've agreed to a meet. He's naturally suspicious.'

'Both you and me know that if I were to say a word about this to anyone, I wouldn't survive either.'

He straightened up. 'If nothing else, I had to make sure you haven't got a monkey wrench in your pocket.'

'How's the knee anyway?' she asked.

'Stiff.'

'Good.' She walked on past him.

When she got to the sea-facing bench, she didn't bother sitting, but moved to the railing and leaned her back against it. McCracken, who was wearing a heavy gabardine coat, a chequered scarf and dark leather gloves, regarded her with low-key interest.

'Peter Janson and Darla Maycroft, eh?' he said. 'Him an amateur football coach . . . Under 16s, no less. Her a fitness instructor at the local gym. But I guess their names'll now go down in history alongside Brady and Hindley, Fred and Rose . . .?'

'They've been charged, not convicted,' Lucy replied. 'I can't discuss it with you.'

'Let me guess.' He spoke on as if she hadn't said anything. 'On the outside a normal, respectable couple, on the inside a pair of arch-pervs. What was he . . . a jealousy freak? Gets off watching blokes ogle his sexy missus . . . but once it comes to the crunch he just can't control the killer instinct it raises?' He pondered. 'She'd have to be a cow too, of course. I can just see it . . . he's lying in wait for them, imagining all sorts, going loopier and loopier, and once the attack starts, she just steps back, happy she's done her bit, content to watch . . .'

'I wouldn't give you the detail even if I was allowed to.'

'No, course not.' McCracken shuddered dramatically. 'The turn-ons some people share though, eh? Was she on the game? Was that where he found her? Bet that was the origin of it. Someone gave him a bad time when he was young. So he's got this inner rage. But then things start looking up. Gets a decent job, gets this peach of a bird. Trouble is there are still blokes lusting after her. "That's no bloody good," he thinks. "We're not standing for that" . . .'

'Why don't we discuss what we're really here for?' Lucy said.

Still McCracken ignored her. 'Perhaps he starts off by giving her other clients a bit of a kicking. And they don't want to report it because they don't want anyone knowing they've been using prozzies. But even that's not enough, because there are still these blokes giving his girlfriend the wicked eye. And you know, kicking the absolute shit out of these bastards is actually quite a lot of fun . . .'

'Okay, why *don't* we talk about it?' Lucy interrupted. 'Why don't we start with you telling me the part *you* played in it?'

McCracken gave a non-too-innocent smirk. 'Me?'

'How long were your people tailing me for?'

He feigned hurt. 'We don't tail people, Lucy. That's your line.'

'You were tailing *me*. You *must* have been.'

'You sound very sure about that.'

'I'm guessing you put a tail on me the moment your plan to get me kicked out of the job didn't work,' she said. 'You must have had someone waiting for me outside the nick on the day I arrested those two maniacs. Outside the bloody police station. Isn't that a no-no even by your circle's standards?'

McCracken shrugged. 'That depends whether it's a good tail or a bad tail.'

'Come again?'

'Just suppose . . .' He briefly seemed amused. 'I'm purely saying this for argument's sake, you understand, but just *suppose* the intent was not to give you a hard time, but to help you?'

'Help me?' she scoffed. 'I'm a copper, I'm the shit on your shoes.'

'You misheard. I said suppose the intent was to help *you* . . . as in you personally, not the police.'

'And why would you do that?'

'Again suppose, just *suppose* . . . someone had decided that getting you in trouble at work, stitching you up with your bosses, was . . . well, a bit mean?'

'Someone?' Lucy snorted. 'You mean my mum?'

'We both know your mum wasn't happy about it. I mean, the truth is your mum doesn't know what she wants. She hates you being a copper because she's worried about you, but at the same time she's proud of you too . . . I suspect it's because she thinks you're doing something worthwhile with your life.' He sniffed as though disappointed. 'I know a few people who'd strongly disagree, but that's by the by. But you're basically right. Your mum was hopping mad that you were suddenly in a bad place professionally.'

'So, let me get this straight?' Lucy's tone remained scornful. 'You changed your entire plan because my mum, a woman you haven't shacked up with for thirty years, gave you a load of earache about it?'

'Hey . . . she's a persuasive woman.'

'And as well as being henpecked by a lass you no longer

even want . . . you're now telling a pack of lies to your own daughter. Not quite what I'd expect from an underworld hardman.'

McCracken sniffed. 'Some truths are better left unsaid, Lucy.'

'Level with me, McCracken. That's all I'm asking. These last few weeks have changed my life in ways I can't even quantify. I need to know *exactly* what happened.'

'You *need* to know? I see.' A gust of wind swept over them, laden with sleet. McCracken huddled deeper into his coat. 'Okay, try this for size . . . when your mum came to see me last month and revealed to me that our daughter is a *detective* . . .'

'I wish,' Lucy said.

'Wishes come true, as you're probably about to find out. Which won't make my life any easier. But the situation was as follows . . .' He eyed her closely. 'I was stunned, gobsmacked. My first thought was "how the hell are the lads going to respond to this?" Then imagine how I felt when your mum told me you were involved in this Jill the Ripper case, which somehow or other was bringing you closer and closer to people I might know. There are very few problems I can't fix, Lucy . . .'

'I've heard that,' she said. 'You're the Shakedown, aren't you?'

'That's the title, yeah. We run the north-west pretty much any way we want, love. But that doesn't mean there aren't plenty of headcases out there who occasionally need reminding they have to pay for their privileges. So that's basically my role, yes, and I undertake it using any method I see fit. But the truth was I didn't know what I was supposed to do with *you*. I couldn't just grease you, like I normally would with a copper getting a sniff. And I couldn't kill you. I'd never have heard the last of it from your mother. So framing you with a foul-up your gaffers couldn't ignore seemed like a plan.'

'You mean beating up Des Barton?' she said disgustedly. 'Knowing full well I'd arrest you? And that it would probably get violent?'

'Well, you can't say it didn't work out that way.' McCracken sighed. 'And then look what flaming happened – Suzy McIvar, flying off the handle as usual, decides that she isn't going through the Executive . . .'

'The Executive?'

'You need to live and learn, darling. You really do.'

'Learn what?' She made no effort to conceal the mockery in her voice. 'That you and your mates think you're the Mafia?'

His smile tightened; and briefly she wondered if anyone ever tested his patience this much and got away with it.

'Good business is essential,' he explained. 'It's why we're all here. But good business isn't possible in a state of war. So no one gets rubbed out without permission. And don't bother quoting me on that, by the way . . . I'll simply deny it.'

'So what are you saying . . . that hit on Tammy would never have been sanctioned?'

'Who knows?' McCracken shrugged. 'That'd be above even my pay grade. But it certainly wouldn't have been cowboyed. And Suzy McIvar would have been nowhere near it. Anyway, the upshot was that not only did Suzy's rash act give you a chance to save your job, it also enabled you to bag the Twisted Sisters and their nasty little side-line. Not a bad night's work for a copper who might have been about to get shown the door. So all's well that ends well.' He shrugged again. 'You're happy, we're happy.'

'How can you be happy? Seriously, how the hell can you? Have you seen the charges the McIvars are facing?'

'They've earned them, love. Look . . . I told you at the time that the rest of us would never have condoned what they were up to, even if we'd known about it. And that we certainly weren't going down for it. So why should *I* worry?'

'You can't be sure you aren't going down,' Lucy said. 'Jayne McIvar's still trying to make deals.'

'I *can* be sure, darling . . . because that's not the way we play this game.'

McCracken got to his feet and ambled to the railing. He stood alongside her, watching the thundering surf. Fleetingly, he looked deadly serious.

'Even if you don't believe we had nothing to do with that kiddie-sex racket, Lucy,' he said, 'believe this . . . we have no ownership of these operations. None of them. Whatever they involve, there's never any trail that leads back to us, either on paper or electronic. SugaBabes . . . well, we visited now and then to shag the birds, but which red-blooded fellas wouldn't? And anyway, it'll take a lot more than the Twisted Sisters naming a few names to take *us* down. And later on, when Jayne and Suzy are sharing cells with people who will only require one phone-call to turn very nasty indeed, maybe they'll retract even those statements.'

Despite this obvious bravado, Lucy was actually starting to believe that the Crew had *not* known about the child brothel in Whitefield. She couldn't help recollecting that heated but cryptic conversation between the McIvar sisters back at SugaBabes, when Jayne had pleaded for a trouble-free business, especially when there were Crew soldiers on the premises. With hindsight, Jayne clearly hadn't wanted anything indiscreet said inside the club that might have attracted their bosses' annoyance, because if the Crew had looked at SugaBabes more closely, maybe with a hypercritical eye, they might have found other things they disapproved of even more.

All that said, Frank McCracken hadn't picked this out-of-the-way rendezvous point because he wanted to see the Christmas lights. Clearly, he felt they, or rather *he*, still had some vulnerabilities. And she – Lucy Clayburn – was probably one of them.

'The main thing where I was concerned,' McCracken added, 'was that even after the Twisted Sisters were arrested, it was obvious *you* weren't going anywhere till you'd nabbed this Jill the Ripper. And like I said, *we* didn't want her either. So, well . . . the best thing to do was help you get on with it. Give you a shadow maybe. Someone to watch your back, just in case there were still one or two McIvar loyalists knocking around after their bosses were locked up. Wouldn't have done for one of them to get in your way, would it?'

Until now, Lucy hadn't considered that there might have been retribution for her personally. That rarely happened to police officers, even when it was organised crime you were dealing with. But as McCracken had now more or less admitted, someone had followed her from Robber's Row when she'd set out to check the home address of Darla Maycroft. Thankfully on that occasion, it had been someone with a remit to assist rather than obstruct – even if it did only extend to him slashing the tyres of her chief-suspects.

'You strike me, Lucy, as a good honest copper,' McCracken said. 'I suppose I always knew there had to be one of those knocking around somewhere. But you also strike me as someone who needs to look over her shoulder a bit more.'

'I'd have spotted your man eventually,' she retorted. 'Though I suppose it depends how long he was planning to shadow me for.'

'That's hypothetical now.' McCracken moved away from the railing, tugging at his gloves to straighten them. 'You caught your killers . . . you've not just saved your job, you'll probably get that promotion you've been looking for.'

'Am I supposed to thank you?'

'Well . . .' McCracken pursed his lips. 'It could be the start of a healthy symbiosis.'

'Symbiosis?'

'Of course. I helped you nab a pair of serial killers. In return, you confirmed that Jayne McIvar is trying to cut deals. Not a bad way to get a partnership off the ground.'

'Let's get one thing straight!' she stated flatly. 'There is *no* partnership. I never want to hear from you again, I never want to speak to you again, I never want to see you again unless it's on a Wanted poster. We're strangers, you understand? Total and complete strangers.'

'Well . . . that works too.' He treated her to another of those infuriatingly bland smiles. 'There's only Mick knows about us at my end. At your end there's only your mum. We keep it to that select band and get on with our lives, happily not talking to each other, we should all be fine.' He gave her a long, frank stare. 'So . . . are we done?'

'Yes . . . I suppose we are.'

'See you around.' And using only the fingers of his left hand, he waved her goodbye.

Lucy felt like she ought to say something else, but he turned away from her to stare at the sea again. The interview was over.

She walked back across the prom, feeling vaguely diminished. She hadn't intended to let it slip that Jayne McIvar was still trying to grass people up, though no doubt McCracken would have guessed that for himself. The main thing was that Lucy clearly had a lot still to learn when it came to dealing with these major players.

It made her feel even grumpier.

There was no longer any sign of Shallicker, but as she approached the kerb her mother's yellow Honda pulled up in front of her. Lucy climbed into the front passenger seat.

Initially, they drove in silence, negotiating the complex Blackpool streets en route back to the M55.

'Well?' Cora asked, when they were finally free of the conurbation. 'What did you say to him?'

Lucy gazed sullenly ahead. 'Told him I never want to speak to him again.'

'That's what I thought.'

'And I never want to speak to *you* again either, Mum.'

'Ah . . . still?'

'Yeah. Still.'

'Okay.' Cora glanced at the dashboard clock. 'It'll be well after teatime when we get home. Fancy grabbing a Chinese on the way?'

'Sure,' Lucy said. 'Why not?'

7

Get your hands on the first five instalments
of the DS Mark Heckenburg series.
Available in all good bookshops now.